Baroness Orczy was born in Hur
of Baron Felix Orczy, a landed
composer and conductor. Orczy n.
Budapest to Brussels and Paris, where she was educated. She
studied art in London and exhibited work in the Royal
Academy.

Orczy married Montagu Barstow and together they worked
as illustrators and jointly published an edition of Hungarian
folk tales. Orczy became famous in 1905 with the publication
of *The Scarlet Pimpernel* (originally a play co-written with her
husband). Its background of the French Revolution and
swashbuckling hero, Sir Percy Blakeney, was to prove
immensely popular. Sequel books followed and film and TV
versions were later made. Orczy also wrote detective stories.

She died in 1947.

THE FIRST
SIR PERCY

Baroness Orczy

HOUSE OF
STRATUS

This edition published in 2003 by House of Stratus, an imprint of Stratus Books Ltd., 21 Beeching Park, Kelly Bray, Cornwall, PL17 8QS, UK.

www.houseofstratus.com

Typeset, printed and bound by House of Stratus.

A catalogue record for this book is available from the British Library and the Library of Congress.

ISBN 0-7551-165-93

CONTENTS

1

A Night on the Veluwe

A moonless night upon the sandy waste – the sky a canopy of stars, twinkling with super-radiance through the frosty atmosphere; the gently undulating ground like a billowy sea of silence and desolation, with scarce a stain upon the smooth surface of the snow; the mantle of night enveloping every landmark upon the horizon beyond the hills in folds of deep, dark indigo, levelling every chance hillock and clump of rough shrub or grass, obliterating road and wayside ditch, which in the broad light of day would have marred the perfect evenness of the wintry pall.

It was a bitterly cold night of mid-March in that cruel winter of 1624, which lent so efficient a hand to the ghouls of war and of disease in taking toll of human lives.

Not a sound broke the hushed majesty of this forgotten corner of God's earth, save perhaps at intervals the distant, melancholy call of the curlew, or from time to time the sigh of a straying breeze, which came lingering and plaintive from across the Zuyder Zee. Then for awhile countless particles of snow, fanned by unseen breaths, would arise from their rest, whirl and dance a mad fandango in the air, gyrate and skip in a glistening whirlpool lit by mysterious rays of steel-blue light, and then sink back again, like tired butterflies, to sleep once

1

more upon the illimitable bosom of the wild. After which Silence and Lifelessness would resume their ghostlike sway.

To right and left, and north and south, not half a dozen leagues away, humanity teemed and fought, toiled and suffered, unfurled the banner of Liberty, laid down life and wealth in the cause of Freedom, conquered and was down-trodden and conquered again; men died that their children might live, women wept and lovers sighed. But here, beneath that canopy dotted with myriads of glittering worlds, intransmutable and sempiternal, the cries of battle and quarrels of men, the wail of widows and the laughter of children appeared futile and remote.

2

But to an eye trained to the dreary monotony of winter upon the Veluwe, there were a few faint indications of the tracks, which here and there intersect the arid waste and link up the hamlets and cities which lie along its boundaries. There were lines – mere shadows upon the even sheet of snow – and tiny white hillocks that suggested a bordering of rough scrub along the edges of the roads.

That same trained eye could then proceed to trace those shadowy lines along their erratic way 'twixt Amersfoort and the Neder Rhyn, or else from Barneveld as far as Apeldoorn, or yet again 'twixt Utrecht and Ede, and thence as far as the Ijssel, from the further shores of which the armies of the Archduchess, under the command of Count Henri de Berg, were even then threatening Gelderland.

It was upon this last, scarcely visible track that a horse and rider came slowly ambling along in the small hours of the morning, on this bitterly cold night in March. The rider had much ado to keep a tight hold on the reins with one hand, whilst striving to keep his mantle closely fastened round his shoulders with the other.

The horse, only half-trusting his master, suspicious and with nerves a-quiver, ready to shy and swerve at every shadow that loomed out of the darkness, or at every unexpected sound that disturbed the silence of the night, would more than once have thrown his rider but for the latter's firm hand upon the curb.

The rider's keen eyes were searching the gloom around him. From time to time a forcible ejaculation, indicative of impatience or anxiety, escaped his lips, numb with cold, and with unconsidered vehemence he would dig his spurs into his horse's flanks, with the result that a fierce and prolonged struggle 'twixt man and beast would ensue, and, until the quivering animal was brought back to comparative quietude again, much time was spent in curses and recriminations.

Anon the rider pulled up sharply at the top of the rising ground, looked round and about him, muttered a few more emphatic '*Dondersteens*' and '*verdommts.*'

Then he veered his mount right round and started to go back down hill again – still at foot-pace – spied a sidetrack on his right, turned to follow it for a while, came to a halt again, and flung his head back in a futile endeavour to study the stars, about which he knew nothing.

Then he shook his head dolefully; the time had gone by for cursing – praying would have been more useful, had he known how to set about it – for in truth he had lost his way upon this arid waste, and the only prospect before him was that of spending the night in the saddle, vainly trying by persistent movement to keep the frost out of his limbs.

For the nonce, he had no idea in which direction lay Amersfoort, which happened to be his objective. Apparently he had taken the wrong road when first he came out of Ede, and might now be tending towards the Rhyn, or have left both Barneveld and even Assel considerably behind.

The unfortunate wayfarer did not of a surety know which to rail most bitterly against: his want of accurate knowledge as to the disposal of the stars upon a moonless firmament, so that he could not have told you, gaze on them how he might, which way lay the Zuyder Zee, the Ijssel, or the Rhyn; or that last mug of steaming ale of which he had partaken ere he finally turned his back on the hospitable doors of the 'Crow's Nest' at Ede.

It was that very mug of delicious spiced liquor – and even in this hour of acute misery, the poor man contrived to smack his half-frozen lips in retrospective enjoyment – which had somehow obscured his vision when first he found himself outside the city gates, confronted by the *verfloekte* waste, through which even a cat could not have picked its way on a night like this.

And now, here he was, hopelessly stranded, without drink or shelter, upon the most desolate portion of the Veluwe. In no direction could the lights of any habitation be seen.

'*Dondersteen!*' he muttered to himself finally, in despair. 'But I must get somewhere in time, if I keep following my nose long enough!'

3

In truth, no more lonely spot could be imagined in a civilized land than that wherein the stranded traveller now found himself. Even by day the horizon seems limitless, with neither tower nor city nor homestead in sight. By night the silence is so absolute that imagination will conjure up strange and impossible sounds, such as that of the earth whistling through space, or of ceaseless rolls of drums and trampings of myriads of feet thousands of leagues away.

Strangely enough, however, once upon a time, in the far long ago and the early days of windmills, a hermit-miller – he must have been a hermit in very truth – did build one here upon the highest point of the Veluwe, close to the junction of the road which runs eastward from Amersfoort and Barneveld, with the one which tends southward from Assel, and distant from each a quarter of a league or so. Why that windmill was erected just there, far from the home of any peasant or farmer who might desire to have his corn ground, or who that hermit-miller was who dwelt in it before flocks of wild geese alone made it their trysting-place, it were impossible to say.

No trace of it remains these days, nor were there any traces of it left a year after the events which this veracious chronicle will presently unfold, for reasons which will soon appear obvious to anyone who reads. But there it stood in this year of grace 1624, on that cold night in March, when a solitary horseman lost his way upon the Veluwe, with serious consequences, not only to himself, but to no less a person than Maurice, Prince of Nassau, Stadtholder of the United Provinces of the Netherlands, and mayhap to the entire future history of that sorely tried country.

On a winter's night such as this, the mill looked peculiarly weird and ghost-like, looming out of the darkness against the background of a star-studded firmament, and rising, sombre and dense, from out the carpet of glabrous snow, majestic in its isolation, towering above the immensity of the waste, its domed roof decked in virgin white like the mother-bosom of the wild. Built of weather-worn timber throughout, it had a fenced-in platform supported by heavy rafters all around it, like a girdle, at a height of twenty feet and more from the ground; and the gaunt, skeleton wings were stretched out to the skies, scarred, broken, and motionless, as if in piteous appeal for protection against the disfiguring ravages of time.

There were two small windows close under the roof on the south side of the building, and a large, narrow one midway up the same side. The disposal of these windows, taken in conjunction with the door down below, was so quaint that, viewed from a certain angle, they looked for all the world like the eyes, nose, and pursed-up mouth of a gargantuan, grinning face.

4

If a stranger travelling through Gelderland these days had thought fit to inquire from a native whether that particular *molen* upon the Veluwe was doing work or was inhabited, he would of a certainty have been told that the only possible inhabitants of the *molen* were gnomes and sprites, and that if any corn was ground there it could only be in order to bake bread for the devil's dinner.

The mill was disused and uninhabited, had been for many years – a quarter of a century or more probably – so any and every native of Gelderland and Utrecht would have emphatically averred. Nevertheless, on this same memorable night in March, 1624, there were evident signs of life – human life – about that solitary and archaic *molen* on the Veluwe. Tiny slits of light showed clearly from certain angles through the chinks of the wooden structure; there were vague sounds of life and movement in and about the place; the weather-worn boards creaked and the timber groaned under more tangible pressure than that of the winds. Nay, what's more, two horses were tethered down below, under the shelter afforded by the overhanging platform. These horses were saddled; they had nosebags attached to their bridles, and blankets thrown across their withers; all of which signs denoted clearly, methinks, that for once the mill was inhabited by something more material than ghosts.

More ponderous, too, than ghoulish footsteps were the sounds of slow pacing up and down the floor of the millhouse, and of two voices, now raised to loud argument, now sunk to a mere cautious whisper.

Two men were, in effect, inside the millhouse at this hour. One of them – tall, lean, dark, in well-worn, almost ragged, black doublet and cloak, his feet and legs encased in huge boots of untanned leather which reached midway up his long thighs, his black bonnet pushed back from his tall, narrow forehead and grizzled hair – was sitting upon the steps of the steep, ladder-like stairs which led to the floor above; the other – shorter, substantially, even richly clad, and wearing a plumed hat and fur-lined cloak, was the one who paced up and down the dust-covered floor. He was younger than his friend, had fair, curly hair, and a silken, fair moustache, which hid the somewhat weak lines of his mouth.

An old, battered lanthorn, hanging to a nail in the wall, threw a weird, flickering light upon the scene, vaguely illuminated the gaunt figure of the man upon the steps, his large hooked nose and ill-shaven chin, and long thin hands that looked like the talons of some bird of prey.

'You cannot stay on here for ever, my good Stoutenburg,' the younger of the two men said, with some impatience. 'Sooner or later you will be discovered, and – '

He paused, and the other gave a grim laugh.

'And there is a price of two thousand guilders upon my head, you mean, my dear Heemskerk?' he said drily.

'Well, I did mean that,' rejoined Heemskerk, with a shrug of the shoulders. 'The people round about here are very poor. They might hold your father's memory in veneration, but there is not one who would not sell you to the Stadtholder if he found you out.'

Again Stoutenburg laughed. He seemed addicted to the habit of this mirthless, almost impish laugh.

'I was not under the impression, believe me, my friend,' he said, 'that Christian charity or loyalty to my father's memory would actuate a worthy Dutch peasant into respecting my sanctuary. But I am not satisfied with what I have learned. I must know more. I have promised De Berg,' he concluded firmly.

'And De Berg counts on you,' Heemskerk rejoined. 'But,' he added, with a shrug of the shoulders, 'you know what he is. One of those men who, so long as they gain their ambitious ends, count every life cheap but their own.'

'Well,' answered Stoutenburg, ''tis not I, in truth, who would place a high price on mine.'

'Easy, easy, my good man,' quoth the other, with a smile. 'Hath it, perchance, not occurred to you that your obstinacy in leading this owl-like life here is putting a severe strain on the devotion of your friends?'

'I make no appeal to the devotion of my friends,' answered Stoutenburg curtly. 'They had best leave me alone.'

'We cannot leave you to suffer cold and hunger, mayhap to perish of want in this God-forsaken eyrie.'

'I'm not starving,' was Stoutenburg's ungracious answer to the young man's kindly solicitude; 'and have plenty of inner fire to keep me warm.'

He paused, and a dark scowl contracted his gaunt features, gave him an expression that in the dim and flickering light appeared almost diabolical.

'I know,' said Heemskerk, with a comprehending nod. 'Still those thoughts of revenge?'

'Always!' replied the other, with sombre calm.

'Twice you have failed.'

'The third time I shall succeed,' Stoutenburg affirmed with fierce emphasis. 'Maurice of Nassau sent my father to the scaffold – my father, to whom he owed everything: money, power, success. The day that Olden Barneveldt died at the hands of that accursed ingrate I, his son, swore that the Stadtholder should perish by mine. As you say, I have twice failed in my attempt.

'My brother Groeneveld has gone the way of my father. I am an outlaw with a price upon my head, and my poor mother has three of us to weep for now, instead of one. But I have not forgotten mine oath, nor yet my revenge. I'll be even with Maurice of Nassau yet. All this fighting is but foolery. He is firmly established as Stadtholder of the United Provinces – the sort of man who sees others die for him. He may lose a town here, gain a city there, but he is the sovereign lord of an independent State, and his sacred person is better guarded than was that of his worthier father.'

'But it is his life that I want,' Stoutenburg went on fiercely, and his thin, claw-like hand clutched an imaginary dagger and struck out through the air as if against the breast of the hated foe. 'For this I'll scheme and strive. Nay, I'll never rest until I have him at my mercy as Gérard in his day held William the Silent at his.'

'Bah!' exclaimed Heemskerk hotly. 'You would not emulate that abominable assassin!'

'Why not call me a justiciary?' Stoutenburg retorted drily. 'The Archduchess would load me with gifts. Spain would proclaim me a hero. Assassin or executioner – it only depends on the political point of view. But doubt me not for a single instant, Heemskerk. Maurice of Nassau will die by my hand.'

'That is why you intend to remain here?'

'Yes. Until I have found out his every future plan.'

'But how can you do it? You dare not show yourself abroad.'

'That is my business,' replied Stoutenburg quietly, 'and my secret.'

'I respect your secret,' answered Heemskerk, with a shrug of the shoulders. 'It was only my anxiety for your personal safety and for your comfort that brought me hither tonight.'

'And De Berg's desire to learn what I have spied,' Stoutenburg retorted, with a sneer.

'De Berg is ready to cross the Ijssel, and Isembourg to start from Kleve. De Berg proposes to attack Arnheim. He wishes to know what forces are inside the city and how they are disposed, and if the Stadtholder hath an army wherewith to come to their relief or to offer us battle, with any chance of success.'

'You can tell De Berg to send you or another back to me here when the crescent moon is forty-eight hours older. I shall have all the information then that he wants.'

'That will be good news for him and for Isembourg. There has been too much time wasted as it is.'

'Time has not been wasted. The frosts have in the meanwhile made the Veluwe a perfect track for men and cannon.'

'For Nassau's men and Nassau's cannon, as well as for our own,' Heemskerk rejoined drily.

'A week hence, if all's well, Maurice of Nassau will be too sick to lead his armies across the Veluwe or elsewhere,' said Stoutenburg quietly, and looked up with such a strange, fanatical glitter in his deep-sunk eyes that the younger man gave an involuntary gasp of horror.

'You mean – ' he ejaculated under his breath; and instinctively drawing back some paces away from his friend, stared at him with wide, uncomprehending eyes.

'I mean,' Stoutenburg went on slowly and deliberately, 'that De Berg had best wait patiently a little while longer. Maurice of Nassau will be a dying man ere long.'

His harsh voice, sunk to a strange, impressive whisper, died away in a long-drawn-out sigh, half of impatience, wholly of satisfaction. Heemskerk remained for a moment or two absolutely motionless, still staring at the man before him as if the latter were some kind of malevolent and fiend-like wraith, conjured up by devilish magic to scare the souls of men. Nor did Stoutenburg add anything to his last cold-blooded pronouncement. He seemed to be deriving a grim satisfaction in watching the play of horror and of fear upon Heemskerk's usually placid features.

Thus for the space of a few moments the old moles appeared to sink back to its habitual ghost-haunted silence, whilst the hovering spirits of Revenge and of Hate called up by the sorcery of a man's evil passions held undisputed sway.

'You mean – ' reiterated Heemskerk after awhile, vaguely, stupidly, babbling like a child.

'I mean,' Stoutenburg gave impatient answer, 'that you should know me well enough by now, my good Heemskerk, to realize that I am no swearer of futile oaths. Last year, when I was over in Madrid, I cultivated the friendship of one Francis Borgia. You have heard of him, no doubt; they call him the Prince of Poets over there. He is a direct descendant of the illustrious Cesare, and I soon discovered that most of the secrets possessed by his far-famed ancestor were known to my friend the poet.'

'Poisons!' Heemskerk murmured, under his breath.

'Poisons!' the other assented drily. 'And other things.' With finger and thumb of his right hand, he extracted a couple of tiny packets from a secret pocket of his doublet, toyed with them for awhile, undid the packets and gazed meditatively on their contents. Then he called to his friend. 'They'll not hurt you,' he said sardonically. 'Look at this powder, now. Is it not innocent in appearance? Yet it is of incalculable value to the man who doth not happen to possess a straight eye or a steady hand with firearms. For add but a pinch of it to the charge in your pistol, then aim at your enemy's head, and if you miss killing him, or if he hold you at his mercy, you very soon have him at yours. The fumes from the detonation will cause instant and total blindness.'

Despite his horror of the whole thing, Heemskerk had instinctively drawn nearer to his friend. Now, at these words, he stepped back again quickly, as if he had trodden upon an adder. Stoutenburg, with his wonted cynicism, only shrugged his shoulders.

'Have I not said that it would not hurt you?' he said, with a sneer. 'In itself it is harmless enough, and only attains its useful properties when fired in connection with gunpowder. But when used as I have explained it to you, it is deadly and unerring. I saw it at work once or twice in Spain. The Prince of Poets prides himself on its invention. He gave me some of the precious powder, and I was glad of it. It may prove useful one day.'

He carefully closed the first packet and slipped it back into the secret receptacle of his doublet; then he fell to contemplating the contents of the second packet – half a dozen tiny pillules, which he kept rolling about in the palm of his hand

'These,' he mused, 'are of more proved value for my purpose. Have not De Berg,' he added, with a sardonic grin, as he looked once more on his friend, 'and the Archduchess, too, heard it noised abroad that Maurice of Nassau hath of late suffered of a mysterious complaint which already threatens to cut him off in his prime, and which up to now hath baffled those learned leeches who were brought over specially from England to look after the health of the exalted patient? Have not you and your friends, my good Heemskerk, heard the rumour, too?'

The young man nodded in reply. His parched tongue seemed to cleave to the roof of his mouth; he could not utter a word. Stoutenburg laughed.

'Ah!' he said, with a nod of understanding. 'I see that the tale did reach your ears. You understand, therefore, that I must remain here for awhile longer.'

And, with absolute calm and a perfectly steady hand, he folded up the pillules in the paper screw and put them back in his pocket.

'I could not leave my work unfinished,' he said simply.

'But how –' Heemskerk contrived to stammer at last; and his voice to his own ears sounded hoarse and toneless, like a voice out of the grave.

'How do I contrive to convey these pillules into the Stadtholder's stomach?' retorted Stoutenburg, with a coarse chuckle. 'Well, my friend, that is still my secret. But De Berg and the others must trust me a while longer – trust me and then thank me when the time comes. The Stadtholder once out of the way, the resistance of the United Provinces must of itself collapse like a house of cards. There need be no more bloodshed after that – no more sanguinary conflicts. Indeed, I shall be acclaimed as a public benefactor – when I succeed.'

'Then – then you are determined to – to remain here?' Heemskerk murmured, feeling all the while that anything he said was futile and irrelevant.

But how can a man speak when he is confronted with a hideous spectre that mocks him, even whilst it terrifies?

'I shall remain here for the present,' Stoutenburg replied, with perfect coolness.

'I – I'd best go, then,' the other suggested vaguely.

'You had best wait until the daylight. 'Tis easy to lose one's way on the Veluwe.'

The young man waited for a moment, irresolute. Clearly he was longing to get away, to put behind him this ghoul-infested *molen*, with its presiding genii of hatred and of crime. Nay, men like Heemskerk, cultivated and gently nurtured, understood the former easily enough. Men and women knew how to hate fiercely these days, and there were few sensations more thoroughly satisfying than that of holding an enemy at the sword's point.

But poison! The slow, insidious weapon that works like a reptile, stealthily and in the dark! Bah! Heemskerk felt a dizziness overcome him; sheer physical nausea threatened to rob him of his faculties.

But there was undoubted danger in venturing out on the arid wild, in the darkness and with nought but instinct and a few half-obliterated footmarks to guide one along the track. The young man went to the door and pulled it open. A gust of ice-laden air blew into the great, empty place, and almost knocked the old lanthorn off its peg. Heemskerk stepped out into the night. He felt literally frightened, and, like a nervous child, had the sensation of someone or something standing close behind him and on the point of putting a spectral hand upon his shoulder.

But Stoutenburg had remained sitting on the steps, apparently quite unmoved. No doubt he was accustomed to look his abominable project straight in the face. He even shrugged his shoulders in derision when he caught sight of Heemskerk's white face and horror-filled eyes.

'You cannot start while this blind man's holiday lasts,' he said lightly. 'Can I induce you to partake of some of the refreshment you were good enough to bring for me?'

But Heemskerk gave him no answer. He was trying to make up his mind what to do; and Stoutenburg, with another careless laugh, rose from his seat and strode across the great barn-like space. There, in a remote corner, where sacks of uncrushed grain were wont to be stacked, stood a basket containing a few simple provisions; a hunk of stale bread, a piece of cheese and two or three bottles of wine. Stoutenburg stooped and picked one of these up. He was whistling a careless tune. Then suddenly he paused, his long back still bent, his arm with the hand that held the bottle resting across his knee, his face, alert and hawk-like, turned in an instant towards the door.

'What was that?' he queried hurriedly.

Heemskerk, just as swiftly, had already stepped back into the barn and closed the door again noiselessly.

'Useless!' commented Stoutenburg curtly. 'The horses are outside.'

'Where is Jan?' he added after an imperceptible pause, during which Heemskerk felt as if his very heart-beats had become audible.

'On the watch, outside,' replied the young man.

Even whilst he spoke the door was cautiously opened from the outside, and a grizzled head wrapped in a fur bonnet was thrust in through the orifice.

'What is it, Jan?' the two men queried simultaneously.

'A man and horse,' Jan replied in a rapid whisper. 'Coming from over Amersfoort way. He must have caught sight of the *molen*, for he has left the track and is heading straight for us.'

'Some wretched traveller lost on this God-forsaken waste,' Stoutenburg said, with a careless shrug of the shoulders. 'I have seen them come this way before.'

'But not at this hour of the night?' murmured Heemskerk.

'Mostly at night. It is easier to follow the track by day.'

'What shall we do?'

'Nothing. Let the man come. We'll soon see if he is dangerous. Are we not three to one?'

The taunt struck home. Heemskerk looked abashed. Jan remained standing in the doorway, waiting for further orders. Stoutenburg went on quietly collecting the scanty provisions. He found a couple of mugs, and with a perfectly steady hand filled first one and then the other with the wine.

'Drink this, Heemskerk,' he said lightly; and held out the two mugs at arm's length. 'It will calm your nerves. You too, Jan.'

Jan took the mug and drank with avidity, but Heemskerk appeared to hesitate.

'Afraid of the poison?' Stoutenburg queried with a sneer. Then, as the other, half-ashamed, took the mug and drank at a draught, he added coolly: 'You need not be afraid. I could not afford to waste such precious stuff on you.'

Then he turned to Jan.

'Remain outside,' he commanded; 'well wrapped in your blanket, and when the traveller hails you pretend to be wakened from pleasant dreams. Then leave the rest to chance.'

Jan at once obeyed. He went out of the *molen*, closing the door carefully behind him.

5

Five minutes later, the hapless traveller had put his horse to a trot. He had perceived the *molen* looming at the top of the rising ground, dense and dark against the sky, and looking upon it as a veritable God-sent haven of refuge for wearied tramps, was making good haste to reach it, fearing lest he himself dropped from sheer exhaustion out of his saddle ere he came to his happy goal. That terrible contingency, however, did not occur, and presently he was able to draw rein and to drop gently if somewhat painfully to the ground without further mishap. Then he looked about him. The mill in truth appeared to be uninhabited, which was a vast pity, seeing that a glass of spiced ale would – but no matter, 'twas best not to dwell on such blissful thoughts! A roof over one's head for the night was the most urgent need.

He led his horse by the bridle, and tethered him to a heavy, supporting rafter under the overhanging platform; was on the point of ministering to the poor, half-frozen beast, when his ear caught a sound which caused him instantly to pause first and then to start on a tour around the *molen*. He had not far to go. The very next moment he came upon a couple of horses tethered like his own, and upon Jan, who was snoring lustily, curled up in a horseblanket in the angle of the porch.

To hail the sleeper with lusty shouts at first, and then with a vigorous kick, was but the work of a few seconds; after which Jan's snores were merged in a series of comprehensive curses against the disturber of his happy dreams.

'*Dondersteen!*' he murmured, still apparently half asleep. 'And who is this *verfloekte plepshurk* who ventures to arouse a weary traveller from his sleep?'

'Another weary traveller, *verfloekte plepshurk* yourself,' the other cried aloud. Nor were it possible to render with any degree of accuracy the language which he subsequently used when Jan persistently refused to move.

'Then, *dondersteen,*' retorted Jan thickly, 'do as I do – wrap yourself up in a blanket and go to sleep.'

'Not until I have discovered how it comes that one wearied traveller happens to be abroad with two equally wearied and saddled horses. An I am not mistaken, *plepshurk*, thou art but a varlet left on guard outside, whilst thy master feasts and sleeps within.'

Whereupon, without further parley, he strode across Jan's outstretched body and, with a vigorous kick of his heavy boot, thrust open the door which gave on the interior of the mill.

Here he paused, just beneath the lintel, took off his hat, and stood at respectful attention; for he had realized at once that he was in the presence of his betters – of two gentlemen, in fact, one of whom had a mug of wine in his hand and the other a bottle. These were the two points which, as it were, jumped most directly to the eye of the weary, frozen, and thirsty traveller: two gentlemen who haply were now satiated, and would spare a drop even to a humble varlet if he stood before them in his full, pitiable plight.

'Who are you, man? And what do you want?' one of these gentlemen queried peremptorily. It was the one who had a bottle of wine – a whole bottle – in his hand; but he looked peculiarly stern and forbidding, with his close-cropped, grizzled head and hard, bird-like features.

'Only a poor tramp, my lord,' replied the unfortunate wayfarer, in high-pitched, flute-like tones, 'who hath lost his way, and has been wandering on this *verdommte* plain since midnight.'

'What do you want?' reiterated Stoutenburg sternly. 'Only shelter for the rest of the night, my lord, and – and – a little drink – a very little drink – for I am mightily weary, and my throat is as dry as tinder.'

'What is your name?'

At this very simple question the man's round, florid face with the tiny, upturned nose, slightly tinged with pink, and the small, round eyes, bright and shiny like new crowns, took on an expression of comical puzzlement.

He scratched his head, pursed up his lips, emitted a prolonged and dubious whistle.

'I haven't a name, so please your lordship,' he said, after a while. 'That is, not a name such as other people have. I have a name, in truth, a name by which I am known to my friends; a name – '

'Thy name, *plepshurk*,' commanded Stoutenburg roughly, 'ere I throw thee out again into the night.'

'So please your lordship,' replied the man, 'I am called Pythagoras – a name which I believe belongs by right to a philosopher of ancient times, but to which I will always answer, so please your High and Mightiness.'

But this time his High and Mightiness did not break in upon the worthy philosopher's volubility. Indeed, at the sound of that highly ludicrous name – ludicrous, that is, when applied to its present bearer – he had deliberately put mug and bottle down, and then become strangely self-absorbed, even whilst his friend had given an involuntary start.

'H'm! Pythagoras!' his lordship resumed, after a while. 'Have I ever seen thine ugly face before?'

'Not to my knowledge, my lord,' replied the other, marvelling when it would please these noble gentlemen to give him something wherewith to moisten his gullet.

'Ah! Methought I had once met another who bore an equally strange name. Was it Demosthenes, or Euripides, or – '

'Diogenes, no doubt, my lord,' replied the thirsty philosopher glibly. 'The most gallant gentleman in the whole wide world, one who honours me with his friendship, was pleased at one time to answer to that name.'

Now, when Pythagoras made this announcement he felt quite sure that lavish hospitality would promptly follow. These gentlemen had no doubt heard of Diogenes, his comrade in arms, the faithful and gallant friend for whom he – Pythagoras – would go through fire and water and the driest of deserts. They would immediately accord a welcome to one who had declared himself honoured by the friendship of so noble a cavalier. Great was the unfortunate man's disappointment, therefore, when his glib speech was received in absolute silence; and he himself was still left standing under the lintel of the door, with an icy cold draught playing upon him from behind.

It was only after a considerable time that my lord deigned to resume his questionings again.

'Where dost come from, fellow?' he asked.

From Ede, so please your lordship,' Pythagoras replied dolefully, 'where I partook – '

'And whither art going?' Stoutenburg broke in curtly. 'I was going to Amersfoort, my lord, when I lost my way.'

'To Amersfoort?'

'Yes, my lord.'

'Mynheer Beresteyn hath a house at Amersfoort,' Stoutenburg said, as if to himself.

'It was to Mynheer Beresteyn's house that I was bound, my lord, when I unfortunately lost my way.'

'Ah!' commented my lord drily. 'Thou wast on thy way to the house of Mynheer Beresteyn in Amersfoort?'

'Yes, my lord.'

'With a message?'

'No, my lord. Not with a message; I was just going there for the wedding.'

'The wedding?' ejaculated Stoutenburg, and it seemed to Pythagoras as if my lord's haggard face took on suddenly an almost cadaverous hue. 'Whose wedding, fellow?' he added more calmly.

'That of my friend Diogenes, so please your lordship, with the Jongejuffrouw Beresteyn, he – '

'Take care, man, take care!' came with an involuntary call of alarm from Heemskerk; for Stoutenburg, uttering a hoarse cry like that of a wounded beast, had raised his arm and now strode on the unfortunate philosopher with clenched fist and a look in his hollow eyes which boded no good to the harbinger of those simple tidings.

19

At sound of his friend's voice, Stoutenburg dropped his arm. He turned on his heel, ashamed no doubt that this stranger-varlet should see his face distorted as it was with passion.

This paroxysm of uncontrolled fury did not, however, last longer than a moment or two; the next instant the lord of Stoutenburg, outwardly calm and cynical as before, had resumed his haughty questionings, looked the awestruck philosopher up and down; and he, somewhat scared by the danger which he only appeared to have escaped through the timely intervention of the other gentleman, was marvelling indeed if he had better not take to his heels at once and run, and trust his safety and his life to the inhospitable wild, rather than in the company of this irascible noble lord.

I think, in fact, that he would have fled the very next moment, but that my lord with one word kept him rooted to the spot.

'So,' resumed Stoutenburg coolly after awhile, 'thou, fellow, art a bidden guest at the marriage feast, which it seems is to be solemnized 'twixt the Jongejuffrouw Beresteyn and another *plepshurk* as low as thyself. Truly doth democracy tread hard on the heels of such tyranny as the United Provinces have witnessed of late. Dost owe allegiance, sirrah, to the Stadtholder?'

'Where Diogenes leads, my lord,' replied Pythagoras, with a degree of earnestness which sat whimsically upon his rotund person, 'there do Socrates and I follow unquestioningly.'

'Which means that ye are three rascals, ready to sell your skins to the highest bidder. Were ye not in the pay of the lord of Stoutenburg during the last conspiracy against the Stadtholder's life?'

'We may have been your honour,' the man replied naively; 'although, to my knowledge, I have never set eyes on the lord of Stoutenburg.'

' 'Twere lucky for thee, knave, if thou didst,' rejoined Stoutenburg with a harsh laugh, 'for there's a price of two thousand guilders upon his head, and I doubt not but thy scurrilous friend Diogenes would add another two thousand to that guerdon.'

Then, as Pythagoras, almost dropping with fatigue, was swaying upon his short, fat legs, he jerked his thumb in the direction where the tantalizing bottles and mugs were faintly discernible in the gloom. My lord continued curtly:

'There! Drink thy fill! Amersfoort is not far. My man will put thee on thy way when thou hast quenched thy thirst!'

Quench his thirst! Where was that cellar which could have worked this magic trick? In the corner to which my lord was pointing so casually there was but the one bottle, which my lord had put down a while ago, and that, after all, was only half full.

Still, half a bottle of wine was better than no wine at all, and my lord, having granted his gracious leave, took no more notice of the philosopher and his unquenchable thirst, turned to his friend, and together the two gentlemen retired to a distant corner of the place and there whispered eagerly with one another.

Pythagoras tiptoed up to the spot where unexpected bliss awaited him. There was another bottle of wine there beside the half-empty one – a bottle that was full up to the neck, and the shape of which proclaimed that it came from Spain. Good, strong, heady Spanish wine!

And my lord had said 'Drink thy fill!' Pythagoras did not hesitate, save for one brief second, while he marvelled whether he had accidentally wandered into Elysian fields or whether he was only dreaming. Then he poured out for himself a mugful of wine.

Twenty minutes later, the last drop of the second bottle of strong, heady Spanish wine had trickled down the worthy Pythagoras' throat. He was in a state of perfect bliss, babbling words of supreme contentment, and seeing pleasing visions of gorgeous feasts in the murky angles of the old millhouse.

' 'Tis time the *plepshurk* got to horse,' Stoutenburg said at last.

He strode across to where Pythagoras, leaning against the raftered wall, his round head on one side, his sugarloaf hat set at the back of his head, was gazing dreamily into his empty mug.

'To horse, fellow!' he commanded curtly. ' 'Tis but a league to Amersfoort, and thy friend will be awaiting thee.'

The old instinct of deference and good behaviour before a noble lord lent some semblance of steadiness to Pythagoras' legs. He struggled to his feet, vainly endeavoured to keep an upright and dignified position – an attempt which, however, proved utterly futile.

Whereupon my lord called peremptorily to Jan, who appeared so suddenly in the doorway that, to Pythagoras' blurred vision, it seemed as if he had been put there by some kind of witchery. He approached his master, and there ensued a brief, whispered colloquy between those two – a colloquy in which Heemskerk took no part. After which, the lord of Stoutenburg said aloud:

'Set this worthy fellow on his horse, my good Jan, and put him on the track which leads to Amersfoort. He has had a rest and a good warm drink. He is not like to lose his way again.'

Vaguely Pythagoras felt that he wished to protest. He did not want to be set on his horse, nor yet to go to Amersfoort just yet. The wedding was not until the morrow – no, the day after the morrow – and for the nonce he wanted to sleep. Yes, sleep! Curled up in a blanket in any corner big enough and warm enough to shelter a dog.

Sleep! That was what he wanted; for he was so confoundedly sleepy, and this *verfloekte* darkness interfered with his eyes so that he could not see very clearly in front of him. All this he explained with grave deliberation to Jan, who had him tightly by the elbow and was leading him with absolutely irresistible firmness out through the door into the white, inhospitable open.

'I don't want to get to horse,' the philosopher babbled thickly. 'I want to curl up in a blanket and I want to go to sleep.'

But, despite his protestations, he found himself presently in the saddle. How he got up there, he certainly could not have told you. Instinct, however, kept him there. Never could it be said that Pythagoras had tumbled off a horse. Anon he felt that the horse was moving, and that the air around him was bitterly cold.

The dull, even carpet of snow dazzled him, though it was pitch dark now both overhead and down below; of darkness that enveloped one like a mantle, and which felt as if it could have been cut through with a knife.

The horse went on at a steady trot, and another was trotting by its side, bearing a cavalier who wore a fur bonnet. Pythagoras vaguely imagined that this must be Jan. He owed Jan a grudge for taking him away from that hospitable *molen*, where half-bottles of wine were magically transformed into large ones, filled to overflowing with delicious liquor.

Presently Pythagoras began to feel cold again after the blissful warmth produced by that super-excellent Spanish wine.

'Is it far to Amersfoort?' he queried drowsily from time to time.

But he never seemed to get a reply. It appeared to him as if he had been hours in the saddle since last he had felt comfortable and warm over in that hospitable *molen*. And he was very sleepy. His head felt heavy and his eyes would not keep open as hours and hours went by and the cold grew more and more intense.

'Is it far to Amersfoort?' he questioned whenever his head rolled forward with a jerk that roused him to momentary consciousness.

'Less than half a league now,' Jan replied presently, and brought his own horse to a halt. 'Follow the track before you and it will lead you straight to the city gates.'

Pythagoras opened his eyes very wide. Straightway in front of him he perceived one or two tiny lights, which were too low down on the horizon for stars. The road, too, on which he found himself appeared straighter and more defined than those upon that *verfloekte* waste.

'Are those the lights of Amersfoort?' he murmured vaguely, and pointed in as straight a direction as his numbed arm would allow.

He expected an answer from Jan, but there came none. The darkness appeared to have swallowed up horse and rider. Anyway, they had disappeared. Good old Jan! Pythagoras would have liked to thank him for his company, even though he did owe him a grudge for taking him away from the *molen* where there had been such wonderful –

The horse followed the track for a minute or two longer. Pythagoras, left to his own devices, tried to keep awake. Suddenly the sharp report of a pistol rent the silence of the night. It was immediately followed by another.

Pythagoras felt a strange, sinking sensation in his stomach, a dizzy feeling in his head, a feeling which was no longer blissful like the one he had experienced after the third mugful of Spanish wine. A moment later, he fell forward on his horse's neck, then rolled out of the saddle down upon the bed of snow.

And at this spot, where the poor philosopher lay, the white pall which covered the Veluwe was dyed with a dark crimson stain.

6

A grey, dull light suffused the sky in the East when Jan once more knocked at the door of the old *molen*.

Stoutenburg's voice bade him enter.

'All well?' my lord queried, at sight of his faithful servant.

'All quiet, my lord,' replied Jan. 'That windbag, I'll warrant, will tell no tales.'

'How far did you take him?'

'Nearly as far as Lang Soeren. I had to keep to a track for fear of losing my way. But he lies eight leagues from Amersfoort now and six from Ede. His friends, I imagine, won't look for him thus far.'

'And his horse?'

'It did not follow me. No doubt it will get picked up by some one in the morning.'

Heemskerk shivered. It was certainly very cold inside this great, barn-like place at this hour just before sunrise; and the passing wayfarer had consumed the last measure of wine. The young man looked grimy, too, and untidy, covered with dust from the floor, where he had lain stretched out for the past three hours, trying to get a wink of sleep; whilst Stoutenburg, restless and alert, had kept his ears open and his nerves on the stretch for the first sound of Jan's return.

'You have been a long time getting to Lang Soeren and back,' the latter remarked further to Jan.

'I was guiding a drunken man on a wearied horse,' the man replied curtly. 'And I myself had been in the saddle all day.'

'Then get another hour's rest now,' Stoutenburg rejoined. 'You will accompany my lord of Heemskerk back to Doesburg as soon as the sun is up.'

Jan made no reply. He was accustomed to curt commands and to unquestioning obedience. Tired, saddlesore and wearied, he would be ready to ride again, go anywhere until he dropped. So he turned on his heel and went out into the cold once more, in order to snatch that brief hour's rest which had been graciously accorded him.

Heemskerk gave an impatient sigh.

'I would the dawn were quicker in coming!' he murmured under his breath.

'The atmosphere of the Veluwe is getting oppressive for your fastidious taste,' Stoutenburg retorted with a sneer. Then, as his friend made no other comment, he continued lightly: 'Dead men tell no tales. I could not risk that blabbering fool going back to Amersfoort and speaking of what he saw. Even your unwonted squeamishness, my good Heemskerk, would grant me that.'

'Or, rather,' rejoined the other, almost involuntarily, 'did not the unfortunate man suffer for being the messenger of evil tidings?'

Stoutenburg shrugged his shoulders with an assumption of indifference.

'Perhaps,' he said. 'Though I doubt if the news was wholly unexpected. Yet I would have deemed Gilda Beresteyn too proud to wed that *plepshurk.*'

'A man with a future,' Heemskerk rejoined. 'He is credited with having saved the Stadtholder's life, when the lord of Stoutenburg planned to blow up the bridge under his passage.'

'And Beresteyn is grateful to him too,' added Stoutenburg with a sarcastic curl of his thin lips, 'for having rescued the fair Gilda from the lord of Stoutenburg's fierce clutches. But Nicolaes might have told me that his sister was getting married.'

'Nicolaes?' ejaculated Heemskerk, with obvious surprise. 'You have seen Nicolaes Beresteyn, then, of late?'

For the space of a few seconds – less perhaps – Stoutenburg appeared confused, and the look which he cast on his friend was both furtive and searching. The next moment, however, he had recovered his usual cool placidity.

'You mistook me, my friend,' he said blandly. 'I did not say that I had seen Nicolaes Beresteyn of late. I have not seen him, in fact, since the day of our unfortunate aborted conspiracy. Rumour reached me that he himself was about to wed the worthy daughter of some prosperous burgher. I merely wondered how the same rumour made no mention of the other prospective bride.'

Once again the conversation flagged. Heemskerk regarded his friend with an anxious expression in his pale, wearied face. He knew how passionately, if somewhat intermittently, Stoutenburg had loved Gilda Beresteyn. He knew of the original girl and boy affection between them, and of the man's base betrayal of the girl's trust. Stoutenburg had thrown over the humbler burgher's daughter in order to wed Walburg de Marnix, whom he promptly neglected, and who had since set him legally free. Heemskerk knew, too, how Stoutenburg's passion for the beautiful Gilda Beresteyn had since then burst into a consuming flame, and how the obscure soldier of fortune who went by the nickname of Diogenes had indeed snatched the fair prize from his grasp.

Nigh on three months had gone by since then. Stoutenburg was still nurturing thoughts of vengeance and of crime, not only against the Stadtholder, but also against the girl who had scorned him. Well, this in truth was none of his friend's business. Hideous as was the premeditated coup against Maurice of Nassau, it would undoubtedly, if successful, help the cause of Spain in the Netherlands, and Heemskerk himself was that unnatural monster – a man who would rather see his country ruled by a stranger than by those of her sons whose political or religious views differed from his own.

Thus, when an hour later he took leave of Stoutenburg, he did so almost with cordiality, did not hesitate to grasp the hand of a man whom he knew to be a scheming and relentless murderer.

'One of us will come out to wait on you in two days' time,' he said at the last. 'I go back to camp satisfied that you are not so lonely as you seem, and that there is some one who sees to it that you do not fare so ill even in this desolation. May I say this to De Berg?'

'If you like,' Stoutenburg replied. 'Anyway, you may assure him, and through him the Archduchess, that Maurice of Nassau will be in his grave before I, his judge and executioner, perish of hunger or of cold.'

He accompanied his friend to the door, and stood there while the latter and Jan were getting to horse. Then, as they went out into the open, he waved them a last adieu. On the far distant east, the pale, wintry sun had tinged the mist with a delicate lemon gold. The vast immensity of the waste lay stretched out as if limitless before him. As far as the eye could see not a tower or column of smoke broke the even monotony of the undulating ground. The shadow of the great *molen* with its gaunt, maimed wings lay, like patches of vivid blue, upon the vast and glistening pall of snow.

The two riders put their horses to a trot. Soon they appeared like mere black specks upon a background of golden haze, whilst in their wake, upon the scarce visible track, the traces of their horses' hoofs, in stains of darker blue upon the virgin white, were infinitely multiplied.

Stoutenburg watched them until the mist-laden distance had completely hidden them from his view. Then, with a sigh of relief, he went within.

2

The Double Wedding

It was one of those days when earth and heaven alike appear to smile. A day almost warm, certainly genial; for the wind had dropped, the sky was of a vivid blue, and the sun had a genuine feeling of warmth in its kiss. From the overhanging eaves the snow dropped down in soft, moist lumps, stained by the thaw, and the quay, where a goodly crowd had collected, was quickly transformed under foot into a sea of mud.

It almost seemed as if the little town was out on a holiday. People came and went, dressed in gay attire, stood about all along the bank of the river, staring up at the stately gabled house which looked so wonderfully gay with its decorations of flags and valuable tapestries and stuffs hanging from the numerous windows.

That house on the quay – and it was the finest house in the town – was indeed the centre of attraction. It was from there that the air of holiday-making emanated, and certainly from there that the gay sounds of music and revelry came wafted on the crisp, wintry air.

Mynheer Beresteyn had come to his house in Amersfoort, of which city he was chief civic magistrate, in order to celebrate the double wedding. No wonder such an event was made an excuse for a holiday. Burgomaster Beresteyn never did things by halves, and his hospitality was certain to be lavish. Already doles and largesse had been poured out at the porch of St. Maria Kerk; a crowd of beggars more or less indigent, crippled, sick, or merely greedy, had assembled there very early in the morning. Whoever was there was sure to get something. And there was plenty to see besides: the brides and bridegrooms and the wedding party; and of course His Highness the Stadtholder was a sight in himself. He did not often go abroad these days, for his health was no longer as good as it was. He had aged considerably, looked moody and ailing for the most part. There had been sinister rumours, too. The widowed Archduchess Isabella, Mistress of Flanders and Brabant, hated him because he held the United Provinces of the Netherlands free from the bondage of Spain. And in Spain the arts of poison and of secret assassination were carried on with as much perfection as they had ever been in Italy in the days of the Borgias.

However, all such dark thoughts must be put away for the day. This is a festive occasion for Amersfoort, when every anxiety for the fate of the poor fatherland – ever threatened and ever sore-pressed – must be laid to rest. Let the brides and bridegrooms see naught but merry faces – happy auguries of the auspicious days to come.

Here they come – the entire wedding party – walking down the narrow streets from the quay to the St. Maria Kerk. Every one is walking, even the Stadtholder. He is conspicuous by his great height, and the richness of his attire: embroidered doublet, slashed sleeves, priceless lace. His face looks thin and drawn, but he has lost nothing of his martial bearing, nor have his eyes lost their eagle glance. He had come over the previous afternoon from Utrecht, where he was in camp, and had deigned to grace Mynheer Beresteyn's house by sleeping under its roof. It was understood that he would return to Utrecht after the banquet which was to follow the religious ceremony, and he, too, for this one day was obviously making a valiant attempt to cast off the load of anxiety attendant upon ceaseless campaigning. In truth, the Archduchess Isabella, not content with the fairest provinces of Belgium, with Flanders, Brabant, and the Hainault, which her father, King Philip of Spain, had ceded to her absolutely, was even now striving to force some of the United Provinces back under the domination of Spain.

Small wonder then that the Stadtholder, wearied and sick, the shadow of his former self, was no longer sure of a whole-hearted welcome when he showed himself abroad. Nor had the people forgiven him the judicial murder of Olden Barneveldt – the trusted councillor in the past, afterwards the bitter opponent of his master's ambitions – or his severity towards Barneveldt's sons. His relentless severity towards those who offended him, his reckless ambition and stern disciplinarianism, had made him an object of terror rather than of affection. Nevertheless, he still stood for the upholder of the liberties of the United Provinces, the finest captain of his age, who by his endurance, his military skill, and his unswerving patriotism, kept his country's frontiers free from the incursions of the most powerful armies of the time. He still stood as the man who had swept the sacred soil of the Netherlands free from Spanish foes and Spanish tyranny, who had amplified and consolidated the work of his father and firmly established the independence of the Republic. Because of what he had done in the past, men like Mynheer Beresteyn and those of his kind still looked upon him with grave respect, as the chosen of God, the prophet sent to them from Heaven to keep the horrors of a new Spanish invasion away from their land.

And when Maurice of Nassau came to a small city like Amersfoort, as he had done today, he was received with veneration, if not with the old cheers and acclamations.

His arbitrary temper was momentarily forgotten, his restless ambition condoned, in the joy of beholding the man who had fought for them, never spared himself until he had won for them all those civil and religious liberties which they prized above all the treasures of the earth.

All heads, then, were bowed in respectful silence as he walked by, with the brides one on each side of him. But the loving glances of the crowd, the jokes and whispered words of cheer and greeting, were reserved for Mynheer Beresteyn and for his family.

2

Two brides, and both comely! Jongejuffrouw Katharina van den Poele, the only child of the wealthy shipowner, member of the Dutch East India Company, a solid burgher both physically and financially, and one of the props of his country's overseas commerce. His daughter in rich brocade, with stiff stomacher that vainly strove to compress her ample proportions, splashed through the mud on her high pattens beside the Stadtholder, her heavily beringed hands clinging to the folds of her gown, so as to save them from being soiled. Stolid and complacent, she heard with a satisfied smile the many compliments that rose from out the crowd on her dazzling complexion, her smoothly brushed hair and magnificent jewellery. The fair Katharina beamed with good-nature and looked the picture of happiness, despite the fact that her bridegroom, who walked immediately behind her, appeared somewhat moody, considering the occasion.

Nicolaes Beresteyn, the Burgomaster's only son, had, in truth, no reason for surliness. His bride excited universal admiration, his own private fortune would be more than doubled by the dowry which the good Kaatje brought him along with her plump person, and all the disagreements between himself and his father, all the treachery and the deceit of the past three months, had been amply forgiven. It was all the more strange; therefore, that on this day his face alone should appear as a reflection of the Stadtholder's silent mood, and more than one comment was made thereon as he passed.

Of the other bride and bridegroom it is perhaps more difficult to speak. We all know the beautiful picture of Gilda Beresteyn which Frans Hals made of her some three months previously. That incomparable master of portraiture has rendered that indescribable air of force, coupled with extreme youthfulness, which was her greatest charm. Often she hath been called ethereal, yet I do not see how that description could apply to one who was so essentially alive as Gilda Beresteyn. Her blue eyes always sparkled with vitality, and whenever she was moved – which was often enough – they became as dark as sloes. Probably the word came to be applied to her because there was always a little something mysterious about her – an enigmatic little smile, which suggested merriment that came from within rather than in response to an outside joke. Many have remarked that her smile was the gentle reflex of her lover's sparkling gaiety.

Him – that ardent lover, sobered bridegroom now – you cannot forget, not whilst Frans Hals' immortal work, whom he hath called *The Laughing Cavalier*, depicts him in all his irrepressible joyousness, and gladdens the eye with its exhilaration and its magnificent *gaité de coeur* – a veritable nepenthe for jaded seek-sorrows.

For once in his life, as he walks gravely behind his bride, there is a look of seriousness not unmixed with impatience in his laughing eyes. A frown, too, between his brows. The crowd have at once taken him to its heart – especially the women. Those who have no sons wish for one at once, who would grow up just like him: tall and stately as a young sapling, with an air of breeding seldom seen in the sons of the Low Countries, and wearing his magnificent bridal attire as if he had never worn leather jerkin or worsted doublet in his life. The women admire the richly wrought doublet, the priceless lace at neck and wrists, the plumed hat that frames a face alike youthful and determined. But everyone marvels why a bridegroom should go to church in high riding-boots that reach midway up his thighs, and why he should be belted and spurred at this hour. Many whispered comments are exchanged as he goes by.

'A stranger, so they say.'

'Though he has fought in the Netherlands.'

'Ah, but he really comes from England.'

'A romantic story. Never knew his father until recently.'

Some said the bridegroom's name was really Blakeney, and that his father was a very rich and very great gentleman over in England. But there were others who remembered him well when he was just a penniless soldier of fortune who went by the name of Diogenes. No one knew him then by any other, and no one but Frans Hals, the painter over in Haarlem, knew whence he had come and what was his parentage. In those days his merry laughter would rouse the echoes of the old city where he and his two boon companions – such a quaint pair of loons ! – were wont to dwell in the intervals of selling their swords to the highest bidders.

Ay, Jongejuffrouw Beresteyn's stranger bridegroom had fought in France and in Flanders, in Groningen and Brabant and 'twas said that recently he had saved the life of the Stadtholder at great risk of his own. Many more tales were whispered about him, which would take too long to relate, while the crowd stood agape all down the quay and up the Korte Gracht as far as the St Maria Kerk.

3

Indeed, Mynheer Beresteyn had not done things by halves. He had chosen that the happy double event should take place at the old house at Amersfoort, where his children had been born, and where he had spent the few happy years of his married life, rather than at Haarlem, which was his business and official residence. He wished, for the occasion, to be just a happy father rather than the distinguished functionary, the head of the Guild of Armourers, one of the most important burghers of the Province, and second only in the council chamber to the Stadtholder.

The religious ceremony was over by noon. It was now mid-afternoon, and the wedding guests had assembled in the stately home on the quay for a gargantuan feast. The Stadtholder sat at a magnificently decked-out table at the far end of the panelled room, on a raised dais surmounted by a canopy of Flemish tapestry, all specially erected for the occasion. Around this privileged board sat the wedding party; Mynheer Beresteyn, grave and sedate, a man who had seen much of life, had suffered a great deal, and even now scarcely dared to give his sense of joy full play. He gazed from time to time on his daughter with something of anxiety as well as of pride. Then the worthy shipowner, member of the Dutch East India Company, and *mejuroffuw*, his wife – the father and mother of Nicolaes Beresteyn's bride, pompous and fleshy, and with an air of prosperous complacence about their persons which contrasted strangely with Mynheer Beresteyn's anxious earnestness. Finally, the two bridal couples, of whom more anon.

In the body of the nobly proportioned banqueting-hall, a vast concourse of guests had assembled around two huge tables, which were decked out with costly linen and plate, and literally groaned under the succulent dishes which serving-men repeatedly placed there for the delectation of the merry party. Roast capons and geese, fish from the Rhyn and from the sea, pasties made up of oysters and quails, and, above all, a constant supply of delicious Rhine or Spanish wines, according as the guests desired light or heady liquor.

A perpetual buzz of talk, intermingled with many an outburst of hilarity and an occasional song, filled the somewhat stuffy air of the room to the exclusion of any individual sound.

The ladies plied their fans vigorously, and some of the men, warmed by good cheer, had thrown their padded doublets open and loosened their leather belts.

The brides-elect sat one on each side of the Stadtholder; a strange contrast, in truth. Kaatje van den Poele, just a young edition of her mother, her well-rounded figure already showing signs of the inevitable coming stoutness, comely to look at, with succulent cheeks shining like rosy apples, her face with the wide-open, prominent eyes, beaming with good-nature and the vigorous application of cold water. Well-mannered, too, for she never spoke unless spoken to, but sat munching her food with naive delight, and whenever her somewhat moody bridegroom hazarded a laboured compliment or joke, she broke into a pleasant giggle, jerked her elbow at him, and muttered a 'Fie, Klaas!' which put an end to further conversation.

Gilda Beresteyn, who sat at the Stadtholder's right hand, was silent, too; demure, not a little prim, but with her, even the most casual observer soon became conscious that beneath the formal demeanour there ran an undercurrent of emotional and pulsating life. The terrible experience which she had gone through a few brief months ago had given to her deep blue eyes a glance that was vividly passionate, yet withal reposeful, and with a curiously childlike expression of trust within its depths.

The stiff bridal robes which convention decreed that she should wear gave her an air of dignity, even whilst it enhanced the youthfulness of her personality. There was all the roundness in her figure which is the attribute of her race; yet, despite her plump shoulders and full throat, her little round face and firm bosom, there remained something ethereal about her, a spirituality and a strength which inspired reverence, even whilst her beauty provoked admiring glances.

'Your Highness is not eating,' she remarked timidly.

'My head aches,' Maurice of Nassau replied moodily. 'I cannot eat. I think I must be over-tired,' he went on more pleasantly as he met the girl's kind blue eyes fixed searchingly upon him. 'A little fresh air will do me good. Don't disturb any one,' he continued hastily, as he rose to his feet and turned to go to the nearest open window.

Beresteyn quickly followed him. The prince looked faint and ill, and had to lean on his host's arm as he tottered towards the window. The little incident was noticed by a few. It caused consternation and the exchange of portentful glances.

A grave-looking man in sober black velvet doublet and sable hose quickly rose from the table and joined the Stadtholder and Mynheer Beresteyn at the window. He was the English physician especially brought across to watch over the health of the illustrious sufferer.

Gilda turned to her neighbour. Her eyes had suddenly filled with tears, but when she met his glance the ghost of a smile immediately crept around her mouth.

'It seems almost wicked,' she said simply, 'to be so happy now.'

Unseen by the rest of the company, the man next to her took her tiny hand and raised it to his lips.

'At times, even today,' she went on softly, 'it all seems like a dream. Your wooing, my dear lord, hath been so tempestuous. Less than three months ago I did not know of your existence – '

'My wooing hath been over-slow for my taste!' he broke in with a short, impatient sigh. 'Three months, you say? And for me you are still a shadow, an exquisite sprite that eludes me behind an impenetrable, a damnable wall of conventions, even though my very sinews ache with longing to hold you in mine arms for ever and for aye!'

He looked her straight between the eyes, so straight and with such a tantalizing glance that a hot blush rose swiftly to her cheeks; whereupon he laughed again – a merry, careless, infectious laugh it was – and squeezed her hand so tightly that he made her gasp.

'You are always ready to laugh, my lord,' she murmured reproachfully.

'Always,' he riposted. 'And now, how can I help it? I must laugh, or else curse with impatience. It is scarce three o'clock now, and not before many hours can we be free of this chattering throng.'

Then, as she remained silent, with eyes cast down now and the warm flush still lingering in her cheeks, he went on, with brusque impatience, his voice sunk to a quick, penetrating whisper:

'If anything should part me from you now, *ma donna*, I verily believe that I should kill someone or myself!'

He paused, almost disconcerted. It had never been his wont to talk of his feelings. The transient sentiments that in the past had grazed his senses, without touching his heart, had only led him to careless protestations, forgotten as soon as made. He himself marvelled at the depth of his love for this exquisite creature who had so suddenly come into his life, bringing with her a fragrance of youth and of purity, and withal of fervid passion, such as he had never dreamed of through the many vicissitudes of his adventurous life.

Still she did not speak, and he was content to look on her, satisfied that she was in truth too completely happy at this hour to give vent to her feelings in so many words. He loved to watch the play of emotions in her tell-tale face, the pursed-up little mouth, so ready to smile, and those violet-tinted eyes, now and then raised to him in perfect trust and abandonment of self, then veiled once more demurely under his provoking glance.

He loved to tease her, for then she blushed, and her long lashes drew a delicately pencilled shadow upon her cheeks. He loved to say things that frightened her, for then she would look up with a quick, inquiring glance, search his own with a palpitating expression that quickly melted again into one of bliss.

'You look so demure, *ma donna*,' he exclaimed whimsically, 'that I vow I'll create a scandal – leap across the table and kiss Kaatje, for instance – just to see if it would make you laugh!'

'Do not make fun of Kaatje, my lord,' Gilda admonished. 'She hath more depth of feeling than you give her credit for.'

'I do not doubt her depth of feeling, dear heart,' he retorted with mock earnestness. 'But, oh, good St Bavon help me! Have you ever seen so solid a yokemate, or,' he added, and pointed to Nicolaes Beresteyn, who sat moody and sullen, toying with his food, beside his equally silent bride, 'so ardent a bridegroom? Verily, the dear lady reminds me of those succulent fish pasties they make over in England, white and stodgy, and rather heavy on the stomach, but, oh, so splendidly nourishing!'

'Fie! Now you are mocking again.'

'How can I help it, dear heart, when you persist in looking so solemn – so solemn, that, in the midst of all this hilarity, I am forcibly reminded of all the rude things you said to me that night at the inn in Leyden, and I am left to marvel how you ever came to change your opinion of me?'

'I changed my opinion of you,' she rejoined earnestly, 'when I learned how you were ready to give your life to save the Stadtholder from those abominable murderers; and almost lost it,' she added under her breath, 'to save my brother Nicolaes from the consequence of his own treachery.'

'Hush! That is all over and done with now, *ma donna*,' he retorted lightly. 'Nicolaes has become a sober burgher, devoted to his solid Kaatje and to the cause of the Netherlands; and I have sold my liberty to the fairest tyrant that ever enslaved a man's soul.'

'Do you regret it,' she queried shyly, 'already?'

'Already!' he assented gravely. 'I am kicking against my bonds, longing for that freedom which in the past kept my stomach empty and my head erect.'

'Will you never be serious?' she retorted.

'Never, while I live. My journey to England killed my only attempt at sobriety, for there I found that the stock to which I belonged was both irreproachable and grave, had been so all the while that I, the most recent scion of so noble a race, was roaming about the world, the most shiftless and thriftless vagabond it had ever seen. But in England' – he sighed and raised his eyes and hands in mock solemnity – 'in England the climate is so atrocious that the people become grim-visaged and square-toed through constantly watching the rain coming down. Or else,' he added, with another suppressed ripple of that infectious laugh of his, 'the climate in England has become so atrocious because there are so many square-toed folk about. I was such a very little while in England,' he concluded with utmost gravity, 'I had not time to make up my mind which way it went.'

'Methinks you told me,' she rejoined, 'that your home in England is beautiful and stately.'

'It is both, dear heart,' he replied more seriously; 'and I shall learn to love it when you have dwelt therein. I should love it even now if it had ever been hallowed by the presence of my mother.'

'She never went there?'

'No, never. My father came to Holland in Leicester's train. He married my mother in Haarlem, then deserted her and left her there to starve. My friend Frans Hals cared for me after she died. That is the whole of her history. It does not make for deep, filial affection, does it?'

'But you have seen your father now. Affection will come in time.'

'Yes; I have seen him, thanks to your father, who brought us together. I have seen my home in Sussex, where one day, please God, you'll reign as its mistress.'

'I, the wife of an English lord!' she sighed. 'I can scarcely credit it.'

'Nor can I, dear heart,' he answered lightly; 'for that you'll never be. Let me try and explain to you just how it all is, for, in truth, English honours are hard to understand. My father is an English gentleman with no handle to his name. Blake of Blakeney they call him over there; and I am his only son. It seems that he rendered signal services to his king of late, who thereupon desired to confer upon him one of those honours which we over here find it so difficult to apprise. My father, however, either because he is advanced in years or because he desired to show me some singular mark of favour, petitioned King James to bestow the proposed honour upon his only son. Thus am I Sir Percy Blakeney, it seems, without any merit on my part. Funny, is it not? And I who, for years, was known by no name save Diogenes, one of three vagabonds, with perhaps more wits, but certainly no more worth, than my two compeers!'

'Then I should call you Sir Percy?' she concluded. 'Yet I cannot get used to the name.'

'You might even call me Percy,' he suggested; 'for thus was I baptized at my dear mother's wish. Though, in truth, I had forgotten it until my father insisted on it that I could not be called Diogenes by mine own servants, and that he himself could not present me to his Majesty the King of England under so fanciful a name.'

'I like best to think of you as Diogenes,' she murmured softly. 'Thus I knew you first, and your brother philosophers, Socrates and Pythagoras – such a quaint trio, and all of you so unsuited to your names! I wish,' she added with a sigh, 'that they were here now.'

'And they should be here,' he assented. 'I am deeply anxious. But Pythagoras – '

He broke off abruptly. Mynheer Beresteyn's voice called to him from the recess by the open window.

'A goblet of wine!' Mynheer commanded; 'for his Highness.'

Diogenes was about to comply with the order, but Nicolaes forestalled him. Already he had poured out the wine.

'Let me take it,' he said curtly, took up the goblet and went with it to the window. He offered it to the Stadtholder, who drank greedily.

It was but a brief incident. Nicolaes had remained beside the prince while the latter drank; then he returned, with the empty goblet in his hand, to take his place once more beside his stolid and solid bride.

'You were speaking of Pythagoras, sir,' Gilda rejoined, as soon as Diogenes was once more seated beside her. 'I never know which is which of the two dear souls. Is Pythagoras the lean one with the deep, bass voice?'

'No. He is the fat one, with the round, red nose,' Diogenes replied gravely. 'He was at Ede the night before last, and was seen there, at the tavern of the Crow's Nest, somewhere after midnight, imbibing copious draughts of hot, spiced ale. After that all traces of him have vanished. But he must have started to join me here, as this had been pre-arranged, and I fear me that he lost his way on that *verfloekte* waste. I have sent Socrates, my lean comrade – he with the deep, bass voice – together with a search party, to look for poor Pythagoras upon the Veluwe. They should be here, in truth, and –'

But the next word died in his throat. He jumped to his feet.

'The Stadtholder!' he exclaimed. 'He hath fainted.'

4

Indeed, there was quite a commotion now in the window recess, where Prince Maurice had remained all this while by the open casement, inhaling the fresh, keen air. The English physician stood beside him, and Mynheer Beresteyn was gazing with anxious eyes on the master to whom, in spite of all, he had remained so splendidly loyal. The dizziness had apparently come on quite suddenly, while the Stadtholder was acknowledging the acclamations of the crowd who had seen and cheered him. He tottered, and would have fallen but for the physician's supporting arm.

Not many of the guests had noticed the incident. They were for the most part too much absorbed in their enjoyment of the feast to pay attention to what went on in other parts of the room. But Diogenes had seen it, and was already over by the window; and Nicolaes Beresteyn, too, had jumped to his feet. He looked wide-eyed and scared, even whilst the stolid Kaatje, flushed with good cheer, remained perfectly unconcerned, munching some sweetmeats which seemed to delight her palate.

The Stadtholder, however, had quickly recovered. The faintness passed off as suddenly as it came, but it left the illustrious guest more silent and moody than before. His face had become of a yellowish pallor, and his eyes looked sunken as if consumed with fever. But he chose to return to his seat under the daïs, and this time he called to Diogenes to give him the support of his arm.

' 'Twas scarce worth while, eh, my friend,' he said bitterly, 'to risk your precious young life in order to save this precarious one. Had Stoutenburg's bomb done the assassin's work, it would only have anticipated events by less than three months.'

'Your Highness is over-tired,' Diogenes rejoined simply.

'Complete rest in the midst of your friends would fight this insidious sickness far better than the wisest of physicians.'

'What do you mean?' the Stadtholder immediately retorted, his keen, hawk-like glance searching the soldier's smiling face. 'Why should you say "in the midst of your friends?" ' he went on huskily. 'You don't mean – ?'

'What, your Highness?'

'I mean – you said it so strangely – as if – '

'I, your Highness?' Diogenes queried, not a little surprised at the Stadtholder's febrile agitation.

'I myself have oft wondered – '

Maurice of Nassau paused abruptly, rested his elbows on the table, and for a moment or two remained quite still, his forehead buried in his hands. Gilda gazed on him wide-eyed and tearful; even Kaatje ceased to munch. It seemed terrible to be so great a man, wielding such power, commanding such obedience, and to be reduced thus to a mere babbling sufferer, fearing phantoms and eagerly gleaning any words of comfort that might come from loyal lips.

Diogenes had remained silent, too; his eyes, usually so full of light-heartedness and merriment, had a strange, searching glitter in them now. A minute or two later the prince had pulled himself together, tried to look unconcerned, and assumed a geniality which obviously he was far from feeling. But it was to Diogenes that he spoke once more.

'Anyhow, I could not rest yet awhile, my friend,' he said with a sigh; 'whilst the Archduchess threatens Gelderland, and De Berg is making ready to cross the Ijssel.'

'Your Highness's armies under your Highness's command,' rejoined the soldier firmly, 'can drive the Archduchess's hosts out of Gelderland, and send Henri de Berg back across the Ijssel. Maurice of Nassau is still the finest commander in Europe, even –'

He paused, and the Stadtholder broke in bitterly:

'Even though he is a dying man, you mean.'

'No!' here broke in Gilda, with glowing fervour. 'I swear that nothing was further from my lord's thoughts. Sir,' she added, and turned boldly to her lover, 'you spoke with such confidence just now. A toast, I pray you, so that we may all join in expressions of loyalty to our guest and sovereign lord, the Stadtholder!'

She poured out a goblet full of wine. Diogenes gave her a quick glance of approval. Then he picked up the goblet, stood upon his seat, and placed one foot on the table.

'Long life to your Highness!' he cried aloud. 'May it please God to punish your enemies and to give victory unto your cause!'

Then, holding the goblet aloft, he called at the top of his voice:

'Maurice of Nassau and the cause of Liberty!'

Every one rose, and a rousing cheer went echoing round the room. It was heard and taken up lustily by the crowd outside, until the very walls of the ancient city echoed the loyal toast, from the grim towers of Koppel Poort to the Vrouwetoren of St Maria Kerk; from gateway to gateway, and rampart to rampart. And the bells of St Joris and St Maria took up the joyful call and sent peal after peal of bells resounding gleefully through the keen, wintry air.

'Maurice of Nassau!' rang the chimes. 'Nassau and liberty!'

5

But after this manifestation of joy and enthusiasm, comparative silence fell upon the wedding assembly. None but those who had partaken over-freely of Mynheer Beresteyn's good cheer could fail to see that the Stadtholder felt ill, and only kept up asemblance of gaiety by a mighty effort of his iron will. Thereafter, conversation became subdued. People talked in whispers, an atmosphere of constraint born of anxiety reigned there where light-hearted gaiety had a while ago held undisputed sway. The host himself did his best to revive the temper of his guests. Serving-men and maids were ordered to go round more briskly with the wine. One or two of the younger men hazarded the traditional jokes which usually obtained at wedding feasts; but those who laughed did so shamefacedly. It seemed as if a vague terror held erstwhile chattering tongues in check.

The Stadtholder, leaning back against the cushions of his chair, spoke very little. His long, nervy fingers played incessantly with crumbs and pellets of bread. He looked impatient and ill at ease, like a man who wants to get away, yet fears to offend his host. He had kept Diogenes by his side this time, and Beresteyn was able to snatch a few last words with his daughter. Once she was married, her husband would take her to his home in England one day, and the thought of parting from the child he loved was weighing the father's spirits down.

' 'Tis the first time,' he said sadly, 'that you will pass out of my keeping. You were the precious heritage bequeathed to me by your dead mother. Now 'tis to a stranger that I am entrusting my priceless treasure.'

'A stranger, father,' riposted Gilda quietly, 'who hath proved himself worthy of the truth. And when we do go to England,' she went on gaily, 'there will only be a narrow strip of water between us, and that is easily crossed.'

Beresteyn gave a quickly smothered sigh. He looked across at the stranger to whom, as he said, he was about to hand over the most precious gift he possessed. Handsome he was, that erstwhile penniless soldier of fortune; handsome and brave, frank and loyal, and with that saving grace of light-hearted gaiety in him which had helped him through the past terrible crisis in his life, and brought him to the safe haven of a stately home in England and a wealthy father, eager to make amends for the wrongs committed long ago.

But still a stranger for all that, a man who had seen more of the seamy side of the world, who had struggled more, suffered more – ay, perhaps sinned more – than those of his rank in life usually did at his age. Something of that rough-and-tumble life of the soldier of fortune, without home or kindred, who sells his sword to the highest bidder, and knows no master save his own will, must have left its mark upon the temperament of the man. Despite the humorous twinkle in the eyes, the bantering curl on the lip, the man's face bore the impress of the devil-may-care existence that takes no heed of the morrow. And at times, when it was in repose, there was a strangely grim look in it of determination as well as of turbulent passions, not always held in check.

Beresteyn sighed with inward apprehension. His well-ordered mind, the mind of a Dutch middle-class burgher, precise and unemotional, could not quite fathom that of the Anglo-Saxon – the most romantic and the most calculating, the most impulsive and the most studied, the most sensuous and most self-repressed temperament that ever set the rest of the world wondering. He could see the reckless scapegrace, the thoughtless adventurer, fuming and fretting under the restraint put upon him by the cut-and-dried conventions attendant upon these wedding ceremonies, could watch him literally writhing under the knowing looks and time-honoured innuendos which custom deemed allowable on these occasions. His hands indeed must be itching to come in contact with the cheeks of mocking friends and smug relatives, all eager to give advice or to chaff the young bride, until the hot blood rushed to her cheeks and tears of annoyance gathered in her eyes.

The whole atmosphere of noise and drinking – ay, of good-humour and complacency – did, in truth, grate upon Diogenes' nerves. He had not lied to Gilda nor yet exaggerated his sentiments when he said that his sinews ached with longing to seize her and carry her away into solitude and quiet, where nought would come to disturb their love-dream; away upon his horse, her soft arms encircling his neck, her head resting on his shoulder, her dear face turned up to his gaze, with those heavenly eyes closed in rapture; the delicate mouth slightly parted, showing a vision of tiny teeth, a tear mayhap trembling on her lashes, a soft blush mantling on her cheek. Away! Across the ocean to that stately home in England, where in the spring the air was soft with the scent of violets and of fruit blossom, and where beside the river the reeds murmured a soft accompaniment to songs of passion and hymns of love. Away from all save the shrine which he had set up for her in his heart; from all save the haven of his arms.

To feel that, and then be forced to sit and discuss plans for the undoing of the Spanish commander or for the relief of Arnheim, was, in fact, more than Diogenes' restive temperament could stand. His attention began to wander, his answers became evasive; so much so that, after a while, the Stadtholder, eyeing him closely, remarked with the pale ghost of a smile:

' 'Tis no use fretting and fuming, my friend. Your English blood is too mutinous for this sober country and its multitude of stodgy conventions. One of these demands that your bride shall sit here till the last of the guests has departed, and only a few fussy and interfering old *tantes* are left to unrobe her and to commiserate with her over her future lot – a slave to a bullying husband, a handmaid to her exacting lord. Every middle-aged frump in the Netherlands hath some story to tell that will bring tears to a young bride's eyes or a blush to her cheeks.'

'Please God,' Diogenes ejaculated fervently, 'Gilda will be spared that.'

'Impossible, you rogue!' the Stadtholder retorted, amused despite his moodiness by the soldier's fretful temper. 'The conventions – '

'*Verfloekt* will be the conventions as far as we are concerned,' Diogenes rejoined hotly. 'And if your Highness would but help – ' he added impulsively.

'I? What can I do?'

'Give the signal for dispersal,' Diogenes entreated; 'and graciously promise to forgive me if, for the first time in my life, I act with disrespect towards your Highness.'

'But, man, how will that help you?' the Stadtholder demurred.

'I must get away from all this wearying bombast, this jabbering and scraping and all these puppy-tricks!' Diogenes exclaimed with comical fierceness. 'I must get away ere my wife becomes a doll and a puppet, tossed into my arms by a lot of irresponsible monkeys! If I have to stay here much longer, your Highness,' he added earnestly, 'I vow that I shall flee from it all, leave an angel to weep for my abominable desertion of what I hold more priceless than all the world, and an outraged father to curse the day when so feckless an adventurer crossed his daughter's path. But stand this any longer I cannot!' he concluded, and, with a quick sweep of the arm, he pointed to the chattering, guzzling crowd below. 'And if your Highness will not help me – '

'Who said I would not help you, you hotheaded rashling?' the Stadtholder broke in composedly. 'You know very well that I can refuse you nothing, not even the furtherance of one of your madcap schemes. And as for disrespect – why, as you say, in the midst of so much bowing and scraping some of us are as eager for disrespect as an ageing spinster for amorous overtures. By way of a change, you know.'

He spoke quite simply and with an undercurrent of genuine sympathy in his tone, as a man towards his friend. Something of the old Maurice of Nassau seemed for the moment to have swept aside the arbitrary tyrant whom men had learned to hate as well as to obey. Diogenes' irascible mood melted suddenly in the sunshine of the Stadtholder's indulgent smile, the mocking glance faded out of his eyes, and he said with unwonted earnestness:

'No wonder that men have gone to death or to glory under your leadership.'

'Would you follow me again if I called?' the prince retorted.

'Your Highness hath no need of me. The United Provinces are free, her burghers are free men. 'Tis time to sheathe the sword, and a man might be allowed, methinks, to dream of happiness.'

'Is your happiness bound up with the mad scheme for which you want my help?'

'Ay, my dear lord!' Diogenes replied. 'And, secure in your gracious promise, I swear that naught can keep me from that scheme now save mine own demise.'

'There are more arbitrary things than death, my friend,' the Stadtholder mused.

'Possibly, your Highness,' the soldier answered lightly; 'but not for me tonight.'

6

More than one chronicler of the time hath averred that Maurice of Nassau had in truth a soft corner in his heart for the man who had saved him from the bomb prepared by the Lord of Stoutenburg, and would yield to the 'Laughing Cavalier' when others, less privileged, were made to feel the weight of his arbitrary temper. Be that as it may, he certainly on this occasion was as good as his word. Wearied with all these endless ceremonials, he was no doubt glad enough to take his departure, and anon he gave the signal for a general breaking up of the party by rising, and, in a loud voice, thanking Mynheer Beresteyn for his lavish hospitality.

'An you will pardon this abrupt departure,' he concluded with unwonted graciousness, 'I would fain get to horse. By starting within the hour, I could reach Utrecht before dark.'

All the guests had risen, too, and there was the usual hubbub and noise attendant on the dispersal of so large a party. The Stadtholder stepped down from the daïs, Mynheer Beresteyn and the English physician remaining by his side, while the bridal party brought up the rear. Room was made for his Highness to walk down the room, the men standing bareheaded and the women curtseying as he passed. But he did not speak to any one, only nodded perfunctorily to those whom he knew personally. Obviously he felt ill and tired, and his moodiness was, for the most part, commented on with sympathy.

The brides and bridegrooms, on the other hand, had to withstand a veritable fusillade of banter, which Nicolaes Beresteyn received sulkily, and the stolid Kaatje with much complacence. Indeed, this bride was willing enough to be chaffed, had even a saucy reply handy when she was teased, and ogled her friends slily as she went by. But Gilda remained silent and demure. I don't think that she heard a word that was said. She literally seemed to glide across the room like the veritable sprite her ardent lover had called her. Her tiny hand, white and slightly fluttering, rested on his arm, lost in the richly embroidered folds of his magnificent doublet. She was not fully conscious of her actions, moved along as in a dream, without the exertion of her will. She was wont to speak afterwards of this brief progress of hers through the crowded room with the chattering throng of friends all around, as a walk through air. Nothing seemed to her to exist. There was no room, no crowd, no noise. She alone existed, and ethereally. Her lover was there, however, and she was fully conscious of his will. She knew that anon she would be a captive in his arms, to be dealt with by him as he liked; and this caused her to feel half fearful and yet wholly content.

He, Diogenes, on the other hand, was the picture of fretful impatience, squeezing his soft felt hat in his hand as if it were the throat of some deadly enemy. He never once looked at his bride; probably if he had he would have lost the last shred of self-control, would have seized her in his arms and carried her away then and there, regardless of the respect due to the Stadtholder and to his host.

But the trial, though severe to any ebullient temper, was not of long duration. Anon the Stadtholder was in the hall, booted once more and spurred, and surrounded by his equerries and by the bridal party.

His bodyguard encumbered the hall, their steel bonnets and short breastplates reflecting the wintry light which came, many-hued, through the tall, stained-glass windows. In the rear the wedding guests were crowding forward to catch a last glimpse of the Stadtholder, and of the pageant of his departure. The great hall door had been thrown open, and through it, framed in the richness of the heavy oaken jambs, a picture appeared, gay, animated, brilliant, such as the small city had never before seen.

There was the holiday throng, moving ceaselessly in an ever-flowing and glittering stream. The women in huge, winged hoods and short kirtles, the men in fur bonnets and sleeved coats, were strolling up and down the quay. There were the inevitable musicians with pipes, viols, and sackbuts, pushing their way through the dense mass of people, with a retinue behind them of young people and old, and of children, all stepping it to the measure of the tune. There was the swarthy foreigner with his monkey dressed out in gaily coloured rags, and the hawker with his tray full of bright handkerchiefs, of glass beads, chains, and amulets, crying out his wares. It was, in fact, a holiday crowd, drawn thither by Mynheer Beresteyn's largesse; the shopkeepers with their wives, who had been induced to shut down shop for the afternoon, as if some official function had been in progress; the apprentices getting in everybody's way, hilarious and full of mischief, trying to steal the hawkers' wares, or to play impish pranks on their employers; servant maids and sober apothecaries, out-at-elbow scriveners and stolid rustics, together with the rag and tag of soldiery, the paid mercenaries of Maurice of Nassau's army, in their showy doublets and plumed bonnets, elbowing their way through with the air of masters.

And all this brilliant gathering was lit by a pale, wintry sun: and with the sleepy waters of the Eem, and the frowning towers of the Koppel-poort forming just the right natural-tinted background to the scene.

'Make way there!' the prince's herald shouted, whilst another rang a fanfare upon the trumpet. 'Make way for his High and Mightiness, Maurice of Nassau, Prince of Orange, Stadtholder of the United Provinces of Holland, Friesland, Utrecht, Gelderland, Over Yssel, and Groningen! Make way!'

The equerries were bringing the prince's charger, the pikemen followed in gorgeous padded trunks and slashed hose. To the noise of the moving throng, the chatter and the laughter, the scraping of viols and piping of sackbuts, was now added the din of champing horses, rattle of bits and chains, the shouts of the men who were bringing the horses along. The crowd receded, leaving an open space in front of the house, where mounted men assembled so quickly that they seemed as if they had risen out of the ground.

The Stadtholder was taking final leave of his host listening with what patience he could muster to lengthy, loyal speeches from the more important guests, and from the other bride and bridegroom. He had – deliberately methinks – turned his back on Diogenes, who, strangely enough, was booted and spurred too, had his sword buckled to his belt, and carried a dark cloak on his arm, presenting not at all the picture of a bridegroom in holiday attire.

And it all happened so quickly that neither the guests within, nor the soldiers, nor the crowd outside, had time to realize it or to take it in. No one understood, in fact, what was happening, save perhaps the Stadtholder, who guessed; and he engaged the sober fathers near him in earnest conversation.

A mounted equerry, dressed in rough leather jerkin and leading another horse by the bridle, had taken up his stand in the forefront of the crowd. Now at a signal unheard by all save him, he jumped out of the saddle and stood beside the stirrup leathers of the second charger. At that same instant Diogenes, with movements quick as lightning, had thrown the cloak, which he was carrying round Gilda's shoulders, and before she could utter a scream or even a gasp, he had stooped and picked her up in his arms as if she were a weightless doll.

Another second and he was outside the door, at the top of the steps which led down to the quay. For an instant he stood there, his keen eyes sweeping over the picture before him. Like a young lion that hath been caged and now scents liberty once more, he inhaled the biting air; a superb figure, with head tossed back, eyes and lips laughing with the joy of deliverance, the inert figure of the girl lying in his arms.

He felt her clinging more closely to him, and revelled in that intoxicating sense of power when the one woman yields who holds a world of happiness in her tiny hand. He felt the tightening of her hold, watched the look of contentment stealing over her face, saw her eyes close, her lips smile, and knew that they were ready for a kiss.

Then he caught sight of his horse, and of the man in the leather jerkin. He signalled to him to bring the horses near. The crowd understood his meaning and set up a ringing cheer. Many things had been seen in Dutch cities before, but never so romantic an abduction as this. The bridegroom carrying off his bride in the face of scandalized and protesting wedding guests! The Stadtholder even was seen to laugh. He could be seen in the background, reassuring the horrified guests, and trying by kind words and pressure of the hand to appease Mynheer Beresteyn's agonized surprise.

'I knew of his mad project, and I must say I approved,' the prince whispered to the agitated father. 'He is taking her to Rotterdam tonight. Let the child be, Mynheer; she is safe enough in his arms.'

Beresteyn was one of those men who throughout his life had always known how to accept the inevitable. Perhaps in his heart he knew that the Stadtholder was right.

'Give them your blessing, Mynheer,' Maurice of Nassau urged. 'English gentleman or soldier of fortune, the man is a man and deserves it. Your daughter loves him. Let them be.'

Diogenes had encountered Beresteyn's reproachful glance. He did not move from where he stood, only his arms closed tighter still around Gilda's motionless form. It was an instinctive challenge to the father – almost a defiance. What he had he would hold, in spite of all.

Beresteyn hesitated for the mere fraction of a second longer; then he, too, stepped out through the door and approached the man and his burden. He said nothing, but, in the face of the crowd, he stooped and pressed his lips against his daughter's forehead. Then Mynheer Beresteyn murmured something which sounded like a blessing, and added solemnly:

'May God's wrath descend upon you, my lord, if you ever cause her unhappiness.'

'Amen to that!' responded Diogenes lightly. 'She and I, Mynheer, will dream together for awhile in England, but I'll bring her back to you when our orchards are gay with apple-blossom and there is a taste of summer in the air.'

He bowed his head to receive the father's blessing. The crowd cheered again; sackbuts and viols set up a lively tune. At every window of the house, along the quay eager faces were peering out, gazing on the moving spectacle. In the doorway of Mynheer Beresteyn's house the Stadtholder remained to watch. For the moment he seemed better and brighter, more like his former self. The rest of the bridal party was still in the hall, but the wedding guests had gone back into the banqueting-room, whence they could see through the open windows what was going on.

7

Then it was that suddenly a curious spectacle presented itself to view. It was, in truth, so curious an one that those of the crowd who were in the rear withdrew their consideration from the romantic scene before them in order to concentrate it on those two strange-looking cavaliers who had just emerged from under the Koppelpoort, and were slowly forging their way through the throng.

It was the ringing shout, reiterated twice in succession by one of these cavaliers, that had at first arrested the attention of the crowd, and had even caused Diogenes to pause in the very act of starting for his sentimental adventure. To him the voice that uttered such peremptory clamour was familiar enough, but what in St Bavon's name did it all mean?

'Hola! you *verdommte plepshurk!*' came for the third time from the strange cavalier. Make way there! We are for the house of Mynheer Beresteyn, where we are bidden as his guests.'

A loud burst of hilarity greeted this announcement, and a mocking voice retorted lustily:

'Hey! Make way there for the honoured guests of Mynheer Beresteyn!'

In truth, it was small wonder that the aspect of these two cavaliers caused such wild jollity amongst the people, who at this precise moment were over-ready for laughter. One of them, as lean as a gatepost, sat high on his horse with long shanks covered in high leathern boots. A tall sugar-loaf hat sat precariously upon his head, and his hatchet face, with the hooked, prominent nose and sharp, unshaved chin, looked blue with the cold.

Behind him on a pillion rode – or rather clung – his companion, a short man as rotund as the other was lean, with round face which no doubt had once been of a healthy ruddy tint, but was now streaked and blotched with pallor. He, too, wore a sugar-loaf hat, but it had slid down to the back of his head, and was held in place by a piece of black tape, which he had in his mouth like a horse has its bit. He was holding on very tightly with his short, fat arms to his companion's body, and his feet were tied together with thick cord beneath the horse's belly. His doublet and hose were smeared with mud and stained with blood, and altogether he presented a pitiable spectacle, more especially when he rolled his small, beady eyes and looked with a scared expression on the hilarious apprentices who were dancing and screaming around him.

But the other appeared quite indifferent to the jeers and mockeries of the crowd. He passed majestically through the gateway of the Koppelpoort that spans the river, not unlike the figure of that legendary knight of the rueful countenance of whom the Señor Cervantes had been writing of late.

Diogenes had remained on the top of the steps, perfectly still. His keen eyes, frowning now under the straight, square brow, watched the slow progress of those two quaint figures. Who will ever attempt to explain the subtle workings of that mysterious force which men term Intuition? Whence does it come? Where does it dwell? How doth it come knocking at a man's heart with cold, hard knuckles that bruise and freeze? Diogenes felt that sudden call. Gilda was still lying snugly in his arms; she had seen nothing. But he had become suspicious now, mistrustful of that Fate which had but a moment ago smiled so encouragingly upon him. All his exhilaration fell away from him like a discarded mantle, leaving him chilled to the soul and inert, and with the premonition of something evil looming from afar on the horizon of his Destiny.

The two quaint companions came nearer. Soon Diogenes could read every line upon the familiar countenances. He and those men had fought side by side, shoulder to shoulder, had bled together, suffered together, starved and triumphed together. There was but little the one thought that the others could not know. Even now, on Socrates' lean, lantern-jawed face Diogenes read plainly the message of some tragedy as yet uncomprehended by the other, but which Pythagoras' sorry plight had more than suggested. It was a deeper thing than Intuition; it was Knowledge. Knowledge that the hour of happiness had gone by, the hour of security and of repose, and that the relentless finger of Fate pointed once more to paths beset with sorrow and with thorns, to the path of an adventurer and of a soldier of fortune, rather than to the easy existence of a wealthy gentleman.

As Socrates swung himself wearily out of the saddle, Diogenes' piercing glance darted a mute, quick query toward his friend. The other replied by a mere nod of the head. They knew; they understood one another. Put into plain language, question and answer might have been put thus:

'Are we to go on the warpath again, old compeer?'

'So it seems. There's fighting to be done. Will you be in it, too?'

And Diogenes gave that quick impatient sigh which was so characteristic of him, and very slowly, very gently, as if she were a sheaf of flowers, he allowed his beloved to glide out of his arms.

3

The Great Interruption

The next moment Diogenes was down on the quay in time to help Socrates to lift his brother philosopher off the pillion.

Gilda, a little scared at first, not understanding, looked wonderingly around her, blinking in the glare, until she encountered her father's troubled glance.

'What is it?' she murmured, half-stupidly.

He tried to explain, pointed to the group down below, the funny, fat man in obvious pain and distress, being lifted off the horse and received in those same strong arms which had sheltered her – Gilda – but a moment ago.

The Stadtholder, too, was curious, asked many questions, and had to be waited on deferentially with replies and explanations, which were still of necessity very vague.

'Attend to his Highness, father,' Gilda said more firmly. 'I can look to myself now.'

She felt a little strange, a little humiliated perhaps, standing here alone, as if abandoned by the very man who but a moment ago had seemed ready to defy every convention for her sake. Just now she had been the centre of attraction, the pivot round which revolved excitement, curiosity, interest. Even the Stadtholder had, for the space of those few minutes, forgotten his cares and his responsibilities in order to think of her and to plead with her father for her freedom and her happiness. Now she was all alone, seemed so for the moment, while her father and Mynheer van den Poele and the older men crowded around his Highness, and every one had their eyes fixed on the curious spectacle down below.

But that sense of isolation and of disappointment was only transient. Gilda Beresteyn had recently gone through experiences far more bitter than this – experiences that had taught her to think and to act quickly and on her own initiative. She saw her lover remounting the steps now. He was carrying his friend in his arms as if the latter had been a child, his other compeer following ruefully. The rowdy 'prentices had been silenced; two or three kindly pairs of hands had proved ready to assist and to care for the horse, which looked spent. The holiday crowd was silent and sympathetic. Every one felt that in this sudden interruption of the gay and romantic adventure there lurked a something mysterious which might very well prove to be a tragedy.

It was Gilda who led the way into the house, calling Maria to open a guest-chamber forthwith, one where the bed was spread with freshly-aired linen. The English physician, at a word from the Stadtholder, was ready to minister to the sick man, and Mynheer Beresteyn himself showed the young soldier and his burden up the stairs, while the crowd of wedding guests and of the prince's bodyguard made way for them to pass through the hall.

What had been such a merry and excited throng earlier in the day was now more than ever subdued. The happenings in the house of Mynheer Beresteyn, which should have been at this hour solely centred around the Stadtholder and the wedding party, were strange enough indeed to call forth whispered comments and subdued murmurings in secluded corners. To begin with, the Stadtholder had put off his departure for an hour and more, and this apparently at the instance of Diogenes, who had begged for the assistance of the prince's English physician to minister to his friend.

People marvelled why the town leech should not have been called in. Why should a strange *plepshurk*'s sickness interfere with his Highness's movements? Also the Stadtholder appeared agitated and fretful since Diogenes had had a word with him. Maurice of Nassau, acquiescing with unwonted readiness both in his physician remaining to look after the sick man and in the postponement of his own departure, had since then retired to a small private room on a floor above, in the company of Mynheer Beresteyn and several of the more important guests. The others were left to conjecture and to gossip, which they did freely, whilst Gilda was no longer to be seen, and the worthy Kaatje was left pouting and desolate beside her morose bridegroom. Nicolaes Beresteyn, indeed, appeared more moody than any one, although the interruption could not in itself have interfered with his new domestic arrangements. At first he had thought of following his father and the Stadtholder into the private chamber upstairs, but to this Mynheer Beresteyn had demurred.

'Your place, my son,' he said, with a gently mocking smile, 'is beside your Kaatje. His Highness will understand.'

And when Nicolaes, trying to insist, followed his father up the stairs to the very threshold of the council room, Mynheer quite firmly and unceremoniously closed the door in his face.

2

Up in the guest-chamber, Diogenes was watching over his sick friend. The first moment that he was alone with his two old compeers, he had turned to Socrates and queried anxiously:

'What is it? What hath happened?'

'He'll tell you when he can speak,' the other replied. 'We found him lying in the snow outside Lang Soeren with two bullet-wounds in his back, after we had searched the whole *verfloekte* Veluwe for him all day. We took him into Lang Soeren, where there was a leech, who extracted the one bullet that had lodged under his shoulder blade; the other had only passed through the flesh along his ribs, where it made a clean hole but could not otherwise be found.'

'Well, yes – and – ' Diogenes went on impatiently, for the other was somewhat slow of speech.

'The leech,' Socrates rejoined unperturbed, 'said that the patient must lie still for a few days because of the fever; but what must this fool do but shout and rave the moment he is conscious that he must to Amersfoort to see you at once. And so loudly did he shout and so wildly did he rave, that the leech himself got scared and ran away. Whereupon I set the bladder-bellied loon upon the pillion behind me and brought him hither, thinking the ride would do him less harm than all that wild screeching and waving of arms. And here we are!' Socrates concluded blandly, and threw himself into the nearest chair; for he, too, apparently, was exhausted with the fatigue of his perilous journey across the waste.

Just then the leech returned, and nothing more could be said. The sick man groaned a good deal under the physician's hands, and Socrates presently dropped off to sleep.

The noise in the street below had somewhat abated, but there was still the monotonous hubbub attendant on a huge crowd on the move. Diogenes went to the window and gazed out upon the throng. Even now the wintry sun was sinking slowly down in the west in a haze of purple and rose, licking the towers of St Maria and Joris with glistening tongues of fire, and tinting the snow-covered roofs and gables with a rosy hue. The sluggish waters of the Eem appeared like liquid flame.

For a few minutes the Koppelpoort, the bridges, the bastions, the helmets and breastplates of the prince's guard threw back a thousand rays of multi-coloured lights. For a brief instant the earth glowed and blushed under this last kiss of her setting lord. Then all became sombre and dreary, as if a veil had been drawn over the light that illuminated the little city, leaving but the grey shadows visible, and the sadness of evening and the expectance of a long winter's night.

Diogenes gave a moody sigh. His fiery temper chafed under this delay. Not for a moment would he have thought of leaving his sick comrade until he had been reassured as to his fate; but if everything had happened as he had planned and wished, he would be half-way to Utrecht by now, galloping adown the lonely roads with a delicious burden upon his saddle-bow, and feeling the cold wintry wind whistling past his ears as he put the leagues behind him.

He turned away from the window, and tiptoed out of the room. The groans of the sick man, the measured movements of the leech, the snoring of Socrates, were grating on his nerves. Closing the door softly behind him, he strode down the gallery which ran in front of him along the entire width of the house. Up and down once or twice. The movement did him good, and he liked the solitude. The house was still full of a chattering throng; he could hear the murmur of conversation rising from below. Once he peeped over the carved balustrade of the gallery and down into the hall. The prince's bodyguard was still there, and two or three equerries. The clank of their spurs resounded up the stairs as they moved about on the flag-covered floor.

3

When Diogenes resumed his pacing up and down, he suddenly became aware of the soft and distant sound of a woman's voice, singing to the accompaniment of a quaint-toned virginal. He paused and listened. The voice was Gilda's, and the sentimental ditty which she sang had just that melancholy strain in it which is to be found in the songs of all nations that are foredoomed to suffer and to fight. Chiding himself for a fool, Diogenes, nevertheless, felt for a moment or two quite unable to move. It seemed as if Gilda's song – he could not catch the words – was tearing at his heart even whilst it reduced him to a state of silent ecstasy. Much against his will he felt the hot tears welling to his eyes. With his wonted impatience he swept them away with the back of his hand.

'Curse me for a snivelling blockhead!' he muttered; and strode resolutely in the direction whence had come the sweet sad sound.

Then it was that he noticed that one of the doors which gave on the gallery was ajar. It was through this that the intoxicating sound had come to his ears. After an instant's hesitation he pushed the door open. It gave on a small panelled room with deep-embrasured window, through which the grey evening light came in, shyly peeping. On the window-ledge a couple of pots of early tulips flaunted their crude colours against the neutral-tinted background, whilst on the shelves in a corner of the room gleamed the vivid blue of bright-patterned china plates. But the flowers and the china and the grey evening light were but momentary impressions, which did not fix themselves upon the man's consciousness. All that he retained clearly was the vision of Gilda sitting at the instrument, her delicate hands resting upon the keys. She had ceased to play, and was looking straight out before her, and Diogenes could see her piquant profile silhouetted against the pale, silvery light. She had changed her stiff bridal robes for a plain gown of dark-coloured worsted, relieved only by dainty cuffs and collar of filmy Flemish lace.

At the sound of her husband's footsteps she turned to look on him, and her whole face became wreathed in smiles. He was still booted and spurred, ready for the journey, with his long, heavy sword buckled to his belt; but he had put hat and mantle aside. The moment he came in Gilda put a finger to her lips.

'Sh-sh-sh!' she whispered. 'If you make no noise they'll not know you are here.'

She pointed across the room to where a heavy tapestry apparently masked another door.

'The Stadtholder is in there,' she added naively, 'with father and Mynheer van den Poele and a number of other grave seigneurs. Kaatje is weeping and complaining somewhere down In *mejuffrouw* van den Poele's arms. So I sat down to the virginal and left the door open, so that you might hear me sing; for if you heard I thought you would surely come. I was lonely,' she added simply, 'and waiting for you.'

Quite enough in truth to make a man who is dizzy with love ten thousand times more dizzy still. And Diogenes was desperately in love, more so indeed than he had ever thought himself capable of being. He quietly unbuckled his sword, which clanged against the floor when he moved, and deposited it cautiously and noiselessly in an angle of the room. Then he tiptoed across to the virginal and knelt beside his beloved.

For a moment or two he rested his head against her cool white hands.

'To think,' he murmured, with a sigh of infinite longing, 'that we might be half-way to Rotterdam by now! But I could not leave my old Pythagoras till I knew that he was in no danger.'

'What saith the physician, my lord?' she asked.

'I am waiting now for his final verdict. But he gives me every hope. In an hour I shall know.'

He paused, trying to read the varying play of emotions upon her face. From the other side of the tapestry came the low sound of subdued murmurings.

'It would not be too late,' he went on, slightly hesitating, taking her hands in his and forcing her glance to meet his. 'You knew I meant to take you to England – to carry you away – tonight?'

She nodded.

'Yes, I knew,' she replied. 'And I was glad to go!' Will you be afraid to come presently?' he urged, his voice quivering with excitement. 'In the dark – I know the road well. We could make Rotterdam by midnight – and set sail for England tomorrow as I had prearranged – '

'Just as you wish, my dear lord,' she assented simply.

'I could not wait, *ma donna*! I had planned it all – to ride with you to Rotterdam tonight – and then tomorrow on the seas – with you – and England in sight, I could not wait!' he reiterated, almost pathetically, so great was his impatience.

'I am ready to start when you will, my lord,' she said again, with a smile.

'And you'll not be afraid?' he insisted. 'It will be dark – and cold. We could not reach Rotterdam before midnight.'

'How should I be afraid of the darkness or of anything,' she retorted, 'when I am with you. And how should I be cold, when I am nestling in your arms?'

He had his arms round her in an instant. He would have kissed her if he dared. But with the first kiss all restraint would of a surety have vanished, as doth the snow in the warm embrace of the sun. He would have seized her then and there once more and carried her away. And this time no consideration on earth would have stayed him. With a muttered exclamation, he jumped to his feet and passed his slender hand across his forehead.

'Good St Bavoni,' he murmured whimsically. 'Why are you so unkind to me tonight?'

And she, a little disappointed because, in truth, she had been ready for the kiss, rejoined with a quaint little pout:

'You are always appealing to St Bavon, my dear lord! Why is that?'

'Because,' he replied very seriously, 'St Bavon is the patron saint of all men that are weak.'

She fixed great, wondering eyes on him. The reply was ambiguous; she did not quite understand the drift of it.

'But you, my lord, are so strong,' she objected.

It was perhaps too dark for her to see the expression in his face; but even so she felt herself unaccountably blushing under that gaze which she could not clearly see. Whereupon he uttered an ejaculation which sounded almost as if he were angered, and abruptly, without any warning, he turned on his heel and went out of the room, leaving Gilda alone once more beside the virginal.

But she no longer felt the desire to sing. The happiness which filled her entire soul was too complete even for song.

4

One of the equerries had awhile ago found his way to the guest-chamber where the sick man was lying, and had informed Diogenes that the Stadtholder was now ready to start on his way, but desired his presence that he might take his leave. Then it was that Diogenes sent an urgent message to his Highness, entreating him to remain but a little while longer. The sick man was better, would soon wake out of a refreshing sleep. Diogenes would then question him. Poor old Pythagoras had something to say, something that the Stadtholder himself must hear. Of this Diogenes was absolutely convinced.

'I know it,' the young soldier asserted earnestly. 'I seem to feel it in my bones.'

Whereupon the Stadtholder had decided to wait, and Diogenes, after his brief glimpse of Gilda, felt easier in his mind, less impatient. Already he chided himself for his gloomy forebodings. Since his beloved was ready to entrust herself to him, the journey to England would only be put off by a few hours. What need to repine? Joy would be none the less sweet for this brief delay.

A quarter of an hour later Pythagoras was awake, the physician out of the room, and Diogenes was sitting on the edge of the bed holding his faithful comrade's hand, and trying to disentangle some measure of coherence out of the other's tangled narrative, whilst Socrates stood by making an occasional comment or just giving an expressive grunt from time to time. It took both time and patience, neither of which commodities did Diogenes possess in superabundance; but after the first few moments of listening to the rambling of the sick man, he became very still and attentive. The busy house, the noisy guests, the waiting Stadtholder down below, all slipped out from his ken. Holding his comrade's hand, he was with him on the snow-clad Veluwe, and had found his way with him into the lonely mill.

'It was the Lord of Stoutenburg,' Pythagoras averred, with as much strength as he could command. 'I'd stake my life on't! I knew him at once. How could I ever forget his ugly countenance, after all he made you suffer?'

'Well – and?' queried Diogenes eagerly.

'I knew the other man too, but could not be sure of his name. He was one of those who was with Stoutenburg that day at Ryswick, when you so cleverly put a spoke in their abominable wheel. I knew them both, I tell you!' the sick man insisted feverishly; 'but I had the good sense not to betray what I knew.'

'But Stoutenberg did not know you?' Diogenes insisted.

'Yes, he did,' the other replied, sagely nodding his head. 'That is why he ordered his menial to put a bullet into my back. The two noble gentlemen questioned me first,' he went on more coherently; 'then they plied me with wine. They wanted to make me drunk so as to murder me at their leisure.'

'They little knew thee, eh, thou bottomless barrel?' Diogenes broke in with a laugh. 'The cask hath not been fashioned yet that would contain enough liquor even to quench thy thirst, what?'

'They plied me with wine,' Pythagoras reiterated gravely; 'and then I pretended to get very drunk. For I soon remarked that the more drunk they thought I was, the more freely they talked.'

'Well, and what did they say?'

'They talked of De Berg crossing the Ijssel with ten thousand men between Doesburg and Bronchorst; and of Isembourg coming up from Kleve at the same time. I make no doubt that the design is to seize Arnheim and Nijmegen. They talked a deal about Arnheim, which they thought was scantily garrisoned and could easily be taken by surprise and made to surrender. Having got these two cities, the plan is to march across the Veluwe and offer battle to the Stadtholder with a force vastly superior to his, if in the meanwhile – '

He paused. It seemed as if his voice, hoarse with fatigue, was refusing him service. Diogenes reached for the potion which stood on a small table beside the bed. The sick man made a wry face.

'Physic?' he ejaculated reproachfully. 'From you, old compeer? Times were when – '

'There will be a time now,' retorted the other gruffly, 'when you'll sink back into a raging fever, and will be babbling bibulous nonsense if you don't do as you are told.'

'I'll sink into a raging fever now,' the sick man retorted fretfully, 'if I have not something potable to drink ere long.'

'You'll drink this physic now, old compeer,' Diogenes insisted, and held the mug to his friend's parched lips, forcing him to drink. 'Then I'll see what can be done for you later on.'

He schooled himself to patience and gentleness. At all costs Pythagoras must complete his narrative. There was just something more that he wished to say, apparently – something fateful and of deadly import, but which for some obscure reason he found difficult to put into words.

'Now then, old friend, make an effort!' Diogenes urged insistently. 'There is still something on your mind. What is it?'

Pythagoras' round, beady eyes were rolling in their sockets. He looked scared, like one who has gazed on what is preternatural and weird.

'Stoutenburg has a project,' he resumed after a while, and sank his spent voice to the merest whisper. 'Listen, my compeer; for the very walls have ears. Bend yours to me. There! That's better,' he added, as Diogenes bent his long back until his ear was almost on a level with the sick man's lips. 'Stoutenburg hath a project, I

tell you. A damnable project, akin to the one which you caused
to abort three months ago.'

'Assassination?' Diogenes queried curtly.

The sick man nodded.

'Do you know the details?'

'Alas, no! But it is aimed at the Stadtholder. What form it is to
take I know not, and they had evidently talked it all over before.
It seemed almost as if the other man – Stoutenburg's friend – was
horrified at the project. He tried to argue once or twice, and once
I heard him say quite distinctly: "Not that, Stoutenburg! Let us
fight him like men; even kill him, like men kill one another. But
not like that." But my Lord Stoutenburg only laughed.'

Diogenes was silent. He was deep in thought.

'You had no other indication?' he asked reflectively.

'No,' Pythagoras replied. 'All I saw was that my lord kept the
finger and thumb of his right hand in a hidden pocket of his
doublet, and once he said: "The Prince of Poets taught me to
manufacture them; and I supply them to him you know of,
whenever he can find an opportunity to come out here to me. He
uses them at his discretion. But we can judge by results!" And
then he laughed because his friend appeared to shudder. I was
puzzled,' the sick man went on wearily, 'because of it all; and I
marvelled who the Prince of Poets might be, for I am no scholar
and I thought that perhaps – '

'You are quite sure Stoutenburg said "Prince of Poets"?'
Diogenes insisted, frowning. 'Your ears must have been buzzing
by then.'

'I am quite sure,' Pythagoras asserted. 'But I could not see
what he had in his hand.'

Diogenes said nothing more, and silence fell upon the stately
chamber, the sombre panelling and heavy tapestries of which
effectually deadened every sound that came from the outside.
Only the monumental clock up against the wall ticked in a loud
monotone. The sick man, wearied with so much talking, fell back
against the pillows. The shades of evening were quickly gathering

in now; the corners of the room were indistinguishable in the gloom. Only the bedclothes still gleamed white in the uncertain light. From the distant tower of St Maria Kerk a bell chimed the hour of seven. A few minutes went by. Anon there came a scratching at the door.

In response to Diogenes' loud 'Enter!' the physician came in, preceded by a serving-man carrying two lighted candles in massive silver sconces.

'His Highness cannot wait any longer,' the physician said, as soon as he had perceived Diogenes, still sitting pensive on the edge of the bed. 'And as I have no anxiety about the patient now, I will, by your leave, place him in your hands.'

Diogenes appeared to wake as if out of a dream. He rose and looked about him somewhat vaguely. The physician thought he must have been asleep.

'Will you pay your respects to his Highness?' the latter said. 'I think he desires to see you.'

Just for a moment Diogenes remained quite still. The physician had approached the sick man, and was surveying him with critical but obviously reassured attention. Socrates was again snoring somewhere in a far corner of the room, and the serving-man, having placed the candles on the table, stood waiting at the door.

'Yes. I'll to his Highness,' Diogenes said abruptly; and, beckoning to the serving-man to precede him, he strode out of the room.

Outside on the landing he paused. Then, with a characteristic, impulsive gesture, he suddenly beat his forehead with the palm of his hand.

'The Prince of Poets, of course!' he murmured under his breath. 'Francis Borgia, the true descendant of his infamous ancestors! Poison! And a slow one at that! Oh, the miserable assassins! Please God, this knowledge hath not come too late!' he added with earnest fervour.

5

A quarter of an hour later the Stadtholder was in possession of all the facts as they had been revealed to Diogenes by his comrade in arms.

'I seem fated,' he said to Diogenes kindly, yet not without a measure of bitterness, 'to owe my safety to you and your brother philosophers.'

He was discussing De Berg's surprise plans on Arnheim and Nijmegen. Of that abominable crime, hatched with the chance aid of a poison-mongering Borgia, Diogenes had not as yet spoken one word. Accustomed to swift decisions and prompt action, he had already made up his mind that he would speak of it first to the English physician, whose business it would be to see to it that the insidious poison no longer reached the prince's lips, at the same time enjoining the strictest secrecy in the matter; for it would only be by rigid circumspection and ceaseless watching that the assassin's accomplice could be brought to justice.

Mynheer Beresteyn and some of his older friends were in the room with his Highness. They all put their grave heads together, for there was no doubt that the Archduchess's advisers had planned an invasion of the United Provinces on a grand scale.

'Arnheim is insufficiently defended, of that there's no doubt,' the Stadtholder said. 'It was my intention to reinforce all the frontier cities, and to keep their garrisons up to the requisite numbers. If I only had the strength – '

He paused. The feeling of physical weakness consequent on disease caused him endless and acute bitterness.

'It is not too late to send troops to Arnheim and to Nijmegen,' Diogenes broke in, in his usual abrupt manner. 'Three thousand in one city, four thousand in the other would be sufficient, if your Highness can act quickly.'

'I cannot detach seven or eight thousand troops from my forces at the present moment,' the prince rejoined. 'If Spinola were to attack from the south I am only just strong enough to defend myself as it is.'

'Marquet is in Overijssel, I believe,' urged the soldier. 'He hath three or four thousand troops. Let him push on to Arnheim to reinforce the garrison.'

'And De Keysere is at Wageningen,' the prince broke in, fired, despite himself, by the other's enthusiasm. 'He hath three thousand mercenaries from Switzerland and Germany.'

'Excellent fighters and well-seasoned,' Diogenes asserted. 'And trained under Maurice of Nassau, the first captain of this or any epoch!'

'Ay!' sighed Maurice wearily. 'But time is against us. Marquet is at Vorden – '

'But Arnheim and Nijmegen can hold out for awhile,' Diogenes argued forcefully.

'And would hold out to the last man,' Mynheer Beresteyn added, 'if they knew that succour would come in due course.'

' 'Tis only uncertainty that paralyses the endurance of a garrison,' Diogenes went on with firm emphasis. 'Send to Arnheim and to Nijmegen, your Highness! Bid them hold out against any attack until you come with ten thousand troops to their aid. In the meanwhile, send orders to Marquet and to De Keysere to advance forthwith with reinforcements for these two garrisons. Then raise your standard once more in Friesland, Drenthe, and Groningen. I'll warrant you will have twenty thousand men there ready to fight once more for liberty and for you!'

His sonorous voice rang clear and metallic in the small, panelled room. His enthusiasm appeared almost like a living thing, a tangible force that touched the hearts and minds of all the solemn burghers here, causing their eyes to glow and their fists, not yet wholly unskilled in the use of the sword, to clench with inward excitement. The Stadtholder looked up at him with undisguised admiration.

'Is it the English blood in you, man,' he said with a smile, 'that makes you valorous in war and wise in counsel?'

Diogenes shrugged his broad shoulders.

'I fought for your Highness before now,' he rejoined, with a quaint, self-deprecating laugh, 'when I had nothing to lose save my skin, and still less to gain. The English blood in me dearly loves a fight, and all doth hate the Spaniard and all his tyrannies.'

'Then I can reckon on you?' the prince riposted quickly.

'On me, your Highness?' the other exclaimed.

'On you, of course. With your mother's blood in your veins, the United Provinces have a double claim on you. You have fought for us before, as you say, unknown to us then, an obscure soldier of fortune with nothing to lose and but little to gain. Join us now, man, in the field and under the council tent. Get to horse tonight. You will find Marquet at Vorden, on his way south from Overijssel. Tell him to push on at once to Arnheim with all the troops he hath at his command. From thence I would bid you go straightway to De Keysere, who is at Wageningen, and order him to reinforce Nijmegen forthwith with three thousand men, if he have them. Tell both Marquet and De Keysere to fight and hold the towns. I'll to their aid as soon as may be. Then, man, join my brother Frederick, and help him to raise my standard in Gelderland and in Overijssel, and rally ten thousand men to our cause. I feel that success will attend our arms if we keep you by our side.'

Maurice of Nassau had spoken with more vigour and verve than he had shown for the past three months. Indeed, his deeply anxious friends could not help but feel that the old fighting spirit of this peerless commander had not wholly been undermined by disease. Five pairs of eager eyes had scanned his features while he spoke; five hearts beat in response to his enthusiasm. Now, when he had finished speaking, Mynheer Beresteyn and the others turned their expectant gaze upon the stranger who had been so signally honoured; but he looked uncertain, gravely perturbed. In the flickering light of the wax candles his face appeared haggard and drawn, and a set line had crept around his ever-laughing lips.

'You seem to hesitate, my friend,' the Stadtholder remarked, with that tone of bitterness which had become habitual to him. 'Methought you said that the English blood in you dearly loved a fight. But, in truth, I had forgotten! You have other claims upon you now – one, at least, which is paramount. An easy, untroubled life awaits you. No wonder you hesitate to embark on so perilous an adventure!' Then, as if loth to give up the thought that was foremost in his mind, he added, with persuasive insistence: 'If you followed me, you'd have everything to gain – nothing to lose save a sentimental pastime.'

Just then Diogenes caught Mynheer Beresteyn's eyes fixed steadily upon him. The old man knew well enough what was going on in that wayward, turbulent mind – the doubts, the fears, the hideous, horrible disappointment. Nothing to lose! Ye gods, at the hour when a whole life's happiness not only beckoned insistently, but was actually there to hand, like a bunch of ripe and luscious fruit, ready to drop into a yearning hand! Here was the end of a vagabond life, here was love and home and peace, and all to be given up as soon as found to the equally insistent call of honour and of duty!

The others did not speak; perhaps they, too, understood. Men in those days were used to stern sacrifices. They and their forbears had given up their all so that their children's children might live in freedom and security. They only marvelled if this stranger, with the combative English blood in him, would give up what was so infinitely dear to him – the exquisite wife to whom he had plighted his troth but a few hours ago – and if he would fight for them again as he had done in the past.

The Stadtholder remained moody and silent, and the close atmosphere of the heavily curtained room seemed to become suddenly still, hushed, as if expectant of the grave decision to come. The wax candles burned quite steadily, with just a tiny fillet of smoke rising up towards the low-raftered ceiling, almost like the incense of a silent prayer rising unwaveringly to God.

To many the silence appeared absolute, but not to the man who stood in the midst of them all beside a table littered with papers and documents, his slender hand – the hand of an idealist, rendered firm and hard by action – resting lightly upon the board. A tense look in his eyes. Through the silence he could hear his beloved in the little room behind the heavy tapestry. He could hear the soft, insidious sound of the quaint-toned virginal, and her voice, tender and melancholy, as the call of the bird to its mate, humming the sweet refrain gently under her breath. With every note she seemed to tear at his heart with an unendurable regret for what might have been.

Oh, it had been such a perfect dream! Gilda and that stately home over in England, and the ride through the night in pursuit of happiness which had proved as elusive as Fata Morgana, as unreal as the phantoms born in the mind of a rhapsodist.

Then the silence did, indeed, become absolute, even to him. Gilda had ceased her song. Only his straining ears caught the sound of her footsteps as she rose from the virginal, then moved swiftly about the room.

'Well,' the Stadtholder reiterated, after awhile, 'which is it to be, my friend? I start for Utrecht within the hour, and if we are to save Arnheim and Nijmegen, you should be on your way to Vorden with the necessary moneys and my written orders tonight. Of course, I cannot compel you,' he added simply. 'The decision rests with you, and if you – '

The words died on his lips, and in an instant all eyes were turned to that end of the room, where a heavy portière divided it from the room beyond. A faint rustling sound had come from there, then the grating of metal rings upon the cornice-pole that held the tapestry. The next moment Gilda appeared in the doorway, shadowy, wraith-like in her sombre gown that melted into the gloom. Just her small, white face and delicate hands stood out against the murky background, and the gossamer lace at her throat and wrists

For a moment she stood there, one hand still holding back the heavy portière, quite still, taking in the company at a glance. A sigh of longing and of renunciation came from an overburdened heart, and was wafted up to the foot of Him who knows all and understands all. Then Gilda allowed the tapestry to fall together behind her, and she came quickly forward. In the other hand she was holding, firmly clasped, her husband's heavy sword.

She came close to him, and then said simply, with an ingenuous smile:

'I thought you might wonder where you had left it. It was in the other room. You will be wanting it, my dear lord, if you start for Vorden within the hour.'

With deft fingers she buckled the sword to his belt. This, in truth, was her decision, and she had acted with scarce a moment's hesitation, even whilst he marvelled how he could set to work to break her heart by leaving her this night.

Now, when their glances met, they understood one another. The power that lay within both their souls had met and, as it were, clasped hands. They accepted one another's sacrifice. Hers, mayhap, was the more complete of the two, because for her his absence would mean weary waiting, the dull heartache so terrible to bear.

For the man, the wrench would be eased by action, danger, and hard fighting; for her there would be nothing to do but to wait. But she acquiesced. No one had seen the struggle which it had cost her, over there in the little room, all alone with only the dumb virginal and the dying light to see the tears of rebellion and of agony which for one brief moment – for her an eternity – had seared her eyes. By the time the full meaning of what she had overheard from the other side of the portière had entered into her brain, she had recovered full outward calm, and had brought him his sword in token of her resolve.

Gilda Beresteyn came of a race that had learned to fight even from its infancy. She had handled her father's sword at an age when little maids are content with playthings. Now, when she made the buckles of her husband's sword secure, she met his glance with perfect serenity, and said simply and calmly:

'You will find me, as before, in the other room. I will be waiting there to bid you farewell.'

Then she glided out of the room, wraith-like, ethereal, as she had come. And Diogenes woke as if out of a trance.

The Stadtholder jumped to his feet.

'Then you're with us?' he exclaimed.

'If your Highness hath need of me,' the soldier replied. 'Have I not said so?' the prince retorted. 'Henceforth, Sir Percy Blakeney – for that is your name, is it not? – accompanies us as our Master of the Camp where-ever we go!'

'Nay,' the other replied quite firmly, and without even a sigh of regret this time, 'my name is Diogenes, as it hath always been. It is the nameless and homeless adventurer, the son of the poor Dutch tramp, who once again places his sword at your Highness's disposal. Sir Percy Blakeney was only a myth, a shade that hath already been exorcized by the magic of your Highness's call, in the name of our faith and of liberty.'

'Frankly, man,' the Stadtholder retorted with a smile, 'I could not picture you in the character of a placid and uxorious country gentleman, watching with unruffled complacence the life and death struggles of your friends.'

'I should have waxed obese, your Highness,' Diogenes assented whimsically; 'and the horror of it would have sent me to my grave.'

'Then, you inveterate mocker, are you ready to start?'

'Booted and spurred, your Highness, and a sword on my hip,' replied the other lightly. 'And my horse hath been waiting for me these two hours past.'

Already Maurice of Nassau was on his feet. He took the sacrifice, the self-denial, as a matter of course; was unaware of it, probably. Every other thought was completely merged in that of the coming struggle – De Berg crossing the Ijssel, Spinola threatening from the south, and victory beckoning once more. The burghers crowded round him, speaking words of loyalty and of encouragement. He responded with somewhat curt farewells. His thoughts were no longer here; they were across the Veluwe with Marquet and De Keysere; inside Arnheim and Nijmegen.

He kept Diogenes by his side, wrote out his orders in sign-manual, discussed plans, possibilities with the man in whose luck and resource he had unbounded belief.

It took time to get everything ready. There was the financial question, too, for some of the troops were mercenaries, who would be demanding their pay ere they engaged to start on a fresh expedition. For this the aid of the loyal burghers had again to be requisitioned. Arrangements had to be made for credits at Zutphen and Arnheim.

This part of the great adventure the Stadtholder was willing to leave in the hands of Mynheer Beresteyn and his friends. Money to him was dross, save as a means of gaining his great ends. For the nonce he was in a hurry to get away, to get back to his camp at Utrecht, and to make ready for the coming fight.

Then at last there came a moment when everything appeared settled. The messenger had his sealed orders, and the credit notes and the ready money upon his person. The Stadtholder was back in the hall with his equerries around him, ready for departure, giving brief, decisive orders such as soldiers love to hear.

But Diogenes did not follow him immediately, and Mynheer Beresteyn remained behind with him. He was the only one who really understood what the once careless and thoughtless adventurer felt at this moment, in face of the inevitable farewell. It was an understanding born in a staunch heart that had known both love and sorrow.

Beresteyn had idolized his young wife, who had died leaving her baby-girl in his arms. That deep affection the lonely widower had thereupon transferred to his motherless daughter, had cherished and guarded her as his most precious treasure, and had only consented to relinquish her into the guardianship of another because he knew that that other was worthy of the trust.

He knew also what hungering passion means; he knew the bitterness of parting and of a burning disappointment, with the prospect of loneliness through the vista of years. But, with that infinite tact which is the attribute of a selfless heart, he offered no words of consolation or even of comment.

'I will leave you to bid farewell to Gilda alone,' was all that he said.

Diogenes nodded in assent. The most terrible moment of this terrible hour was yet to come, for Gilda, having precipitated his decision, was now waiting for the last kiss.

6

She was, in truth, waiting for him, submissive and composed. What she had done, when she with her own act had mutely bidden him to go, that she did not regret. She had done it not so much perhaps from a sense of duty or of patriotism, but rather because she knew that this course was the only one that he would never rue.

Hers was that perfect love that dwells on the other's happiness, and not on its own. She knew that, though for the time being he would find bliss and oblivion in her arms, he would soon repine in inactivity whilst others fought for that which he held sublime.

So now, when he pushed aside the tapestry and once more stood before her, with the lovelight in his eyes obscured by the shadow of this coming parting, she met him without a tear. The next moment he had her in his arms, and his hand rested lightly across her eyes, lest they should perceive that his were full of tears.

For a long while he could not speak; then he drew her closer to him and pressed his lips against hers, drinking in all the joy and rapture which he might never taste again.

'What is it that hath happened, my lord?' she murmured. 'I could not hear everything, and did not wish to be caught prying. All that I heard was that the Stadtholder needed you, and that in your heart you knew that your place, whilst there was danger to our land, was by his side, and not by mine.'

'Your father will explain more fully, my beloved,' he replied.

'You are right. The Stadtholder hath need of every willing sword. This unfortunate land is gravely threatened. The Archduchess is throwing the full force of her armies against the Netherlands. His Highness thinks that I might help to save the United Provinces from becoming once more the vassals of Spain. As you say, my place is on this soil where I and my mother were born. I should be a coward indeed were I to turn my back now on this land when danger is so grave. So I am going, my beloved,' he continued simply.

'Tonight I go to Vorden on his Highness's business; thence on to Wageningen. I shall go, taking your dear image in my heart, and with your exquisite face before me always. For I love you with every fibre of my being, every bone in my body and with every beat of my heart. Try not to weep, my dear. I shall return one day soon to take you in my arms, as I shall clasp your spirit only until then. I shall return, doubt it not. Such love as ours was not created to remain unfulfilled. Whatever may happen, believe and trust in me, as I shall believe in you, and keep the remembrance of me in your heart without sadness and without regret.'

He spoke chiefly because he dared not trust to the insidiousness of silence. He knew that she wept for the first time because of him. Yet how could it be otherwise? And sorrow made her sacred. When, overcome with grief, she lay half-swooning in his arms, he picked her up quite tenderly and laid her back against the cushions of the chair. Then, as she sat there, pale and wan-looking in the uncertain light of the wax candles, with those exquisite hands of hers lying motionless in her lap, he knelt down before her.

For a second or two he rested his head against those soft white palms, fragrant as the petals of a lily. Then he rose, and, without looking at her again, he walked firmly out of the room.

4

Adder's Fork

Nicolaes Beresteyn accompanied his brother-in-law during the first part of the journey. He had insisted on this, despite Diogenes' preference for solitude. There was not much comradeship lost between the two men. Though the events of that memorable New Year's Day, distant less than three months, were ostensibly consigned to oblivion, nevertheless, the bitter humiliation which Nicolaes had suffered at the hands of the then nameless soldier of fortune still rankled in his heart. Since then so many things had come to light which, to an impartial observer, more than explained Gilda Beresteyn's love for the stranger, and Mynheer her father's acquiescence in a union based on respect for so brave a man.

But Nicolaes had held aloof from the intimacy, and soon his own courtship of the wealthy Kaatje gave him every reason for withdrawing more and more from his own family circle. But tonight, after the tempestuous close of what should have been a merely conventional day, he sought Diogenes' company in a way he had never done before.

'Like you,' he said, 'I am wearied and sick with all this mummery. A couple of hours on the Veluwe will set me more in tune with life.'

Diogenes chaffed him not a little. 'The lovely Kaatje will pout,' he suggested, 'and rightly, too. You have no excuse for absenting yourself from her side at this hour.'

'I'll come with you as far as Barneveld,' Nicolaes insisted. 'A matter of less than a couple of hours' ride. It will do me good. And Kaatje is still closeted with her garrulous mother.'

'You think it will do her good to be kept waiting,' Diogenes retorted with good-natured sarcasm. 'Well, come, if you have a mind. But I'll not have your company further than Barneveld. I am used to the Veluwe, and intend taking a short cut over the upland, through which I would not care to take a companion less well acquainted with the waste than I.'

Thus it was decided. Already the Stadtholder had gone with his numerous retinue, with his bodyguard and his pikemen and his equerries, and those of the wedding-party who had come in his train from Utrecht, friends of Mynheer Beresteyn, who had ridden over for the most part with wife or daughter pillioned behind them, and all glad to avail themselves of the protection of his Highness's escort against highway marauders, none too scarce in these parts. Torch-bearers and linkmen completed the imposing cavalcade, for the night would be moonless, and the tracks across the moorland none too clearly defined.

Diogenes had waited with what patience he could muster until the last of the numerous train had defiled under the Koppelpoort. Then he, too, got to horse. Despite Socrates' many protestations, he was not allowed to accompany him.

'You must look after Pythagoras,' was Diogenes' final word on the subject.

' 'Tis the first time,' the other answered moodily, 'that you go on such an adventure without us. Take care, comrade! The Veluwe is wide and lonely. That swag-bellied oaf up there hath cause to rue his solitary wanderings on the *verfloekte* waste.'

'I'll be careful, old compeer,' Diogenes retorted with a smile. 'But mine errand is not one on which I desire to draw unnecessary attention, and I can remain best unperceived if I am alone. 'Tis no adventure I am embarking on this night. Only a simple errand as far as Vorden, a matter of ten leagues at most.'

'And the whole of the *verdommte* Veluwe to traverse at dead of night!' the other muttered sullenly.

'I know every corner of it,' Diogenes rejoined impatiently. 'And it will not be the first time that I travel on it alone.'

Thus Socrates was left grumbling, and anon Diogenes, accompanied by Nicolaes Beresteyn, started on his way.

2

At first the two men spoke little. The air was still cold and very humid, and the thaw was persisting. The horses stepped out briskly on the soft, sandy earth.

The distance between Amersfoort and Barneveld is but a couple of leagues. Within the hour the lights of the little city could be seen gleaming ahead. After a while Nicolaes Beresteyn became more loquacious, talked quite freely of the past.

'My father no longer trusts me,' he said with ill-concealed bitterness. 'Did you see how he shut me out of the council-chamber?'

'Yet the Stadtholder himself told you everything that occurred subsequently,' Diogenes retorted kindly, ' including his own plans and mine errand at this hour. I think that your conscience troubles you unnecessarily, and you see a deliberate intention in every simple act.'

'If I thought that my father still suspected me –' Nicolaes mumbled under his breath.

'And if he did, you could scarce blame him. 'Tis only in the future you can prove your true worth. And methinks,' he added, more seriously than he was usually wont to speak, 'that you will have occasion to do this very soon.'

'In the meanwhile, here's Barneveld ahead of us,' Nicolaes rejoined, with a quick, undefinable sigh, and giving a sudden turn to the conversation. 'I'll see you across the city, then return to the bosom of my family, there to live in uxorious idleness, whilst you, a stranger, are entrusted with the destinies of our land. A poor outlook for a man who is young and a patriot, you'll own.'

To this Diogenes thought it best to make no reply. He knew well enough that the mistrust of which Nicolaes accused his father was a very real thing, and that it was indeed only time that would soften the proud burgher's heart towards his only son. It was not likely that one who but a brief while ago had conspired against the Stadtholder's life with that abominable Stoutenburg could be admitted readily into the councils of the very man whom he had plotted to assassinate. With every desire to forgive, it was but natural that Mynheer Beresteyn should fail entirely to forget.

No more, however, was said upon the subject now, and Nicolaes soon relapsed into that sullen mood which had of late become habitual to him. Thus Diogenes was glad enough to be rid of his company. At Barneveld he obtained a fresh horse, left his own in charge of a man known to him, with orders to ride it quietly on the morrow as far as Wageningen, where he himself would pick it up a couple of days later. His journey would not lie due east to Zutphen. There he meant to make a halt of a few hours, and thence proceed to Vorden, where Marquet was in camp, with four thousand seasoned troops, trained under Mansfeld, and rested now since the campaign in Groningen.

The Stadtholder's orders were that the general proceed, at once to Arnheim, ere the forces of the Archduchess had time to cross the Ijssel, and to cut off all access to so important a city.

From Vorden to Wageningen, which lies due south from Barneveld, the journey would be a long one, and, with De Berg's army so near, might even prove perilous. But De Keysere was at Wageningen, with three thousand troops and some artillery. His help would be of immense service to Nijmegen if the latter city, too, were to be attacked.

'How will you journey from Vorden to Wageningen?' Nicolaes asked Diogenes in the end. 'You will have to avoid the Ijssel.'

'I'll cut across to Lang Soeren,' the other replied; 'and thence go to Ede.'

'There's scarce a track on the Veluwe just there,' the other urged.

'Such as there is, I know,' Diogenes retorted curtly. 'And I must trust to luck.'

They had brought their horses to a halt about a quarter of a league outside Barneveld, where the two men decided to part. The stretch of the great waste, with its undulating, barren hills, and narrow, scarce visible tracks, lay straight out before them. Diogenes was sniffing the frosty air out towards the east, where lay Vorden, and whence there came to his nostrils the sharp tang of the breeze, that cut like a knife. The thaw which had held sway in the cities and on the low-lying lands had been vanquished ere it reached the arid upland. The snow upon the Veluwe lay as even and as pure as before. Above, a canopy of stars seemed but a diamond-studded veil of mysterious indigo, stretched over a world of light, which it failed altogether to dim. The silence and desolation were absolute; but not so the darkness. To the keen eye of the adventurer, accustomed to loneliness, the vast stretches of open country and limitless horizons, there was no such thing as absolute darkness. He could perceive the slightest accidental upon the smooth carpet of snow, noted every tiny mound that marked a clump of rough shrub or grass and every footmark of beast or bird, mere flecks of blue upon the virgin pall.

'Such track as there is, I know,' he had carelessly asserted awhile ago, in response to a warning from Nicolaes. And now, without an instant's hesitation, and tossing to the other a last curt word of farewell, he gave his horse a slight taste of the spur, and soon became a mere speck upon the illimitable waste.

3

It was close on midnight when, weary, saddle-sore, his boots covered in half-melted snow, Mynheer Nicolaes Beresteyn demanded admittance into his native city.

At first the guard at the Koppelpoort, roused from his slumbers, refused to recognize in the belated traveller the bridegroom of a few hours ago. Had anyone ever heard, I ask you, of a bridegroom absenting himself on the very night of his nuptial until so late an hour? And then returning in a mood that was so irascible and inconsequent that the sergeant in command at the gate was on the point of ordering his detention in the guard-room, pending investigation and the orders of the burgomaster, whose decision on such points was final? But since the burgomaster happened to be Mynheer Beresteyn, and as the weary and pugnacious traveller did, in truth, appear to be his only son – why, it was perhaps best on the whole to take the matter as a joke, and not to say too much about it. The sergeant did, indeed, as Nicolaes was finally allowed to ride over the bridge, essay one or two of the most time-honoured witticisms at the expense of the belated bridegroom; but Mynheer Nicolaes was clearly in no mood for chaff, and when he had passed by, the sergeant and one or two of the men, who had witnessed his strangely sullen mood, shook their heads in ominous prognostication of sundry matrimonial difficulties to come.

The house on the quay, plainly visible from the Koppelpoort, was dark enough to suggest that every one of its inmates was already abed. Nicolaes, however, did not ride up to the front door; but, after he had crossed the bridge, he went straight on through one or two narrow streets which lay at the back of his home until he reached the corner of the Korte Gracht, which, again, abuts on the quay. Thus he had gone round in a semicircle, in obvious avoidance of the paternal house, and now he brought his horse to a halt outside a tall and narrow door which was surmounted by a lanthorn let into the wall. A painted sign which hung from an iron bracket above the door indicated to the passing wayfarer that the place was one where rider and horse could find food and shelter.

Nicolaes dismounted, and going up to the door, he knocked against it with the point of his foot. This he had to do several times before the welcome sound of someone moving inside the house came to his ear. A moment or two later the door was opened cautiously. A man appeared on the threshold, wrapped in a night-robe and still wearing a night-bonnet on his head.

'Is that you, Mynheer?' he queried drowsily.

'Who else should it be, you loon?' Nicolaes replied irritably. 'Here's your horse,' he added, and without waiting for further commend or protest from the unfortunate landlord thus roused from his slumbers, he proceeded to tether the animal by the reins to one of the iron rings in the wall. 'It is so late, mynheer,' the man protested dolefully; 'and so cold. Will you not take the horse round to the stable yourself? It is but a step to your right, and there's the gate – '

'It is late, as you say, and cold,' Nicolaes retorted curtly. 'And when I paid you so liberally for the horse, I did not bargain to take service with you as ostler in the middle of the night.'

'But, mynheer – ' urged the landlord, still protesting.

But Nicolaes did not listen. In faith, he had ceased to hear, for already he was striding rapidly down the Korte Gracht, and the next moment was back on the quay. A few steps brought him to the door of his father's house. Here he paused for a moment ere he mounted the stone steps that led up to the massive front door, stamped his feet so as to shake the melted snow from his boots, and with a few quick touches tried to re-establish some semblance of order in his clothes. Indeed, when presently he rapped vigorously with the iron knocker against the door, he looked no longer like a wearied and querulous traveller, but rather like a man just returned from a short and pleasant ride.

To his astonishment it was Maria, his sister Gilda's faithful tire-woman, who opened the door for him. She anticipated his very first query by a curt:

'Everyone is abed. The *jongejuffrouw* alone chose to wait for you, and I could not let her wait alone.'

Nicolaes uttered an angry exclamation.

'Tell my sister to go to bed, too,' he commanded briefly. 'I'll go to my rooms at once, as it is so late.'

Maria made no audible reply. She mumbled something about 'Shameful conduct!' and 'Wedding-night!' But Nicolaes paid no heed, strode quickly across the hall, and ran swiftly up the stairs.

But on the landing he came abruptly to a halt. He had almost fallen against his sister Gilda, who stood there waiting for him.

Behind her, a little way down the passage, a door stood ajar, and through it there came a narrow fillet of light. At sight of him, and before he could utter a sound, she put a finger to her lip, then led the way along the passage. The door which stood ajar was the one which gave on her own room. She went in, and he followed her, his heart beating with something like shame or fear.

'Hush!' she whispered, and gently closed the door behind him. 'Make no noise! Kaatje has at last sobbed herself to sleep. She hath been put to bed in her mother's room. 'Twere a shame to disturb her.' Then, as Nicolaes muttered something that sounded very like a curse, the girl added reproachfully: 'Poor Kaatje! You have shown very little ardour towards her, Klaas.'

'I lost my way in the dark,' he answered. 'I had no thought it could be so late.'

Just then the tower clock of St Maria Kerk chimed the midnight hour.

Gilda hazarded timidly.

'You should not have thought of accompanying my lord. He was ready to start out alone; and your place, Klaas, was beside your wife!'

'Are you going to lecture me about my duty, Gilda?' he said irritably. 'You must not think that because – '

'I think nothing,' she broke in simply, 'save that Kaatje wept when the evening wore on and you did not return; and that the more she wept the greater was our father's anger against you.'

'He knew that I meant to accompany your husband a part of the way,' Nicolaes retorted. 'In truth, had he done me the justice to read my thoughts, he himself would have bade me go.'

'It was kind of you,' she rejoined somewhat coolly, 'to be concerned as to my lord's safety. But I can assure you – '

' 'Twas not concern for *his* safety,' he broke in gruffly, 'that caused me to accompany him tonight.'

'What then?'

But he gave no reply, bit his lip and turned away from her, with the air of one who fears that he hath said too much and cares not to be questioned again.

'I'd best go now,' he said abruptly.

He looked around for his gloves, which he had thrown down upon the table. His manner seemed so strange that Gilda was suddenly conscious of a nameless kind of fear; the sort of premonition that comes to highly sensitive natures, at times when hitherto unsuspected danger suddenly looms upon the cloudless sky of life. She forced him to return her searching glance.

'You are hiding something from me, Klaas,' she said determinedly. 'What is it?'

'I?' he riposted, feigning surprise. 'Hiding something? Why should I have something to hide?'

'That I know not,' she replied. 'But there was some hidden meaning in your words just now when you said that 'twas not concern for my lord's safety that caused you to accompany him this night. What, then, was it?' she insisted, seeing that he remained silent, even though he met her gaze with a look that appeared both fearful and pitying.

She had her back to the door now, and looked like some timid creature brought to bay by a cruel and hitherto unsuspected enemy.

'You must not ask me for my meaning, Gilda,' Nicolaes said at last. 'There are things which concern men only, and with which women should have no part.'

His tone of ill-concealed compassion stung her like a cut from a whip across the face.

'There is nothing that concerns my lord,' she retorted proudly, 'in which he would not desire me to bear my part.'

'Then let him tell you himself.'

'What?'

She threw the question at him like a challenge, stepped up to him and seized him by the wrist – no longer a timid creature at bay, but a strong, determined woman, who feels in some mysterious way that the man whom she loves is being attacked, and who is prepared, with every known and unknown weapon almighty love can suggest, to defend him, his life or his honour, or both.

'You are not going out of this room, Klaas, until you have explained!' she said with unquestionable determination. 'What is it that my lord should tell me himself?'

'Why he, newly wed and a stranger, was so determined on this, his wedding night, to carry the Stadtholder's message across the Veluwe.'

Nicolaes spoke abruptly, almost fiercely now, as if wearied of this wrangling, and burdened with a secret he could no longer hold. But she did not at first understand his meaning.

'I do not understand what you mean,' she murmured vaguely, a perplexed frown between her eyes.

'There were plenty there eager and willing to go,' Nicolaes went on roughly. 'Nay, the errand was not in itself perilous. Speed was required, yes; and a sound knowledge of the country. But a dozen men at least who were in this house today know the Veluwe as well as this stranger, and any good horse would cover the ground fast enough. But he wanted to go – he, this man whom none of us know, who was married this day, and whose bride had the first call on his attention. He insisted with the Stadtholder, and he went – And I went with him; would have gone all the way if he had not forced me to go back. Why did he wish to go, Gilda? Why did he leave you deliberately this night? Think! Think! And why did he insist on going alone, with not even one of those besotted boon companions of his to share in his adventure? A message to Marquet – my God!' he added with a sneer. 'A message to the Archduchess, more like, to cross the Ijssel ere it be too late!'

'You devil!'

She hissed out the words through set lips and teeth clenched in an access of fierce and overwhelming passion. And before he could recover himself, before he could guess her purpose, she had seized his heavy, leathern gloves, which were lying on the table, and struck him with them full in the face. He staggered, and put his hand up to his eyes.

'Go!' she commanded briefly.

He tried to laugh the situation off, said almost flippantly:

'I'll punish you for this, you young vixen!'

But she did not move, and her glance seemed to freeze the words upon his lips.

'Go!' she commanded once more.

He shrugged his shoulders.

'I understand your indignation, Gilda. Nay, I honour it. But remember my warning! Your stranger lord,' he went on with slow and deliberate emphasis, 'will be returning anon to the Stadtholder's camp, a courted and honoured man; but 'tis the armies of the Archduchess who will have crossed the Ijssel by then, whilst the orders to Marquet will have reached that commander too late.'

Then he turned on his heel and went out of the room, and anon Gilda heard his footsteps resounding along the passage. She listened until she heard the opening and closing of a distant door, after which she sighed and murmured, 'Poor Kaatje!' That was all; but there was a world of meaning in the sorrowful compassion wherewith she said those words.

Then she raised her left hand, round the third finger of which glittered a plain gold ring. The ring she pressed long and lingeringly against her lips, and in her heart she prayed, 'God guard you, my dear lord!'

5

A Race for Life

As for Diogenes, he reached Zutphen in the small hours of the morning, and after a few hours' rest pushed on to Vorden at dawn. He himself would have deprecated any suggestion of making this journey across the Veluwe a romantic adventure. The upland, under its covering of snow, held neither terrors nor secrets for him. The wind, the stars, an unerring instinct and sound knowledge of the scarce visible tracks, guided him across the arid waste. A real child of the open, he had less difficulty in finding his way across such a God-forsaken wild than he would through the intricate streets of a city.

Messire Marquet, encamped outside Vorden, welcomed the Stadtholder's messenger effusively. His troops, for the most part composed of mercenaries from Germany, were getting restive in idleness; once or twice they had used threats when demanding their pay. Diogenes, bringing both money and the prospect of a fight, was doubly welcome. His stay at the camp was brief. By late morning he was once more on his way, with the intention of re-crossing the Ijssel at Dieren and of reaching Wageningen before dark. He had but half a dozen leagues to cover, and eight hours of daylight wherein to do it. Weather, too, and circumstances favoured him. The thaw, which had been so completely vanquished upon the upland, had remained sole monarch in the plain. The air was mild and intensely humid. A dense sea-fog lay over the river and the surrounding marshes. The numerous little tributaries of the Ijssel and the intervening canals and ditches were already free from ice, and as Diogenes put his horse to an easy gallop in the direction of the river, the animal sank fetlock deep in mud.

The road was solitary, and, as far as the eye could reach through the mist, seemed entirely deserted. The countryside here had the desolate appearance peculiar to districts that have been fought over. The few thatched cottages, which from time to time loomed out of the mist, still bore the marks of passing fire and sword; the trees were truncated and sparse, the marshland was riddled with the scars of ceaseless tramping of men, of wagons, and of beasts. The inevitable windmills, gaunt-looking and ghost-like through the humid atmosphere, appeared neglected and forlorn.

But the solitary rider had no eyes for landscape just now. He could have wished for a clearer day, for it was impossible even for his keen eyes to see what was going on behind that impenetrable wall of fog. If Pythagoras' ears had not played him false, De Berg was there, not very far away, waiting to cross the Ijssel when opportunity arose.

Thanks to that faithful hypertrophied loon, the ambitious designs of the Archduchess could still be frustrated. De Berg's armies were still on the right bank of the Ijssel, and if Marquet got his men on the move by midday, as he had promised he would do, the crossing of the enemy troops would become difficult, mayhap impossible.

These were pleasing thoughts for the man on whose speed and resource these important plans depended. All that he chafed against was the imperative slowness of his progress, as the mist enveloped him more closely the nearer he got to the river. But withal it protected him, too, hid him mayhap from the prying eyes of vedettes on the watch. Already, judging by certain landmarks that met him on the way, Brummen was half a league behind him on his right, Hengels far away on the left, and Dieren not more than another league on ahead. For the last quarter of an hour he had heard from time to time the heavy booming sound, akin to the reverberation of distant cannonade, which came from the breaking and cracking of the ice as it drifted down-stream. He put his horse to a slow trot, as he pried through the mist for the first indication of a short cut he knew of, which would take him to the river bank in less than half an hour.

2

The next moment he had spied the narrow track and set his horse to follow it; when suddenly, out of the mist, there came a loud report, and Diogenes heard the whistle of a bullet close to his ear. It almost grazed his shoulder. Without an instant's pause, without turning to look whence had come this unexpected greeting, he set spurs to his horse and galloped at breakneck speed towards the river. Over fields and ditches; no thought of prudence now, only of speed! Mud and water flew out in all directions under the horse's frantic gallopade, the plucky beast sinking at times almost to his knees in the marshy ground. A few minutes later – five, perhaps – Diogenes heard the sound of many hoofs behind him, obviously in pursuit. He turned to look this time, and through the mist vaguely discerned some three or four cavaliers, who were distant from him then less than two hundred yards. So far, so good! The Ijssel was close by now, and if, when be reached the banks, he turned off in the direction of the stream, he could easily reach the ford on this side of Brummen and get across – on foot, if need be, if his horse proved an obstacle to rapid progress.

A few more minutes now and the river was in sight, with, far away on the opposite bank, Brummen, nestling at the foot of the rising ground, the gate of the Veluwe. With renewed vigour the rider sped along, his blood whipped up by the chase, his whole body exhilarated by this sensation of danger and of one of those sportive races for life for which three months of idleness and luxury had given him a hitherto unsuspected longing.

Ah, there was the shore at last, the group of three windmills close to the bank, an unmistakable landmark. Here, too, within two hundred paces on ahead, was the ford, which no amount of drifting ice would cause the daring adventurer to miss. Already he was within a few yards of the low-lying bank, searching the approach to the ford with eyes now doubly keen, when, with staggering suddenness, another cavalier appeared, straight in front of him this time, and barring the way to the river-brink.

No time to note his face; just a second wherein to decide what had best be done, not only to save his own life, but also the message which he must carry to Wageningen, at whatever cost. Then the cavalier turned for one brief second in his saddle, to call to some companions as yet unseen. A brief second, did I say? 'Twas but a fraction. The next moment Diogenes had whipped out a pistol from his saddle-bow, and with a steady hand fired at his foe. The cavalier reeled in his saddle and fell, just as half a dozen others issued with a shout from out the mist, and those in pursuit put fresh spurs to their mounts.

It had been madness to attempt the ford now. The young soldier, sore-pressed, might in truth have sold his life dearly, but with it, too, he would have sold Nijmegen and the possible success of the Stadtholder's plans. Oft-times before, in the course of his adventurous life, had he been in as tight a place, where life and death hung quite evenly in the scales of Fate; but never before had he been quite so anxious to flee. He could not trust to the valour of his sword, his own well-nigh unexampled skill in a fight against odds that would have made the bravest pause. No! It meant running away, away as fast as his horse would take him, and faster if the poor brute gave out. A short gallop along the bank, the cavalier behind him warming to the pursuit; keeping closer and closer to the low-lying bank, till the horse began to flounder in what was sheer morass.

The ford now lay well behind him. The waters of the Ijssel, tossed for awhile upon the shallows, flowed with increased swiftness here. Huge ice-blocks floated seawards upon the heaving bosom of the stream. The foremost of the pursuing cavaliers was then less than fifty yards behind, and more than one bullet had whizzed past the fleeing rider, one of them piercing his hat, the other grazing his thigh, but none doing him serious injury. Already the rallying cry of the pursuers had turned to one of triumph as the distance lessened between them and their quarry, when, with a sudden jerk of the reins, Diogenes plunged headlong into the river.

3

The Ijssel at this point is close on a quarter of a mile wide, her current is no longer sluggish, whilst the drifting ice-blocks constitute a peril which had to be boldly faced. But the mist, which hung thickly over the river, was the daring adventurer's most faithful ally.

Strangely enough, Diogenes' first thought, when his horse, finally losing its foothold upon the rapidly shelving bank, started to swim, was of Gilda, and of that ride which he had promised himself, with her dear arms clinging around him, her fair hair, tossed by the wind, brushing against his face. It was one of those sweet, sad visions which some mocking sprite seems to conjure up at moments such as this, when life – ay, and honour, too! – are trembling in the balance. Sad and swift! It vanished almost as quickly as it came, giving place to thoughts of De Keysere, still unsuspecting at Wageningen, and of Marquet, who haply had already started. Was there a trap waiting for him, too? Was this just an outpost of De Berg's armies; and had they indeed been mysteriously warned by traitor or spy, as Diogenes more than half suspected?

But what was the use of speculating? Indeed, every conjecture was futile, for this now was a supreme struggle – a tussle with

Death, who was watching, uncertain whence and how he would strike. For the moment the adventurer was at grips with the flood and with the ice, guiding his horse as best he could towards mid-stream, where the current kept the threatening floes at bay. His pursuers had come to a halt upon the bank. Indeed, not one of them had the mind to follow his quarry on this perilous adventure. They stood there, some half-dozen of them, holding counsel, their eyes peering through the mist in search of the one black speck – horse and rider – now appearing clearly silhouetted against the silvery water, now vanishing again under cover of the floes. Then one of them raised his musket and took steady aim at the valiant swimmer, who had succeeded at last in reaching midstream.

The bullet whizzed through the mist. Diogenes' horse, hit through the neck, plunged and reared, pawed the waters wildly for a moment, then gave that heartrending scream which is so harrowing to the ears of all animal-lovers. But already the rider had his feet clear of the stirrups, and as the waters finally swept over the head of the stricken beast, he slid out of the saddle and struck out for the opposite shore.

6

A Nest of Scorpions

Of the extraordinary events which threatened to make March 21, 1624, one of the most momentous dates in the history of the Netherlands we have not much in the way of detail. The broad facts we know chiefly through Van Aitzema's ponderous and minute 'Saken *v.* Staet,' whilst De Voocht gives us one or two more intimate touches in his highly interesting, if somewhat obscure, 'Brieven.' De Voocht was, of course, a friend of the Beresteyn family, and, as I understand it, was present in the house at Amersfoort when the terrible catastrophe was so auspiciously and mysteriously averted.

The one thing, however, which neither he nor Van Aitzema have made quite clear is the motive which prompted the Stadtholder to go to Amersfoort in person. He had quite a number of knights and gentlemen around him whom he could have fully trusted to take even so portentous a message and such explicit orders as he desired to send. De Voocht, indeed, suggests that it was Nicolaes Beresteyn who persuaded him, urging the obstinacy of his father, the burgomaster, and of the burghers of the city, who had steadily opposed the Stadtholder's wishes when he – Nicolaes – had been sent to convey them.

Nicolaes Beresteyn had joined his sovereign lord at the camp at Utrecht a couple of days after his wedding. Wearied of sentimental dalliance with the stolid Kaatje, he was glad enough that his duty demanded his presence in camp rather than in the vicinity of his young wife's apron-strings.

It was but natural that, when the Stadtholder desired to send orders to Amersfoort, he should do so through the intermediary of Nicolaes. But on that day, which was March 20, the young man returned, vowing that these were not being obeyed; not a matter of disloyalty, of course, just of tenacity. Civic dignitaries, conscious of their worth and of the sacrifices they had made in the common cause, were wont to wax obstinate where the affairs of their own cities were concerned. But, on the other hand, resistance to his will had invariably the effect of rousing the Stadtholder's arbitrary temper to a point of unreasoning anger. Olden Barneveldt had expiated his contumacy on the scaffold, and I doubt not that, when Nicolaes returned from Amersfoort that evening and delivered his report, the fate of even so trusted a councillor as Mynheer Beresteyn hung for awhile in the balance.

That the matter was one of supreme importance it were impossible to doubt. Maurice of Nassau would not lightly have left his camp at Utrecht that day. The forces of the Archduchess Isabella, who, under the leadership of De Berg and of Isembourg, were threatening Gelderland from two sides, had succeeded on the one part in crossing the Ijssel. His own army was threatened by that of Spinola from the south. On the other hand, the messenger whom he had sent across the Veluwe to urge Marquet and De Keysere to concentrate inside Arnheim and Nijmegen had not yet returned. Nevertheless, he chose, by this suddenly planned excursion to Amersfoort, to expose his valuable person to serious danger; a fact which subsequent events proved only too conclusively.

Nicolaes Beresteyn was sent back at dawn the following morning to warn the burgomaster of the Stadtholder's coming, and enjoining the strictest secrecy. The young man was under orders to say nothing beyond that fact. When closely questioned, however, by his father and also by others, he did admit that fugitives from Ede had succeeded in reaching the camp.

Fugitives from Ede? What did that mean? Why should there be fugitives from Ede, when the armies of the Archduchess were so many leagues away?

Nicolaes Beresteyn shrugged his shoulders.

'The Stadtholder will explain,' was all that he said. He appeared impatient and consequential, made them all feel that he could say more if he cared. He had been kept out of the prince's councils while he was under the paternal roof, but now he had gained a place in the camp which had always been his by right. These solemn burghers – important enough within the purlieus of their own city – had become insignificant, mere civilians, now that the fate of the country rested upon those who were young enough to bear arms.

Nicolaes tried to meet his sister's glance.

Her indifference towards him galled his sense of importance, and he wished her to know that he neither repented nor was ashamed of what he had said the other night. Anon when he had succeeded in forcing her eyes to meet his, he gave her a look charged with a mocking challenge. Up to this hour, she had said nothing to her father; now Nicolaes appeared to dare her to speak. But his sneers had not the power to disturb her sublime trust in the man she loved. That some mystery did cling to his journey across the Veluwe she could no longer doubt; but her fears upon the subject dwelt solely on any personal danger that might have overtaken him.

As for her father and his friends, they had apparently decided to possess their souls in patience. There was, indeed, nothing to do but to wait the Stadtholder's arrival, and in the meanwhile to try and hold those fears in check which had been aroused by the ominous words, 'Fugitives from Ede.'

2

The Stadtholder arrived in the course of the morning. Mynheer Beresteyn did not receive him on the doorstep, as he would have done had the visit been an open one. As it was, the passers-by on the busy quay did not bestow more than a passing glance on the plainly clad cavalier who swung himself out of the saddle outside the burgomaster's house. A message from the camp, probably, they thought. Mynheer Nicolaes had been backwards and forwards from Utrecht several times these past two or three days. The burgomaster awaited his exalted guest in the hall. His attitude and the expression of his face were alike pregnant with eager questionings. The Stadtholder gave curt acknowledgment to the greetings of Mynheer Beresteyn, of his family, and of his friends, and then strode deliberately into the banqueting-hall.

It looked vast and deserted at this early hour of a winter's morning. Nothing of the animation, the riotous gaiety of that day, less than a week ago, seemed to linger in its sombre, panelled walls. The daïs upon which the brides and bridegrooms and the wedding party had sat, and which had crowned so brilliant a spectacle, had been removed, and the magnificent gold and silver plate, the fine linens and priceless crystals been carefully stowed away. Serving-men and sweepers were busy airing and dusting the room when the door was thrown open, and His Highness came in, ushered in by his host. They fled at sight of these great gentlemen, like so many rabbits into carefully hidden burrows.

The Stadtholder went up to the long centre table and faced Mynheer Beresteyn and those who had come in with him – the members of his family and half a dozen burghers, men of importance in the little city. Every one could see that His Highness's anger was bitter against them all.

'And so, mynheer,' he began curtly, and in tones of marked irritation, and addressing himself more particularly to the burgomaster, 'you have thought fit to defy my orders!'

'Your Highness!' protested Mynheer Beresteyn.

'Yet they were clear enough,' the Stadtholder went on, not heeding the interruption. 'Or did your son Nicolaes fail to explain?'

'He told us, your Highness, that it was feared the armies of the Archduchess had crossed the Ijssel – '

'The armies of the Archduchess crossed the Ijssel three days ago,' Maurice of Nassau broke in impatiently. 'Since then they have overrun Gelderland and occupied Ede, putting that city to fire and sword.'

There came a sound like the catching of breath, the rise of a gasp of horror and anguish in every one's throat. But it was quickly suppressed, and His Highness was listened to in silence until the end. Even now, when he paused, no one spoke. All eyes were cast to the ground in self-centred meditation. The whole thing had come as a thunderbolt out of a cloudless sky. Ede had always seemed so safe, so remote. A little city which led nowhere save to the Zuyder Zee, and in the very heart of the United Provinces. What could be the motive of the Archduchess's commanders to adventure thus far into a country which was so universally hostile to them, even to the most miserable peasant, who would pollute every well and stream rather than see the enemy overrun the land? But all these men – ay, and the women, too – had seen so much, suffered so much; fire and sword were such familiar dangers before their eyes, that for them the time had gone when sighs and lamentations would ease their overburdened hearts. They had learned to receive every fresh blow from God's hands in silence, but with determination to fight on, to fight again and to the death once more, if need be, for their liberties, their rights, and the welfare of their children. It was indeed Mynheer Beresteyn who took the next words out of the Stadtholder's mouth.

'Then Amersfoort, too, is threatened?' he said simply.

The prince nodded.

'Think you,' he retorted, 'that I would have ordered the evacuation of the town had there not been imperative necessity for such a course? Now, you may pray God that your wilful disobedience hath not placed your city in jeopardy.'

' 'Twas but yesterday we had the order,' one of the burghers urged. 'And – '

' 'Twas yesterday it should have been obeyed,' the Stadtholder broke in roughly. 'You would then have saved me a perilous journey, for the country already is infested with spies and vedettes, outposts of the Spanish armies.'

'We are all ready to guard your Highness with our lives,' the Burgomaster said quietly.

' 'Tis your wits I want, mynheer,' the prince riposted drily, 'not your blood. Indeed, I do fear that Amersfoort is threatened, though I know not if De Berg will spend his forces on you, or, rather, concentrate them on Arnheim. But you must be prepared,' he added with stern emphasis. 'You are not in a position to defend yourselves, and I cannot detach any of my troops to come to your assistance if you are attacked. Therefore, my orders were: "Evacute the town." You, mynheer burgomaster, must issue your proclamation at once. Let every one go who can, taking women and children with them. Those who remain do so at their risk. Some of you can go north to Amsterdam, others west to Utrecht. Let De Berg find an empty shell when he comes.'

3

Only those who had ever had the sorry task of abandoning a home in the face of an advancing enemy can have any conception of what this peremptory order meant to these burghers – fathers of families for the most part, who, after the terrible privations which they had suffered for over half a century, had begun but a few years ago to reconstitute their country and their homes, to resume their interrupted industries, their commerce, their splendid art, to re-establish the wealth and power which had been their birthright, and which the tyranny of a bigoted and jealous overlord had wilfully wrested from them.

Now it meant laying aside spindles and looms once again, lathes, chisels, or books, in order to buckle on swords which threatened to rust in their scabbards, and to don steel helmets. It meant leaving the women to weep, the children fatherless.

Anxious eyes searched the Stadtholder's drawn, moody face; more than one mind reverted to memories of this peerless and fearless commander, the hero of Turnhout and Ostend. Would he have spoken in those days of 'evacuation' and of 'helplessness'? Would he have dreaded Spinola or the hosts of the Archduchess?

Ah, that subtle, insidious disease had indeed done its work! What mysterious poison was it that had shaken this great man's nerve, made him gloomy and fretful, weakened that indomitable will which had once made the tyrant of Madrid quake for the future of his kingdom?

'De Berg would not dare – ' one of the burghers hazarded timidly.

'He may not,' His Highness answered. 'In which case it might be safe for you all to return to your homes a few days hence. But some of those who fled from Ede believe that De Berg intends to detach some of his troops and with them to push on as far as the Zuyder Zee, leaving it to others to join Isembourg, who is coming up from Kleve, and with his help to capture Nijmegen first and then Arnheim.'

'Marquet by now,' observed Beresteyn, 'must be well on the way to Arnheim, and De Keysere close to Nijmegen. They can intercept Isembourg and cut him off from Ede and De Berg. Your Highness's messenger – '

'Our messenger,' the prince broke in curtly, 'failed to deliver our messages. Marquet is *not* on his way to Arnheim, and De

Keysere was still at Wageningen when the first fugitives from Ede ran terror-stricken into our camp.'

The words were scarce out of his mouth when the sound of a low, quickly suppressed cry came from the rear of the little group that had gathered around His Highness. Few heard it, or guessed whence it had come. Only Mynheer Beresteyn, turning swiftly, caught his daughter's eyes fixed with a set expression upon him. With an almost imperceptible glance he beckoned to her, and she pushed her way through to his side, and slid her cold little hand into his firm grasp. Encouraged by her father's nearness, it was Gilda who uttered the word of protest which had risen to more than one pair of lips.

'Impossible, your Highness!' she said resolutely.

'Impossible!' Maurice of Nassau retorted curtly. 'Why impossible, *mejuffrouw?*'

'Because my lord is a brave man, as full of resource as he is of courage. He undertook to deliver your Highness's commands to Messire Marquet and Mynheer de Keysere. He is not a man to fail.'

She looked brave and determined, without a trace of self-consciousness, even though the rigid education meted out to girls in these times forbade their raising a voice in the councils of their lords. But in this case she had been voicing what was in more than one mind, and when she looked around her with a kind of timid defiance, she only encountered kindly glances.

Her father pressed her hand in tender encouragement. The Stadtholder himself appeared gracious and indulgent. It was only her brother's gaze that was unendurable, for it was charged with sarcasm, not unmixed with malevolence. Did Nicolaes hate her, then? A sickening sense of horror filled the poor girl's soul at the thought. Klaas, her little brother, whom she had loved and mothered, though he was her elder.

Oft-times had she stood between his childish peccadillos and his father's wrath. And now – she could not even bear to meet his glance. She knew that he triumphed, and that he rejoiced in his triumph, even though he must know that she was wounded to the quick. His warning was ringing in her ear, his warning which had, in truth, proved prophetic: 'The orders to Marquet will reach that commander too late!'

As in a dream, she listened to the Stadtholder's words. The whole situation appeared unreal – impossible.

'Your defence of your husband,' the prince was saying, 'does you honour, *mejuffrouw*. But this is not a time for sentiment, but for facts. And these it is our duty to face. We placed our every hope on Marquet's co-operation, but Arnheim and Nijmegen are in peril at this hour because certain messages which I sent failed to reach their destination. We have not the leisure to discuss the causes of this failure; rather must we take immediate measures for the safety of our subjects here.'

Gilda perforce had to remain silent. To the others, in fact, the matter was only important, in so far that the messenger's failure to arrive had placed Arnheim and Nijmegen in jeopardy. What cared they for her heartbreaking anxiety on account of her beloved?

She looked up at her father, because from him she could always expect sympathy. But he, too, was over-preoccupied just now; patted her hand gently, then let it go, absorbed as he was in listening to the Stadtholder's orders for the speedy evacuation of Amersfoort.

She turned away with a bitter sigh, all the more resolutely suppressed as her brother's mocking glance followed her every movement. The men now were in close conference, the Stadtholder sitting at the table, the burgomaster beside him, with pen and ink, drafting the necessary proclamation, the others grouped around, discussing and tendering advice. Every one was busy, every one had something to think about. Gilda, heavy-hearted, took the opportunity of slipping unseen out of the room.

4

What prompted her to run up to the very top of the house, like some stricken bird seeking an eyrie, she could not herself have told you. There is such a thing as instinct, and instinct takes innumerable forms according to the most pressing needs of the heart. For the moment, Gilda's most pressing need was a sight of her beloved. Quite apart from the importance of his presence now with news from the threatened cities, she longed to see him, to feel his arms round her to warm her starved soul in the sunshine of his love and his never absent smile. This longing it was that drove her up to the attic chambers, under the apex of the roof; for these chambers had tiny dormer windows which commanded extensive views of the countryside far beyond the ramparts and beyond the Eem.

Gilda wandered into one of the attic chambers and threw open the narrow casements that gave on the back of the house. Leaning against the window frame, she looked out over the river and beyond it into the mist-laden distance. The sharp, humid air did her good, with its savour of the sea and the tang of spring already lurking in the atmosphere. The sea-fog which had hung over the country for some days still made a dense white veil that enveloped all the life that lay beyond the ramparts, and gave to the little city a strange air of isolation, as if the very world ended on the other side of its walls. From where Gilda stood, high above a forest of roofs and gables, she could see the picturesque fortifications, the monumental gates and turrets, and the Joris Poort and Nieuwpoort, which spanned the Eem on this side. Far away on her right was Utrecht; on her left Barneveld, beyond which stretched the arid upland which held in its cruel breast the secret of her husband's fate.

The girl felt inexpressibly alone, weighted with that sense of forlornness from which only the young are wont to suffer. With the years there comes a more complete self-sufficiency, a greater desire for solitude. Gregariousness is essentially the attribute of youth. And Gilda had no one in whom she could confide. Her father, in truth, had been all to her that a mother might have been; but just now the girl was pining for one of her own sex, for some one who would not be busy with many things, with politics and wars and dissensions, but whose breast would be warm and soft to pillow a head that was weary.

The tears gathered in Gilda's eyes and fell unheeded down her cheeks. It seemed to her as if every moment now she must see a rider galloping swiftly towards her, as if she must hear that merry laugh ringing right across the marshland. But all that she saw was the sleepy little city, stretching out before her until it seemed to melt and merge in the arms of the mist; the network of narrow streets, the crow's foot gables, the dormer windows and ornamental corbellings; and, above everything, the tower of St Maria and St Joris, with the quaint market-place alive with people that looked like ants, fussy and minute.

Even as she gazed, wide-eyed and tearful, the bell of St Maria began to toll. The slow, monotonous reverberation seemed in itself a presage of evil. From the height, Gilda could see the human ants pause awhile in their activities. Their very attitude, the grouping of individual figures, a kind of arrested action in the entire life of the town, proclaimed brooding terror. A moment or two later the sharp clang of the town-crier's bell mingled with the majestic booming, and people started to run toward the market-place from every direction.

Gilda watched this gathering, could see the narrow streets waxing dark with moving forms. She saw the casements thrown open one by one, heads and shoulders filling the dark squares of the window frames. And down below, the arrival of the town-crier, with his halberd and his bell, a crowd of diminutive ant-like forms pressed round his heels. A grey picture, yet all alive with movement, like unto one over which an impatient artist has hastily passed an obliterating brush; the outlines blurred, the colours dull and hazy in the humid atmosphere. It all seemed so dreamlike, so remote. Only a week ago life had appeared so exquisitely gay and so easy! An ardent lover, a happy future, home, adventure! Everything was tumbling out fulsomely from the Cornucopia of Fate.

And now all the tragedy represented by those running people below; the enemy at the gates; the abandoned homes; the devastated city; crying children and starving women – a whole herd of fugitives wandering over the desolate marshland, seeking shelters in cities already over-filled, asking for food where so little was to be had.

It was cruel! Oh, horribly cruel! And awful to see the children dancing around the town-crier, teasing him by pulling at his doublet or trying to steal his bell. The crowd in the market-place had become very dense, and still people came running out of the side streets. The steps of St Maria Kerk were black with the moving throng, and Gilda thought with added heartache of that same crowd, five short days ago, rallying for a holiday, cheering her and her handsome lover, wishing her joy and prosperity in the endless days to come.

Soon the city appeared weltering in confusion. The town-crier continued to ply his bell, and to call the proclamation ordered by the burgomaster. He went on so that every citizen in turn might hear, and now the crowd no longer tended all one way. Some had heard and were hurrying home to consult with their families, to make arrangements either for speedy departure or for weathering the terrible alternative of an invading army. Others lingered in groups on the market-place or at street corners, discussing or lamenting, according to their temperament, pausing to ask of friends what they would do or what they thought of the terrible situation.

Gilda, up at the attic casement, could almost guess by the attitude, the gestures of the scared human ants, just how unsteady had become their mental balance. It was all so unexpected, and there was nothing that anyone could do to help in this terrible emergency. The Stadtholder was going back to camp. He had declared that he could not help. Threatened from every side, he could not spare his forces to come to the aid of so small a place as Amersfoort. And he – the stranger with the happy smile and the gay, inconsequent temper – who had been sent across the Veluwe to obtain succour – had failed to return. There was no garrison at Amersfoort, so there was nothing for it but to flee.

5

At what precise moment Gilda became aware of the solitary rider galloping *tête baissée* toward the city, it were impossible to say. He came out of the mist from the direction of Utrecht, and Gilda saw him long before the sentry at the Joris Poort challenged him. Apparently he had papers and all necessaries in order, for he was admitted without demur; and at the sight Gilda turned away from her point of vantage, ran across the attic-chamber and down the stairs. It was such a very short distance between the Joris Poort and the front door of the burgomaster's house, and she wanted so much to be the first to welcome him.

It was then half an hour before noon. The city by this time was in the throes of a complete upheaval. The noise in the streets had become incessant and deafening. Church bells tolling, town-criers bawling, the clang of the halberds of the city guards mingling with the rattle of cart-wheels upon the cobble-stones, with the tramping of hundreds of feet and stamping of innumerable horses' hoofs. The air was resonant with shrieks and cries, with the grating and jarring of metal, with peal of bells and the hubbub of a throng on the move. Gilda, when she reached the foot of the stairs, found herself facing the wide-open doorway, and through it saw the quay alive with people running, with horses and driven cattle, with crowds scrambling into the boats down below, with carts and dogs and children and barrows piled up with furniture and luggage hastily tied together.

The confusion bewildered her. Determined not to allow futile terror to overmaster her, she, nevertheless, felt within her whole being the sense of an impending overwhelming catastrophe. She could not approach the door, because the crowd was swarming up the stone steps, and her father's serving-men, armed with stout sticks and cudgels, had much ado to keep some of the more venturesome or more terrified among that throng from invading the house.

How that solitary rider whom she had spied in the distance would succeed in forging his way through the dense mass of surging humanity, she could not imagine; and yet through all the turmoil, the din, the terror, she was more conscious of his nearness than of any other sensation. The longing to see him was, in a certain sort of way, appeased. She knew that he lived, and that time alone stood between her present and past longing and the bliss of nestling once more in his arms.

Oh, the crowd! It was rapidly becoming unmanageable. The serving-men plied their cudgels in vain. There were men and women there stronger and bolder than others who were determined to have a word with the burgomaster.

'I am Mynheer Beresteyn's friend!' was shouted authoritatively to the helpless guardians of their master's privacy. Or, 'You know me, Anton? Make way for me there. I must speak with the burgomaster!'

'The burgomaster is busy!' the serving-men bawled out until they were hoarse. 'No one can be admitted!'

But it was difficult for any man to raise a stick against well-known burghers of the city, friends and acquaintances who had supped here in the house at mynheer's own table; and the pressure became more and more difficult to withstand every moment. Some of the people had actually pushed their way into the hall, making it impossible for Gilda to get near the door; and the longing was irresistible to be close at hand when he dismounted, so that her smile might be the first to greet him as he ran up the steps. She pictured it all – his coming, his appearance, the way he would look about him, knowing that she must be near.

Then all at once something awful happened. Gilda, from where she stood, could neither see nor hear what it was; and yet she knew, just from looking at the crowd, that something more immediately terrifying had turned this seething mass of humanity into a horde of scared beasts. Their movements suddenly became more swift; it seemed as if some fearsome goad had been applied to the entire population of the city, and the desire to get away, to run, to flee had become more insistent.

Those who had swarmed up the steps of the burgomaster's house ran down again. They had no longer the desire to speak with anyone, or to appeal to the servants to let them pass. They only wanted to run like the others, the few more grave ones gathering their scattered families around them like a mother hen does her chicks.

And, oh, the awful din! It had intensified a thousandfold, and seemed all of a sudden like hell let loose. So many people shrieked, the women and the children for the most part. And the boatmen down on the water, plying for hire their small craft, already dangerously overloaded with fugitives and their goods. But now everyone on the quay appeared obsessed with the desire to get into the boats. There was scrambling and fighting upon the quay, shrieks of terror followed by ominous splashes in the murky waters. Gilda closed her eyes, not daring to look.

And still the clang of the church bells tolling, and the hideous cacophony of a whole population stampeding in a mad panic.

The hall, the doorway, the outside steps were now deserted. Life and movement and din were all out on the quay and in the streets around. The serving-men even had thrown down their sticks and cudgels. Some of them had disappeared altogether, others stood in groups, skulking and wide-eyed. Gilda tried to frame a query. Her pale, anxious face no doubt expressed the words which her lips could not utter, for one of the men in the hall replied in a husky whisper:

'The Spaniards! They are on us!'

She wanted to ask more, for at first it did not seem as if this were fresh news. The Spaniards were at Ede, the town was being evacuated because of them. What had occurred to turn an ordered evacuation into so redoubtable a stampede?

And still no sign of my lord.

6

Then suddenly the doors of the banqueting-hall were thrown open, and the burgomaster appeared. Had Gilda doubted for a moment that something catastrophic had actually happened, she would have felt her doubts swept aside by the mere aspect of her father. He, usually so grave, so dignified, was trembling like a reed, his hair was dishevelled, his cheeks of a grey, ashen colour. The word 'Gilda' was actually on his lips when he stepped across the threshold, and quite a change came over him the moment he caught sight of his daughter. Before he could call to her she was already by his side, and in an instant he had her by the hand and dragged her with him back into the banqueting-hall.

'What has happened?' she asked, in truth more bewildered than frightened.

'The Spaniards!' her father replied briefly. 'They are on us.'

'Yes,' she ventured, frowning, 'but – '

'Not three leagues away,' he broke in curtly. 'Their vanguard will be here by nightfall.'

She looked round her, puzzled to see them all so calm in contrast to the uproar and the confusion without. The Stadtholder was sitting beside the table, his head resting on his hand. He looked woefully ill. Nicolaes Beresteyn was beside him, whispering earnestly.

'What are you going to do, father dear?' Gilda asked in a hurried whisper.

'My fellow-burghers and I are remaining at our posts,' Beresteyn replied quietly. 'We must do what we can to save our city, and our presence may do some good.'

'And Nicolaes?' she asked again.

'Nicolaes has his horse ready. He will take you to Utrecht in His Highness's train.' Then, as Gilda made no comment on this, only gave his hand a closer pressure, he added tentatively: 'Unless you would prefer to go with Mynheer van den Poele and his family. He is taking Kaatje and her mother to Amsterdam.'

'I would prefer to remain with you,' she said simply.

'Impossible, my dear child!' he retorted.

'My place is here,' she continued firmly, 'and I'll not go. Oh, can't you understand?' she pleaded, with a break in her voice. 'If you sent me away, I should go mad or die!'

'But, Gilda –' the poor man protested.

'My lord is here,' Gilda suddenly broke in more calmly.

'My lord? What do you mean?'

'I saw him awhile ago. I was up in the attic-chamber. He came through the Joris Poort.'

'Your eyes deceived you. He would be here by now.'

'He should be here,' she asserted. 'I cannot understand what has happened. Perhaps the crowd –'

'Your eyes deceived you,' he reiterated, but more doubtfully this time. Then, as just at that moment the Stadtholder rose and caught his eye, Beresteyn called to him, 'My daughter says that my lord has returned.'

'Impossible!' burst forth impulsively from Nicolaes.

'Why should it be impossible?' Gilda retorted quickly, and fixed coldly challenging eyes upon her brother. 'Why should you say that it is impossible?' she insisted, seeing that Nicolaes now looked shamefaced and confused.

'What do you know about my lord?'

'Nothing, nothing!' Nicolaes stammered. 'I did not mean that, of course; it only seems so strange – ' And he added roughly, 'Then why is he not here?'

'The crowd is very dense about the streets,' one of the burghers suggested. 'My lord, mayhap, hath found it difficult to push his way through.'

'Why should he be coming to Amersfoort?' mused Mynheer Beresteyn.

'He came from the direction of Utrecht,' Gilda replied. 'Some one at the camp must have told him that His Highness was here.'

'No one knew I was coming hither,' the Stadtholder broke in impatiently.

'My sister more like hath been troubled with visions,' Nicolaes rejoined with a sneer. 'Nor have we the time,' he added, 'to wait on my lord's pleasure. If your Highness is ready, we should be getting to horse.'

'But surely,' Gilda protested with pitiful earnestness, 'your Highness will wait to see your messenger. He must be bringing news from Messire Marquet. He – '

'Yes,' the Stadtholder broke in decisively, 'I'll see him. Let some one go out into the streets at once and find the man. Tell him that we are waiting – '

'He knows his way about the town,' Nicolaes interposed, with an ill-concealed note of spite in his voice. 'Why should he need a pilot?'

There was a moment's silence. Every one looked nervy and worried. Then the Stadtholder turned once more to the burgomaster, and queried abruptly:

'Are those two companions of my lord's still in your house, mynheer? Can you not send one of them?'

The suggestion met with universal approval. And Mynheer Beresteyn himself urged the advisability of finding my lord's friends immediately. He took his daughter's hand. It was cold as ice, and quivered like a wounded bird in his warm grasp. He patted it gently, reassuringly. Her wild eyes frightened him. He knew what she suffered, and in his heart condemned his son for those insinuations against the absent. But this was not a moment for delicacy or for scruples. The hour was a portentous one, and fraught with peril for a nation and its chief. The individual matters so little at such times. The feelings, the sufferings, the broken heart of one woman or one man – how futile do they seem when a whole country is writhing in the throes of her death agony?

'Go, my dear child,' Beresteyn admonished firmly. 'Obey His Highness's commands. Find my lord's friends and tell them to go at once, and return hither with my lord. Go,' he added; and whispered gently in Gilda's ear, as he led her, reluctant yet obedient, to the door, 'Leave your husband's honour in my hands.'

She gave him a grateful look, and he gave her hand a last reassuring pressure. Then he let her go from him, only urging her to hurry back.

It must not be supposed for a moment that he did not feel for her in her anxiety and her misery. But the man in question was a stranger – an Englishman, what? – and Mynheer Beresteyn was above all a patriot, a man who had suffered acutely for his country, had sacrificed his all for her, and was ready to do it again whenever she called to him. The Stadtholder stood for the safety and the integrity of the United Provinces; he was the champion and upholder of her civil and religious liberties. His personal safety stood, in the minds of Beresteyn and his fellow burghers, above every consideration on earth.

Gilda knew this, and though she trusted her father implicitly, she knew that her beloved would be ruthlessly sacrificed, even by him, if, through misadventure or any other simple circumstance entirely beyond his control, he happened to have failed in the enterprise which had been entrusted to him. Nicolaes, of course, was an avowed enemy. Why? Gilda could not conjecture. Was it jealousy, or petty spite only? If so, what advantage could he reap from the humiliation of one who already was a member of his own family? But she felt herself encompassed with enemies. No one had attempted to defend my lord's honour when it was so ruthlessly impugned save her father, and he was too absorbed, too much centred in thoughts of his country's peril, to do real battle for the absent.

It was with a heavy heart that she turned to go up the stairs in search of the two men who alone were ready to go through fire in the defence of their friend. A melancholy smile hovered round Gilda's lips. She felt that with those two quaint creatures she had more in common at this hour than with her father, whom she idolized. In those two poor caitiffs she had all that her heart had been hungering for: simple hearts that understood her sorrow, loyal souls that never wavered. For evil or for good, through death-peril or through seeming dishonour, their friend whom they reverenced could count upon their devotion. And as Gilda went wearily up the stairs, her mind conjured up the picture of those two ludicrous vagabonds, with their whimsical saws and rough codes of honour, and she suddenly felt less lonely and less sad.

7

Great was her disappointment, therefore, when she reached the guest-chamber, which they still occupied, to find that it was empty. The whole house was by this time in a hopeless state of turmoil and confusion. Serving-men and maids rushed aimlessly hither and thither, up and down the stairs, along the passages, in and out of the rooms; or stood about in groups, whispering or cowering in corners. Some of them had already fled; the few who remained looked like so many scared chickens, fussy and inconsequent – the maids with kirtles awry and hair unkempt, the men striving to look brave and determined, putting on the air of masters, and adding to the maids' distress by their aimless, hectoring ways.

There was nothing in the house now left of that orderly management which is the pride of every self-respecting housewife. Doors stood open, displaying the untidiness of the rooms; there was noise and bustle everywhere, calls of distress and loud admonitions. From no one could Gilda learn what she desired to know. She was forced to seek out Maria, her special tiring-woman, who, it was to be hoped, had some semblance of reason left in her. Maria, however, had no love for the two rapscallions, who were treated in the house as if they were princes, and knew nothing of the respect due to their betters. She replied to her young mistress's inquiries by shrugging her shoulders and calling heaven to witness her ignorance of the whereabouts of those abominable louts.

'Spoilt, they have been,' the old woman asserted sententiously. 'Shamefully spoilt. They have neither order nor decency, nor the slightest regard for the wishes of their betters – '

'But, Maria, whither have the two good fellows gone?' Gilda broke in impatiently.

'Gone? Whither have they gone?' Maria ejaculated, in pious ignorance of such probable wickedness. 'Nay, that ye cannot expect any self-respecting woman to know. They have gone, the miserable roysterers! Went but an hour ago, without saying by your leave. This much I do know. And my firm belief is that they were naught but a pair of Spanish spies, come to hand us all, body and soul, to – '

'Maria, I forbid thee to talk such rubbish!' Gilda exclaimed wrathfully.

And, indeed, her anger and her white and worried look did effectually silence the garrulous woman's tongue.

Even the waiting-maids! Even these ignorant fools! Gilda could have screamed with the horror of it all, as if she had suddenly landed in a nest of scorpions and their poison encompassed her everywhere. This story of spies! God in Heaven, how had it come about? Whose was the insidious tongue that had perverted her brother Nicolaes first, and then every trimmer and rogue in the house? Gilda felt as if it might ease her heart to run round with a whip, and lash all these base detractors into acknowledgment of their infamy. But she forced herself to patience.

A vague instinct had already whispered to her that she must not go back to the banqueting-hall with the news that my lord's friends had gone, and that no one had any knowledge of their whereabouts. She felt that if she did that, her brother's sneers would become unendurable, and that she might then be led to retort with accusations against her only brother which she would afterwards for ever regret.

So she waited for awhile, curtly bade Maria to be gone, and to leave her in peace. She wanted to think, to put a curb on her fears and her just wrath against this unseen army of calumniators; for wrath and fear are both evil counsellors. And above all, she wanted to see her beloved.

He was in the town. She knew it as absolutely as that she was alive. Were her eyes likely to be deceived? Even now, when she closed her eyes, she could see him, as she had done but a few minutes ago, walking his horse through the Joris Poort, his plumed hat shading the upper part of his face. She could see him, with just that slight stoop of his broad shoulders which denoted almost unendurable fatigue. She had noted this at the moment, with a pang of anxiety, and then forgotten it all in the joy of seeing him again. She remembered it all now. Oh, how could they think that she could be deceived?

Just for a second or two she had the mind to run back to the casement in the attic-chamber, and see if she could not from thence spy him again. But surely this would be futile. He must have reached the quay by now,would be at the front door, with no one to welcome him. In truth, the longing to see him had become sheer physical pain.

So Gilda once more made her way down into the hall.

7

A Subtle Traitor

Down below, in the banqueting-hall, Gilda's departure had at first been followed by a general feeling of obsession, which caused the grave men here assembled to remain silent for awhile and pondering. There was no lack of sympathy, I repeat; net even on the part of the Stadtholder, whose heart and feelings were never wholly atrophied. But there had sprung up in the minds of these grave burghers an unreasoning feeling of suspicion toward the man whom they had trusted implicitly such a brief while ago.

Terror at the imminence of their danger, the appearance of the dreaded foe almost at their very gates, had in a measure – as terror always will – blurred the clearness of their vision, and to a certain extent warped their judgements. The man now appeared before them as a stranger, therefore a person to be feared, even despised to the extent of attributing the blackest possible treachery to him. They forgot that the closest possible ties of blood and of tradition bound the English gentleman to the service of the Prince of Orange. Sir Percy Blakeney now, and Diogenes the soldier of fortune of awhile ago, were one and the same. But no longer so to them. The adder's fork had bitten into their soul and left its insidious poison of suspicion and of misbelief.

So none of them spoke, hardly dared to look on Mynheer Beresteyn, who, they felt, was not altogether with them in their distrust. The Stadtholder had lapsed into one of his surly moods. His lean, brown hands were drumming a devil's tattoo upon the table.

Then suddenly Nicolaes broke into a harsh and mirthless laugh.

'It would all be a farce,' he exclaimed with bitter malice, 'if it did not threaten to become so tragic.' Then he turned to the Stadtholder, and his manner became once more grave and earnest. 'Your Highness, I entreat,' he said soberly, 'deign to come away with me at once, ere you fall into some trap set by those abominable spies – '

'Nicolaes,' his father broke in sternly, 'I forbid you to make these base insinuations against your sister's husband.'

'I'll be silent if you command me,' Nicolaes rejoined quietly. 'But methinks that his Highness's life is too precious for sentimental quibbles. Nay,' he went on vehemently, and like one who is forced into speech against his will, 'I have warned Gilda of this before. While we were all waiting here calmly, trusting to that stranger who came God knows whence, he was warning De Berg to effect a quick crossing.'

'It is false!' protested the burgomaster hotly.

'Then I pray you, Nicolaes insisted hotly, tell me how it is that De Berg did forestall his Highness's plans? Who was in the council-chamber when the plans were formulated save yourselves? Who knew of the orders to Marquet? Marquet hath not gone to relieve Arnheim, and the armies of the Archduchess are at our gates!'

He paused, and a murmur of assent went round the room, and when Mynheer Beresteyn once more raised his voice in protest, saying firmly: 'I'll not believe it! Let us wait at least until we've heard what news my lord hath brought!' No one spoke in response, and even the Stadtholder shrugged his shoulders, as if the matter of a man's honour or dishonour had no interest for him.

'Your Highness,' Nicolaes went on with passionate earnestness, 'let me beg of you on my knees to think of your noble father, of the trap into which he fell, and of his assassin, Gerard – a stranger, too – '

'But this man saved my life once!' the Stadtholder said, with an outburst of generous feeling in favour of the man to whom, in truth, he owed so much.

'He hated Stoutenburg then, your Highness,' Nicolaes retorted, and boldly looked his father in the face – his father who knew his own share in that hideous conspiracy three months ago. 'He loved my sister Gilda. It suited his purpose then to use his sword in your Highness's service. But remember, he is only a soldier of fortune after all. Have we not all of us heard him say a hundred times that he had lived hitherto by selling his sword to the highest bidder?'

This time his tirade was greeted by a distinct murmur of approval. Only the burgomaster raised his voice admonishingly once more.

'Take care, Nicolaes!' he exclaimed. 'Take care!'

'Take care of what?' the young man retorted with all his wonted arrogance, and challenged his father with a look. 'Would you give your only son away,' that look appeared to say, 'in order to justify a stranger?'

Then, as indeed Mynheer Beresteyn remained silent, not exactly giving up the contention, but forced into passive acquiescence by the weight of public opinion and that inalienable feeling of family and kindred which makes most men or women defend their own against any stranger, Nicolaes continued, with a magnificent assumption of patriotic fervour:

'Have we the right to hazard so precious a thing as his Highness's life for the sake of sparing my sister's feelings?'

In this sentiment every one was ready to concur. They did not actually condemn the stranger; they were not prepared to call him a traitor and a potential assassin, or to believe one half of Nicolaes Beresteyn's insinuations. They merely put him aside, out of their minds, as not entering into their present schemes. And even the burgomaster could not gainsay the fact that his son was right.

The most urgent thing at the present juncture was to get the Stadtholder safely back to his camp at Utrecht. Every minute spent in this garrisonless city was fraught with danger for the most precious life in the United Provinces.

'Where is his Highness's horse?' he asked.

'Just outside,' Nicolaes replied glibly; 'in charge of a man I know. Mine is ready, too. Indeed, we should get to horse at once.'

The Stadtholder did not demur.

'Have the horses brought to,' he said quickly. 'I'll be with you in a trice.'

2

Nicolaes hurried out of the room, his Highness remaining behind for a moment or two, in order to give final instructions, a last admonition or two to the burghers.

'Do not resist,' he said earnestly. 'You have not the means to do aught but to resign yourselves to the inevitable. As soon as I can, I will come to your relief. In the meanwhile, conciliate De Berg by every means in your power. He is not a harsh man, and the Archduchess has learnt a salutary lesson from the discomfiture of Alva. She knows by now that we are a stiff-necked race, whom it is easier to cajole than to coerce. If only you will be patient! Can you reckon on your citizens not to do anything rash or foolish that might bring reprisals upon your heads?'

'Yes,' the burgomaster replied. 'I think we can rely on them for that. When your Highness has gone, we'll assemble on the market place, and I will speak to them. We'll do our best to stay the present panic, and bring some semblance of order into the town.'

Their hearts were heavy. 'Twas no use trying to minimize the deadly peril which confronted them. There was a century of oppression, of ravage, and pillage, and bloodshed to the credit of the Spanish armies. It was difficult to imagine that the spirit of an entire nation should have changed suddenly into something more tolerant and less cruel.

However, for the moment, there was nothing more to be said, and alas! it was not as if the whole terrible situation was a novel one. They had all been through it before, at Leyden and Bergen-op-Zoom, at Haarlem and Delft, when they were sweeping their land free from the foreign tyrant; and it was useless at this hour to add to the Stadtholder's difficulties by futile lamentations. All the more as Nicolaes had now returned with the welcome news that the horses were there, and everything ready for his Highness's departure. He appeared more excited than before, anxious to get away as quickly as may be.

'There is a rumour in the town,' he said, 'that Spanish vedettes have been spied less than a league away.'

'And have you heard any rumour as to the arrival of our Diogenes?' the Stadtholder asked casually.

Nicolaes hesitated a moment ere he replied:

'I have heard nothing definite.'

3

A minute later the Stadtholder was in the hall. The doors were open and the horses down below in charge of an equerry.

Nicolaes, half way down the outside stone steps, looked the picture of fretful impatience. With a dark frown upon his brow, he was scanning the crowd, and now and again a curse broke through his set lips when he saw the Stadtholder still delayed by futile leave-takings.

'In the name of heaven, let us to horse!' he exclaimed almost savagely.

Just at that moment his Highness was taking a kindly farewell of Gilda.

'I wish, *mejuffrouw*,' he was saying, 'that you had thought of taking shelter in our camp.'

Gilda forced herself to listen to him, her lips tried to frame the respectful words which convention demanded. But her eyes she could not control, nor yet her thoughts, and they were fixed upon the crowd down below, just as were those of her brother Nicolaes. She thought that every moment she must catch sight of that plumed hat, towering above the throng, of those sturdy shoulders, forging their way to her. But all that she saw was the surging mass of people. A medley of colour. Horses, carts, the masts of ships. People running. And children. Numberless children, in arms or on their tiny feet; the sweet, heavy burdens that made the present disaster more utterly catastrophic.

Then suddenly she gave a loud cry.

'My lord!' she called, at the top of her voice. Then something appeared to break in her throat, and it was with a heart-rending sob that she murmered almost inaudibly: 'Thank God! It is my lord!'

The Stadtholder turned, was across the hall and out in the open in a trice.

'Where?' he demanded.

She ran after him, seized his surcoat with a trembling hand, and with the other pointed in the direction of the Koppelpoort.

'A plumed hat!' she murmured vaguely, for her teeth were chattering so that she could scarcely speak. 'All broken and battered with wind and weather – a torn jerkin – a mud-stained cloak. He is leading his horse. He has a three days' growth of beard on his chin, and looks spent with fatigue. There! Do you not see him?'

But Nicolaes already had interposed.

'To horse, your Highness!' he cried.

He would have given worlds for the privilege to seize the Stadtholder then and there by the arm, and to drag him down the steps and set him on his horse before the meeting which he dreaded could take place. But Maurice of Nassau, torn between his desire to get out of the threatened city as quickly as possible and his wish to speak with the messenger whom an inalienable instinct assured him that he could trust, was lingering on the steps trying in his turn to catch sight of Diogenes.

'Beware of the assassin's dagger, your Highness!' Nicolaes whispered hoarsely in his ear. 'In this crowd, who can tell? Who knows what deathly trap is being laid for you?'

'Not by that man, I'll swear!' the Stadtholder affirmed.

'Nay, if he is loyal he can follow you to the camp and report to you there. But for God's sake remember your father and the miscreant Gerard. There, too, a crowd; the hustling, the hurry! In the name of your country, come away!'

There was no denying the prudence of this advice. Another instant's hesitation, the obstinacy of an arbitrary temperament that abhors being dictated to, and the Stadtholder was ready to go. Gilda, on the top of the steps, was more like a stone statue of expectancy than like a living woman. Nay, all that she had alive in her were just her eyes, and they had spied her beloved. He was then by the Koppelpoort, some hundred yards or more on the other side of the quay, with a seething mass of panic-stricken humanity between him and the steps of Mynheer Beresteyn's house.

He had dismounted and was leading his horse. The poor beast, spent with fatigue, looked ready to drop, and, indeed, appeared too dazed to pick his own way through the crowd. As it was, he was more than a handful for his equally wearied master, whose difficulties were increased a hundredfold by the number of small children who were for ever getting in the way of the horse's legs, and were in constant danger of being kicked or trampled on.

But Gilda never lost sight of him now that she had seen him. With every beat of her heart she was measuring the footsteps that separated him from the Stadtholder. And the more Nicolaes fretted to hurry his Highness away, the more she longed and yearned for the quick approach of her beloved.

4

Amongst all those here present, Gilda was the only one who scented some unseen danger for them all in Nicolaes' strangely feverish haste. What the others took for zeal, she knew by instinct was naught but treachery. What form this would take she could not guess; but this she knew, that for some motive as sinister as it was unexplainable, Nicolaes did not wish the Stadtholder and his messenger to meet. That same motive had caused him to utter all those venomous accusations against her husband, and was even now wearing him into a state of fretfulness which bordered on dementia.

'My lord!' she cried out to her beloved at one time; and felt that even through all the din and clatter her voice had reached his ear, for he raised his head, and it even seemed to her as if his eyes met hers above the intervening crowd and as if the supernal longing for him which was in her heart had drawn him with its mystic power over every obtruding obstacle.

For, indeed, the next moment he was right at the foot of the steps, not five paces from the Stadtholder.

Nicolaes spied him in a moment, and a loud curse broke from his lips.

'That skulking assassin!' he cried; and with a magnificent gesture covered the Stadtholder with his body. 'To horse, your Highness, and leave me to deal with him!'

Maurice of Nassau, indeed, was one of the bravest men of his time, but the word 'assassin' was bound to ring unpleasantly in the ears of a man whose father had met his death at a murderer's hand. Half-ashamed of his fears, he nevertheless did take advantage of Nicolaes' theatrical attitude to slip behind him and mount his horse as quickly as he could. But with his foot already in the stirrup compunction appeared to seize him. Wishing to palliate the gross insult which was being hurled at the man who had once saved his life at imminent peril of his own, he now turned and called to him in gracious, matter-of-fact tones:

'Why, man, what made you tarry so long? Come with us to Utrecht now. We can no longer wait.'

With this he swung himself in the saddle.

'Not another step, man, at your peril!'

This came from Nicolaes Beresteyn, who was still standing in a dramatic pose between Diogenes and the Stadtholder, with his cloak wrapped around his arm.

'Stand back, you fool!' retorted the other loudly, and would have pushed past him, when suddenly Nicolaes disengaged his arm from his cloak.

For one fraction of a second the gleam of steel flashed in the humid air; then, without a word of warning, swift as a hawk descending on its prey, he struck at Diogenes with all his might.

It had all happened in a very few brief seconds. Diogenes, spent with fatigue, or actually struck, staggered and half fell against the bottom step. But Gilda, with a loud cry, was already by his side, and as Nicolaes raised his arm to strike once again, she was on him like some lithe pantheress.

She seized his wrist, and gave it such a violent twist that he uttered a cry of pain, and the dagger fell with a clatter to the ground. After which everything became a blur. She heard her brother's loudly triumphant shout:

'His Highness's life was threatened. Mine was but an act of justice!' even as he in his turn swung himself into the saddle.

5

The Stadtholder looked dazed. It had all happened so quickly that he had not the time to visualize it all. De Voocht, who was in the hall of the burgomaster's house from the moment when the Stadtholder bade farewell to Gilda until that when he dug his spurs into his horse and scattered the crowd in every direction, tells us in his 'Brieven' – the one which is dated March 21, 1624 – that the incidents followed on one another with such astounding rapidity that it was impossible for any one to interfere.

All that he remembers very clearly is seeing his Highness getting to horse, then the flash of steel in the air and Nicolaes Beresteyn's arm upraised ready to strike. He could not see if any one had fallen. The next moment he heard Gilda's heart-piercing shriek, and saw her running down the stone steps – almost flying, like a bird.

Mynheer Beresteyn followed his daughter as rapidly as he could. He reached the foot of the steps just as his son put his horse to a walk in the wake of his Highness. He was wont to say afterwards that at the moment his mind was an absolute blank. He had heard his daughter's cry and seen Nicolaes strike; but he had not actually seen Diogenes. Now he was just in time to see his son's final dramatic gesture and to hear his parting words:

'There, father,' Nicolaes shouted to him, and pointed to the ground, 'is the pistol which the miscreant pointed at the Stadtholder when I struck him down like a dog!'

The people down on the quay had hardly perceived anything. They were too deeply engrossed in their own troubles and deadly peril.

When the horses reared under the spur they scattered like so many hens out of the way of immediate danger; but a second or two later they were once more surging everywhere, intent only on the business of getting away.

Gilda, at the foot of the steps, saw and heard nothing more. The sudden access of almost manlike strength wherewith she had fallen on her brother and wrenched the murderous dagger from his grasp had as suddenly fallen from her again. Her knees were shaking; she was almost ready to swoon.

She put out her arms and encountered those of her father, which gave her support. Her brother's voice, exultant and cruel, reached her ears as through a veil.

'My lord!' she murmured, in a pitiful appeal.

She did not know how severely he had been struck; indeed, she had not seen him fall. Her instinct had been to rush on Nicolaes first and to disarm him. In this she succeeded. Then only did she turn to her beloved.

But the crowd, cruelly indifferent, was all around like a surging sea. They pushed and they jostled; they shouted and filled the air with a medley of sounds. Some actually laughed. She saw some comely faces and ugly ones; some that wept and others that grinned. It seemed to her even for a moment that she caught sight of a round red face and of lean and lanky Socrates. She tried to call to him, to beg him to explain. She turned to her father, asking him if in truth she was going mad.

For she called in vain to her beloved. He was no longer here.

8

Devil's-writ

When Diogenes, taken wholly unawares by Nicolaes' treacherous blow, had momentarily lost his balance, he would have been in a precarious position indeed had not his faithful friends been close at hand at the moment.

It is difficult to surmise how terribly anxious the two philosophers had been these past few days. Indeed, their anxiety had proved more than a counterpart to that felt by Gilda, and had, with its simple-hearted sympathy, expressed in language more whimsical than choice, been intensely comforting to her.

Both these worthies had been inured to blows and hurts from the time when, as mere lads, they first learned how to handle a sword, and Pythagoras' wound, which would have laid an ordinary man low for a fortnight, was, after four days, already on the mend. To keep a man of that type in bed, or even within four walls, when he began to feel better was more than any one could do. And when he understood that Diogenes had been absent four days on an errand for the Stadtholder, that the *jongejuffrouw* was devoured with anxiety on his behalf, and that that spindle-legged gossoon Socrates was spending most of the day and one half of the night on horseback, patrolling the ramparts watching for the comrade's return; when he understood all that, I say, it was not likely that he – Pythagoras –

an able-bodied man and a doughty horseman at that, would be content to lie abed and be physicked by any grovelling leech.

Thus the pair of them were providentially on the watch on that memorable March 21, and they both saw their comrade-in-arms enter the city by the Joris Poort. They followed him as best they could through the crowd, cursing and pushing their way, knowing well that Diogenes' objective could be none other than a certain house they wot of on the quay, where a lovely *jongejuffrouw* was waiting in tears for her beloved.

Remember that to these two caitiffs the fact that the Spaniards were said to be at the very gates of Amersfoort was but a mere incident. With their comrade within the city, they feared nothing, were prepared for anything. They had been in far worse plights than this many a time in their career, the three of them, and had been none the worse for it in the end.

Of course, now matters had become more complicated through the *jongejuffrouw*. She had become the first consideration, and though it was impossible not to swear at Diogenes for thus having laid this burden on them all, it was equally impossible to shirk its responsibilities.

The *jongejuffrouw* above all. That had become the moral code of these two philosophers, and with those confounded Spaniards likely to descend on this town – why, the *jonge-juffrouw* must be got out of it as soon as may be! No wonder that Diogenes had turned up just in the nick of time! Something evidently was in the wind, and it behoved for comrades-in-arms to be there, ready to help as occasion arose.

A simple code enough, you'll admit; worthy of simple, unsophisticated hearts. Socrates,, being the more able-bodied of the two, then took command, dismounted, and left his lubberly compeer in charge of the horses at a comparatively secluded corner of the market-place.

'If you can get hold of one more horse,' he said airily, 'one that is well-saddled and looks sprightly and fresh, do not let your super-sensitive honesty stand in your way. Diogenes' mount looked absolutely spent, and I'm sure he'll need another.'

With which parting admonition he turned on his heel and made his way toward the quay.

2

Thus it was that Socrates happened to be on the spot, or very near it, when Diogenes was struck by the hand of a traitor, and, wearied, sick, and faint, lost his footing and fell for a moment helpless against the steps, whilst Nicolaes Beresteyn dug his spurs into his horse's sides and urged the Stadtholder to immediate haste.

A second or two later these two were lost to sight in the crowd. It was Socrates who received his half-swooning friend in his arms, and who dragged him incontinently into the recess formed by the side of the stone steps and the wall of the burgomaster's house.

By great good fortune, the dagger-thrust aimed by the abominable miscreant had lost most of its virulence in the thick folds of Diogenes' cloak. The result was just a flesh wound in the neck, nothing that would cause so hardened a soldier more than slight discomfort. His scarf, tied tightly around his shoulders by Socrates' rough, but experienced, hands, was all that was needed for the moment. It had only been fatigue, and perhaps the unexpectedness of the onslaught, that had brought him to his knees for that brief second, and rendered him momentarily helpless. Time enough, by mischance for Nicolaes to drag the Stadtholder finally out of sight.

But by the time Diogenes' faithful comrade had found shelter for him in the angle of the wall the feeling of sickness had passed away.

'The Stadtholder,' he queried abruptly, 'where is he?'

'Gone!' Socarates grunted through clenched teeth. 'Gone, together with that spawn of the devil who – '

'After him!' Diogenes commanded, speaking once more with that perfect quietude which is the attribute of men of action at moments of acute peril. 'Get me a horse, man! Mine is spent.'

'In the market-place,' Socrates responded laconically. 'Pythagoras is in charge. You can have the best, and we'll follow.' Then he added, under his breath: 'And the *jongejuffrouw*? She was so anxious – '

Diogenes made no reply, gave one look up at the house which contained all that for him was dearest on God's earth. But he did not sigh. I think the longing and the disappointment were too keen even for that. The next moment he had already started to push his way through the throng along the quay, and thence into Vriese Straat in the direction of the market-place, closely followed by his long-legged familiar.

As soon as the Groote Market lay open before him, his sharp eyes searched the crowd for a sight of the Stadtholder's plumed bonnet. Soon he spied his Highness right across the place, with Nicolaes riding close to his stirrup.

The two horsemen were then tending toward Joris Laan, which leads straight to the *poort*.

At that end of the *markt* the crowd was much less dense, and Joris Laan beyond appeared practically deserted. It was, you must remember, from that side that the enemy would descend upon the city when he came, and the moving throng, if viewed from a height, would now have looked like a column of smoke when it is all blown one way by the wind. Already the Stadtholder and Nicolaes had been free to put their horses to a trot.

Another moment and they would be galloping down Joris Laan, which is but three hundred yards from the *poort*.

'Oh, God, grant me wings!' Diogenes muttered, between his teeth.

'What are you going to do?' Socrates asked.

'Prevent the Stadtholder from falling into an abominable trap, if I can,' the other replied briefly.

Socrates pointed to the distant corner of the *markt,* where Pythagoras could be dimly perceived waiting patiently beside three horses.

'I see the ruffian has stolen a horse,' be said. 'So long as it is a fresh one – '

'I shall need it,' Diogenes remarked simply.

'I told him only to get the best, but you can't trust that loon since good fortune hath made him honest.'

The next few seconds brought them to the spot. Pythagoras hailed them with delight. He was getting tired of waiting. Three horses, obviously fresh and furnished with excellent saddlery, were here ready. Even Socrates had a word of praise for his fat compeer's choice.

'Where did you get him from?' he queried, indicating the mount which Diogenes had without demur selected for himself.

Pythagoras shrugged his shoulder. What did it matter who had been made the poorer by a good horse? Enough that it was here now, ready to do service to the finest horseman in the Netherlands. Already Diogenes had swung himself into the saddle, and now he turned his horse toward Nieuwpoort.

'Where do we go?' the others cried.

'After me!' he shouted in reply.

3

Nose to heels, the three riders thundered through the city. It was deserted at this end of it, remember. Thank God for that! And now for a host of guardian angels to the rescue! Down the Oude Straat they galloped, their horses' hoofs raising myriads of sparks from the uneven cobblestones. 'God grant me wings!' the leader had cried ere he set spurs to his horse, and the others followed without an instant's thought as to the whither or the wherefore. 'After me!' he had called; and they who had fought beside him so often, who had bled with him, suffered with him, triumphed at times, been merry always, were well content to follow him now and forget everything in the exhilaration of this chase.

A chase it was! They could not doubt it, even though they seemed at this moment to be speeding in the opposite direction to that pursued by the Stadtholder and Nicolaes Beresteyn. But they well knew their friend's way, when he let his mount have free rein and threw up his head with that air of intense vitality which in him was at its height when life and death were having a tussle somewhere at the end of a ride.

Down the Oude Straat, which presently abuts on the ramparts. Then another two hundred yards to Nieuwpoort. No one in sight now. This part of the city looks like one of the dead. Doors open wide, litter of every sort encumbering the road. The din from afar, even the ceaseless tolling of St Maria bell, seem like dream-sounds, ghost-like and unreal. Now the *poort*. Still no one in sight. No guard. No sentry. The gate left open. Here two or three halberds hastily thrown down in some hurried flight. There a culverin, forlorn looking, gaping wide-mouthed like some huge toad yawning as if astonished or wearied to find itself deserted. Then, again, a pile of muskets. It must have been a sudden panic that drove the guard from their post. But, thank God, the gate!

Diogenes is already through; after him his two cornpeers. A quarter of a league further on they suddenly draw rein. The horses rear, snorting and tossing, panting with the excitement and fretted with the curb. The riders blink for a second or two in the glare. The white mist is positively blinding here, where its sovereignty is unfettered. Just a clump of trees, way out on the right, here and there a hut with thatched roof and a piece of low fencing, or the gaunt arms of a windmill stretched with eerie stillness to the silvery sky. And above it all the mist – a pale shroud that envelops everything.

To the east and the south the arid upland plunges headlong through it into infinity, cloaks within its stern bosom the secrets of the lurking enemy – the armies of De Berg, the Spanish outposts, the ambuscades. To the west Utrecht, unseen – and just now two tiny specks speeding along its road – the Stadtholder and Nicolaes Beresteyn. They came out into the open through Joris Poort, and are now some four hundred yards or less from the spot where three panting but exhilarated philosophers were now filling their lungs with the crisp, humid air.

They looked neither to right nor left. The Stadtholder, easily recognizable by his plumed bonnet, rides a length or less in advance of his companion. The fog has not yet swallowed them up. Diogenes takes all this in. A simple enough picture – the sea-fog and two riders speeding towards Utrecht. But a swift intaking of his breath, a tight closing of his firm lips, indicate to the others that all is not as simple as it seems.

4

Then a very curious thing happened. At first it seemed nothing. But to the watchers outside Nieuwpoort it had the same effect as a flash of lightning would have in an apparently cloudless sky. It began with Nicolaes Beresteyn drawing his horse close up to the Stadtholder, on his Highness's right. Then for another few seconds the two riders went along side by side, like one black speck now, still quite distinguishable through the fog. Socrates and Pythagoras had their eyes on Diogenes. But Diogenes did not move. He was frowning, and his face bad a set and tense expression. He had his horse tightly on the curb, and appeared almost wilfully to fret the animal, who was pawing the wet, sandy ground and covering itself with lather – a picture of tearing impatience.

'What do we do now?' Pythagoras exclaimed at last, unable, just like the horse, to contain his excitement.

'Wait,' Diogenes replied curtly. 'All may be well after all.'

'In which case?' queried Socrates.

'Nothing!'

A groan of disappointment rose to a couple of parched throats; but it was never uttered. What went on in the mist on the road to Utrecht, four hundred yards away, had stifled it at birth.

The Stadtholder's horse had become restive. A simple matter enough; but in this case unexplainable, because Maurice of Nassau was a splendid horseman. He could easily have quietened the animal if there had not been something abnormal in its sudden antics. It reared and tossed for no apparent reason, would have thrown a less experienced rider.

'The brute is being teased with a goad,' Pythagoras remarked sententiously.

That was clear enough. Even in the distance, an experienced eye could have perceived that the horse became more and more unmanageable every moment, and the Stadtholder's seat more and more precarious. Then suddenly there came the sharp report of a pistol. The horse, goaded to madness, took the bit between its teeth, and with a final plunge bolted across country, away from that strident noise, which, twice repeated at intervals, had turned its fretfulness into blind panic.

It was at the first report that Socrates and Pythagoras again glanced at their leader. A gurgle of delight escaped them when they caught his eye. They had received their orders. The next moment all three had dug their spurs in their horses' flanks and were galloping over sand and ditch.

Diogenes' horse, given free rein at last, after the maddening curb of a awhile ago, was soon half a dozen lengths ahead of the others, tearing along with all its might at right angles to the direction in which the Stadtholder's panic-stricken animal was rushing like one possessed. That direction was Ede.

5

In truth, the low-lying land veiled in sea-fog must at that moment have presented a very curious spectacle. Maurice of Nassau, Prince of Orange, the hope and pride of the Netherlands, helpless upon a horse that was running away with him straight in the direction of the nearest Spanish outposts.

Three soldiers of fortune, strangers, in the land hastening to intercept him, and a couple of hundred yards or so behind the Stadtholder, Nicolaes Beresteyn, puzzled and terror-filled at this unexpected check to his manoevure, pushing along for dear life.

It had been such a splendid scheme, evolved over there in the lonely mill on the Veluwe, between a reprobate and a traitor. The Spaniards on the watch. The Stadtholder helpless, whilst his mount carried him headlong into their hands. What a triumph for Stoutenburg, who had planned it all, and for Nicolaes Beresteyn, the worker of the infamous plot! The Stadtholder prisoner in the hands of the Archduchess! His life the price of the subjection of the Netherlands!

And all to be frustrated by a foolish mischance! Three riders intent upon intercepting that runaway horse! Who in thunder were they? The mist, remember, would have blurred Nicolaes' vision. His thoughts were not just then on the man whom he hated. They were fixed upon the possibility – remote, alas! – of convincing the Stadtholder after this that the goaded horse had been the victim of a series of accidents.

Even at this moment the foremost of the three riders had overtaken the runaway. He galloped for a length or two beside it, then, with a dexterous and unerring grip, he seized the panic-stricken animal by the bridle. A few seconds of desperate struggle 'twixt man and beast. Then man remained the conqueror. The horse, panting, quivering in every limb, covered in sweat and foam, was finally brought to a standstill, and the Stadtholder in an instant had his feet clear of the stirrups and swung himself out of the saddle.

6

Then, and then only, did Nicolaes Beresteyn recognize the man who for the second time had frustrated his nefarious plans – the man whom, because of his easy triumphs, the humiliation which he had inflicted upon him, because of his careless gaiety and his very joy of life, he hated with a curious, sinister intensity.

A ferocious imprecation rose to his lips. For awhile everything became a blank. The present, the future, even the past. Everything became chaos in his mind. He could no longer think. All that he had planned became a blur, as if the sea-fog had enveloped his senses as well as the entire landscape.

But this confused mental state only lasted a very little while – a few seconds, perhaps. Slowly, while he gazed on that distant group of men and horses, his perceptions became clearer once more. And even before the imprecation had died on his lips it gave place to a smile of triumph. Nicolaes Beresteyn had remembered that his Majesty the devil might well be trusted to care for his own. Had he not served the hell-born liege lord well?

For the nonce he brought his horse to a halt. It would be worse than folly to go on. With recognition of those three horsemen over there had also come the certainty that he was now irretrievably unmasked. The Stadtholder, his father, his sister, even his young wife, would turn from him in horror, as from a traitor and an outcast – a pariah, marked with the brand of Cain.

No! Henceforth, for good or for evil, his fortunes must be linked openly with Stoutenburg – with the man who wielded such a strange, cabalistic power over him that he (Nicolaes) – rich, newly wed, in a highly enviable worldly position – had been ready to sacrifice his all in his cause, and to throw in the last shred of his honour into the bargain. In Stoutenburg's cause – ay, and in order to be revenged on the man who had never wronged him save in his conceit – that most vulnerable spot in the moral armour of such contemptible rogues as was Nicolaes Beresteyn.

The spot where he had brought his horse to a halt was immediately behind a low, deserted hut, which concealed him from view. Here he dismounted and, throwing the reins over his arm, advanced cautiously to a point of vantage at the angle of the little building, whence he could see what those four men were doing over there and yet himself remain unseen.

They, too, had dismounted, and were obviously intent on examining the Stadtholder's horse. A sinister scowl spread over Nicolaes Beresteyn's face. There was still a chance, then, of putting a bullet in one or other of those two men – the hated enemy or the Stadtholder. Nicolaes pondered; the scowl on his face became almost satanic in its expression of cruelty. Awhile ago, be had replaced his pistol in the holster, after it had served its nefarious purpose. Now he took it out again and examined it thoroughly.

It had one more charge in it, the devilish charge invented by the Borgias, the secret of which one of that infamous race had confided to Stoutenburg. The fumes from the powder when it struck the eyes must cause irretrievable blindness. Indeed, it had proved its worth already.

Nicolaes, from his hiding-place, could see those four men quite clearly. The Stadtholder, Diogenes, the two caitiffs, all standing round the one horse. Then Diogenes took something out of his belt. He raised his arm, and the next moment a sharp report rang through the mist-laden air. The poor animal rolled over instantly into the mud.

The scowl on Nicolaes' face now gave place once more to a smile of triumph – more sinister than the frown. With the gesture of a conqueror, he clutched the pistol more firmly. The potent fumes had, in truth, wrought their fiendish work on the innocent beast. Diogenes had just put it out of its misery, and his two familiars were preparing to mount one of the horses, whilst he and the Stadtholder had the other two by the reins.

Why not?

The miscreant was sure enough of his aim, and the others would be unprepared. He was sure, too, of the swiftness of his horse, and the Spanish outposts were less than a quarter of a league away, whilst within half that distance Stoutenburg was on the watch with a vedette, waiting to capture the Stadtholder on his runaway horse as it had been prearranged.

Once there he – Nicolaes – would be amongst friends.

Then, why not?

Already the riders had put their horses to a trot. Diogenes and the Stadtholder on ahead, the two loons some few lengths in their rear. In less than three minutes they would be within range of Nicolaes' pistol and its blinding fumes. And Diogenes was riding on the side nearest to his enemy.

Nicolaes Beresteyn grasped his weapon more firmly. He realized with infinite satisfaction that his arm was perfectly steady. Indeed, he had never felt so absolutely calm. The measured tramp of the horses keyed him up to a point of unswerving determination. He raised his arm. The horses were galloping now. They would pass like a flash within twenty paces of him.

The next moment the sharp report of the pistol rang stridently through the mist. There was a burst, a flash, a column of smoke. Nicolaes jumped into the saddle and set spurs to his horse. The other riders went galloping on for a few seconds – not more. Then one of them swayed in his saddle. Nicolaes then was a couple of hundred yards away.

'You are hit, man!' the Stadtholder exclaimed. 'That abominable assassin – '

But the words died in his throat. The reins had slipped out of Diogenes' grasp, and he rolled down into the mud.

A sudden jerk brought the Stadtholder's horse to a halt. He swung himself out of the saddle, and ran quickly to his companion.

'You are hit, man!' he reiterated; this time with an unexplainable feeling of dread.

The other seemed so still, and yet his clothes and the soft earth around him showed no stains of blood.

Pythagoras now was also on the spot. He had slid off the horse as soon as the infamous assassin had started to ride away. Socrates was trying to give chase. Even now two pistol-shots rang out in quick succession right across the moorland. But the hell-hound was well mounted, and the avenging bullets failed to reach their mark. All this the Stadtholder took in with a rapid glance, even whilst Pythagoras, round-eyed and scared, was striving with gentle means to raise the strangely inert figure.

'He hath swooned,' the Stadtholder suggested.

The stricken man had one arm across his face. His hat had fallen from his head, leaving the fine, square brow free and the crisp hair weighted by the sweat of some secret agony. The mouth, too, was visible, and the chin, with its four days' growth of beard, the mouth that was always ready with a smile. It was set now in an awesome contraction of pain, and, withal, that terrible immobility.

Now Socrates was arriving. A moment or two later he, too, had dismounted, cursing lustily that he had failed to hit the hell-hound. A mute query, an equally mute reply, was all that passed between him and Pythagoras.

Then the stricken man stirred as if suddenly roused to consciousness.

'Are you hit, man?' the Stadtholder queried again.

'No – no!' he replied quickly. 'Only a little dazed. That is all.'

He raised himself to a sitting posture, helping himself up with his hands, which sank squelching into the mud; whereat he gave a short laugh, which somehow sent a cold shiver down the listeners' spines.

'Where is my hat?' he asked. 'Pythagoras, you lazy loon, get me my hat.'

He must indeed have been still dazed, for when his friend picked up the hat and gave it to him, his hand shot out for it quite wide of the mark. He gave another laugh, short and toneless as before, and set the hat on his head, pulling it down well over his eyes.

'I had a mugful of hot ale at Amersfoort before starting,' he said. 'It must have got into my head.'

He made no attempt to get to his feet, but just sat there, with his two slender hands all covered with mud, tightly clasped between his knees.

'Can you get to horse?' his Highness queried at last.

'No,' Diogenes replied, 'not just yet, an it please you. I verily think that I would roll out of my saddle again, which would, in truth, be a disgusting spectacle.'

'But we cannot leave you here, man,' the Stadtholder rejoined, with a slight tone of impatience.

'And why not, I pray you?' he retorted. 'Your Highness must get to Utrecht as quickly as may be. A half-drunken lout like me would only be a hindrance.'

His voice was thick now and halting, in very truth like that of a man who had been drinking heavily. He rested his elbows on his knees and held his chin between his mud-stained hands.

'Socrates, you lumpish vagabond,' he exclaimed all of a sudden, 'don't stand gaping at me like that! Bring forth his Highness's horse at once, and see that you accompany him to Utrecht without further mishap, or 'tis with us you'll have to deal on your return!'

'But you, man!' the Stadtholder exclaimed once more.

He felt helpless and strangely disturbed in his mind, not understanding what all this meant; why this man, usually so alert, so keen, so full of vigour, appeared for the moment akin to a babbling imbecile.

'I'll have a good sleep inside that hut, so please you,' the other replied more glibly. 'These two ruffians will find me here after they have seen your gracious Highness safely inside your camp.'

Then, as the Stadtholder still apppeared to hesitate, and neither of the others seemed to move, Diogenes added, with an almost desperate note of entreaty:

'To horse, your Highness, I beg! Every second is precious. Heaven knows what further devilry lies in wait for you, if you linger here.'

'Or for you, man,' the Stadtholder murmured involuntarily.

'Nay, not for me!' the other retorted quickly. 'The Archduchess and her gang of vultures fly after higher game than a drunken wayfarer lost on the flats. To horse I entreat!'

And once more he pressed his hands together, and so tightly that the knuckles shone like polished ivory, even through their covering of mud.

The Stadtholder then gave a sign to the the two men. It was obviously futile to continue arguing here with a man who refused to move. He himself had very rightly said that every second was precious. And every second, too, was fraught with danger. Already his Highness had well-nigh been the victim of a diabolical ambuscade, might even at this hour have been a prisoner in the hands of the enemy, a hostage of incalculable value, even if his life had been spared, but for the audacious and timely interference of this man, who now appeared almost like one partially bereft of reason.

'We'll see you safely inside the hut, at any rate,' was his Highness's last word.

'And I'll not move,' Diogenes retorted with a kind of savage obstinacy, 'until the mist has swallowed up your gracious Highness on the road to Utrecht.'

After that there was nothing more to be said. And we may take it that the Stadtholder got to horse with unaccountable reluctance. Something in that solitary figure sitting there, with the plumed hat tilted over his eyes and the slender, mud-stained hands tightly locked together, gave him a strange feeling of nameless dismay, like a premonition of some obscure catastrophic tragedy.

But his time and his safety did not belong to himself alone. They were the inalienable property of a threatened country, that would be gasping in her death-throes if she were deprived of him at this hour of renewed and deadly danger. So he gathered the reins in his hands and set spurs to his horse, and once he had started he did not look behind him, lest his emotion got the better of his judgment.

The two gossoons immediately followed in his wake. This they did because the friend they had always been wont to obey had thus commanded, and his seeming helplessness rendered his orders doubly imperative at this hour. They rode a length or two behind the Stadtholder, who presently put his horse to a gallop. Utrecht now was only a couple of leagues away.

The three horsemen galloped on for a quarter of a league or less at the same even, rapid pace. Then Pythagoras slackened speed. The others did not even turn to look at him, he seemed to have done it by tacit unspoken consent. The Stadtholder and Socrates sped on in the direction of Utrecht, and Pythagoras turned his horse's head round toward the direction whence he had come.

8

The afternoon lay heavy and silent upon the plain. There was as yet no sign of the approach of the enemy from the south, and the low-lying land appeared momentarily hushed under its veil of mist, as if conscious of the guilty secret enshrined within its bosom. The fog, indeed, had thickened perceptibly. It lay like a wall around that lonely figure, still sitting there on the soft earth, with its head buried in its hands.

Far away, the gaunt-looking carcase of the dead horse appeared as the only witness of a hideous deed as yet unrecorded. Each a blurred and uncertain mass – the dead horse and the lonely figure, equally motionless, equally pathetic – were now the sole occupants of the vast and silent immensity.

Not far away, in the little town of Amersfoort, humanity, panic-stricken and terrorized, filled the air with clamour and with wails. Here, beneath the ghostly shroud of humid atmosphere, everything was stilled as if in ghoulish expectancy of something mysterious, indiscernible which was still to come. It was like the arrested breath before the tearing cry, the hush which precedes a storm.

Overhead, a flight of rooks sent their melancholy cawing through the air.

When Pythagoras was within fifty yards of his friend he dismounted, and, leading his horse by the bridle, he walked towards him. When he was quite near, Diogenes put out a hand to him.

'I knew you would come back, you fat-witted nonny,' he said simply.

'Socrates had to go on with the Stadtholder,' the other remarked, 'or he'd be here, too.' Then he added tentatively: 'Will you lean on my arm?'

'Yes, I'll have to do that now, old crony, shall I not?' Diogenes replied. 'That devil,' he murmured under his breath, 'has blinded me!'

9

Mala Fides

Nicolaes Beresteyn, riding like one possessed, had reached Stoutenburg's encampment one hour before nightfall. He brought the news of the failure of his plan for the capture of the Stadtholder, spoke with many a muttered oath of the Englishman and his two familiars, and of how they had interposed just in the nick of time to stop the runaway horse.

'But for that cursed rogue!' he exclaimed savagely, 'Maurice of Nassau would now be a prisoner in our hands. We would be holding him to ransom, earning gratitude, honours, wealth at the hands of the Archduchess. Whereas – now – '

But there was solace to the bitterness of this disappointment. The blinding powder, invented by the infamous Borgia, had done its work. The abominable rogue, the nameless adventurer, who had twice succeeded in thwarting the best-laid schemes of his lordship of Stoutenburg, had paid the full penalty for his audacity and his arrogant interference.

Blind, helpless, broken, an object now of contemptuous pity rather than of hate, he was henceforth powerless to wreak further mischief.

'Just before I put my horse to a swift gallop,' Nicolaes Beresteyn had concluded, 'I saw him sway in the saddle and roll down into the mud. One of the vagabonds tried to chase me; but my horse bore me well, and I was soon out of his reach.'

That news did, indeed, compensate Stoutenburg for all the humiliation which he had endured at the hands of his successful rival in the past. A rival no longer; for the Laughing Cavalier, blind and helpless, was not like ever to return to claim his young wealthy wife and to burden her with his misery. This last tribute to the man's pluck and virility Stoutenburg paid him unconsciously. He could not visualize that splendid creature, so full of life and gaiety, and conscious of mighty strength, groping his way back to the side of the woman whom he had dazzled by his power.

'He would sooner die in a ditch,' he muttered to himself, under his breath, 'than excite her pity!'

'Then the field is clear for me!' he added exultantly; and fell to discussing with Nicolaes his chances of regaining Gilda's affections. 'Do you think she ever cared for the rogue?' he queried, with a strange quiver of emotion in his harsh voice.

Nicolaes was doubtful. He himself had never been in love. He liked his young wife well enough; she was comely and rich. But love? No, he could not say.

'She'll not know what has become of him,' Stoutenburg said, striving to allay his own doubts. 'And women very quickly forget.'

He sighed, proud of his own manly passion that had survived so many vicissitudes, and was linked to such a tenacious memory.

'We must not let her know,' Nicolaes insisted.

Stoutenburg gave a short, sardonic laugh.

'Are you afraid she might kill you if she did?' he queried.

Then, as the other made no reply, but stood there brooding, his soul a prey to a sudden horror, which was not unlike a vague pang of remorse, Stoutenburg concluded cynically:

'I'll give the order that every blind beggar found wandering around the city be forthwith hanged on the nearest tree. Will that allay your fears?'

Thereafter he paid no further heed to Nicolaes, whom, in his heart, he despised for a waverer and a weakling; but he gave orders to his master of the camp to make an immediate start for Amersfoort.

2

Amersfoort had, in the meanwhile, so De Voocht avers, become wonderfully calm. Those whose nerves would not stand the strain of seeing the hated tyrants once more within the gates of their peace-loving little city, those who had no responsibilities, and those who had families, fled at the first rumour of the enemy's approach. Indeed, for many hours the streets and open places, the quays and the sleepy, sluggish river, had on the first day been nothing short of a pandemonium. Then everything gradually became hushed and tranquil. Those who were panic-stricken had all gone by nightfall; those who remained knew the risk they were taking, and sat in their homes, waiting and pondering. Amersfoort that evening might have been a city of the dead.

Darkness set in early, and the sea-fog thickened at sundown. Some wiseacres said that the Spaniards would not come until the next day. They proved to be right. The dawn had hardly spread o'er the whole of the eastern sky on the morning of the twenty-second, when the master of the enemy's camp was heard outside the ramparts, demanding the surrender of the city.

The summons was received in absolute silence. The gates were open, and the mercenaries marched in. In battle array, with banners flying, with pikemen, halberdiers and arquebusiers; with fifes and drums and a train-load of wagons and horses, and the usual rabble of beggarly camp followers, they descended on the city like locusts; and soon every tavern was filled to overflowing with loud-voiced, swarthy, ill-mannered soldiery, and all the streets and places encumbered with their carts and their horses and their trappings.

They built a bonfire in the middle of the market-place, and all around it a crowd of out-at-elbows ruffians, men, women, and children, filled the air with their shrieks and their bibulous songs. Some four thousand troops altogether, so De Voocht states, spread themselves out over the orderly, prosperous little town, invaded the houses, broke open the cellars and storehouses, made the day hideous with their noise and their roistering.

As many as could found shelter in the deserted homes of the burghers; others used the stately kerks as stabling for their horses and camping ground for themselves. The inhabitants offered no resistance. A century of unspeakable tyranny ere they had gained their freedom had taught them the stern lesson of submitting to the inevitable. The Stadtholder had ordered them to submit. Until he could come to their rescue they must swallow the bitter cup of resignation to the dregs. It could not be for long. He who before now had swept the Spanish hordes off the sacred soil of the United Provinces could do so again. It was only a case for a little patience. And patience was a virtue which these grave sons of a fighting race knew how to practise to its utmost limit.

And so the burghers of Amersfoort who had remained in the city in order to watch over its fate and over their property submitted without murmur to the arrogant demands of the invaders. Their wives ministered in proud silence to the wants of the insolent rabble. They saw their dower-chests ransacked, their effects destroyed or stolen, their provisions wasted and consumed. They waited hand and foot, like serving wenches, upon their tyrants; for, indeed, it had been the proletariat who had been the first to flee.

They even succeeded in keeping back their tears when they saw their husbands – the more noted burghers of the town – dragged as hostages before the commander of the invading troops, who had taken up his quarters in the burgomaster's house.

That commander was the Lord of Stoutenburg. In high favour with the Archduchess now, he had desired leave to carry through this expedition to Amersfoort. Private grudge against the man who had robbed him of Gilda, or lust for revenge against the Stadtholder for the execution of Olden Barneveldt, who can tell? Who can read the inner workings of a tortuous brain, or appraise the passions of an embittered heart?

Attended by all the sinister paraphernalia which he now affected, the Lord of Stoutenburg entered Amersfoort in the late afternoon as a conqueror, his eyes glowing with the sense of triumph over a successful rival and of power over a disdainful woman. The worthy citizens of the little town gazed with astonishment and dread upon his sable banner, broidered in silver with a skull and crossbones – the emblem of his relentlessness, now that the day of reckoning had come.

He rode through the city, hardly noticing its silent, death-like appearance. Not one glance did he bestow on the closed shutters to the right or left of him. His eyes were fixed upon the tall pinnacled roof of the burgomaster's house, silhouetted against the western sky, the stately abode on the quay where, in the days long since gone by, he had been received as an honoured guest.

Since then what a world of sorrow, of passion, of endless misery had been his lot! It seemed as if, on the day when he became false to Gilda Beresteyn in order to wed the rich and influential daughter of Marnix de St Aldegonde, fickle fortune had finally turned her back on him. His father and brother ended their days on the scaffold; his wife, abandoned by him and broken-hearted; he himself a fugitive with a price upon his head, a potential assassin, and that vilest thing on earth, a man who sells his country to her enemies.

No wonder that, at a comparatively early age, the Lord of Stoutenburg looked a careworn and wearied man. The lines on his face were deep and harsh, his hair was turning grey at the temples. Only the fire in his deep-set eyes was fierce and strong, for it was fed with the fire of an ever-enduring passion – hatred. Hatred of the Stadtholder; hatred of the nameless adventurer who had thwarted him at every turn ; hatred of the woman who had shut him out wholly from her heart.

But now the hour of triumph had come. For it he had schemed and lied and striven, and never once given way to despair. It had come, crowned with immeasurable success. The Stadtholder – thanks to the subtle poison of an infamous Borgia, administered by a black-hearted assassin – was nothing but a physical wreck; whilst those who had brought him – Stoutenburg – to his knees three short months ago were at his mercy at last. A longing as cruel as it was vengeful had possession of his soul whenever he thought of these two facts.

His schemes were not yet mature, and he had not yet arrived at any definite conclusion as to how he would reach the ultimate goal of his desires; but this he did know – that the Stadtholder was too sick to put up a fight for Amersfoort, and that Gilda and her stranger lover were definitely parted, and both of them entirely in his power. Their fate was as absolutely in his hands as his had once been in theirs. And the Lord of Stoutenburg, with his eyes raised to the pinnacled roof of the house that sheltered the woman whom he still loved with such passionate ardour, felt that for the first time for this many a year he might count himself almost happy.

3

Nicolaes Beresteyn was among the last to enter his native city. He did so as a shameless traitor, a dishonoured gambler who had staked his all upon a hellish die. Indeed, now he seemed like a man possessed, careless of his crime, exulting in it even. The vague fear of meeting his father and Gilda eye to eye seemed somehow to add zest to his adventure. He did not know how much they knew, or what they guessed, but felt a strange thrill within his tortuous soul at thought of standing up before them as their master, of defying them and deriding their reproaches.

His young wife he knew to be away. Her father had started off for Amsterdam with his family and his servants at the first rumour of the enemy's approach. In any case she was his. She and her wealth, and Mynheer van den Poele's influence and business connexions. He – Nicolaes – who had always been second in his father's affections, always subservient to Gilda and to Gilda's interests, and who since that affair in January had been treated like a skulking schoolboy in the paternal home, would now rule there as a conqueror, a protector on whose magnanimity the comfort of the entire household would depend.

These and other thoughts – memories, self-pity, rage, too, and hatred, and imputations against fate – coursed through his mind as he rode into his native city at the head of the rearguard of Stoutenburg's troops. He drew rein outside his father's house. Not the slightest stirring of his dormant conscience troubled him as he ran swiftly up the familiar stone steps.

With the heavy basket-hilt of his rapier he rapped vigorously against the stout oak panels of the door, demanding admittance in the name of the Archduchess Isabella, Sovereign Liege Lady of the Netherlands. At once the doors flew open, as if moved by a spring. Two elderly serving-men stood alone in the hall, silent and respectful.

At sight of their young master they both made a movement as if to run to him, deluded for the moment into hopes of salvation, relief from this awful horror of imminent invasion. But he paid no heed to them. His very look chilled them and froze the words of welcome upon their lips, as he strode quickly past them into the hall.

The shades of evening were now rapidly drawing in. Except for the two serving-men, the house appeared deserted. In perfect order, but strangely still and absolutely dark. As he looked about him, Nicolaes felt as if he were in a vault. A cold shiver ran down his spine. Curtly he bade the men bring lighted candles into the banqueting-hall.

Here, too, silence and darkness reigned. In the huge monumental hearth a few dying embers were still smouldering, casting a warm glow upon the red tiles, and flicking the knobs and excrescences of the brass tools with minute crimson sparks.

Nicolaes felt his nerves tingling. He groped his way to one of the windows, and with an impatient hand tore at the casement. Stoutenburg's troops were now swarming everywhere. The quay was alive with movement. Some of the soldiers were bivouacking against the house, had built up a fire, the ruddy glow of which, together with the flicker of resin torches, threw a weird and uncertain light into the room. Nicolaes felt his teeth chattering with cold. His hands were like fire. Could it be that he was afraid – afraid that in a moment or two he would hear familiar footsteps coming down the stairs, that in a moment or two he would have to face the outraged father, come to curse his traitor son?

Bah! This was sheer cowardice! But a brief while ago he had exulted in his treachery, gloried in his callous disregard of his monstrous crime. Now it seemed to him that a pair of sightless yet still mocking eyes glared at him from out the gloom. With a shudder and a quickly smothered cry of horror, Nicolaes buried his face in his hands.

The next moment the two serving men came in, carrying lighted candles in heavy silver candelabra. These they set upon the table; and one of them, kneeling beside the hearth, plied the huge bellows, coaxing the dying embers into flame. After which they stood respectfully by, awaiting further commands. Obviously they had had their orders – absolute obedience and all those outward forms of respect which they were able to accord. Nicolaes looked at them with a fierce, defying glance. He knew them both well. Greybeards in the service of his father, they had seen the young master grow up from the cradle to this hour when he stood, a rebel and a skunk, on the paternal hearth.

But they did not flinch under his glance. They knew that they had been specially chosen for the unpleasant task of waiting upon the enemy commanders because their tempers had no longer the ebullience of youth, and they might be trusted to remain calm in the face of arrogance or even of savagery – even in the face of Mynheer Nicolaes, the child they had loved, the youth they had admired, now a branded traitor, who had come like a thief in the night to barter his honour for a crown of shame.

4

A certain commotion outside on the quay proclaimed the fact that the commander of the troops, the Lord of Stoutenburg, had entered the town at the head of his bodyguard, and followed by his master of the camp and his equerries.

He, too, made straight for the burgomaster's house, brought his horse to a halt at the foot of the stone steps. With a curt nod, Nicolaes bade the old crones to run to the front door and receive his Magnificence. In this, as in everything else, the men obeyed at once and in silence.

But already Stoutenburg, preceded by his equerries and his torchbearers, had stepped across the threshold. He knew his way well about the house. As boys, he and his brother Groeneveld had played their games in and around the intricate passages and stairs. As a young man he had sat in the deep window embrasures, holding Gilda's hand, taking delight in terrifying her with his impetuous love, and forcing her consent to his suit by his masterful wooing. A world of memories, grave and gay, swept over him as he entered the banqueting-hall where but for his many misfortunes – as he callously called his crimes – he would one day have sat at the bridegroom's table beside Gilda, his plighted wife.

Both he and Nicolaes felt unaccountably relieved at meeting one another here. For both of them, no doubt, the silence and gloom of this memory-haunted house would in the long run have proved unendurable.

'I did not know that I should meet you here,' Stoutenburg exclaimed, as he grasped his friend by the hand.

'I thought it would be best,' Nicolaes replied curtly. But this warm greeting from the infamous arch-traitor, in the presence of the two loyal old servants, brought a hot flush to the young man's brow. The last faint warning from his drugged conscience, mayhap. But the feeling of shame faded away as swiftly as it had come, and the next moment he was standing by, impassive and seemingly unconcerned, while the Lord of Stoutenburg gave his orders to the men.

These orders were to prepare the necessary beds for my lord and for Mynheer Nicolaes Beresteyn, also for the two equerries, and proper accommodation for my lord's bodyguard, which consisted of twenty musketeers with their captain. Moreover, to provide supper for his Magnificence and mynheer in the banqueting-hall, and for the rest of the company in some other suitable room, without delay.

The two old crones took the orders in silence, bowed, and prepared to leave the room.

'Stay,' my lord commanded. 'Where is the burgomaster?'

'In his private apartments, so please you,' one of the men replied.

'And his daughter?'

'The *jongejuffrouw* is with Mynheer the Burgomaster.'

'Tell them both I want them to sup here with me and Mynheer Nicolaes.'

Again the men bowed with the same silent dignity. It was impossible to gather from their stolid, mask-like faces what their thoughts might be at this hour. When they had gone, Stoutenburg peremptorily dismissed his equerries.

'If you have anything to complain of in this house,' he said curtly, 'come and report to me at once. Tomorrow we leave at dawn.'

Both the equerries gave a gasp of astonishment.

'Tomorrow?' one of them murmured, apparently quite taken aback by this order.

'At dawn,' Stoutenburg reiterated briefly.

This was enough. Neither did the equerries venture on further remarks. They had served for some time now under his Magnificence, knew his obstinacy and the irrevocableness of his decisions when once he had spoken.

'No further commands until then, my lord?' was all that the spokesman said.

'None for you,' Stoutenburg replied curtly. 'But tell Jan that the moment – the moment, you understand – that the burgomaster enters this room, he is to be prevented from doing any mischief. If he carries a weapon, he must at once be disarmed; if he resists, there should be a length of rope handy wherewith to tie his hands behind his back. But otherwise I'll not have him hurt. Understand?'

'Perfectly, my lord,' the equerry gave answer. ' 'Tis simple enough.'

5

Now the two friends – brothers in crime – were alone in the vast, panelled hall.

Nicolaes had said nothing, made no movement of indignation or protest, when the other delivered his monstrous and treacherous commands against the personal liberty of the burgomaster. He had sat sullen and glowering, his head resting against his hand.

Stoutenburg looked down on him for a moment or two, his deep-set eyes full of that contempt which he felt for this weak-kneed and conscience-plagued waverer. Then he curtly advised him to leave the room.

'You might not think it seemly,' he remarked with a sneer, 'to be present when I take certain preventive measures against your father. These measures are necessary, else I would not take them. You would not have him spitting some of our men, or mayhap do himself or Gilda some injury now, would you?'

'I was not complaining,' Nicolaes retorted drily.

Indeed, he obeyed readily enough. Now that the time had come to meet his father, he shrank from the ordeal with horror. It would have to come, of course; but, like all weak natures, Nicolaes was always on the side of procrastination. He rose without another word, and, avoiding the main door of the banqueting-hall, he went out by the back one, which gave on a narrow antechamber and thence on the service staircase.

'I'll remain in the antechamber,' he said. 'Call me when you wish.'

Stoutenburg shrugged his shoulders. He was glad to remain alone for awhile – alone with that wealth of memories which would not be chased away. Memories of childhood, of adolescence, of youth untainted with crime; of love, before greed and ambition had caused him to betray so basely the girl who had believed in him.

'If Gilda had remained true to me,' he sighed, with almost cynical inconsequence, exacting fidelity where he had given none. 'If she had stuck to me that night in Haarlem everything would have been different.'

He went up to the open window, and, leaning his arm against the mullion, he gazed upon the busy scene below. The current of cold, humid air appeared to do him good. His arquebusiers and pikemen, bivouacking round the spluttering fires, striving to keep the damp air out of their stiffening limbs; the shouts, the songs, the peremptory calls; the shrieks of frightened women and children; the loud Spanish oaths; the medley of curses in every tongue – all this confused din pertaining to strife seemed to work like a tonic upon his brooding spirit. A blind beggar soliciting alms among the soldiery chased all softer thoughts away.

'Hey, there!' he shouted fiercely, to one of the soldiers who happened just then to have caught his eye. 'Have I not given orders that every blind beggar lurking around the city be hung to the nearest tree?'

The men laughed. A monstrously tyrannical order such as that suited their present mood.

'But this one was inside the city, so please your Magnificence,' one of them protested with a cynical laugh, 'when we arrived.'

'All the more reason why he should be hung forthwith!' Stoutenburg riposted savagely in reply.

A loud guffaw greeted this inhuman order. His Magnificence was loudly cheered, his health drunk in deep goblets of stolen wine. Then a search was made for the blind beggar. But he, luckily for himself, had in the meanwhile taken to his heels.

6

The next moment a slight noise behind him caused the Lord of Stoutenburg to turn on his heel. The door had been thrown open, and the burgomaster, having his daughter on his arm, stood upon the threshold. He was dressed in his robes of office, with black cloak and velvet bonnet; but he wore a steel gorget round his neck and rapier by his side.

At sight of his arch enemy, he had paused under the lintel, and the ashen pallor of his cheeks became more marked. But he had no time to move, for in an instant Jan and three or four men were all around him.

At this treacherous onslaught a fierce oath escaped Beresteyn's lips. In an instant his sword was out of its scabbard, he himself at bay, covering Gilda with his body, and facing the men who had thus scurrilously rushed on him out of the gloom. But obviously resistance was futile. Already he was surrounded and disarmed, Gilda torn forcibly away from him, thrust into a corner, whilst he himself was rendered helpless, even though he fought and struggled magnificently. The whole unequal combat had only lasted a few seconds; and now the grand old man stood like a fettered lion, glowering and defiant, his hands tied behind his back with a length of rope, against which he was straining with all his might.

One of the most disloyal pitfalls ever devised against an unsuspecting civilian – and he the chief dignitary of a peace-loving city. Stoutenburg, watched the scene with an evil glitter in his restless eyes. Shame and compunction did, in truth, bear no part in his emotions at this moment. He was exulting in the thought of his vile stratagem, pleased that he had thought of enticing Gilda hither by summoning her father at the same time. It was amusing to watch them both – the burgomaster still dignified, despite his helplessness, and Gilda beautiful in her indignation. By St Bavon, the girl was lovely, and still desirable. And thank Beelzebub and all the powers of darkness who lent their aid in placing so exquisite a prize in the hands of the conqueror.

Stoutenburg could have laughed aloud with glee. As it was, he made an effort to appear both masterful and indifferent. He knew that he could take his time, that any scheme which he might formulate for his own advancement and the satisfaction of his every ambition was now certain of success. The future was entirely his, to plan and mould at will.

So now he deliberately turned back to the window, closed it with a hand that had not the slightest tremor in it. Then he returned to the centre of the room, sat down beside the table, and took on a cool and judicial air. All his movements were consciously slow. He looked at the burgomaster and at Gilda with ostentatious irony, remained silent for awhile as if in pleasant contemplation of their helplessness. 'You are in, suspense,' his silence seemed to express. 'You know that your fate is in my hands. But I can afford to wait, to take mine ease. I am lord of the future, and you are little better than my slaves.'

'Was it not foolishness to resist, mynheer?' he said at last, in a tone of gentle mockery. 'Bloodshed, eh? In truth, the role of fire-eater ill becomes your dignity and your years.'

'Spare me your insults; my lord,' Beresteyn retorted, with calm dignity. 'What is your pleasure with my daughter and with me?'

'I will tell you anon,' Stoutenburg replied coolly, 'when you are more composed.'

'I am ready now to hear your commands.'

'Quite submissive, eh?' the other retorted with a sneer.

'No; only helpless, and justly indignant at this abominable outrage.'

'Also surprised – what? – at seeing me here tonight?'

'In truth, my lord, I had not expected to see the son of Olden Barneveldt at the head of enemy troops.'

'Or *your* son in his train, eh?'

The burgomaster winced at the taunt. But he rejoined quite simply:

'If what rumour says is true, my lord, then I have no son.'

'If,' Stoutenburg retorted drily, 'rumour told you that Nicolaes Beresteyn hath returned to his allegiance, then the jade did not lie. Your son, mynheer, hath shown you which way loyalty lies. Not in the service of a rebel prince, but in that of the Archduchess Isabella, our Sovereign Liege.'

He paused, as if expecting some word of reply from the burgomaster; but as the latter remained silent, he went on more lightly:

'But enough of this. Whether you, Mynheer Beresteyn, and your son do make up your differences presently is no concern of mine. You will see him anon, no doubt, and can then discuss your family affairs at your leisure. For the nonce, I do desire to know whether your city intends to be submissive. I have exercised great leniency up to this hour; but you must remember that I am equally ready to punish at the slightest sign of contumely or of resistance to my commands.'

'For the leniency to which the Lord of Stoutenburg lays claim,' Beresteyn rejoined with perfect dignity, 'in that, up to this hour he has not murdered our peaceful citizens, burned down our houses, or violated our homes, we tender him our thanks. As for the future, the treacherous pitfall into which I have fallen, and the unwarrantable treatment that is meted out to me, will mayhap prove to my unfortunate fellow-citizens that resistance to overwhelming force is worse than useless.'

'Excellent sentiments, mynheer!' Stoutenburg retorted. 'Dictated, I make no doubt, by one who knows the usages of war.'

'We do all of us,' the burgomaster gave quiet answer, 'obey the behests of our Stadtholder, our Sovereign Liege.'

'The rebel prince, mynheer, who, by commanding you to submit, hath for once gauged rightly the temper of the Sovereign whom he hath outraged. Will you tell me, I pray you,' Stoutenburg added, with a sardonic grin, 'whether the *jongejuffrouw* your daughter is equally prepared to obey Maurice of Nassau's behests and submit to my commands?'

At this cruel thrust an almost imperceptible change came over the burgomaster's calm, dignified countenance; and even this change was scarce noticeable in the uncertain, flickering light of the wax candles. Perhaps he had realized, for the first time, the full horror of his position, the full treachery of the snare which had been laid for him, and which left him, pinioned and helpless, at the mercy of an unscrupulous and cowardly enemy. Not only him, but also his daughter.

A groan like that of a wounded beast escaped his lips, and his powerful arms and shoulders strained at the cords that fettered him. Nevertheless, after a very brief moment of silence he rejoined with perfect outward calm:

'My daughter, my lord, was under my protection until vile treachery rendered me helpless. Now that her father can no longer watch over her, she is under the protection of every man of honour.'

'That is excellently said, mynheer,' Stoutenburg replied. 'And in a few words you have put the whole situation tersely and clearly. You have orders from the Stadtholder to obey my commands; therefore I do but make matters easier for you by having you removed to your apartments, instead of merely commanding you to return thither – an order which, if you were free, you might have been inclined to disobey.'

'A truce on your taunts, my lord!' broke in the burgomaster firmly. 'What is your pleasure with us?'

'Just what I have had the honour to tell you,' Stoutenburg replied coolly. 'That you return forthwith to your apartments.'

'But my daughter, my lord?'

'She sups here, with her brother Nicolaes and with me.'

' 'Tis only my dead body you'll drag away from here,' the burgomaster rejoined quietly.

Once more Stoutenburg broke into that harsh, mirthless laugh which had become habitual to him and which seemed to find its well-spring in the bitterness of his soul.

'Fine heroics, mynheer!' he said derisively. 'But useless, I fear me, and quite unnecessary. Were I to assure you that your daughter hath ceased to rouse the slightest passion in my heart or to stir my senses in any way, you would mayhap not credit me. Yet such is the case. The *jongejuffrouw*, I'll have you believe, will be as safe with me as would the ugliest old hag out of the street.'

'Nevertheless, my lord,' Beresteyn rejoined with calm dignity, 'whilst I live I remain by my daughter's side.'

Stoutenburg shrugged his shoulders.

'Jan,' he called, 'take mynheer the burgomaster back to his apartments. I have no further use for him.'

7

Mynheer Beresteyn was still a comparatively young and vigorous man. In his day, he had been counted one of the finest soldiers in the armies of the Prince of Orange, and had accomplished prodigies of skill and valour at Turnhout and Ostend. The feeling that at this moment, when he would have given his life to protect his daughter, he was absolutely helpless, was undoubtedly the most cruel blow he had ever had to endure at the hands of Fate. His eyes, pathetic in their mute appeal for forgiveness, sought those of Gilda. She had remained perfectly still all this while, silent in the dark corner whither Jan and the soldiers had thrust her at their first onslaught on the burgomaster. But she had watched the whole scene with ever-increasing horror, not at thought of herself, of her own danger, only of her father and all that he must be suffering. Now her one idea was to reassure him, to ease the burden of sorrow and of wrath which his own impotence must have laid upon his brave soul.

Before any of the men could stop her, she had evaded them. Swift and furtive as a tiny lizard, she had wormed her way between them to her father's side. Now she had her arms round his neck, her head against his breast.

'Do not be anxious because of me, father dear,' she whispered under her breath. 'God hath us all in His keeping. Have no fear for me.'

A deep groan escaped the old man's breast. His eyes, fierce and indignant rested with an expression of withering contempt upon his enemy.

'Jan,' Stoutenburg broke in harshly, 'didst not hear my commands?'

Four pairs of hands immediately closed upon the burgomaster. He, like a creature at bay, started to struggle.

'Some one knock that old fool on the head!' his lordship shouted with a fierce oath.

And Jan raised his fist, over-willing to obey. But, with a loud cry of indignation, Gilda had already interposed. She seized the man's wrist with her own small hands and turned flaming eyes upon Stoutenburg.

'Violence is unnecessary, my lord,' she said, vainly striving to speak coolly and firmly. 'My father will go quietly, and I will remain here to listen to what you have to say.'

'Bravely spoken!' Stoutenburg rejoined with a sneer. 'And you, Mynheer Beresteyn, would do well to learn wisdom at so fair a source. You and your precious daughter will come to no harm if you behave like reasonable beings. There is such a thing,' he added cynically, 'as submitting to the inevitable.'

'Do not trust him, Gilda,' the old man cried. 'False to his country, false to his wife and kindred, every word which he utters is a lie or a blasphemy.'

'Enough of this wrangle,' Stoutenburg exclaimed, wrathful and hoarse. 'Jan, take that ranting dotard away!'

Then it was that, just before the men had time to close in all round the burgomaster, Gilda, placing one small, white hand upon her father's arm, pointed with the other to the door at the far end of the room. Instinctively the old man's glance turned in that direction. The door was open, and Nicolaes stood upon the threshold. He had heard his father's voice, Stoutenburg's brutal commands, his sister's cry of indignation.

'Nicolaes is here, father dear,' Gilda said simply. 'God knows that he is naught but an abominable traitor yet methinks that even he hath not fallen so low as to see his own sister harmed before his eyes.'

At sight of his son an indefinable look had spread over the burgomaster's face. It seemed as if an invisible and ghostly hand had drawn a filmy grey veil all over it. And a strange, hissing sound – the intaking of a laboured sigh – burst through his tightly set lips.

'Go!' he cried to his son, in a dull, toneless voice, which nevertheless could be heard, clear and distinct as a bell, from end to end of the vast hall. 'A father's curse is potent yet, remember!'

Nicolaes broke into a forced and defiant laugh, tried to assume a jaunty, careless air, which ill agreed with his pallid face and wild, scared eyes. But, before he could speak, Jan and the soldiers had finally seized the burgomaster and forcefully dragged him out of the room.

10

A Prince of Darkness

Gilda had seen her father dragged away from her side without a tear. Whatever tremor of apprehension made her heart quiver after she had seen the last of him, she would not allow these two men to see.

She was not afraid. When a woman has suffered as Gilda had suffered during these past two days, there is no longer in her any room for fear. Not for physical fear, at any rate. All her thoughts, her hopes, her anxieties were concentrated on the probable fate of her beloved. That unerring instinct which comes to human beings when they are within measurable distance of some acute, unknown danger amounts at times to second sight. This was the case with Gilda. With the eyes of her soul she could see and read something of what went on in her enemy's tortuous brain. She could see that he knew something about her beloved, and that he meant to use that knowledge for his own abominable ends. What these were she could not divine. Prescience did not go quite so far. But it had served her in this, that when her father was taken away she had just sufficient time and strength of will to brace herself up for the ordeal which was to come.

It is always remarkable when a woman, young and brought up in comparative seclusion and ignorance, is able to face moral danger with perfect calm and cool understanding. It was doubly remarkable in the case of a young girl like Gilda. She was only just twenty, had been the idol of her father; motherless, she had had no counsels from those of her own sex, and there are always certain receptacles in a woman's soul which she will never reveal to the most loving, most indulgent father.

Three months ago, this same absolutely innocent, unsophisticated girl had suddenly been confronted with the vehement, turbulent passions of men. She had seen them in turmoil all round her – love, hatred, vengeance, treachery – she herself practically the pivot around which they raged. Out of the deadly strife she had emerged pure, happy in the arms of the man whom her wondrous adventures as much as his brilliant personality had taught her to love.

Since then her life had been peaceful and happy. She had allowed herself to be worshipped by that strangely captivating lover of hers, whose passionately wilful temperament, tempered by that persistent, sunny gaiety she had up to now only half understood. He made her laugh always, made her taste a strange and exquisite bliss when he held her in his arms. But withal she had up till now kept an indulgent smile in reserve for his outbursts of vehemence, for his wayward, oft-times irascible moods, his tearing impatience when she was away from him. Her love for him in the past had been almost motherly in its tenderness.

Somehow, with his absence, with the danger which threatened him, all that had become changed, intensified. The tenderness was still in her heart for him, an exquisite tenderness which caused her sheer physical ache now, when her mind conjured up that brief vision which she had had of him yesterday morning, wearied, with shoulders bent, his face haggard above a three-days' growth of beard, his eyes red-rimmed and sunken. But with that tenderness there was mingled at this hour a feeling which was akin to fierceness – the primeval desire of the woman to defend and protect her beloved – that same tearing impatience with Fate, of which he had been wont to suffer, for keeping him away from her sheltering arms.

Oh, she understood his vehemence now! No longer could she smile at his fretfulness. She, too, was a prey at this hour to a wildly emotional mood, tempest-tossed and spirit-stirring; her very soul crying out for him. And she hated – ay, hated with an intensity which she herself scarcely could apprise – this man whom she knew to be his deadly enemy.

2

'Sit down, sister; you are overwrought.'

Nicolaes' cool, casual words brought her straightway back to reality. Quietly, mechanically she took the seat which he was offering – a high-backed, velvet-covered chair – the one in which the Stadtholder had sat at her wedding feast. She closed her eyes, and sat for a moment or two quite still. Visions of joy and of happiness must not obtrude their softly insidious presence beside the stern demands of the moment.

Stoutenburg brought a footstool, and placed it to her feet. She felt him near her, but would not look on him, and he remained for awhile on his knees close beside her, she unable to move away from him.

'How beautiful you are!' he murmured, under his breath.

Her hand was resting on the arm of her chair. She felt his lips upon it, and quickly drew it back, wiping it against her gown as if a slimy worm had left its trail upon her fingers. Seeing which, he broke into a savage curse and jumped to his feet.

'I thank you for the reminder, *mejuffrouw*,' he said coldly.

After which he sat down once more beside the long centre table, at some little distance from her, but so that the light from the candles fell upon her dainty figure, graceful and dignified against the background of the velvet-covered chair; the whole of his own face remained in shadow. Nicolaes, nervous and restless, was pacing up and down the room.

3

'Allow me, *mejuffrouw*,' Stoutenburg began coolly after awhile, 'to tender you my sincere regrets for the violence to which necessity alone compelled me to subject the burgomaster; a worthy man, for whom, believe me, I entertain naught but sincere regard.'

'I pray you, my lord,' she retorted with complete self-possession, 'to spare me this mockery. Had you not determined to put an insult upon me, an insult which, apparently, you dared not formulate in the presence of my father, you had not, of a certainty, subjected him to such an unwarrantable outrage.'

'You misunderstand my motives, *mejuffrouw*. There was, and is, no intention on my part to insult you. Surely, as you yourself very rightly said just now, your brother's presence is sufficient guarantee for that.'

'I said that, in order to quieten my father's fears. The treacherous snare which you laid for him, my lord, is proof enough of your cowardly intentions.'

'You do yourself no good, *mejuffrouw*,' rejoined the lord of Stoutenburg harshly, 'by acrimony or defiance. I had to lure your father hither, else he would not have allowed you to come. Violence to you – though you may not believe it – would be repellent to me. But, having got you both here, I had to rid myself of him, using what violence was necessary.'

'And why, I pray you, had you, as you say, to rid yourself of my father? Were you afraid of him?'

'No,' he replied; 'but I am compelled to put certain matters before you for your consideration, and did not desire that you should be influenced by him.'

A quick sigh of satisfaction – or was it excitement? – escaped her breast. Fretful of all these preliminaries, which she felt were but the opening gambits of his dangerous game, she was thankful that, at last, he was coming to the point.

'Let us begin, *mejuffrouw*,' Stoutenburg resumed, after a moment's deliberation, 'by assuring you that the whereabouts of that gallant stranger who goes by the name of Diogenes are known to me and to your brother Nicolaes. To no one else.'

He watched her keenly while he spoke. Shading his eyes with his hand, he took in every transient line of her face, noted the pallor of her cheeks, the pathetic droop of the mouth. But he was forced to own that at that curt announcement, wherewith he had intended to startle and to hurt, not the slightest change came over her. She still sat there, cool and impassive, her head resting against the velvet cushion of the chair, the flickering light of the candle playing with the loose tendrils of her golden hair. Her eyes he could not see, for they were downcast, veiled by the delicate, blue-veined lids; but of a surety, not the slightest quiver marred the perfect stillness of her lips.

In truth, she had expected some such statement from that execrable traitor. Her intuition had not erred when it told her that, in some subtle, devilish way, he would use the absence of her beloved as a tool wherewith to gain what he had in view. Now what she realized most vividly was that she must not let him see that she was afraid. Not even let him guess if she were hurt. She must keep up a semblance of callousness before her enemy for as long as she could. With her self-control, she would lose her most efficacious weapon. Therefore, for the next minute or two, she dared not trust herself to speak, lest her voice, that one uncontrollable thing, betrayed her.

'I await your answer, *mejuffrouw*,' Stoutenburg resumed impatiently, after awhile.

'You have asked me no question, my lord,' she rejoined simply. 'Only stated a fact. I but wait to hear your further pleasure.'

'My pleasure, fair one,' he went on lightly, 'is only to prove to you that I, as ever before, am not only your humble slave but also your sincere friend.'

'A difficult task, my lord. But let me see, without further preamble, I pray you, how you intend to set about it.'

'By trying to temper your sorrow with my heartfelt sympathy,' he murmured softly.

'My sorrow?'

'I am forced to impart sad news to you, alas!'

'My husband is dead?'

The cry broke from her heart, and this time she was unable to check it. Will and pride had been easy enough at first. Oh, how easy! But not now. Not in the face of this! She would have given worlds to appear calm, incredulous. But how could she? How could she, when such a torturing vision had been conjured up before her eyes?

For a moment it seemed as if reason itself began to totter. She looked on the man before her, and he appeared like a ghoulish fiend, with grinning jaws and sinister eyes, the play of light behind him making his face appear black and hideous. She put her hands up to her face, closed her eyes, and, oh, Heaven, how she prayed for strength!

None indeed but an implacable enemy, a jealous suitor, could have seen such soul-agony without relenting. But Stoutenburg was one of those hard natures which found grim pleasure in wounding and torturing. His love for Gilda, intensely passionate but never tender, was nothing now but fierce desire for mastership of her and vengeance upon his successful rival. The girl's involuntary cry of misery had been as balm to his evil soul. Now her hands dropped once more on her lap. She looked at him straight between the eyes, her own still a little wild, lit by a feverish brightness.

'You have killed him,' she said huskily. 'Is that it? Answer me! You have killed him?'

He put up his hand, smiling, as if to soothe a crying child.

'Nay! On my honour!' he replied quietly. 'I have not seen that gallant adventurer these three months past.'

'Well, then?'

'Ask your brother Nicolaes, fair one. He saw him but a few hours ago.'

'Ay, yesterday,' she retorted. 'When he tried to assassinate him. I saw the murderous hand uplifted; I saw it all, I tell you! And in my heart I cursed my only brother for the vile traitor that he is. But, thank Heaven, my lord was only hurt. I believe – ' She paused, put her hand up to her throat. The glance in Stoutenburg's eyes gave her a feeling as if she were about to choke.

'You are quite right, *mejuffrouw*,' he broke in drily, 'in believing that the intrepid Englishman who, for reasons best known to himself, hath chosen to meddle in the affairs of this country – that he, I say, was only hurt when your brother interposed yesterday betwixt him and the Stadtholder. The two ragamuffins who usually hang around him did probably save him from further punishment at the moment. But not altogether. Nicolaes will tell you that, half an hour later, that same intrepid and meddlesome English gentleman did once more try to interfere in the affairs of our Sovereign Liege the Archduchess Isabella. This time with serious consequences to himself.'

'My brother Nicolaes,' she murmured, more quietly this time, 'hath killed my husband?'

'No, no!' here broke in Nicolaes at last. 'The whole thing, I vow, was the result of an accident.'

'What whole thing?' she reiterated slowly. 'I pray you to be more explicit. What hath happened to my husband?'

'The explosion of a pistol,' Nicolaes stammered, shamed out of his defiance at seeing his sister's misery, yet angered with himself for this weakness. 'He is not dead, I swear!'

'Maimed?' she asked.

'Blind,' Nicolaes replied, 'but otherwise well. I swear it!' he protested, shutting his ears to Stoutenburg's scornful laugh, his eyes to the other's sardonic grin, his miserably weak nature swaying like a pendulum 'twixt his ambition, his hatred of the once brilliant soldier of fortune, and his dormant tenderness for the sweet and innocent sister to whom his treacherous hand had dealt such a devilish blow.

There was silence in the room now. Gilda had uttered no cry when that same blow fell on her like a crash. It had seemed to snap the very threads that held her to life. One sigh, and one only, came through her lips, like the dying call of a wounded bird. All feeling, all emotion, seemed suddenly to have died out of her, leaving her absolutely numb, scarcely conscious, with wide, unseeing eyes staring straight out before her, striving to visualize that splendid creature, that embodiment of gaiety, of laughter, of careless insouciance, stricken with impotence; those merry, twinkling eyes sightless. The horror of it was so appalling that it placed her for the moment beyond the power of suffering. She was not a human being now at all; she had no soul, no body, no life. Her senses had ceased to be. She neither saw nor heard nor felt. She was just a thing, a block of insentient stone into which life would presently begin to trickle slowly, bringing with it a misery such as could not be endured even by lost souls in hell.

How the time went by she did not know.

Just before this awful thing had happened she had chanced to look at the clock. It was then five minutes to eight. But all this was in the past. She no longer heard the ticking of the clock, nor her enemy's laboured breathing, nor Nicolaes' shuffling footsteps at the far end of the room. Fortunately, she could not see the triumph, the ominous sparkle, which glittered in Stoutenburg's eyes. He knew well enough what she suffered, or would be suffering anon when consciousness would return. Knew and revelled in it. He was like those inquisitors, the unclean spirits that waited on Spanish tyranny, who found their delight in watching the agony of their victims on the rack; who treasured every groan, exulted over every cry, wrung by unendurable bodily pain. Only with him it was the moral agony of those whom he desired to master that caused him infinite bliss. His stygian nature attained a demoniacal satisfaction out of the mental torture which he was able to inflict.

It is an undoubted fact that even the closest scrutiny of contemporary chronicles has failed to bring to light a single redeeming feature in this man's character, and all that the most staunch supporters of the Barneveldt family can bring forward in mitigation of Stoutenburg's crimes is the fact that his whole soul had been warped by the judicial murder of his father and of his elder brother, by his own consequent sufferings and those of his unfortunate mother.

4

'You will, I hope, *mejuffrouw*, give me the credit of having tried to break this sad news to you as gently as I could.'

These words, spoken in smooth, silky tones, were the first sounds that reached Gilda's returning perceptions. What had occurred in between she had not the vaguest idea. She certainly was still sitting in the same chair, with that sinister creature facing her, and her brother Nicolaes skulking somewhere in the gloom. The fire was still crackling in the hearth, the clock still ticking with insentient monotony. A tiny fillet of air caused the candle-light to flicker, and sent a thin streak of smoke upwards in an ever-widening spiral.

That streak of smoke was the first thing that Gilda saw. It arrested her eyes, brought her back slowly to consciousness. Then came Stoutenburg's hypocritical tirade. Her senses were returning one by one. She even glanced up at the clock. It marked three minutes before eight. Only two minutes had gone by. One hundred and twenty seconds. And they appeared longer than the most phantasmagoric conception of eternity. Two minutes! And she realized that she was alive, that she could feel, and that her beloved was sightless. Was it at all strange that, with return to pulsating life, there should arise within her that indestructible attribute of every human heart – a faint germ of hope?

When first the awful truth was put before her by her bitterest foe, she had not been conscious of the slightest feeling of doubt. Nicolaes' stammering protests, his obvious desire to minimise his own share of responsibility, had all helped to confirm the revelation of a hideous crime.

'He is not dead, I swear!' and 'He is not otherwise hurt!' which broke from the dastard's quaking lips at the moment, had left no room for doubt or hope. At least, so she thought. And even now that faint ray of light in the utter blackness of her misery was too elusive to be of any comfort. But it helped her to collect herself, to look those two craven miscreants in the face. Nicolaes obviously dared not meet her glance, but Stoutenburg kept his eyes fixed upon her, and the look of triumph in them whipped up her dormant pride.

And now, when his double-tongued Pharisaism reached her ear, she swallowed her dread, bade horror be stilled. She knew that he was about to place an 'either – or' before her which would demand her full understanding, and all the strength of mind and body that she could command. The fate of her beloved was about to be dangled before her, and she would be made to choose – what?

'You began, my lord,' she said, with something of her former assurance – and God alone knew what it cost her to speak – 'by saying that you desired to place certain matters before me for my consideration. I have not yet heard, remember, what those matters are.'

'True – true!' he rejoined, with hypocritical unction. 'But I felt it my duty – my sad duty, I may say – '

'A truce on this hollow mockery!' she riposted. 'I pray you, come to the point.'

'The point is, fair one, that both Nicolaes and I desire to compass your welfare,' he retorted blandly.

'This you can best do at this hour, my lord, by allowing me to return to the privacy of mine apartments.'

'So you shall, *myn engel* – so you shall,' he rejoined suavely. 'You will need time to prepare for departure.'

She frowned, puzzled this time.

'For departure?' she asked, a little bewildered.

'I leave this town tomorrow at the head of my troops.'

'Thank God for that!' she rejoined earnestly.

'And you, *mejuffrouw*,' he added curtly, 'will accompany us.'

'I?' she asked, not altogether understanding, the frown more deeply marked between her brows.

'Methought I spoke clearly,' he went on, in his habitual harsh, peremptory tone. 'I only came to this town in order to fetch you, *myn engel*. Tomorrow we go away together.'

'The folly of human grandeur hath clouded your brain, my lord!' she said coldly.

'In what way?' he queried, still perfectly bland and mild.

'You know well that I would sooner die than follow you.'

'I know well that most women are over-ready with heroics. But,' he added, with a shrug of the shoulders, 'these tantrums usually leave me cold. You are an intelligent woman, *mejuffrouw*, and you have seen your valiant father resign himself to the inevitable.'

'I pray you waste no words, my lord,' she rejoined coolly. 'Three months ago, when at Ryswick, your crimes found you out, and you strove to involve me in your own disgrace and ruin, I gave you mine answer – the same that I do now. My dead body you can take with you, but I, alive, will never follow you!'

' 'Twas different then,' he retorted, with a cynical smile. 'You had a fortune-hunting adventurer to hand who was determined to see that your father's shekels did not lightly escape his grasp. Today – '

'Today,' she retorted, and rose to her feet, fronted him now, superb with indignation, 'he is sightless, absent, impotent, you would say, to protect me against your villainy! You miserable, slinking cur!'

Stoutenburg's harsh, forced laugh broke in upon her wrath.

'Ah!' he exclaimed lightly. 'You little spit-fire! In very truth, I like you better in that mood. Heroics do not become you, *myn schat*, and they are so unnecessary. Did you perchance imagine that it was love for you that hath influenced my decision to take you away from here?'

'I pray God, my lord, that I be not polluted by as much as a thought from you!'

'Your prayers have been granted, fair one,' he retorted with a sneer. ' 'Tis but seldom I think of you now, save as an exquisite little termagant whom it will amuse me to tame. But this is by the way. That pleasure will lose nothing by procrastination. You know me well enough by now to realise that I am not likely to be lenient with you after your vixenish treatment of me. For the nonce, I pray you to keep a civil tongue in your head,' he added roughly. 'On your conduct at this hour will depend your future comfort. Nicolaes will not always be skulking in dark corners, ready to interfere if my manner become too rough.'

'He is here now,' she said boldly, 'and if there is a spark of honour left in him he will conduct me to my rooms!'

With this she turned and walked steadily across the room. Even so his harsh laugh accompanied her as far as the door. When her hand was upon the knob, he called lightly after her:

'The moment you step across the threshold, *myn schat*, Jan will bring you back here – in his arms!'

5

Instinctively she paused, realizing that the warning had come just in time – that the next moment, in very truth, she would be in the hands of those vile traitors who were there ready to obey their master's every command. She paused, too, in order to murmur a quick prayer for Divine guidance, seeing that human protection was denied her at this hour. What could she do? She was like a bird caught in a snare from which there seemed to be no issue. Stoutenburg's sneering laugh rang in her ear. He, too, had risen and had followed her. He was beside her now, took her hand from the knob and held it for a moment forcibly in his. His glance, charged with cruel mockery, took in every line of her pallid face.

'Heroics again, fair one!' he said, with an impish grin. 'Must I assure you once more that you are perfectly safe with me? See, if you were in danger from me, would not your brother interfere? Bah! Nicolaes knows well enough that passion doth not enter into my schemes at this hour. My plans are too vast to be swayed by your frowns or your smiles. I have entered this city as a conqueror. As a conqueror I shall go out of it tomorrow, and you will come with me. I shall go hence because I choose, and for reasons which I will presently make clear to you.

'But you shall come with me. When you are with me in my camp, I may honour you as my future wife, or cast you from me as I would a beggar. That will depend upon my mood, and upon your temper. Nicolaes will not be there to run counter to my will. Therefore, understand me, my pretty fire-eater, that from this hour forth you are as absolutely my property as my dogs are, my horse, or the boots which I wear. I am the master here,' he concluded, with strangely sinister calm, 'and my will alone is law.'

'A law unto yourself,' she retorted, faced him with absolute composure, neither defiant nor afraid, her nerves quiescent, her voice perfectly steady, 'and mayhap unto your cringing sycophants. But above your will, my lord, is that of God; and neither death nor life are your slaves.'

'Ay! But methinks they are, *myn engel*,' he answered drily. 'Yours, in any case.'

'No human being, my lord, can lose the freedom to die.'

'You think not?' he sneered. 'Well, we shall see.' He let go her hand, then quietly turned and walked to the window, threw open the casement once more, then beckoned to her. Strangely stirred, she followed, moved almost mechanically by something she could not resist.

At a sign from him she looked out upon the busy scene on the quay below – the enemy soldiers in possession, their bivouac fires, their comings and goings, the unfortunate citizens running hither and thither at their bidding, fetching and carrying, hustled, pushed, beaten, ordered about with rough words or the persuasive prod of pike or musket. A scene, alas, which already as a child had been familiar to her. A peaceable town in the hands of ruthless soldiery; the women fleeing from threatened insults, children clinging to their mother's skirts, men standing by, grim and silent, not daring to protest lest mere resentment brought horrible reprisals upon the city.

Gilda looked out for awhile in silence, her heart aching with the misery which she beheld, yet could not palliate. Then she turned coldly inquiring eyes on the prime mover of it all.

'I have seen a reign of terror such as this before, my lord,' she said. 'I was at Leyden, as you well know, and I have not forgotten.'

'A reign of terror, you call it, *mejuffrouw*?' he retorted coolly. 'Nay, you exaggerate. What is this brief occupation? Tomorrow we go, remember. Is there a single house demolished at this hour, a single citizen murdered. You are too young to recollect Malines or Ghent, the reign of Alva over these recalcitrant countries. I have been lenient so far. I have spared fire and sword. Amersfoort still stands. It will stand tomorrow, even after my soldiers have gone,' he went on, speaking very slowly, 'if – '

'If what, my Lord?' she asked, for he had paused. The moment had come, then, the supreme hour when that dreaded 'either – or' would be put before her. Even now he went on with that same sinister quietude which seemed like the voice of some relentless judge, sent by the King of Darkness to sway her destiny.

'If,' Stoutenburg concluded drily, 'you, *mejuffrouw*, will accompany me. Oh,' he added quickly, seeing that at once she had resumed that air of defiance which irritated even whilst it amused him, 'I do not mean as an unwilling slave, pinioned to my chariot-wheel or strapped into a saddle, nor yet as a picturesque corpse, with flowing hair and lilies 'twixt your lifeless hands. No, no, fair one! I offer you the safety of your native city, the immunity of your fellow-citizens, in exchange for a perfectly willing surrender of your live person into my charge.'

She looked on him for awhile, mute with horror, then murmured slowly:

'Are you a devil, that you should propose such an execrable bargain?'

He laughed and shrugged his shoulders.

'I am what you and my native land have made me,' he replied. 'As to that, the Stadtholder never offered to bargain with me for my father's life.'

'Who but a prince of darkness would dream of doing so?' she retorted.

'Call me that, an you wish, fair one,' he put in lightly, 'and come back to the point.'

'And the point is, my Lord?'

'That I will respect this city if you come tomorrow, willing and submissive, with me.'

'That, never!' she affirmed hotly.

'In that case,' he riposted coldly, 'my soldiers will have a free hand ere they quit the town, to sack it at their pleasure. Pillage, arson, will be rewarded; looting will be deemed a virtue, as will murder and outrage. Even your father – '

'Enough, my lord!' she exclaimed, with passionate indignation. 'Tell me, I pray, which of the unclean spirits of Avernus did suggest this infamy to you?' Then, as he met her burning glance with another careless shrug and a mocking laugh, she turned to

Nicolaes, and cried out to him, almost with entreaty: 'Klaas! You at least are not a party to such hideous villainy!'

But he, sullen and shamefaced, only threw her an angry look.

'You make it very difficult for us, Gilda,' he said moodily, 'by your stupid obstinacy.'

'Obstinacy?' she retorted, puzzled at the word. Then reiterated it once or twice, 'Obstinacy – obstinacy? My God, hath the boy gone mad?'

'What else is it but obstinacy?' he rejoined vehemently. 'You know that, despite all he says, Stoutenburg hath never ceased to love you. And now that he is the master here you are lucky indeed to have him as a suitor. He means well by you, by us all, else I were not here. Think what it would mean to me, to father, to every one of us, if you were Stoutenburg's wife. But you jeopardize my future and the welfare of us all by those foolish tantrums.'

She gazed on him in utter horror – on this brother whom she loved; could scarce believe her ears that it was he – really he – who was uttering such odious words. She felt her gorge rising at this callous avowal of a wanton and insulting treachery. And he, feeling the contempt which flashed on him from her glowing eyes, avoided her glance, tried to shift his ground, to argue his point with the sophistry peculiar to a traitor, and sank more deeply every moment into the mire of dishonour.

'It is time you realized, Gilda,' he said, 'that our unfortunate country must sooner or later return to her true allegiance. The Stadtholder is sick. His arbitrary temper hath alienated some of his staunchest friends. The Netherlands are the unalienable property of Spain; though two rebel princes have striven to wrest them from their rightful master, the might of Spain was sure to be felt in the end. 'Twas folly ever to imagine that this so-called Dutch Republic would ever abide; and the hour, though tardy, has struck at last when such senseless dreams must come to an end.'

'Well spoken, friend Nicolaes!' Stoutenburg put in lustily. 'In verity, our Liege Lady the Archduchess Isabella, whom may God protect, could with difficulty find a more eloquent champion.'

'Or our noble land so vile a traitor!' Gilda murmured, burning now with shame. 'Thank Heaven, Nicolaes, that our poor father is not here, for the disgrace of it all would have struck him dead at your feet. Would to God,' she murmured under her breath, 'that it killed me now!'

'An undutiful prayer, *myn engel*,' Stoutenburg rejoined, 'seeing that its fulfilment would mean that Amersfoort and her citizens would be wiped off the face of the earth.'

This time he spoke quite quietly, without any apparent threat, only with determination, like one who knows that he is master and hath full powers to see his will obeyed. She looked at him keenly for a moment or two, wondering if she could make him flinch, if she could by word or prayer shake him in that devilish purpose which in truth must have found birth through the whisperings of uncanny fiends.

Gilda gazed critically at his lean, hard face with the sunken, restless eyes that spoke so eloquently of disappointed hopes and frustrated ambitions; the mouth, thin-lipped and set; the unshaven chin; the hollow temples and grizzled hair. She took in every line of his tall, gaunt figure; the shoulders already bent, the hands fidgety and claw-like; the torn doublet and shabby boots, all proclaiming the down-at-heel adventurer who has staked his all – honour, happiness, eternity – for ambition; has staked all he possessed and played a losing game.

But for pity or compunction Gilda sought in vain. The glance which after awhile was raised to hers revealed nothing but unholy triumph and a cruel, callous mockery. In truth, that glance had told her that she could expect neither justice nor mercy from him, and had spared her the humiliation of a desperate and futile appeal.

A low moan escaped her lips. She tottered slightly, and felt her knees giving way under her.

Vaguely she put out her hand, fearing that she might fall. Even so, she swayed backwards, feeling giddy and sick. But the dread of losing consciousness before this man whom she loathed and despised kept up both her courage and her endurance. She felt the panelling of the window-embrasure behind her, and leaned against it for support.

6

Stoutenburg had made no effort to come to her assistance, neither had Nicolaes. Probably both of them knew that she would never allow either of them to touch her. But Stoutenburg's mocking glance had pursued her all through her valiant fight against threatening unconsciousness. Now that she leaned against the framework of the window, pale and wraithlike, only her delicate profile vaguely distinguishable in the semi-gloom, her lips parted as if to drink in the cold evening air, she looked so exquisite, so desirable, that he allowed his admiration of her to override every other thought.

'You are lovely, *myn schat*,' he said quietly. 'Exquisite and worthy to be a queen. And, by Heaven,' he exclaimed with sudden passion, 'you'll yet live to bless this hour when I broke your obstinacy. Hand in hand, *myn engel*, you and I, we'll be masters of this beautiful land. I feel that I could do great things if I had you by my side. Listen, Gilda,' he went on eagerly, thinking that because she remained silent and motionless she had given up the fight, and was at last resigned to the inevitable – 'listen, my beautiful little vixen! The Archduchess will wish to reward me for this; the capture of Amersfoort is no small matter, and I have further projects in mind. In the meanwhile, De Berg hath already hinted that she might re-establish the republic under the suzerainty of Spain, and appoint me as her Stadtholder. Think, *myn Geliefde* : think what a vista of glorious, satisfied ambition lies before us both! Nay, before us all. Your father, chief pensionary; Nicolaes, general of our armies; your family raised above every one in the land. You'll thank me, I say; thank me on your knees for my constancy and for my unwavering loyalty to you. And even tonight, presently, when you are quite calm and at rest, you'll pray to your God, I vow, for His blessing upon your humble and devoted slave.'

He bent the knee when he said this, still scornful even in this affectation of humility, and raised the hem of her gown to his lips. She did not look down on him, nor did she snatch her skirts out of his hand. She just stared straight out before her, and said slowly, with great deliberation:

'Tonight – presently – when I am at rest – I will pray God to kill you ere you put your monstrous threat into execution.'

With a light laugh he jumped to his feet.

'Still the shrewish little vixen, what?' he said carelessly. 'Yet, see what a good dog I am. I'll not bear resentment, and you shall have the comfort of your father's company at the little supper party which I have prepared. Only the four of us, you and the burgomaster, and Nicolaes and I; and we can discuss the arrangements for our forthcoming wedding, which shall be magnificent, I promise you. But be sure of this, fair one,' he went on harshly, drew up his gaunt figure to its full height, 'that what I've said I've said. Tomorrow at sunrise I go hence, and you come with me, able-bodied and willing, to a place which I have in mind. But this city will be the hostage for your good behaviour. My soldiers remain here under the command of one Jan, who obeys all my behests implicitly and without question, because he hates the Stadtholder as much as I do, and hath a father's murder to avenge against that tyrant just as I have. Jan will stay in Amersfoort until I bid him go. But at one word from me, this city will be reduced to ashes, and not one man, woman or child shall live to tell the tale of how the *jongejuffrouw* Gilda Beresteyn set her senseless obstinacy above the lives of thousands.'

'Think not that I'll relent,' he concluded, and once more turned to the open window; gazed down upon the unfortunate city which he had marked as the means to his fiendish ends. His restless eyes roamed over the busy scene; his soldiers, his – the executioners who would carry out his will! Never had he been so powerful; never had his ambition been so near its goal! It had all come together – the humiliation of the Stadtholder, his own success in this daring enterprise, Gilda entirely at his mercy! Success had crowned all his nefarious schemes at last. 'Nothing will change me from my purpose,' he said, with all the harsh determination which characterized his every action – 'nothing! Neither your tears nor your frowns nor your prayers. There is no one, understand me, no one who can stand between me and my resolve.'

'No one but God,' she murmured under her breath. 'Oh, God, protect me now! My God, save me from this!'

Dizzy, moving like a sleep-walker, she tried to hold herself erect, tried to move from the window, and from the propinquity of that execrable miscreant.

'Have I your permission to go now?' she murmured faintly.

'Yes,' he replied; 'to your father. I'll order Jan to release our worthy burgomaster, and you and he can pray for my demise at your leisure. Whether you confide in him or not is no concern of mine. I would have you remember that my promise to respect this city and her inhabitants only holds good if you, of your own free will, come with me tomorrow. Amersfoort shall live if you come willingly. You are the best judge whether your father would be the happier for this knowledge. Methinks it would be kinder to let him think that you come tomorrow as my willing bride. But that is for you to decide. I want him here anon to give his blessing upon our future union in the presence of your brother Nicolaes. I wish the bond to be made irrevocable as soon as may be. If you or your father break it afterwards, it will be the worse for Amersfoort. Try and believe that the alternative is one of complete indifference to me. I have everything in the world now that I could possibly wish for. My ambition is completely satisfied. To have you as my wife would only be the pandering to a caprice. And now you may go, *myn schat,*' he concluded. 'The destinies of your native city are in your dainty hands.'

He watched her progress across the room with a sarcastic grin. But in his heart he was conscious of a bitter disappointment. Unheard by her, he muttered under his breath:

'If only she would care, how different everything might be!'

Aloud he called to Nicolaes:

'Escort your sister, man, into the presence of the burgo-master! And see that Jan and a chosen few form a guard of honour on the passage of the future Lady of Stoutenburg.'

Nicolaes hastened to obey. Gilda tried to check him with a brief:

'I thank you; I would prefer to go alone!'

But already he had thrown open the door, and anon. his husky voice could be heard giving orders to Jan.

Gilda, at the last, turned once more to look on her enemy. He caught her eye, bowed very low, his hand almost touching the ground ere he brought it with a sweeping flourish back to his breast, in the most approved fashion lately brought in from France.

'In half an hour supper will be served,' he said. 'I await the honour of the burgomaster's company and of your own!'

And he remained in an attitude of perfect deference whilst she passed silently out of the room.

11

The Danger-spoke

Gilda had refused her brother's escort, preferring to follow Jan; and Nicolaes, half indifferent, half ashamed, watched her progress up the stairs, and when she had disappeared in the gloom of the corridor above, he went back to his friend.

The two old serving-men were now busy in the banqueting-hall, bringing in the supper. They set the table with silver and crystal goblets, with jugs of Spanish and Rhenish wines, and dishes of cooked meats. They came and went about their business expeditiously and silently, brought in two more heavy candelabra with a dozen or more lighted candles in their sconces, so that the vast room was brilliantly lit. They threw fresh logs upon the fire, so that the whole place looked cosy and inviting.

Stoutenburg had once more taken up his stand beside the open window. Leaning his arm against the mullion, he rested his head upon it. Bitterness and rage had brought hot tears to his eyes. Somehow it seemed to him as if in the overflowing cup of his triumph something had turned to gall. Gilda eluded him. He could not understand her. The experience which he had of women had taught him that these beautiful and shallow creatures, soulless for the most part and heartless, were easily to be cajoled with soft words and bribed with wealth and promises. Yet he had dangled before Gilda's eyes such a vision of glory and exalted position as should have captured, quite unconditionally, the citadel of her affections, and she had remained indifferent to it all.

He had owned himself still in love with her, and she had remained quite callous to his ardour. He had tried indifference, and had only been paid back in his own coin. To a man of Stoutenburg's intensely egotistical temperament, there could only be one explanation to this seeming coldness. The wench's senses – it could be nothing more – were still under the thrall of that miserable adventurer who, thanks to Beelzebub and his horde, had at last been rendered powerless to wreak further mischief. There could be he argued to himself, no aversion in her heart for one who was so ready to share prosperity, power, and honour with her, to forgive and forget all that was past, to raise her from comparative obscurity to the most exalted state that had ever dazzled a woman's fancy and stormed the inmost recesses of her soul.

She was still infatuated with the varlet, and that was all. A wholly ununderstandable fact. Stoutenburg never could imagine how she had ever looked with favour on such an adventurer, whose English parentage and reputed wealth were, to say the least, problematical. Beresteyn had been a fool to allow his only daughter to bestow her beauty and her riches on a stranger, about whom in truth he knew less than nothing. The girl, bewitched by the rascallion, had cajoled her father and obtained his consent. Now she was still under the spell of a handsome presence, a resonant voice, a provoking eye. It was, it could be, nothing more than that. When once she understood what she had gained, how utterly inglorious that once brilliant soldier of fortune had become, she would descend from her high altitude of disdain and kiss the hand which she now spurned. But, in anticipation of that happy hour, the Lord of Stoutenburg felt moody and discontented.

2

Nicolaes' voice, close to his elbow, roused him from his gloomy meditations.

'You must be indulgent, my friend,' he was saying, in a smooth, conciliatory voice. 'Gilda had always a wilful temper.'

'And a tenacious one,' Stoutenburg retorted. 'She is still in love with that rogue.'

'Bah!' the other rejoined, with a note of spite in his tone. 'It is mere infatuation! A woman's whimsey for a good-looking face and a pair of broad shoulders! She should have seen the scrubby rascal as I last caught sight of him – grimy, unshaven, broken. No woman's fancy would survive such a spectacle!'

Then, as Stoutenburg, still unconsoled, continued to stare through the open window, muttering disjointed phrases through obstinately set lips, he went on quite gaily:

'You are not the first by any means, my friend, whose tempestuous wooing hath brought a woman, loving and repentant, to heel. When I was over in England with my father, half a dozen years ago, we saw there a play upon the stage. It had been writ by some low-born mountebank, one William Shakespeare. The name of the play was *The Taming of the Shrew*. Therein, too, a woman of choleric temper did during several scenes defy the man who wooed her. In the end he conquered; she became his wife, and as tender and submissive an one as e'er you'd wish to see. But, by St Bavon, how she stormed at first! How she professed to hate him! I was forcibly reminded of that play when I saw Gilda defying you awhile ago; and I could have wished that you had displayed the same good-humour over the wrangle as did the gallant Petruchio – the hero of the piece.'

Stoutenburg was interested.

'How did he succeed in the end?' he queried. 'Your Petruchio, I mean.'

'He starved the ranting virago into submission,' Nicolaes replied, with an easy laugh. 'Gave her nothing to eat for a day and a night; swore at her lackeys; beat her waiting-maids. She was disdainful at first, then terrified. Finally, she admired him, because he had mastered her.'

'A good moral, friend Nicolaes!'

'Ay! One you would do well to follow. Women reserve their disdain for weaklings, and their love for their masters.'

'And think you that Gilda –'

'Gilda, my friend, is but a woman after all. Have no fear, she'll be your willing slave in a week.'

Stoutenburg's eyes glittered at the thought.

'A week is a long time to wait,' he murmured. 'I wish that now –'

He paused. Something that was happening down below on the quay had attracted his attention – unusual merriment, loud laughter, the strains of a bibulous song. For a minute or two his keen eyes searched the gloom for the cause of all this hilarity. He leaned far out of the window, called peremptorily to a group of soldiers who were squatting around their bivouac fire.

'Hey!' he shouted. 'Peter! Willem! – whatever your confounded names may be! What is that rascallion doing over there?'

'Making us all laugh, so please your lordship,' one of the soldiers gave reply; 'by the drollest stories and quips any of us have ever heard.'

'Where does he come from?'

'From nowhere, apparently,' the man averred. 'He just fell among us. The man is blind, so please you,' he added after a moment's hesitation.

Stoutenburg swore.

'How many times must I give orders,' he demanded roughly, 'that every blind beggar who comes prowling round the camps be hanged to the nearest post?'

'We did intend to hang him,' the soldier replied coolly; 'but when first he came along he was so nimble that, ere we could capture him, he gave us the slip.'

'Well,' Stoutenburg rejoined harshly, 'it is not too late. You have him now.'

'So we have, Magnificence,' the man replied, hesitated for a second or two, then added: 'But he is so amusing, and he seems a gentleman of quality, too proud for the hangman's rope.'

'Too proud is he?' his lordship retorted with a sneer. 'A gentleman of quality, and amusing to boot? Well, let us see how his humour will accommodate itself to the gallows. Here, let me have a look at the loon.'

There was much hustling down below after this; shouting and prolonged laughter ; a confused din, through which it was impossible to distinguish individual sounds, Stoutenburg's nerves were tingling. He was quite sure by now that he had recognised that irrepressibly merry voice. A gentleman of quality! Blind! Amusing! But, if Nicolaes' report of yesterday's events were true, the man was hopelessly stricken. And what could induce him to put his head in the jackal's mouth, to affront his triumphing enemy, when he himself was so utterly helpless and abject?

Not long was the Lord of Stoutenburg left in suspense. Even whilst he gazed down upon the merry, excited throng, he was able to distinguish in the midst of them all a pair of broad shoulders that could only belong to one man. The soldiers, laughing, thoroughly enjoying the frolic, were jostling him not a little for the sheer pleasure of measuring their valour against so hefty a fellow. And he, despite his blindness, gave as good as he got; fought valiantly with fist and boot and gave his tormentors many a hard knock, until, with a loud shout of glee, some of the men succeeded in seizing hold of him, and hoisted him up on their shoulders and brought him into the circle of light formed by the resin torches.

A double cry came in response – one of amazement from Stoutenburg and one of horror from Nicolaes. But neither of them spoke. Stoutenburg's lips were tightly set; a puzzled frown appeared between his brows. In truth, for once in the course of his devilish career, he was completely taken aback and uncertain what to do. The man whom he saw there before him, in ragged clothes, unshaved and grimy, blinking with sightless eyes, was the man whom he detested above every other thing or creature on earth – the reckless soldier of fortune of the past, for awhile the proud and successful rival; now just a wreck of humanity, broken, ay, and degraded, and henceforth an object of pity rather than a menace to his rival's plans. His doublet was in rags, his plumed hat battered, his toes shone through the holes in his boots. The upper part of his face was swathed in a soiled linen bandage. This had, no doubt, been originally intended to shield the stricken eyes; but it had slipped, and those same eyes, with their horrible fixed look, glittered with unearthly weirdness in the flickering light.

'Salute his Magnificence, the lord and master of Amersfoort and of all that in it lies!' one of the soldiers shouted gaily.

And the blind man forthwith made a gesture of obeisance; swept with a wide flourish his battered plumed hat from off his head.

'To his Magnificence!' he called out in response. 'Though mine eyes cannot see him, my voice is raised in praise of his nobility and his valour. May the recording angels give him his full deserts.'

3

The feeling of sheer horror which had caused Nicolaes to utter a sudden cry was, in truth, fully justified.

'It can't be!' he murmured, appalled at what he saw.

Stoutenburg answered with a hoarse laugh.

'Nay, by Satan and all his myrmidons it is!' Already he was leaning out of the window, giving quick orders to the men down below to bring that drunken vagabond forthwith into his presence. After which he turned once more to his friend.

'We'll soon see,' he said, ' if it is true, or if our eyes have played us both an elusive trick. Yet methinks,' he added thoughtfully, 'that the pigwidgeon who of late hath taken my destiny in hand is apparently intent on doing me a good turn.'

'In what way?' the other asked.

'By throwing my enemy across my path,' Stoutenburg replied drily.

'You'll hang him of course?' Nicolaes rejoined.

'Yes; I'll hang him!' Stoutenburg retorted, with a snarl. 'But I must make use of him first.'

'Make use of him? How?'

'That I do not know as yet. But inspiration will come, never you fear, my friend. All that I want is a leverage for bringing the Stadtholder to his knees and for winning Gilda's love.'

'Then, in Heaven's name, man,' Nicolaes rejoined earnestly, 'begin by ridding yourself of the only danger-spoke in your wheel!'

'Danger-spoke?' Stoutenburg exclaimed, threw back his head and laughed. 'Would you really call that miserable oaf a serious bar to mine ambition or a possible rival in your sister's regard?'

And, with outstretched hand he pointed to the door. There, under the lintel – pushed on by Jan and two or three men who, powerfully built though they were, looked like pigmies beside the stricken giant, drunk as an owl, his hat awry above that hideous bandage, dirty, unkempt, and ragged – appeared the man who had once been the brilliant inspiration of Franz Hals' immortal *Laughing Cavalier*.

At sight of him Nicolaes Beresteyn gave a loud groan and collapsed into a chair, burying his face in his hands. He was ever a coward, even in villainy; and when the man whom he had once hated so bitterly, and whom his craven hand had struck in such a dastardly manner, lurched into the room, and as he fell against the table uttered an inane and bibulous laugh, his nerve completely forsook him.

At a peremptory sign from Stoutenburg, Jan closed the doors which gave on the hall; but he and two of the men remained at attention inside the room.

The blind man groped with his hands till they found a chair, into which he sank, with powerful limbs outstretched, snorting like a dog just come out of the water. With an awkward gesture he pushed his hat from off his head, and in so doing he dislodged the grimy bandage so that it sat like a scullion's cap across his white forehead.

Stoutenburg watched him with an expression of cruel satisfaction. It is not often given to a man to have an enemy and a rival so completely in his power, and the exultation in Stoutenburg's heart was so great that he was content to savour it in silence for awhile. Nicolaes was beyond the power of speech, and so the silence for a moment or two remained absolute.

Then the blind man suddenly sat up, craning his neck and rolling his sightless eyes.

'I wonder where the devil I am!' he murmured through set lips. He appeared to listen intently; no doubt caught the sound of life around him, for he added quickly:

'Is anybody here?'

'I am here,' Stoutenburg replied curtly. 'Do you know who I am, sirrah?'

'In truth, I do not,' Diogenes replied. 'But by your accent I would judge you to be a man who at this moment is mightily afraid.'

'Afraid?' Stoutenburg retorted, with a loud laugh. 'I, afraid of a helpless vagabond who has been fool enough to run his head into a noose which I had not even thought of preparing for him?'

'Yet you are afraid, my lord,' the other rejoined quietly, 'else you would not have ordered your bodyguard to watch over your precious person whilst you parleyed with a blind man.'

'My bodyguard is only waiting for final orders to take you to the gallows,' Stoutenburg rejoined roughly. 'You may as well know now as later that it is my intention to hang you.'

'As well now as later,' the blind man assented, with easy philosophy. 'I understand that for the nonce, whoever your Magnificence may be, you are master in Amersfoort. As such, you have a right to hang anyone you choose. Me, or another. What matters? I was very nearly hung once, you must know, by the Lord of Stoutenburg. I did not mind much then; I'd mind it still less now. People talk of a hereafter. Well, whatever it is, it must be a better world than this, so I would, just as soon as not, go and find out for myself.'

He struggled to his feet, still groping with his hands for support, found the edge of the table and leaned up against it.

'Let's to the hangman, my lord,' he said thickly. 'If I'm to hang, I prefer it to be done at once. And if we tarry too long I might get sober ere I embark on the last adventure. But,' he added, and once more appeared to search the room with eyes that could not see, 'there's someone else here besides your lordship. Who is it?'

'My friend and yours,' Stoutenburg replied. 'Mynheer Nicolaes Beresteyn.'

There was a second or two of silence. Nicolaes made as if he would speak, but Stoutenburg quickly put a finger up to his lips, enjoining him to remain still. The blind man passed his trembling hand once or twice in front of his eyes, as if to draw aside an unseen veil that hid the outer world from his gaze.

'Ah!' he murmured contentedly. 'My friend Klaas! He is here too, is he? That is indeed good news. For Nicolaes was ever my friend. That time, three months ago – or was it three years, or three centuries? I really have lost count – that time that the Lord of Stoutenburg was on the point of hanging me, Klaas would have interposed on my behalf, only something went wrong with his heart at the moment, or his nerves, I forget which.'

' 'Twere no use to rely on mynheer's interference this time,' Stoutenburg put in drily. 'There is but one person in the world now who can save you from the gallows.'

'You mean the Lord of Stoutenburg himself?' the blind man queried blandly.

'Nay! He is determined to hang you. But there is another.'

'Then I pray your lordship to tell me who that other is,' Diogenes replied.

'You might find one, sirrah, in the *jongejuffrouw* Gilda Beresteyn, the Lord of Stoutenburg's promised wife.'

Diogenes made no reply to this. He was facing the table now, still clinging to it with one hand, whilst the other wandered over the objects on the table. Suddenly they encountered a crystal jug which was full of wine. An expression of serene beatitude overspread his face. He raised the goblet to his lips, but ere he drank he said carelessly:

'Ah, the *jongejuffrouw* Beresteyn is the promised wife of the Lord of Stoutenburg?'

'My promised wife!' Stoutenburg put in roughly. 'Methought you would ere this have recognised the man whom you tried to rob of all that he held most precious.'

'Your lordship must forgive me,' the blind man rejoined drily. 'But some unknown miscreant – whom may the gods punish – interfered with me yesterday forenoon, when I was trying to render assistance to my friend Klaas. In the scuffle that ensued, I received a cloud of stinking fumes in the face, which has totally robbed me of sight.'

As he spoke he raised his eyes, blinking in that pathetic and inconsequent manner peculiar to the blind. Nicolaes gave an audible groan. He could not bear to look on those sightless orbs, which in the flickering light of the wax candles appeared weird and unearthly.

'Oh,' Stoutenburg put in carelessly, 'is that how the – er – accident occurred?'

'So, please your lordship, yes,' Diogenes replied. 'And I was left stranded on the moor, since those two unreclaimed varlets, Pythagoras and Socrates by name, did effectually ride off in the wake of the Stadtholder, leaving me in the lurch. A pitiable plight, your lordship will admit.'

'So pitiable,' the other retorted with a sneer, 'that you thought to improve your condition by bearding the Lord of Stoutenburg in his lair.'

'I did not know your lordship was in Amersfoort,' Diogenes replied imperturbably. 'I thought – I hoped – '

He paused, and Stoutenburg tried in vain to read what went on behind that seemingly unclouded brow. The blind man appeared serene, detached, perfectly good-humoured. His slender hand, which looked hard beneath its coating of grime, was closed lovingly around the crystal jug. Stoutenburg vaguely wondered how far the man was really drunk, or whether his misfortune had slightly addled his brain. So much unconcern in the face of an imminent and shameful death gave an uncanny air to the whole appearance of the man. Even now, with a gently apologetic smile, he raised the jug once more to his lips. Stoutenburg placed a peremptory hand upon his arm.

'Put that down, man,' he said harshly. 'You are drunk enough as it is, and you'll have need of all your wits tonight.'

'There you are wrong, my lord,' Diogenes retorted, and quietly transferred the jug to his other hand. 'A man, meseems, needs no wits to hang gracefully. And I feel that I could do that best if I might quench my thirst ere I met my friend the hangman.'

'You may not meet him at all.'

'But just now you said – '

'That it was my intention to hang you,' Stoutenburg assented. 'So it is. But I am in a rare good humour tonight, and – '

'So it seems, my lord,' the blind man put in carelessly. 'So it seems.'

He appeared to be swaying on his feet, and to have some difficulty in retaining his balance. He still clung to the edge of the table with one hand. In the other he had the jug full of wine.

'The *jongejuffrouw* Gilda Beresteyn,' Stoutenburg went on, 'will sup with me this night to celebrate our betrothal. The fulfilment of this, my great desire, hath caused me to feel lenient toward mine enemies.'

'Have I not always asserted,' Diogenes broke in with comical solemnity – 'always ass-asserted that your lordship was a noble and true gentleman?'

'Women, we know,' his lordship continued, ignoring the interruption, 'are wont to be tender-hearted where their – their former swains are concerned. And I feel that if the *jongejuffrouw* herself did make appeal to me on your behalf, I would relent towards you.'

'B-b-but would that not be an awkward – a very awkward decision for your lordship?' Diogenes riposted, turning round vacant eyes on Stoutenburg.

'Awkward? How so?'

'If I do not hang, the *jongejuffrouw*,' stead of being my widow, would still be my wife. And the laws of this country – '

'I have no concern with the laws of this country,' Stoutenburg rejoined drily, 'in which, anyhow, you are an alien. As soon as the Archduchess our Liege Lady is once more mistress here, we shall again be at war with England.'

'Poor England!'

Diogenes sighed, and solemnly wiped a tear from his blinking eyes.

'And every English *plepshurk* will be kicked out of the country. But that is neither here nor there.'

'Neither here nor there,' the other assented, with owlish gravity. 'But before England is s-sh-s-swept off the map by lordship, what will happen?'

'My marriage to the *jongejuffrouw*,' Stoutenburg replied curtly. 'She hath consented to be my wife, and my wife she will be as soon as I have a mind to take her. So you may drink to our union, sirrah. I'll e'en pledge you in a cup.'

He poured himself out a goblet of wine, laughing to himself at his own ingenuity. That was the way to treat the *smeerlap*. Make him feel what a pitiable, abject knave he was! Then show him up before Gilda, just as he was – drunk, ragged, unkempt, an object of derision in his misfortune rather than of pity.

'Nay,' the rascal objected, his speech waxing thicker and his hand more unsteady, 'I cannot pledge you, my lord, in drinking to your union with my own wife, unless – unless my friend Klaas will drink to that union too. Mine own brother by the law, you see, my lord, and – '

'Mynheer Nicolaes will indeed drink to his sister's happy union with me,' Stoutenburg retorted, with a sneer. 'His presence here is a witness to my good intentions toward the wench. So you may drink, sirrah. The *jongejuffrouw* herself is overwilling to submit to my pleasure – '

But the impious words were smothered in his throat, giving place to a fierce exclamation of choler. The blind man had at his invitation raised the jug of wine to his lips, but in the act his feet apparently slipped away from under him. The jug flew out of his hand, would have caught the Lord of Stoutenburg on the head had he not ducked just in time. But even so his Magnificence was hit on the shoulder by the heavy crystal vessel, and splashed from head to foot with the wine, whilst Diogenes collapsed on the floor with a shamed and bibulous laugh.

A string of savage oaths and tempestuous abuse poured from Stoutenburg's lips, which were in truth livid with rage. Already Jan had rushed to his assistance, snatched up a serviette from the table, and soon contrived to wipe his lordship's doublet clean.

The blind man in the meanwhile did his best to hoist himself up on his feet once more, clung to the edge of the table; but the sight of him released the last floodgate of Stoutenburg's tempestuous wrath. He turned with a vicious snarl upon the unfortunate man, and it would indeed have fared ill with the defenceless creature, for the Lord of Stoutenburg was not wont to measure his blows by the helplessness of his victims, had not a sudden exclamation from Nicolaes stayed the hand that was raised to strike.

'Gilda!' the young man cried impulsively.

Stoutenburg's arm dropped to his side. He turned toward the door. Gilda had just entered with her father, and was coming slowly down the room.

12

Tears, Sighs, Hearts

Gilda caught sight of her beloved the moment she entered. To say that their eyes met would indeed be folly. Certain it is, however, that the blind man turned his sightless gaze in her direction. She only gave a gasp, pressed her hands to her heart as if the pain there was unendurable, and at the moment even the beauty of her face was marred by the look of soul-racking misery in her eyes and the quivering lines around her mouth.

The next moment, even while Jan and the soldiers retired, closing the doors behind them, she was in her husband's arms. Ay, even though Stoutenburg tried to intercept her. She did not hear his mocking laugh, or her brother's vigorous protest, nor yet her father's cry of horror. She just clung to him who, blind, fallen, degraded an you will, was still the beloved of her heart, the man to whom she had dedicated her soul.

She swallowed her tears, too proud to allow those who had wrought his ruin to see how mortally she was hurt.

She passed her delicate hands, fragrant as the petals of flowers, over his grimy face, those poor, stricken eyes, the noble brow so deeply furrowed with pain. She murmured words of endearment and of tenderness such as a mother might find to soothe the troubles of a suffering child. All in a moment. Stoutenburg had not even the time to interfere, to utter the savage oaths which rose from his vengeful heart at sight of the loving pity which this beautiful woman lavished on so contemptible an object.

Nor had the blind man time to encircle that exquisite form in his trembling arms. He had put them out at first, with a pathetic gesture of infinite longing. It was just a flash, a vision of his past self, an oblivion of the hideous, appalling present. Her arms at that moment were round his neck, her head against his breast, her soft, fair hair against his lips.

2

Then something happened. A magnetic current seemed to pass through the air. Diogenes freed himself with a sudden jerk from Gilda's clinging arms, staggered back against the table, swaying on his feet and uttering an inane laugh; whilst she, left standing alone, turned wide, bewildered eyes on her brother Nicolaes, who happened to be close to her at the moment. I think that she was near to unconsciousness then, and that she would have fallen, but that the burgomaster stepped quickly to her side and put his arms round her.

'May God punish you,' he muttered between his teeth, and turned to Stoutenburg, who had watched the whole scene with a sinister scowl, 'for this wanton and unnecessary cruelty!'

'You wrong me, mynheer,' Stoutenburg retorted, with a shrug. 'I but tried to make your daughter's decision easier for her.'

Then, as the burgomaster made no reply, but, with grim, set look on his face, drew his daughter gently down to the nearest chair, Stoutenburg went on lightly, speaking directly to Gilda:

'In the course of my travels, *mejuffrouw*, I came across a wise philosopher in Italy. He was a man whom an adverse fate had robbed of most things that he held precious; but he told me that he had quite succeeded in conquering adversity by the following simple means. He would gaze dispassionately on the objects of his past desires, see their defects, appraise them at their just value, and in every case he found that their loss was not so irreparable as he had orginally believed.'

'A fine moral lesson, my lord,' the burgomaster interposed, seeing that Gilda either would not or could not speak as yet. 'But I do not see its point.'

' 'Tis a simple one, mynheer,' Stoutenburg retorted coldly. 'I pray you, look on the man to whom, an you had your way, you would even now link your daughter.'

Instinctively Beresteyn turned his lowering gaze in the direction to which his lordship now pointed with a persuasive gesture. Diogenes was standing beside the table, his powerful frame drawn up to its full height, his sightless eyes blinking and gleaming with weird inconsequence in the flickering light of the candles. His hands were clasped behind his back, and on his face there was a curious expression which the burgomaster was not shrewd enough to define – one of self-deprecation, yet withal of introspection and of detachment, as if the helpless body alone was present and the mind had gone a-roaming in the land of dreams. The burgomaster tried manfully to conceal the look of half-contemptuous pity which, much against his will, had crept into his eyes.

'The man,' he rejoined calmly, 'is what Fate and a dastard's hand have made him, my lord. Many a fine work of God hath been marred by an evildoer's action.'

'That is as may be, mynheer,' Stoutenburg riposted coolly. 'But 'tis of the present and of the future you have to think now – not of the past.'

'Even so, my lord, I would sooner see my daughter in the arms of that stricken lion than in those of a wily jackal.'

'Am I the wily jackal?' Stoutenburg put in, with a sneer. Then, as the burgomaster made no reply, he added tersely: 'I see that the *jongejuffrouw* hath told you – '

'Everything,' Beresteyn assented calmly.

'And that I await your blessing on our union?'

'My blessing you cannot have, my lord, as you well know,' the burgomaster retorted firmly. ' 'Twere blasphemy to invoke the name of God on such an unholy alliance. My daughter is the lawfully wedded wife of an English gentleman, Sir Percy Blakeney by name, and until the law of this country doth sever those bonds she cannot wed another.'

Stoutenburg gave a strident laugh.

'That is, indeed, unfortunate for the English gentleman with the high-sounding name,' he said, with a sneer, 'whom I gravely suspect of being naught but the common varlet whom we all know so well in Haarlem. But, gentleman or churl,' he added, with a cynical shrug, ' 'tis all one to me. He hangs tomorrow, unless – '

A loud cry of burning indignation escaped the burgomaster's lips.

'You would not further provoke the wrath of God,' he exclaimed, 'by this foul and cowardly crime!'

'And why not, I pray you?' the other coolly retorted. 'Nor do I think that the Almighty would greatly care what happened to this drunken knave. The refuse of human kind, the halt, the lame, and the blind, are best out of the way.'

'A man, my lord,' the burgomaster protested, 'who, when he had you in his power, generously spared your life!'

'The more fool he!' Stoutenburg riposted drily.

' 'Tis my turn now. He hangs tomorrow, unless, indeed – '

'Unless, what, my lord?'

'Unless,' Stoutenburg went on, with an evil leer, 'my future wife will deign to plead with me for him – with a kiss.'

A groan like that of a wounded beast broke from the burgomaster's heavy heart. For a moment a light that was almost murderous gleamed in his eyes. His fists were clenched; he murmured a dark threat against the man who goaded him wellnigh to madness. Then, suddenly, he met Stoutenburg's mocking glance fixed upon him, and a huge sob rose in his throat, almost choking him. Gilda, with a pitiful moan, had hidden her face against her father's sleeve.

' 'Tis but anticipating the happy time by a few hours,' Stoutenburg went on, with calm cynicism. 'But I have a fancy to hold my future wife in my arms now – at this moment – and to grant her in exchange for her first willing kiss the life of a miserable wretch whose life or death are, in truth, of no account to me.'

He took a step or two forward in the direction where Gilda sat, clinging with desperate misery to her father. Then, as the burgomaster, superb with indignation, grand in his dignity, instinctively interposed his burly figure between his daughter and the man whom she loathed, Stoutenburg added, with well-assumed carelessness:

'If the *jongejuffrouw* prefers to put off the happy moment until we are alone in my camp tomorrow, we'll say no more about it. Let the rogue hang; I care not!'

'My lord,' – the burgomaster spoke once more in a vigorous protest, which, alas, he knew to be futile – 'what you suggest is monstrous, inhuman! God will never permit – '

'I pray you, mynheer,' Stoutenburg broke in fiercely, 'let us leave the Almighty out of our affairs. I have read my Bible as assiduously as you when I was younger, and in it I learned that God hath enjoined all wives to submit themselves to their husbands. A kiss from my betrothed, a word of gentle pleading, are little enough to ask in exchange for an act of clemency. And you, Heer Burgomaster, do but stiffen my will by your interference. Will you, at least, let the *jongejuffrouw* decide on the matter for herself, and, in her interests and your own, give to all that she does your unqualified consent!'

'My consent you'll never wring from me, as you well know, my lord. I and my daughter are powerless to withstand your might, but if we bend to the yoke it is because it hath pleased God that we should wear it, not because we submit with a free will. By exulting in such a monstrous crime you do but add to the loathing which we both feel for you – '

'Silence!' Stoutenburg broke in fiercely. 'Silence, you dolt! What good, think you, you do yourself or your daughter by provoking me beyond endurance? She knows my decision, and so, methinks, do you. If the *jongejuffrouw* feels such unqualified hatred for me, let her return to your protecting arms and leave Amersfoort to its fate. As for that sightless varlet, let him hang, I say! I am a fool, indeed, to listen to your gibberish! Jan!' he called, and strode to the door with a great show of determination, staking his all now on this card which he had decided to play.

But the card was a winning one, as well he knew. Already Gilda, as if moved by an unseen voice, had jumped to her feet and intercepted him ere he reached the door. Her whole appearance had changed – the expression of her eyes, her tone, her gestures.

'My father is overwrought, my lord,' she said firmly.

'He hath already promised me that he would offer no opposition to my wishes.'

She looked him straight in the eyes, and he returned her gaze, his restless eyes seeming to search her very soul. She had, in truth, changed most markedly. She was, of course, afraid – afraid for that miserable *plepshurk*'s life. But the change was something more than that – at least, Stoutenburg chose to think so. There was something in her glance at this moment that he did not quite understand, that he did not dare understand. A wavering – almost he would have called it a softness, had he dared. He came nearer to her, and, though at first she drew back from him, she presently held her ground, still gazing on him like a bird when it is fascinated and cannot move.

Now he was quite sure that her blue eyes looked less hard, and certainly her mouth was less tightly set. Her lips were slightly parted, and her breath came quick and panting. Ah, women were queer creatures! Had Nicolaes been right when he quoted the English play? Gilda had certainly begun by falling against that contemptible rascal's breast, but since then? Had her wayward fancy been repelled by that whole air of physical degradation which emanated from the once brilliant cavalier, or had it been merely dazzled by visions of power and of wealth, which had their embodiment in him who was her future lord?

He himself could not say. All that he knew, all that he felt of a certainty now, was that he held more than one winning card in this gamble for possession of an exquisite and desirable woman. Still holding her gaze, he took her hands. She did not resist, did not attempt to draw away from him, and he murmured softly:

'What are your wishes, *myn engel?*'

'To submit to your will, my lord,' she replied firmly.

'At last!' he exclaimed, on a note of triumph, drew her still closer to him. 'A kiss, fair one, to clinch this bargain, which hath made me the happiest of men!'

He had lost his head for the moment. Satisfaction, and an almost feverish sense of exultation, had turned his blood to liquid fire. All that he saw was this lovely woman, whom he had nearly conquered. Nearly, but not quite. At his desire for a kiss he felt that she stiffened. She closed her eyes, and even her lips became bloodless. She appeared on the verge of a swoon. Bah! Even this phase would pass away. Nicolaes was right. Women reserved their contempt for weaklings. In the end 'twas the master whom they adored.

'A kiss, fair one!' he called again. 'And the rogue shall live or hang according as your lips are sweet or bitter!'

He was on the point of snatching that kiss at last, when suddenly there came so violent a crash that the whole room shook with the concussion, and even the windows rattled in their frames. The blind man, more unsteady than ever on his feet, had tried to get hold of a chair, lost his balance in the act, and, in the endeavour to save himself from falling, had lurched so clumsily against the table that it overturned, and all the objects upon it – silver, crystal, china dishes, and candelabra – fell with a deafening clatter on the floor.

Stoutenburg, uttering one of his favourite oaths, had instinctively turned to see whence had come this terrific noise. In turning, his hold on Gilda's wrists had slightly relaxed; sufficiently, at any rate, to enable her to free herself from his grasp and to seek shelter once more beside her father. Diogenes alone had remained unruffled through the commotion. Indeed, he appeared wholly unconscious that he had brought it about. He had collapsed amidst the litter, and now sprawled on the floor, surrounded by a medley of broken glass, guttering candles, hot food and liquor, convulsed with laughter, whilst his huge, dark eyes, with the dilated pupils and pale, narrow circles of blue light, looked strangely ghostlike in the gloom.

'Who in thunder,' he muttered inarticulately, 'is making this confounded din?'

3

At the noise, too, the men had come running in from the hall. The sound had been akin to the detonation of a dozen pistols, and they had rushed along, prepared for a fight. With the fall of the candelabra, the vast banqueting hall had suddenly been plunged into semi-darkness. Only a couple of wax candles in tall sconces, which had been orignally set on the sideboard, vaguely illumined the disorderly scene.

Diogenes, with his infectious laugh, did in truth succeed in warding off the punishment which his Magnificence already held in preparation for him. As it was, Stoutenburg caught sight of Gilda's look of anxiety, and this at once put him into rare good humour. He had had his wish. Gilda had been almost kind, had practically yielded to him in the very presence of the man whom he desired to humiliate and to wound, as he himself had been humiliated and wounded in the past.

Whether the blind man's keen sense of hearing had taken in every detail of the scene, it was of course impossible to say. But one thing he must have heard – the brief soliloquy at the door, when Gilda, in response to his ardent query: 'What are your wishes, *myn engel?*' had replied quite firmly: 'To submit to your will, my lord!' That moment must, in truth, have been more galling and more bitter to the once gallant Laughing Cavalier than the rattle of the rope upon the gallows, or the first consciousness that he was irremediably blind.

Indeed, Stoutenburg had had something more than his wish. To make a martyr of the rogue, he would have told you, was not part of his desire. All that he wanted was to obliterate the man's former brilliant personality from Gilda's mind; that he should henceforth dwell in her memory as she last saw him, abject in his obvious impotence, owing his life to the woman whom he had wooed and conquered in the past with the high hand of a reckless adventurer. After that, the rogue might hang or perish in a ditch: his lordship did not care. What happened to blind men in these days of fighting, when none but the best men had a chance to live at all, he had never troubled his head to inquire. At any rate, he knew that a sightless lion was less harmful than a keen-eyed mouse. Ah, in truth he had had more than his wish, and satisfied now as to the present and the future, he thought that the moment had come to let well alone, and to remove from Gilda's sight the spectacle which, by some subtle reaction, might turn her heart back to pity for the knave. He gave Jan a significant nod.

But Gilda, whose glowing eyes had watched his every movement, was quick to interpose.

'My lord,' she cried in protest. 'I hold you to your bargain!'

'Have no fear, *myn schat,*' he answered suavely. 'I will not repudiate it. The fellow's life is safe enough whilst you and the Heer Burgomaster honour me by supping with me. After that, the decision rests with you. As I said just now, he shall live or hang according as your lips are sweet or bitter. For the nonce, I am wearied and hungry. We'll sup first, so please you.'

And Gilda had to stand by whilst she saw her husband dragged away from her presence. He offered no resistance; indeed, accepted the situation with that good-humoured philosophy which was so characteristic of him.

But, oh, if she could have conveyed to him by a look all the tenderness, the sorrow, the despair, that was torturing her heart! If she could have run to him just once more, to whisper into his ear those burning words of love which would have eased his pain and hers!

If she could have defied that abominable tyrant who gloated over her misery, and, hand in hand with her beloved, have met death by his side, with his arms around her, her spirit wedded to his, ere they appeared together before the judgment seat of God!

But, as that arrogant despot had reminded her, she had even lost the freedom to die. The destinies of her native city were in her hands. Unless she bowed her willing neck to his will, Amersfoort and all its citizens would be wiped off the face of the earth. And as she watched the chosen of her heart led like a captive lion to humiliation if not to death, those monstrous words rang in her ears, that surely must provoke the wrath of God.

Therefore, she watched his departure dry-eyed and motionless. Ay! envying him in her heart, that he, at least, was not called upon to make such an appalling sacrifice as lay now before her. She had indeed come to that sublimity of human suffering that she almost wished to see those dear, sightless eyes closed in their last long sleep, rather than that he should be forced to endure what to him would be ten thousand times worse than death – her submission to that miscreant – her willing union; and he, ignorant of how the tyrant had wrung this submission from her.

13

The Stygian Creek

The Lord of Stoutenburg was conscious of a great feeling of relief when the blind man was finally removed from his presence. While the latter stood there, even in the abjectness of his plight, Stoutenburg felt that he was a living menace to the success of all his well-thought-out schemes. He kept his eyes fixed on Gilda with a warning look, that should be a reminder to her of the immutability of his resolve. He tried, in a manner, to surround her with a compelling fluid that would engulf her resistance and leave her weak and passive to his will.

There was of necessity a vast amount of confusion and din ere order was restored among the debris; and conversation was impossible in the midst of the clatter that was going on – men coming and going, the rattle of silver and glass. Gilda, the while, sat quite still, her blue eyes fixed with strange intensity on the door through which her beloved had disappeared. Her father stood beside her, holding her hand, and she rested her cheek against his.

The burgomaster, throughout the last scene, had not once looked at Diogenes. A dark, puzzled frown lingered between his brows whilst he stared moodily into the fire. He absolutely ignored the presence of his son, putting into practice his stern dictum that henceforth he had no son, whilst Nicolaes, who was becoming inured to his shameful position, put on a careless and jaunty air, spoke with easy familiarity to Stoutenburg, and peremptorily to the men.

Then at last the table was once more set, the candles relit, and the board again spread for supper. Stoutenburg, with an elegant flourish, invited his guests to sit, offered his arm to Gilda to lead her to the table. She, moved by a pathetic desire to conciliate him, a forlorn hope that a great show of submission on her part would soften his cruel heart and lighten the fate of her beloved, placed her hand upon his sleeve, and when she met his admiring glance a slight flush drove the pallor from her cheeks.

'You are adorable, *myn geloof!*' he murmured.

He appeared highly elated, sat at the head of the table, with Gilda on his right and the burgomaster on his left, whilst Nicolaes sat beside his sister.

The two old crones served the supper, coming and going with a noiselessness and precision acquired in long service in the well-conducted house of the burgomaster. They knew the use of the two pronged silver utensils which Mynheer Beresteyn had acquired of late direct from France, where they were used at the table of gentlemen of quality for conveying food to the mouth. They knew how to remove each service from the centre of the table without unduly disturbing the guests, and how to replace one cloth with another the moment it became soiled with sauce or wine.

Jan stood at the Lord of Stoutenburg's elbow and served him personally and with his own hands. Every dish, before it was handed to his lordship, was placed in front of the burgomaster, who was curtly bidden to taste of it. His Magnificence, adept in the poisoner's art, was taking no risks himself.

The cook had done his best, and the supper was, I believe, excellent. The Oille, that most succulent of dishes, made up of quails, capons, and ducks and other tasty meats, was a marvel of gastronomic art, and so were the tureens of beef with cucumber and the breast of veal larded and garnished with hard-boiled eggs. In truth, it was all a terrible waste, and sad to see such excellent fare laid before guests who hardly would touch a morsel. Gilda could not eat, her throat seemed to close up every time she tried to swallow. Indeed, she had to appeal to the very last shred of her pride to keep up a semblance of dignity before her enemy. The burgomaster, too, flushed with shame at the indignity put upon him, did no more than taste of the dishes as they were put before him by the surly Jan.

The Lord of Stoutenburg, on the other hand, put up a great show of hilarity, talked much and drank deeply, discussed in a loud, arrogant voice with Nicolaes the Archduchess's plans for the subduing of the Netherlands. And Nicolaes, after he had imbibed two or three bumpers of heady Spanish wine, felt more assured, returned Gilda's reproachful glances with indifference, and his father's contempt with defiance.

2

What Gilda suffered it were a vain attempt to describe. How she contrived to remain at the table; to appear indifferent, almost gay; to glance up now and again at a persuasive challenge from Stoutenburg, will for ever remain her secret. She never spoke of that hour, of that hateful, harrowing supper, like an odious nightmare, which was wont in after years to send a shudder of horror right through her whenever she recalled it.

The burgomaster remained at first obstinately silent, whilst the Lord of Stoutenburg talked with studied insolence of the future of the Netherlands. The happy times would now come back, the traitor vowed, when the United Provinces, dissolved into feeble and separate entities, without form or governance, would once more return to their allegiance and bow the knee before the might of Spain; when the wholesome rule of another Alva would teach these stiffnecked and presumptuous burghers that comfort and a measure of welfare could only be obtained by unconditional surrender and submission to a high, unconquerable Power.

'Freedom! Liberty!' he sneered. 'Ancient Charters! Bah! Empty, swaggering words, I say, which their masters will soon force them to swallow. Then will follow an era more suited to all this beggarly Dutch rabble, one that will teach them a lesson which will at last stick in their memories. The hangman, that's what they want! The stake! The rack! Our glorious Inquisition, and the relentlessness which, alas, for the nonce hath lain buried with our immortal Alva!'

He drank a loyal toast to the coming new era, to the Archduchess, to King Philip IV, who in his glorious reign would see Spain once more unconquered, the Netherlands subdued, England punished at last. Nicolaes joined him with many a lustful shout, whilst the burgomaster sat with set lips, his eyes glowing with suppressed indignation. Once or twice it seemed as if his stern self-control would give way, as if his burning wrath would betray him into words and deeds that might cause abysmal misery to hundreds of innocent people, whilst not serving in any way the cause which he would have given his life to uphold.

Indeed, in the book of heroic deeds of which God's angel hath a record, none stand out more brilliantly than the endurance of the Burgomaster of Amersfoort and of his daughter on this memorable occasion. Nor is there in the whole valorous history of the Netherlands a more glorious page than that which tells of the sacrifice made by father and daughter in order to save the city which they loved from threatened annihilation.

3

But like all things, good and evil, the trial came to an end at last. The Lord of Stoutenburg gave the signal, and the burgomaster and Gilda rose from the table, both, in truth, with a deep sigh of thankfulness.

Stoutenburg remained deferential until the end – deferential, that is, with an under-current of mockery, which he took no pains to conceal. His bow, as he finally took leave of his guests, bidding the burgomaster a simple farewell and Gilda *au revoir* until the dawn on the morrow, was so obviously ironical that Beresteyn was goaded into an indignant tirade, which he regretted almost as soon as he had uttered it.

'Let him who stands,' he said firmly, and with all of his wonted dignity, 'take heed lest he fall. The Netherlands are not conquered yet, my lord, because your mercenary troops have succeeded, for the time being, in overrunning one of her provinces. Ede may have fallen. Amersfoort may for the moment, be under your heel – '

'Arnheim and Nijmegen may have capitulated by now,' Stoutenburg broke in derisively. 'Sold to De Berg, like Amersfoort and Ede, by the craven *smeerlap* to whom you have given your daughter.'

'Even that may have happened,' the burgomaster riposted hotly, 'if so be the will of God. But we are a race of fighters. We have beaten and humiliated the Spaniard and driven him from off our land before now. And Maurice of Nassau, the finest captain of the age, is unconquered still!'

'Mightily sick, so I'm told,' the other put in carelessly. 'He was over-ready, methinks, to abandon Amersfoort to its fate.'

'Only to punish you more effectually in the end. Take heed, my lord, take heed! The multiplicity of your crimes will find you out soon enough.'

' 'Sblood!' retorted Stoutenburg, unperturbed; 'but you forget, mynheer burgomaster, that, whate'er betide me, your daughter's fate is henceforth linked to mine own.'

Then it was that Beresteyn repented of his outburst, for indeed he had gained nothing by it, and Stoutenburg had used the one argument which was bound to silence him. What, in truth, was the use of wrangling? Dignity was sure to suffer, and that mocking recreant would only feel that his triumph was more complete.

Even now he only laughed, pointed with an ironical flourish of his arm to the widely open doors, through which, in the dimly lighted hall, a group of men could be perceived, sitting or standing around the centre table, with Diogenes standing in their midst, his fair head crowned by the hideous bandage, and his broad shoulders towering above the puny, swarthy Spanish soldiery. He had a mug of ale in his hand, and holding it aloft he was singing a ribald song, the refrain of which was taken up by the men. In the vague and flickering light of resin torches, his sightless orbs looked spectral, like those of a wraith.

'You should be grateful to me, mynheer,' Stoutenburg added with a sneer, 'for freeing your daughter from such a yoke.'

He turned to Gilda, took her unresisting hand and raised it to his lips. Above it, he was watching her face. She was looking beyond him, straight at the blind man; and though Stoutenburg at that moment would have bartered much for the knowledge of what was in her thoughts, he could not define the expression of her eyes. At one time he thought that they softened, that the fulfilment of all his hopes was hanging once more in the balance. It seemed for the moment as if she would snatch away her hand and seek shelter, as she had done before, against the heart of her beloved; that right through that outer husk of misery and degradation she saw something that puzzled her rather than repelled. A question seemed to be hovering on her lips. A question or a protest. Or was it a mute appeal for forgiveness?

Stoutenburg could not tell. But he felt that for a space of a few seconds the whole edifice of his desires was tottering, that Fate might, after all, still be holding a thunderbolt in store for him, which would hurl him down from the pinnacle of this momentary triumph. Gilda – as a woman – was still unconquered. Neither her heart nor her soul would ever be his.

Somehow, it was the glance wherewith she regarded the blind man that told the Lord of Stoutenburg this one unalterable fact.

The sortilege which he had tried to evoke, by letting her look on the pitiful wreck who had once been her lover, had fallen short in its potent charm. His own brilliant prospects, his masterful personality, ay, his well-assumed indifference, had all failed to cast their spells over her. Unlike the valiant Petruchio of the English play, he had not yet succeeded in taming this beautiful shrew. In the past she had resisted his blandishments; if she succumbed at all, it would be beneath the weight of his tyranny.

Well, so be it! Nicolaes, no doubt, had been right when he said that women reserved their disdain for weaklings. It was the man of iron who won a woman's love. The thought sent a fierce glow of hatred coursing through his blood. Mythical and fatalistic as he was, he believed that his lucky star would only begin to rise when he had succeeded in winning Gilda for his own. He had deemed women an easy conquest in the past. This one could not resist him for long. Even men were wont to come readily under his sway – witness Nicolaes Beresteyn, who was as wax in his hands. In the past, he had delighted in wielding a kind of cabalistic power, which he undoubtedly possessed, over many a weak or shifty character. His mother even was wont to call him a magician, and stood not a little in awe of the dark-visaged, headstrong child, and later on of the despotic, lawless youth, who had set the crown on her manifold sorrows by his callousness and his crimes.

That power had been on the wane of late. But it was not – could not – be gone from him for ever. Nicolaes was still his sycophant. Jan and his kind were willing to go to death for him. His own brain had devised a means for bringing that obstinate burgomaster and the beautiful Gilda to their knees. Then, of a surety, in the Cornucopia of Fate there was something more comforting, more desirable, than a thunderbolt!

Was not a man the master of his destiny?

Bah! What was a woman's love, after all? Why not let her go – be content with worldly triumphs? The sacking of Amersfoort, which would yield him wealth and treasure; the gratitude of the Archduchess: a high – if not the highest – position in the reconquered provinces! Why not be content with those? And Stoutenburg groaned like a baffled tiger, because in his heart of hearts he knew these things would not content him in the end. He wanted Gilda! Gilda, of the blue eyes and the golden hair, the demure glance and fragrant hands. His desire for her was in his bones, and he felt that he would indeed go raving mad if he lost her after this – if that beggarly drunkard, unwashed, dishonoured, and stricken with blindness, triumphed through his very abasement and the magnitude of his misfortune.

'This, at any rate, I can avert!' he murmured under his breath. And somehow the thought eased the racking jealousy that was torturing him – jealousy of such an abject thing. He waited until Gilda had passed out of the room, and when she was standing in the hall, so obviously bidding a last farewell in her heart to the man she loved so well, he called peremptorily to Jan:

'Take the varlet,' he commanded roughly, 'and hang him on the Koppelpoort!'

At the word Gilda turned on him like an infuriated tigress. Pushing past her father, past the men, who recoiled from her as if from a madwoman she was back beside the execrable despot who thus put the crown on his hideous cruelties.

'Your bargain, my lord!' she cried hoarsely. 'You dare not – you dare not – '

'My bargain, fair one?' Stoutenburg retorted coolly. 'Nay, you were so averse to fulfilling your share of it, that I have repented me of proposing it. The varlet hangs. That is my last word.'

His last word! And Jan so ready to obey! The men were already closing in around her beloved; less than a minute later they had his hands securely pinioned behind his back. Can you wonder that she lost her head, that she fought to free herself from her father's arms, and, throwing reserve, dignity to the winds, threw herself at the feet of that inhuman monster and pleaded with him as no woman on earth had, mayhap, ever pleaded before?

We do not like to think of that exquisite, refined woman kneeling before such an abominable dastard. Yet she did it! Words of appeal, of entreaty, poured from her quivering lips. She raised her tear-stained face to his, embraced his knees with her arms. She forgot the men that stood by, puzzled and vaguely awed – Jan resolute, her father torn to the heart. She forgot everything save that there was a chance – a remote chance – of softening a cruel heart, and she could not – no, could not! – see the man she loved dragged to shameful death before her eyes.

She promised – oh, she promised all that she had to give!

'I'll be your willing slave, my lord, in all things,' she pleaded, her voice broken and hoarse. 'Your loving wife, as you desire. A kiss from me? Take it, an you will. I'll not resist! Nay, I'll return it from my heart, in exchange for your clemency.'

Then it was that the burgomaster succeeded at last in tearing her away from her humiliating position. He dragged her to her feet, drew her to his breast, tried by words and admonition to revive in her her sense of dignity and her self-control. Only with one word did he, in his turn, condescend to plead.

'An you have a spark of humanity left in you, my lord,' he said loudly, 'order your executioners to be quick about their business.'

For the Lord of Stoutenburg had, with a refinement of cruelty almost unbelievable, were it not a matter of history, stayed Jan from executing his inhuman order.

'Wait!' his glittering eyes appeared to say to the sycophant henchman who hung upon his looks. 'Let me enjoy this feast until I am satiated.'

Then, when Gilda lay at last, half-swooning in the shelter of her father's arms, he said coolly:

'Have I not said, fair one, that if you deigned to plead the rascal should not hang? See! The potency of your charm upon my sensitive heart! The man who hath always been my most bitter enemy, and whom at last I have within my power, shall live because your fair arms did encircle my knees, and because of your free will you offered me a kiss. Mynheer Burgomaster,' he added, with easy condescension, 'I pray you lead your daughter to her room. She is overwrought and hath need of rest. Go in peace, I pray you. That drunken varlet is safe now in my hands.'

The burgomaster could not trust himself to reply. Only his loving hands wandered with a gentle, soothing gesture over his beloved daughter's hair, whilst he murmured soft, endearing words in her ear. Gradually she became more calm, was able to gather her wits together, to realize what she had done and all that she had sacrificed, probably in vain. Stoutenburg had spoken soft words, but how could she trust him, who had ever proved himself a liar and a cheat? She was indeed like a miserable, captive bird, held, maimed and bruised, in a cruel trap set by vengeful and cunning hands. It seemed almost incredible why she should be made to suffer so.

What had she done? In what horrible way had she sinned before God, that His hand should lie so heavily upon her? Even her sacrifice – sublime and selfless – failed to give her the consolation of duty nobly accomplished. Everything before her was dreary and dark. Life itself was nought but torture. The few days – hours – that must intervene until she knew that Amersfoort was safe confronted her like the dark passage into Gehenna. Beyond them lay death at last, and she, a young girl scarce out of adolescence, hitherto rich, beautiful, adulated, was left to long for that happy release from misery with an intensity of longing akin to the sighing of souls in torment.

14

Treachery

Throughout this harrowing scene the blind man had stood by, pinioned, helpless, almost lifeless in his immobility. The only sign of life in him seemed to be in those weird, sightless orbs, in which the flickering light of the resin torches appeared to draw shafts of an unearthly glow. He was pinioned and could not move. Half a dozen soldiers had closed in around him. Whether he heard all that went on, many who were there at the time declared it to be doubtful. But, even if he heard, what could he have done? He could not even put his hands up to his ears to shut out that awful sound of his beloved wife's hoarse, spent voice pleading desperately for him.

One of the men who was on guard over him told De Voocht afterwards that he could hear the tough sinews cracking against the bonds that held the giant captive, and that great drops of sweat appeared upon the fine, wide brow. When Gilda, leaning heavily upon her father's arm, finally mounted the stairs which led up to her room, the blind man turned his head in that direction. But the *jongejuffrouw* went on with head bent and did not glance down in response.

All this we know from De Voocht, who speaks of it in his 'Brieven.' But he was not himself present on the scene and hath it only from hearsay. He questioned several of the men subsequently as he came in contact with them, and, of course, the burgomaster's testimony was the most clear and the most detailed. Mynheer Beresteyn admitted that, throughout that awful, never-to-be-forgotten evening, he could not understand the blind man's attitude, was literally tortured with doubts of him. Was he, in truth, the craven wretch which he appeared to be – the miserable traitor who had sold the Stadtholder's orginal plans to De Berg, betrayed Marquet and De Keysere, and hopelessly jeopardized the whole of Gelderland, if not the entire future of the Nederlands? If so, he was well-deserving of the horrible punishment which had already been meted out to him – well-deserving of the gallows, which would not fail to be his lot.

But was he? Was he?

The face, of course, out of which the light of the eyes had vanished, was inscrutable. The mouth, remember, was partially hidden by the three days' growth of beard, and grime and fatigue had further obliterated all other marks of expression. Of course, the man must have suffered tortures of humiliation and rage, which would effectually deaden all physical pain. But at the time he seemed not to suffer. Indeed, at one moment it almost seemed as if he were asleep, with sightless eyes wide open, and standing on his feet.

2

After Gilda and her father had disappeared on the floor above, the Lord of Stoutenburg, like a wild and caged beast awaiting satisfaction, began pacing up and down the long banqueting-hall. The doors leading into it from the hall had been left wide open, and the men could see his lordship in his restless wanderings, his heavy boots ringing against the reed-covered floor. He held his arms folded across his chest, and was gnawing – yes, gnawing – his knuckles in the excess of his excitement and his choler.

Then he called Jan, and parleyed with him for awhile, consulted Mynheer Nicolaes, who was more taciturn and gloomy than ever before.

The soldiers knew what was coming. They had witnessed the scene between the *jongejuffrouw* and his Magnificence, and some of them who had wives and sweethearts of their own, had felt uncomfortable lumps, at the time, in their throats. Others, who had sons, fell to wishing that their offsprings might be as finely built, as powerful as that poor, blind, intoxicated wretch who, in truth, now had no use for his magnificent muscles.

But what would you? These were troublous times. Life was cheap – counted for nothing in the sight of such great gentlemen as was the Lord of Stoutenburg. The varlet, it seems, had offended his lordship awhile ago. Jan knew the story, and was very bitter about it, too. Well, no man could expect to be treated with gentleness by a great lord whom he had been fool enough to offend. The blind rascallion would hang, of that there could be no doubt. The *jongejuffrouw* had been pacified with soft words and vague promises, but the rascal would hang. Any man there would have bet his shirt on that issue. You had only to look at his lordship. A more determined, more terrifying look it were impossible to meet. Even Jan looked a little scared. When his Magnificence looked like that it boded no good to any one. All the rancour, the gall, that had accumulated in his heart against everything that pertained to the United Provinces and to their Stadtholder would effectively smother the slightest stirring of conscience or pity. Perhaps, when the *jongejuffrouw* knelt at his feet, he had thought of his mother, who, equally distraught and equally humiliated, had knelt equally in vain at the Stadtholder's feet, pleading for the life of her sons. Oh, yes, all that had made the Lord of Stoutenburg terribly hard and callous.

But the men were sorry for the blind vagabond, for all that. He had had nothing to do with the feuds between the Stadtholder and the sons of Olden Barneveldt. He had done nothing, seemingly, save to win the love of the beautiful lady whom his Magnificence had marked for his own. He was brave, too. You could not help admiring him as he stood between you and your comrades, his head thrown back, a splendid type of virility and manhood. Half-seas over he may have been. His misfortunes were, in truth, enough to make any man take to drink; but you could not help but see that there was an air of spirituality about the forehead and the sensitive nostrils which redeemed the face from any suggestion of sensuality. And now and again a quaint smile would play round the corners of his mouth, and the whole wan face would light up as if with a sudden whimsical thought.

Then all at once he threw back his head and yawned. Such a droll fellow! Yawning on the brink of eternity! It was, in truth, a pity he should hang!

3

Yes, the blind man yawned, loudly and long, like one who is ready for bed. And the harmless sound completed Stoutenburg's exasperation. He once more gave the harsh word of command:

'Take the varlet out and hang him!'

Obviously this time it would be irrevocable. There was no one here to plead, and there was Jan, stolid and grim as was his wont, already at attention under the lintel – a veritable tower of strength in support of his chief's decisions.

Jan was not in the habit of arguing with his lordship. This, or any other order, was as one to him. As for the blind vagabond – well, Jan was as eager as his Magnificence to get the noose around the rascal's throat. There were plenty of old scores to settle between them – the humiliation of three months ago, which had sent Stoutenburg, disgraced and a fugitive, out of the land, had hit Jan severely, too. And that never-to-be-forgotten discomfiture was entirely due to this miserable caitiff, who, indeed, would get naught but his deserts.

The task, in truth, was a congenial one to Jan. A blind man was easy enough to deal with, and this one offered but little resistance. He had been half-asleep, it seems, and only woke to find himself on the brink of eternity. Even so, his good-humour did not forsake him.

'Odd's fish!' he exclaimed when, roughly shaken from his somnolence, he found himself in the hands of the soldiery. 'I had forgotten this hanging business. You might have left a man to finish his dreams in peace.'

He appeared dazed, and his speech was thick. He had been drinking heavily all the evening, and, save for an odd moment or so of lucid interval, he had been hopelessly fuddled all along. And he was merry in his cups; laughter came readily to his lips; he was full of quips and sallies, too, which kept the men in rare good-humour. In truth, the fellow would joke and sing apparently until the hangman's rope smothered all laughter in his throat.

But he had an unquenchable thirst; entreated the men to bring him a jug of wine.

'Spanish wine,' he pleaded. 'I dote on Spanish wine, but had so little of it to drink in my day. That villianous rascal Pythagoras – some of you must have known the pot-bellied loon – would always seize all there was to get. He and Socrates. Two scurvy runagates who should hang 'stead o' me. Give me a mug of wine, for mercy's sake!'

The men had none to give, and the matter was referred to Jan.

'Not another drop!' Jan declared with unanswerable finality. 'The knave is quite drunk enough as it is.'

'Ah!' the blind man protested with ludicrous vehemence. 'But there thou'rt wrong, worthy Jan. No man is ever – is ever drunk enough. He may be top-heavy, he may be as drunk as a lord, or as fuddled as David's sow. He may be fuzzy, fou, or merely sottish; but sufficiently drunk? No!'

A shout of laughter from the men greeted this solemn pronouncement. Jan shrugged his shoulders impatiently.

'Well, that is as may be!' he rejoined gruffly. 'But not another drop to drink wilt thou get from me.'

'Oh, Jan,' the poor man protested, with a pitiable note of appeal, 'my good Jan, think on it! I am about to hang! Wouldst refuse the last request of a dying man?'

'Thou'rt about to hang,' Jan assented, unmoved. 'Therefore, 'twere a pity to waste good liquor on thee.'

'I'll pay thee well, my good Jan,' Diogenes put in, with a knowing wink of his sightless eyes.

'Pay me?' Jan retorted, with a grim laugh. ' 'Tis not much there's left in thy pockets, I'm thinking.'

'No,' the blind man agreed, nodding gravely. 'These good men here did, in truth empty my pockets effectually awhile ago. 'Twas not with coin I meant to repay thee, good Jan – '

'With what, then?'

'Information, Jan!' the blind man replied, sinking his voice to a hoarse whisper. 'Information for the like of which his Lordship of Stoutenburg would give his ears.'

Jan laughed derisively. The men laughed openly. They thought this but another excellent joke on the part of the droll fellow.

'Bah!' Jan said, with a shrug of the shoulders. 'How should a varlet like thee know aught of which his lordship hath not full cognisance already?'

'His lordship,' the other riposted quickly, even whilst a look of impish cunning overspread his face – 'his lordship never was in the confidence of the Stadtholder. I was!'

'What hath the Stadtholder to do with the matter?'

'Oh, nothing, nothing!' the blind man replied airily. 'Thou art obstinate, my good Jan, and 'tis not I who would force thee to share a secret for the possession of which, let me assure thee, his lordship would repay me not only with a tankard of his best wine, but with my life! Ay, and with a yearly pension of one thousand guilders to boot.'

These last few words he had spoken quite slowly and with grave deliberation, his head nodding sagely while he spoke. The look of cunning in those spectral orbs had lent to his pale, wan face an air of elfin ghoulishness. He was swaying on his feet, and now and again the men had to hold him up, for he was on the very point of measuring his length on the hall floor.

Jan did not know what to make of it all. Obviously the man was drunk. But not so drunk that he did not know what he was talking about. And the air of cunning suggested that there was something alive in the fuddled brain. Jan looked across the hall in the direction of the banqueting-room.

The doors were wide open, and he could see that his lordship, who at first had paced up and down the long room like a caged beast, had paused quite close to the door, then advanced on tip-toe out into the hall, where he had remained for the last minute or two, intent and still, with eager, probing glance fixed upon the blind man. Now, when Jan questioned him with a look, he gave his faithful henchman a scarce perceptible sign, which the latter was quick enough to interpret correctly.

'Thou dost set my mouth to water,' he said to the blindman, with well-assumed carelessness, 'by all this talk of yearly pensions and of guilders. I am a poor man, and not so young as I was. A thousand guilders a year would keep me in comfort for the rest of my life.'

'Yet art so obstinate,' Diogenes riposted with a quaint, inane laugh, 'as to deny me a tankard of Spanish wine which might put thee in possession of my secret – a secret, good Jan, worth yearly pensions and more to his lordship.'

'How do I know thou'rt not a consummate liar?' Jan protested gruffly.

'I am!' the other riposted, wholly unruffled. 'I am! Lying hath been my chief trade ever since I was breeched. Had I not lied to the Stadtholder he would not have entrusted his secrets to me, and I could not have bartered those secrets for a tankard of good Spanish wine.'

'Thy vaunted secrets may not be worth a tankard of wine.'

'They are, friend Jan, they are! Try them and see.'

'Well, let's hear them and, if they are worth it, I'll pay thee with a tankard of his lordship's best Oporto.'

But the blind man shook his head with owlish solemnity. 'And then sell them to his lordship,' he retorted, 'for pensions and what not, whilst thine own hand, mayhap, puts the rope around my neck. No, no, my good Jan, say no more about it. I'd as lief see his lordship and thee falling into the Stadtholder's carefully laid trap, and getting murdered in your beds, even while I am on my journey to kingdom come.'

'Who is going to murder us?' Jan queried, frowning and puzzled, trying to get his cue once more from his master. 'And how?'

'I'll not tell thee,' the blind man replied, with a quick turn to that obstinacy which so oft pertains to the drunkard, 'not if thou wert to plunge me in a bath of best Oporto.'

Some of the men began to murmur.

'We might all share?' one or two of them suggested.

'Let's hear what it is,' others declared.

'I'll tell thee, knave, what I'll do,' Jan rejoined decisively. 'I'll bring thee a tankard of Oporto to loosen thy tongue. Then, if thy secret is indeed as important as thou dost pretend, I'll see that the hangman is cheated of thy carcase.'

For awhile the blind man pondered.

'Loosen my hands then, friend Jan,' he said, 'for, in truth, I am trussed like a fowl; then let's feel the handle of that tankard. After that we'll talk.'

4

The soldiers sat around the table, watching the blind man with grave attention. At a sign from Jan they soon loosened his bonds. There was something magnetic in the air just then, something that sent sensitive nerves aquiver, and of which these rough fellows were only vaguely conscious. They could not look on that drunken loon without laughing. He was more comical than ever now, with that air of bland beatitude upon his face as his slender fingers closed around the handle of the tankard which Jan had just placed in his hand.

'I would sell my soul for a butt of this nectar,' he said; and drank in the odour of the wine with every sign of delight, even before he raised the tankard to his lips.

The Lord of Stoutenburg watched the blind man, too. A deep furrow between his brows testified to the earnest concentration of his thoughts. The man knew something, or thought he knew, of that his lordship could not be in doubt. The question was, was that knowledge of such importance as the miserable wretch averred, or was he merely, like any rogue who sees the rope dangling before his eyes, trying to gain a respite by proposing vain bargains or selling secrets that had only found birth in his own fuddled brain. Stoutenburg, remember, was no psychologist. Indeed, psychology did not exist as a science in these days when men were overbusy with fighting, and had no time or desire to probe into the inner workings of one another's soul.

On the other hand, here was a man, thus his lordship argued to himself, who might know something of the Stadtholder's plans. He was wont before he rolled so rapidly down the hill of manhood and repute, to be an intimate of Maurice of Nassau. He might, as lately as yesterday, have been initiated into the great soldier's plans for repelling this sudden invasion of the land which he had thought secure. The Stadtholder, in truth, was not the man to abandon all efforts at resistance just because his original plans had failed. True, the attempt to rescue Arnheim and Nijmegen had ended in smoke. Marquet and De Keysere were, thanks to timely warning, being held up somewhere by the armies of Isembourg and De Berg. But Maurice of Nassau would not, of a certainty, thus lightly abandon all hopes of saving Gelderland. He must have formulated a project, and Stoutenburg, who was no fool, was far from underestimating the infinite brain power and resourcefulness of that peerless commander. Whether he had communicated that project to this besotted oaf was another matter.

Stoutenburg searched the blind man's face with an intent glance that seemed to probe the innermost thoughts behind the fine, wide brow. For the moment, the face told him nothing. It was just vacant, the sightless eyes shone with delight, and the tankard raised to the lips effectually hid all expression around the mouth.

Well, there was not much harm done, the waste of a few moments, if the information proved futile. Jan was ready with the rope, if the whole thing proved to be a mere trick for putting off the fateful hour. As the Lord of Stoutenburg gazed on the blind man, trying vainly to curb his burning impatience, he instinctively thought of Gilda. Gilda, and his hopeless wooing of her, her coldness toward him, and her passionate adherence to this miserable caitiff, who, in truth, had thrown dust in her eyes by an outward show of physical courage and a mock display of spurious chivalry.

What if the varlet had been initiated in the Stadtholder's projects? What if he betrayed them now – sold them in exchange for his own worthless life, and stood revealed, before all the world, as an abject coward, as base as any Judas who would sell his master for thirty pieces of silver? The thought turned the miscreant giddy, so dazzling did this issue appear before his mental vision. What a revelation for a fond and loyal woman, who had placed so worthless an object on a pinnacle of valour! What a disillusionment! She had staunchly believed in his integrity up to now. But after this?

In truth, what more can a man desire than to see the honour of a rival smirched in the eyes of the woman who spurns him? That was the main thought that coursed through Stoutenburg's brain, driving before it all obstinacy and choler, ay, even soothing his exacerbated nerves.

He gave a sign to Jan.

'Bring that varlet here to me,' he commanded. 'I'll speak to him myself.'

The sound of his voice chased the look of beatitude from the blind man's face, which took on an expression of bewildered surprise.

'I had no thought his lordship was here,' he said, with a self-conscious, inane laugh.

The men were murmuring more audibly. Some of them had seen visions of good reward, shared amongst them all, after the blind man had been made to speak.

But Jan paid no heed to their discontent. In a trice he had the blind man secure once more, with arms tied as before behind his back. Diogenes had uttered a loud cry of protest when the empty tankard was torn out of his hand.

'Jan,' he shouted, in a thick, hoarse voice, 'if thou'rt a knave and dost not keep faith with me, the devil himself will run away with thee.'

'His Magnificence will hear what thou hast to say,' Jan retorted gruffly. 'After that, we'll see.'

He led the prisoner through into the banqueting-hall, and despite the men's murmurings, he closed the door upon them. He sat the blind man down in a chair, opposite his lordship. The poor loon had begun to whimper softly, just like a child, and continued to appeal pitiably to Jan.

'If his lordship is satisfied,' he murmured confidingly, 'you'll see to it, Jan, that I do not hang.'

'Jan has his orders!' his lordship put in roughly. 'But take heed, sirrah! If your information is worth having, you may go to hell your own way; I care nought! But remember,' he added, with slow and stern emphasis, 'if you trick me in this, 'twill not be the rope for you at dawn – but the stake!'

Diogenes gave a quick shudder.

'By the lord,' he said blandly, 'how very unpleasant! But I am a man of my word. Jan put good wine into me. He shall be paid for it. And I'll tell you what the Stadtholder hath planned for the defeat of the Lord of Stoutenburg.'

'Well,' his lordship retorted curtly. 'I wait!'

There was silence for a moment whilst the blind man apparently collected his thoughts. He sat, trussed and helpless in the chair, with his head thrown back, and the full light of the candles playing upon his pale face – the latter still vacant and with a childish expression of excitement about those weird, dark orbs. The Lord of Stoutenburg, master of the situation, sat in a high-backed chair opposite him, his chin resting in his hand, his eyes, glowering and fierce, searching that strange, mysterious face before him. Strange and mysterious, in truth, with those sightless eyes, that glittered uncannily whenever the flickering candle-light caught the abnormally dilated pupils, and those quavering lips which every moment broke into a whimsical and inane smile.

'Jan, my friend,' the blind man asked after a while, 'art here?'

'Ay!' Jan replied gruffly. 'I'm here right enough, to see that thou'rt not up to mischief.'

'How can I be that, worthy Jan?' the other retorted blandly, 'since thou hast again trussed me like a capon?'

'Well, the sooner thou hast satisfied his lordship,' Jan rejoined with stolid indifference, 'the sooner thou wilt be free –'

'To go to hell mine own way!' Diogenes put in with a hiccough. 'So his lordship hath pledged his word. Let all those who are my friends bear witness that his lordship did pledge his word.'

He paused, and once again a look of impish cunning overspread his face. He seemed to be preparing for a fateful moment which literally would mean life or death for him. An exclamation of angry impatience from Stoutenburg recalled him to himself.

'I am ready,' he protested with eager servility, 'to do his lordship's pleasure.'

'Then speak, man!' Stoutenburg retorted savagely, 'ere I wring the words from thee with torture!'

'I was only thinking how to put the matter clearly,' Diogenes protested blandly. 'The Stadtholder only outlined his plan to me. There was so little time. My friend Klaas will remember that after his Highness's horse bolted across the moor I was able to stop it – '

'Yes – curse your interference!' Stoutenburg muttered between his teeth.

'Amen to that!' the blind man assented. 'But for it, I should still have the privilege of beholding your lordship's pleasing countenance. But at the moment I had no thought save to stop a runaway horse. The Stadtholder was mightily excited, scented that a trap had been laid for him. My friend Klaas again will remember that, after his Highness dismounted he stopped to parley with me upon the moor.'

Nicolaes nodded.

'Then it was,' Diogenes went on, 'that he told me what he meant to do. I was, of course, to bear my part in the new project, which was to make a feint upon Ede – '

'A feint upon Ede?'

'Ay! A surprise attack, which would keep De Berg, who is in Ede, busy whilst the Stadtholder – '

'Bah!' Stoutenburg broke in contemptuously, 'De Berg is too wary to be caught by a feint.'

'So he is, my lord, so he is!' Diogenes rejoined with solemn gravity. 'But if I were to tell you that the surprise attack is to be made in full force, and that the weight will fall on the south side of the town, what then?'

'I do not see with what object.'

'Yet you, my lord, would know the Stadtholder's tactics of old. You fought under his banner – once.'

'Before he murdered my father, yes!' Stoutenburg broke in impatiently. He did not relish this allusion to his former fighting days, before black treachery had made him betray the ruler he once served. 'But what of that?'

'For then your lordship would remember,' the blind man went on placidly, 'that the Stadtholder's favourite plan was always to draw the enemy away by a ruse from his own chief point of attack.'

'But where would the chief point of attack be in this case?' Stoutenburg queried, with a frown.

'At a certain *molen* your lordship wots of on the Veluwe.'

'Impossible!'

'Oh, impossible? Your lordship is pleased to jest. Some days ago, spies came into Utrecht with the information that the Lord of Stoutenburg had his camp at an old *molen*, which stands disused and isolated on the highest point of the Veluwe, somewhere between Apeldoorn and Barneveld.'

'My camp? Bah! The mill was only a halting-place – '

'The spies averred, my lord,' the blind man broke in blandly, 'that vast stores of arms and ammunition are accumulated in that halting-place. And that the attack on Amersfoort was planned within its rickety walls.'

Then, as the Lord of Stoutenburg made no comment on this – indeed, he had cast a rapid, significant glance on Nicolaes, who throughout this colloquy had appeared as keen, as interested, as his friend – the blind man went on slowly:

'The Stadtholder's objective is the *molen* on the Veluwe.'

'What? From Ede!' Nicolaes exclaimed.

'No, no! Have I not said that the attack on Ede would be a feint? It will be the Stadtholder himself who, with a comparatively small force, will push on toward Barneveld and the *molen*, and at once cut off all communication between Ede and Amersfoort.'

'I understand,' Stoutenburg rejoined, with a grave nod. 'But if it is a small force we can easily – '

'You can now,' Diogenes assented coolly, 'since you are warned.'

'Quite right! Eh, friend Nicolaes?' his lordship retorted, and strove to let his harsh voice express a world of withering contempt. 'If all this is not a trick yon varlet hath served us well. What say you? Shall we let him go to hell his own way, and save the hangman a deal of pother?'

'If it all prove true,' Nicolaes put in cautiously. 'But what proof have we?'

'None, in truth. Nor would I let this craven vagabond out of Jan's sight until we do make sure that he hath not lied. But there'll be no harm in being prepared. Here, sirrah!' his lordship continued, once more addressing the blind man. 'With how strong a force doth the Stadtholder propose to cut us off from Ede?'

But, during this brief colloquy between the two friends, the blind man had begun to nod. His head fell forward on his chest, the heavy lids veiled the stricken eyes, and anon a peaceable snore came through the partially open mouth. Stoutenburg swore, as was his wont, the moment his choler was roused, and Jan shook the prisoner roughly by the shoulder.

'Eh? Eh? What?' the latter queried, blinked his sightless eyes, and turned a pale and startled face vaguely from side to side. 'What is it? Where's that confounded – '

'Answer his lordship's question!' Jan commanded briefly.

'Question? What question? Your lordship must forgive me. I am so fatigued, and that tankard of – '

'I asked thee, knave,' Stoutenburg broke in impatiently, 'with how strong a force the Stadtholder proposed to cut us off from Ede?'

'Call it four thousand, my lord,' the blind man babbled, 'and let me go to sleep.'

'You shall sleep till Judgment Day when I've done with you, sirrah! Will the Stadtholder lead that force in person?'

The blind man winked and blinked, tried to collect his thoughts, which apparently had all wandered off toward the Land of Nod. Then he said:

'The plan was to leave the bulk of that force to menace Arnersfoort. But the Stadtholder himself meant to push on as far as the *molen*, with but a few hundred of his picked men. He thought to seize the stores of arms and ammunition there and then to await the coming of the Lord of Stoutenburg, who, driven out of Amersfoort and cut off from Ede, would make of necessity for his headquarters.'

'Ah!'

The exclamation, deep and prolonged, came from three pairs of lips. Stoutenburg, Nicolaes and Jan looked at one another, and there was triumph and satisfaction depicted in their glance. The same thought had occurred simultaneously to these three traitors; the Stadtholder, with a comparatively small force, pushing on to the lonely *molen* on the Veluwe, not knowing that some of De Berg's troops were holding the Ijssel beyond.

He would be caught like a rat in a trap; and the question was whether it would not be better to allow him to carry out his plan, not to oppose him on his way, to let him reach the *molen* and then close in behind him, so that he would have but two alternatives before him – to surrender in the *molen* or to turn his small force in the direction of the Zuider Zee, and therein seek a watery grave.

'I must have a little time to think,' Stoutenburg muttered to himself, after a while.

The blind man had apparently dropped off to sleep again. His head had once more fallen forward on his chest. Jan was prepared to give him another rude awakening, but his lordship stopped him with a sign.

'Let the muckworm sleep,' he said. 'I must think out the whole position. If what the knave says is true – '

'I am inclined to believe it true,' Nicolaes interposed. 'The man is too fuddled to have invented so circumstantial a story. And I have it in my mind,' he added reflectively, 'that when the Stadtholder visited Amersfoort yesterday he said something to my father about devising a plan later on if the city were seriously threatened.'

'Then, by Satan! all would be well indeed!' And Stoutenburg drew up his gaunt figure to its full height, looked already every inch a conqueror, with heel set upon the neck of his foes. Jan alone looked dubious.

'I wouldn't trust the rogue,' he said grimly.

'Would you hang him now?' Stoutenburg retorted. 'No; I would wait to make sure. Let him sleep awhile now. When he wakes out of his booze, he might be able to give us further details.'

'In the meanwhile,' his lordship rejoined, 'keep the men under arms, Jan. I have not yet thought the matter over; but this I know – that I'll start for the *molen* with a few hundred musketeers and pikemen as soon as I am sure that this rascallion hath not spun a tissue of lies. Do you send out spies at once in every direction, with orders to bring back information immediately. We must hear if an attack hath indeed been made on Ede, and if the Stadtholder is moving out of Utrecht. Have you some men you can trust?'

'Oh, yes, so please your lordship,' Jan replied. 'I can send Piet Walleren in the direction of Ede, and I myself will push on towards Utrecht. We'd both be back long before dawn.'

'And 'tis not you who could be nousled, eh, good Jan?' his lordship was pleased to say.

'If we have been tricked by this tosspot,' Jan riposted gruffly, 'I'll see him burnt alive, and 'tis mine own hand will set the brand to the stake.'

He paused, and drew in his breath with a shudder; for he had turned to look on the blind man whom he was threatening with so dire a fate and whom he had thought asleep, and encountered those sightless orbs fixed upon him as if they could see something through and beyond him, some ghoul or spectre lurking in a distant corner of the room. So uncanny and terrifying did the rascal look, indeed, that instinctively Jan, who believed neither in God nor the devil, remembered his mother's early teachings, and made sundry and vague signs of the Cross upon his breast, with a view to exorcising those evil spirits which must be somewhere lurking about, unseen by all save by the man who had lost his sight.

'What is it now?' Stoutenburg queried with a scowl. The blind man indeed appeared to be listening – listening so intently, with head now craned forward and eyes fixed into vacancy – that instinctively the three recreants listened too. To what, they could not have told. Through the open casement the sound of life – camp life, of the sentries' challenging call, of bivouac fires, and rowdy soldiery – came in as before. A little less roisterous, perhaps, seeing that most of the men, tired after long days of marching and hours of carousing, had settled themselves down to sleep.

Inside the room, the monumental clock up against the wall ticked off each succeeding second with tranquil monotony. It was now close upon midnight. Nothing had happened, nothing could have happened, to disturb the wonted tenor of the life of an army in temporary occupation of an unresisting city.

Nothing, in fact, unless that blind tatterdemalion over there had indeed spoken the truth.

And still he listened. A vague anxiety seemed to have completely banished sleep, even momentarily to have dissipated the potent effect of that excellent Oporto; and on his face there was that strained look peculiar to those who have been robbed of one sense and are at pains to exert the others to their utmost power. It seemed as if his sightless orbs must pierce some hidden veil which kept vital secrets hidden from ordinary human gaze. And these three men – traitors all – whose craven hearts, weighted with crime, were sensitive to every uncanny spell, felt their own senses unaccountably thrilled by that motionless, stony image of a man whose very soul appeared on the alert, and in whom life itself was, as it were, momentarily arrested.

The spell continued for a moment or two. A minute, perhaps, went by; then, with an impatient curse, Stoutenburg jumped to his feet, strode rapidly to the window, and, leaning out far over the sill, he listened.

Indeed, at first it was naught but the habitual confused sounds that reached his ear. But as he, in his turn, strained every sense to hear, something unusual seemed to mingle with the other sounds. A murmuring. Strange voices. A few isolated words that rose above the others, louder than the sentries' call; also a patter of feet, like men running and a clang of arms that at this hour should have been stilled.

The Lord of Stoutenburg could not have told you then why those sounds should have suddenly filled his mind with foreboding – why, indeed, he heard them at all. Beneath the window, ranged against the wall, the men of his picked company were sleeping peacefully. Their bivouac fire fed by those on guard, shed a pleasant glow over the familiar scene. Beyond its ruddy gleam everything looked by contrast impenetrably dark. The river beyond the quay appeared like a yawning abyss of tenebration. And beyond it, nothing; only blackness – a blackness that could be felt. The lights of the city had long since been extinguished, only one tiny glimmer, which came from a small oil-lamp, showed above the Koppelpoort.

But that confused sound, that murmuring, came from the rear of the burgomaster's house, from the direction of the Market Place, where the bulk of his lordship's army was encamped.

'What in thunder does it mean?' Stoutenburg muttered.

Nicolaes came and joined him by the window. He, too, strained his ears to hear, feeling his nerves vaguely stirred by a kind of superstitious dread. But Stoutenburg turned to the blind man, and tried to read an answer in the latter's white, set face.

Jan shook Diogenes fiercely by the shoulder.

'Dost hear, knave?' he said harshly. 'What does it all mean?'

'What does what mean, worthy Jan?' the blind man queried blandly.

'Thou art listening for something. What is it? His lordship desires to know.'

'Canst *thou* hear anything, friend Jan?' the other riposted serenely.

'Only the usual sounds. What should I hear?'

'The armies of the Stadtholder on the move.'

An exclamation of incredulity broke from Stoutenburg's lips. Nevertheless, he turned imperatively to Jan.

'Go or send at once into the town,' he commanded. 'Let us hear if anything has happened.'

In a moment Jan was out of the room; and soon his gruff voice could be heard from outside, questioning and giving orders. He had gone himself to see what was amiss.

And Stoutenburg, half incredulous, yet labouring under strong excitement, once more approached the window and, leaning far out into the night, set his ears to listen.

His senses, too, were keyed up now, detached as they were from everything else except just what went on outside. The subdued murmurings reached his perceptions independently of every other sound. A hum of voices, and through it that of Jan, questioning and commanding; and others that talked agitatedly, with many interruptions.

After awhile he felt that he could stand the strain no longer. Very obviously something had happened, something was being discussed out on the Market Place, and there was a kind of buzzing in the air, as if around the hive of bees that have been disturbed by a company of robber-wasps. And to him – Stoutenburg – for whom that buzzing might mean the first step up towards the pinnacle of his desires, the turning point of his destiny, beyond which lay power, dominion, ambition, satisfied, and passion satiated, every moment of suspense and silence became positive torture. A primeval, savage instinct would, but for the presence of Nicolaes, have driven him to seizing the helpless prisoner by the throat, and thus to ease the tension on his nerves and still the wild hammering of blood on his temples.

But Nicolaes did, as it happened, exercise in this instance a restraining influence on his friend; quite unknowingly, of course, as his was the weaker nature. But the last half-hour had wrought a marked change in Stoutenburg – a subtle one, which he himself could not have defined. Before then, he had been *striving* for great things – for revenge, for power, for the satisfaction of his passions. But now he felt that he had *attained* all that, and more. Obviously his stricken enemy had not lied. The Stadtholder was about to fall into a trap which was easy enough to set. The once brilliant Laughing Cavalier had sunk to a state of moral and physical degradation from which he could never now recover. And Gilda! Gilda had but to realize the slough of turpitude into which her former lover had sunk to turn gratefully and with a sigh of infinite relief to the man who had freed her from such a yoke.

In truth, Stoutenburg felt that he no longer needed to climb. He had reached the summit. The summit of ambition, of power, of sentimental satisfaction. He was a conqueror now ; master in the land of his birth; the future Stadtholder of the United Provinces, wedded to the richest heiress in the Netherlands; happy, feared, and obeyed.

That was his position now, and that was the cause of the subtle change in him – a change which forced him to keep his savage instincts in check before his servile friend; forced him to try and appear before others as above petty passions; a justiciary and not a terrorist.

6

The minutes sped by, leaden-footed for the impatience of these two men. Nicolaes and Stoutenburg, each trying to appear calm, hardly dared to speak with one another lest their speech betrayed the exacerbation of their nerves.

It was Nicolaes' turn now to pace up and down the room, to halt beside the window and peer out into the darkness in search of Jan's familiar figure. Stoutenburg had once more taken a seat on the highbacked chair, striving to look dignified and detached. His arm was thrown over the table, and with his sharply pointed nails he was drumming a devil's tatoo on the board.

Alone, the blind man appeared perfectly serene. After that brief moment of comparative lucidity, he had relapsed into somnolence. Occasional loud snores testified that he was once more wandering in the Elysian fields of unconsciousness.

Half an hour after midnight Jan returned.

'There is no doubt about it,' were the first words he spoke. 'An attack on Ede appears to be in progress, and the Stadtholder left his camp at Utrecht a couple of hours ago with a force of four thousand men.'

He was out of breath, having run, he said, all the way from the Joris Poort, where he had gleaned the latest information.

'Who brought the news?' his lordship asked.

'No one seems to know, my lord,' Jan replied. 'But every one in the town has it. The rumour hath spread like wildfire. It started at opposite quarters of the city. The Nieuw Poort had it that a surprise attack had been delivered on Ede earlier in the evening, and the Joris Poort that the Stadtholder and his force are on the move. The captains at the gates had heard the news from runners who had come direct from Utrecht and from Ede.'

'Where are those runners now?'

'In both cases the captains sent them back for further information. The fellows were willing enough to go, for a consideration; but the business has become a dangerous one, for the roads to Utrecht and Ede, they averred, are already full of the Stadtholder's vedettes.'

'Bah!' Stoutenburg ejaculated contemptuously. 'A device for extorting money!'

'Probably,' Jan riposted dryly. 'But the money will be well spent if we get the information. The men are not to be paid until they return. And if they do not return –' Jan shrugged his shoulders. If the spies did not return, it would go to prove that the Stadtholder's vedettes were not asleep.

'I sent Piet Wallerin and one or two others out, too,' he added, 'with orders to push on both roads as far as possible, and bring back any information they can obtain – the sooner the better.'

'They have not yet returned?' Stoutenburg asked.

'Oh, no! They have only been gone half an hour.'

'Is the night very dark?'

'Very dark, my lord.'

'Piet may never get back.'

'In that case we shall know that the Stadtholder's vanguard has sighted him,' Jan rejoined coolly. 'Nothing else would keep Piet from getting back.'

Stoutenburg nodded approval.

'You think, then, that this varlet here spoke the truth?' he asked again.

'I have no longer any doubt of it, my lord,' Jan gave reply. 'Though I did not actually speak with the men who seem originally to have brought the news, the captains at the Poorts had no doubt whatever as to its authenticity. But we shall know for certain before dawn. Piet and the others will have returned by then – or not, as the case may be. But we shall know.'

'And, of course we are prepared?'

'To do just what your lordship commands. The men will be under arms within the next two hours, and I can seek the Master of the Camp, and send him at once to your lordship for instructions.'

'Mine instructions are simple enough, good Jan; and thou canst convey them to the Master of the Camp thyself. They are, to remain quiescent, under arms but asleep. To surrender the town if it be attacked – '

'To surrender?' Jan protested with a frown.

'We must throw dust in the Stadtholder's eyes,' Stoutenburg riposted. 'Give the idea that we are feeble and unprepared, and that I have fled out of Amersfoort. The surrender of the city and its occupation will keep the main force busy, whilst Maurice of Nassau, anxious to possess himself of our person, will push on as far as the *molen*, where I, in the meanwhile, will be waiting for him.'

His voice rang with a note of excitement and of triumph.

'With the Stadtholder a prisoner in my hands,' he exclaimed, 'I can command the surrender of all his forces. And then the whole of the Netherlands will be at my feet!'

Never, in his wildest dreams had he hoped for this. Fate, in very truth, had tired of smiting him, had an overfull cornucopia for him now and was showering down treasures upon him, one by one.

7

It was Nicolaes who first remembered the blind man.

During the last momentous half-hour he had been totally forgotten. Stoutenburg during that time had been in close confabulation with Jan, discussing plans, making arrangements for the morrow's momentous expedition. Neither of them seemed to feel the slightest fatigue. They were men of iron, whom their passions kept alive. But Nicolaes was a man of straw. He had been racked by one emotion after the other all day, and now he was so tired that he could hardly stand. He envied the blind man every time that a lusty snore escaped the latter's lips, and tried to keep himself awake by going to the fire from time to time and throwing a log or two upon it. But he stood in too great an awe of his friend to dare own to fatigue when the future of his native land was under discussion.

It was really in order to divert Stoutenburg's attention from these interminable discussions on what to do and what not to do on the morrow, that presently, during a pause, he pointed to Diogenes.

'What is to happen to this drunken loon?' he asked abruptly.

Stoutenburg grinned maliciously.

'Have no fear, friend Nicolaes,' he said. 'The fate of our valued informer will be my special care. I have not forgotten him. Jan knows. While you were nodding, he and I arranged it all. You did not hear?'

Nicolaes shook his head.

'No,' he said. 'What did you decide?'

'You shall see, my good Klaas,' Stoutenburg replied with grim satisfaction. 'I doubt not but what you'll be pleased. And, since we have now finished the discussion of our plans, Jan will at once go and bid the Heer Burgomaster rise from his bed and attend upon our pleasure.'

'My father?' Nicolaes exclaimed in surprise. 'Why? What hath he – '

'You will see, my good Klaas,' the other broke in quietly. 'You will see. I think that you will be satisfied.'

Jan, at his word, had already gone. Nicolaes, really puzzled, tried to ask questions, but Stoutenburg was obviously determined to keep the secret of his intentions awhile longer to himself.

It was long past one o'clock now, and bitterly cold. Even the huge blazing logs in the monumental hearth failed to keep the large room at a pleasing temperature. Nicolaes, shivering and yawning, crouched beside the blaze, knocked his half-frozen hands one against the other. He would at this moment have bartered most of his ambitions for the immediate prospect of a good bed. But Stoutenburg was as wide awake as ever, and evidently some kind of inward fever kept the cold out of his bones.

After Jan's departure he resumed that restless pacing of his up and down the long room. Up and down, until Nicolaes, exasperated beyond endurance, could have screamed with choler.

Less than a quarter of an hour later, the burgomaster arrived, ushered in by Jan. He had apparently not taken off his clothes since he had been upstairs. It was indeed more than likely that he had spent the time in prayer, for Mynheer Beresteyn was a pious man, and the will of God in fortune or in adversity was a very real thing to him. With that same dignified submission which he had displayed throughout, he had immediately followed Jan when curtly ordered to do so. But he came down to face the arrogant tyrant for the third time tonight with as heavy a heart as before, not knowing what fresh indignity, what new cruel measure, would be put upon him. Grace or clemency he knew that he could not expect.

The look of malignant triumph wherewith Stoutenburg greeted him appeared to justify his worst forebodings. The presence, too, of Diogenes, fettered and asleep, filled his anxious heart with additional dread. As he stepped out into the room he took no notice of his son, but only strove to face his arch-enemy with as serene a countenance as he could command.

'Your lordship desired that I should come,' he said quietly. 'What is your lordship's pleasure?'

But Stoutenburg was all suavity. A kind of feline gentleness was in his tone as he replied:

'Firstly, to beg your forgiveness, mynheer, for having disturbed you again – and at this hour. But will you not sit? Jan,' he commanded, 'draw a chair nearer to the hearth for the Heer Burgomaster.'

'I was not asleep, my lord,' Beresteyn rejoined coldly. 'And by your leave, will take your commands standing.'

'Oh, commands, mynheer!' Stoutenburg rejoined blandly. ' 'Tis no commands I would venture to give you. It was my duty – my painful duty – not to keep you in ignorance of certain matters which have just come to my knowledge, and which will have a momentous bearing upon all my future plans. Will you not sit?' he added, with insidious urbanity. 'No? Ah, well, just as you wish. But you will forgive me if I – '

He sat down in his favourite chair, with his back to the table and the candle-light and facing the fire, which threw ruddy gleams on his gaunt face and grizzled hair. His deep-set eyes were inscrutable in the shadow, but they were fixed upon the burgomaster, who stood before him dignified and calm, half-turned away from the pitiful spectacle which the blind man presented in somnolent helplessness.

'Since last I had the pleasure of addressing you, mynheer,' Stoutenburg began slowly, after awhile, 'it hath come to my knowledge that the Stadtholder, far from abandoning all hope of reconquering Gelderland from our advancing forces, did in truth not only devise a plan whereby he intended to deliver Ede and Amersfoort from our hands, but his far-reaching project also embraced the possibility of seizing my person, and once for all ridding himself of an enemy – a justiciary, shall we say ? – who is becoming mighty inconvenient.'

'A project, my lord,' the burgomaster riposted earnestly, 'which I pray God may fully succeed.'

Stoutenburg gave a derisive laugh.

'So it would have done, mynheer,' he said with a sardonic grin. 'It would have succeeded admirably, and by this hour tomorrow I should no doubt be dangling on a gibbet, for Maurice of Nassau hath sworn that he would treat me as a knave and as a traitor, unworthy of the scaffold.'

'And the world would have been rid of a murderous miscreant,' the burgomaster put in coldly, 'had God so willed it.'

'Ah, but God – your God, mynheer,' Stoutenburg retorted with a sneer, 'did not will it, it seems. And forewarned is forearmed, you know.'

Instinctively, as the full meaning of Stoutenburg's words reached his perceptions, the burgomaster's eyes had sought those of his son, whilst a ghastly pallor overspread his face even to his lips.

'The Stadtholder's schemes have been revealed to you,' he murmured slowly. 'By whom?'

Then, as Stoutenburg made no reply, only regarded him with a mocking and quizzical gaze, he added more vehemently:

'Who is the craven informer who hath sold his master to you?'

'What would you do to him if you knew?' Stoutenburg retorted coolly.

'Slay him with mine own hand,' the burgomaster replied calmly, 'were he my only son!'

' 'Twas not I!' Nicolaes cried involuntarily.

Stoutenburg appeared vastly amused.

'No,' he said. 'It was not your son Klaas, whose merits, by the way, you have not yet learned to appreciate. Nicolaes hath rendered me and the Archduchess immense services, which I hope soon to repay adequately. But,' he added with mocking emphasis, 'this most signal service of all, which will deliver the Stadtholder into my hands and re-establish thereby the dominion of Spain over the Netherlands, was rendered to me by the varlet whom, but for me, you would have acclaimed as your son.'

And, with a wide flourish of the arm, Stoutenburg turned in his chair and pointed to Diogenes, who, sublimely unconscious of what went on around him, was even in the act of emitting a loud and prolonged snore. Instinctively the burgomaster looked at him. His glance, vague and puzzled, wandered over the powerful figure of the blind man, the nodding head, the pinioned shoulders, and from him back to Stoutenburg, who continued to regard him – Beresteyn – with a malicious leer.

'I fear me,' the latter murmured after awhile, 'that your lordship will think me over-dull; but – I don't quite understand – '

'Yet, 'tis simple enough,' Stoutenburg rejoined; rose from his chair, and approached the burgomaster, as he spoke with a sudden, fierce tone of triumph. 'This miserable cur on whom Gilda once bestowed her love, seeing the gallows dangling before his bleary eyes, hath sold me the secrets which the Stadtholder did entrust to him – sold them to me in exchange for his worthless life! I entered into a bargain with him, and I will keep my pledge. In very truth, he hath saved my life by his revelations, and jeopardized that of the Stadtholder – my most bitter enemy. Maurice of Nassau had thought to trap me in the lonely *molen* on the Veluwe which is my secret camp. Now 'tis I who will close the trap on him there, and hold his life, his honour, these provinces, at my mercy. And all,' he concluded with a ringing shout, 'thanks to the brilliant adventurer, the chosen of Gilda's heart, her English milor, mynheer! – the gay and dashing Laughing Cavalier!'

He had the satisfaction of seeing that the blow had gone home. The burgomaster literally staggered under it, as if he had actually been struck in the face with a whip. Certain it is that he stepped back and clutched the table for support with one hand, whilst he passed the other once or twice across his brow.

'My God!' he murmured under his breath.

Stoutenburg laughed as a demon might, when gazing on a tortured soul. Then he shrugged his shoulders and went on airily:

'You are surprised, mynheer Burgomaster? Frankly, I was not. You believed this fortune-hunter's tales of noble parentage and English ancestry. I did not. You doubted his treachery when he went on a message to Marquet, and sold that message to de Berg. I knew it to be a fact. My love for Gilda made me clear-sighted, whilst yours left you blind. Now you see him at last in his true colours – base, servile, without honour and without faith. You are bewildered, incredulous, mayhap? Ask Jan. He was here and heard him. Ask my captains at the gate, my master of the camp. The Stadtholder is heading straight for the trap which he had set up for me, because the cullion who sits there did sell his one-time master to me.'

The burgomaster, overcome with horror and with shame, had sunk into a chair and buried his face in his hands. The echo of Stoutenburg's rasping voice seemed to linger in the noble panelled hall, its mocking accents to be still tearing at the stricken father's aching heart, still deriding his overwhelming sorrow. Gilda! His proud, loving, loyal Gilda! If she were to know! A great sob, manfully repressed, broke from his throat and threatened to choke him.

And for the first time in this day of crime and of treachery, Nicolaes felt a twinge of remorse knocking at the gates of his heart. He could not bear to look on his father's grief, and not feel the vague stirrings of an affection which had once been genuine, even though it was dormant now. His father had been perhaps more just toward him than indulgent. Gilda had been the apple of his eye, and he – Nicolaes – had been brought up in that stern school of self-sacrifice and self-repression which had made heroes of those of his race in their stubborn and glorious fight for liberty.

No doubt it was that rigid bringing-up which had primarily driven an ambitious and discontented youth like Nicolaes into the insidious net spread out for him by the wily Stoutenburg. Smarting under the discipline imposed upon his self-indulgence by the burgomaster, he had lent a willing ear to the treacherous promises of his masterful friend, who held out dazzling visions before him of independence and of aggrandisement. Even at this moment Nicolaes felt no remorse for his treachery to his country and kindred. He was only sentimentally sorry to see his father so utterly broken down by sorrow.

And then there was Gilda. Already, when Stoutenburg had placed that cruel 'either – or' before her, Nicolaes had felt an uncomfortable pain in his heart at sight of her misery. Stoutenburg would have called it weakness, and despised him for it. But Stoutenburg's was an entirely warped and evil nature, which revelled in crime and cruelty as a solace to past humiliation and disappointment, whereas Nicolaes was just a craven time-server, who had not altogether succeeded in freeing himself from past teachings and past sentiments.

And Gilda's pale, tear-stained face seemed to stare at him through the gloom, reproachful and threatening, whilst his father's heartrending sob tore at his vitals and shook him to the soul with a kind of superstitious awe. The commandment of Heaven, not wholly forgotten, not absolutely ignored, seemed to ring the death-knell of all that he had striven for, as if the Great Judge of All had already weighed his deeds in the balance, and decreed that his punishment be swift and sure.

But Stoutenburg, in this the hour of his greatest triumph, had none of these weaknesses. Nor indeed did he care whether the burgomaster was stricken with sorrow or no. What he did do now was to go up to Jan, and from the latter's belt take out a pistol. This he examined carefully, then he put it down upon the table close to where the burgomaster was sitting.

At the metallic sound made by the contact of the weapon upon the board, the burgomaster had instinctively looked up. Stoutenburg caught his eye, then quietly pointed to the pistol.

'My friend Nicolaes and I,' he said, 'will leave you to deal with the informer as you think best.'

He stayed quite still a moment, looking down into the horror-stricken yet determined face of the burgomaster, and then at the blind man, who apparently was fast asleep. Then he curtly ordered Jan and Nicolaes to follow him, and strode leisurely out of the room.

8

A quarter of an hour later the stately house on the quay appeared wrapped in the mantle of sleep. The soldiers, wearied and discontented, had after a good deal of murmuring, finally settled down to rest. They had collected what clothes, blankets, curtains even, that they could lay their hands on, and, wrapped up in these, they had curled themselves up upon the floor.

We may take it, however, as a certainty that Jan remained wide awake, with one ear on that door which gave on the banqueting-hall, and which he, at the command of his master, had carefully closed behind him.

Upstairs, Nicolaes had thrown himself like an insentient and wearied mass upon his own bed in the room wherein he had slept as a child, as an adolescent, as a youth, now as a black-hearted traitor, haunted by memories and the ghoulish shadows of his crime. He could not endure the darkness, so left a couple of wax candles burning in their sconces. Whether he actually fell asleep or no, he could not afterwards have told you. Certain it is that he was not fully awake, but rather on that threshold of dreams which for those that are happy is akin to the very gate of paradise, but unto souls that are laden with crime is like the antechamber of hell. Half consciously Nicolaes could hear Stoutenburg pacing up and down an adjoining room, restless and fretful, like some untamed beast on the prowl.

Then suddenly the sharp report of a pistol rang through the silence of the night. Nicolaes jumped from his bed, with a feeling of sheer physical nausea, which turned him dizzy and faint. Stoutenburg had paused abruptly in his febrile wanderings. To the listener it almost seemed as if he could hear his friend's laboured breathing, the indrawing of a sigh that spoke of torturing suspense.

A few minutes went by, and then a heavy step was heard ascending the stairs, after that, the closing and shutting of a door. Then nothing more.

In that heavy step, Nicolaes had recognized his father's. Even now he could hear the burgomaster moving about in the room close by, which had always been his. Gilda's was further along, down the passage. Everything now seemed so still. Just for awhile, after the burgomaster had gone upstairs, Nicolaes had heard the soldiers moving down below. Rudely awakened from their sleep, they had done a good deal of muttering. Voices could be heard, and then a rattle, like the shaking of a door. But apparently the men had been quickly reassured by Jan.

The silence acted as a further irritant on Nicolaes' nerves. Taking up a candle, he went out of the room in search of Stoutenburg. Outside on the landing he came upon Jan, who was on the same errand bent.

'What has happened?' the young man queried hoarsely.

Jan shook his head.

'Which is His Lordship's room?' was all that he said.

Nicolaes led the way, and Jan followed. They found Stoutenburg standing in the middle of the room which he had selected for his own use. He was still fully dressed, had not even taken off his boots. Apparently he was waiting for news, but otherwise he seemed quite calm.

'Well?' he queried curtly, as soon as he caught sight of Jan.

'We cannot get into the room,' Jan replied. 'After we heard the shot fired, we saw the burgomaster come out of it; but he locked the door and, with the key in his hand he walked steadily up the stairs.'

'How did he look?'

'Like a man who had seen a ghost.'

'Well?' Stoutenburg queried again, impatiently. 'What did you do after that?'

'I tried the door, of course. It is a stout piece of oak, and I had no orders to break it down. It would take a heavy joist, and the men are already grumbling –'

'Yes!' Stoutenburg put in curtly. 'But the windows?'

'I thought of them, and myself went round to look. Of course we could climb up to them, but they appeared to be barred and shuttered.'

'So much the better!' his lordship retorted with a note of grim spite in his rasping voice. 'Let the varlet's carcase rot where it is. Why should we trouble? Go back to bed, Nicolaes,' he added after a slight pause. 'And you too, Jan. As for me, I feel that I could sleep peacefully at last!'

He threw himself on the bed with a long sigh of satisfaction, and when spoken to again by one of the others, he curtly ordered them to leave him in peace. So Jan did leave him, and went back to his men. But Nicolaes, terrified of solitude, which he felt would for him be peopled with ghouls, elected to find what rest he could in an armchair beside his friend. And a few minutes later the house was once more wrapped in the mantle of sleep.

15

The Molen *on the Veluwe*

Again it is to de Voocht's highly interesting and reliable 'Brieven' that we like to turn for an account of the Lord of Stoutenburg's departure out of Amersfoort. It occurred at dawn of a raw, dull March morning, and was effected with all the furtiveness, the silence, usually pertaining to a surprise attack.

The soldiers bivouacking inside that part of the city knew nothing of the whole affair. But few of them did as much as turn in their sleep when his lordship rode through the Koppelpoort, together with four companies of cavaliers. Jan was an adept at arranging these expeditions, and the Lord of Stoutenburg had made a speciality of marauding excursions ever since he had started on his career of treachery against his own country.

His standard-bearer preceded the companies, carrying the sable standard embroidered in silver, with the skull and cross-bones, which his lordship had permanently adopted as his device. But they went without drums or pipes, and with as little clatter as may be, choosing the unpaved streets whereon the mud lay thick and effectually deadened the sound of horses' hoofs.

A litter taken from the burgomaster's coach-house and borne by two strong Flemish horses, bore the *jongejuffrouw* Gilda Beresteyn in the train of her future lord. She had offered no resistance, no protest of any kind when finally ordered by her brother to make herself ready. She had spent the greater part of the night in meditation and in prayer. Her father, hearing her move about in her room, had come to her in the small hours of the morning and had sat with her for some time. Nicolaes, wakeful and restless, had wandered out into the corridor on which gave most of the sleeping rooms, and had heard the subdued murmurings of the burgomaster's voice, and occasionally that of his sister. What they said he could not hear, but he was able subsequently to assure Stoutenburg that the burgomaster's tone was distinctly one of admonition, and Gilda's one of patience and resignation.

Just before dawn, one of the old serving men, who had remained on the watch in the house all through the night, brought her some warm milk and bread, which she swallowed eagerly. The burgomaster was with her then. But later on, when the Lord of Stoutenburg desired her presence in the living-room, she went to him alone.

That room was the one where, a little more than a week ago, the Stadtholder had held council with the burgomaster and his friends, on the day of her wedding. Her wedding! And she had sat in the little room next to it and played on the virginal so as to attract her beloved to her side. Then had come the hour of parting, and she had with her own hands taken his sword to him and buckled it to his side, and bade him go whither honour and duty beckoned.

My God, what memories!

But she met Stoutenburg's mocking glance with truly remarkable serenity. She felt neither faint nor weak. Her communion with God, her interview with her father had given her all the strength she needed, not to let her enemies see what she suffered or if she were afraid. And when Stoutenburg with callous irony reminded her of his decision, she answered quite calmly:

'I am ready to do your wish, my lord.'

'And you'll not regret it, Gilda,' he vowed with sudden earnestness; and his sunken eyes lighted up with a kind of fierce ardour which sent a cold shudder coursing down her spine. 'By Heaven! you'll not regret it! You shall be the greatest lady in Europe, the most admired, the most beloved. Aye! With you beside me, I feel that I shall have the power to create a throne, a kingdom, for us both. Queen of the Netherlands, *myn engel*! What say you to this goal? And I your king – '

He paused and closely scrutinized her face, marvelled what she knew of that drunken oaf, once her lover, who now lay dead in the room below, slain by the avenging hand of an outraged father and an indignant patriot. But she looked so serene that the came to the conclusion that she knew nothing. The burgomaster had apparently desired to spare her for the moment this additional horror and shame.

Well, no doubt it was all for the best. She was ready to come with him, and that, after all, was the principal thing. In any event she knew the alternative.

'Jan remains here,' he said, 'in command of the troops. He will not leave until I send him word.'

Until then, Amersfoort and the lives of all its citizens were in jeopardy. The quick, scared look in her eyes, when he reminded her of this, was sufficient to assure him that she fully grasped the position. Of the Stadtholder's plans, as betrayed by the informer, she knew, of course, nothing. Better so, he thought. The whole thing, when accomplished, when he – Stoutenburg – was made master of Gelderland, the Stadtholder a prisoner in his hands, the United Provinces ready to submit to him, would be a revelation to her – a revelation which would make her, he doubted not, a proud and happy woman, rather than a mere obedient slave.

2

In the meanwhile, he had strictly enjoined Jan to leave the banqueting hall undisturbed.

'Let the locked door and close shutters guard the grim secret within,' he said decisively. 'Apparently the Heer Burgomaster intends for the nonce to hold his tongue.'

In the hurry and excitement of the departure, the soldiers, who in the night had been roused by the pistol shot, forgot that unimportant event. Certain it is that not one of them did more than cursorily wonder what it had been about. Then, as no one gave reply, the matter was soon allowed to fall into oblivion. At one moment, Stoutenburg, who was standing in the hall waiting for Gilda, felt tempted to go and have a last look on his dead enemy; but the key was not in the lock and he would not send to the burgomaster for it.

It was better so.

Just then Gilda came down the stairs. She was accompanied by her old waiting woman, Maria, and was wrapped in fur cloak and hood ready for the journey. Apparently she had taken final leave of her father, and had quite resigned herself to parting from him.

'The burgomaster is well, I trust, this morning?' Stoutenburg asked with great urbanity, as soon as he had formally greeted her.

'I thank you, my lord,' she replied coolly. 'My father is as well as I can desire.'

The litter was her own. Oft had she travelled in it between Haarlem and Amersfoort, when the weather was too rough for riding. Those had been happy journeys to and fro, for both homes were dear to her. Both now had become hallowed through the presence in them of her beloved. To Stoutenburg, who watched her keenly while she crossed the hall, it seemed as if once she glanced round in the direction of the banqueting room, and craned her neck as if trying to catch whatever faint sound might be coming from there. She appeared to shiver, and drew her fur cloak closer round her shoulders, her lips moved slightly as if murmuring. Stoutenburg thought that she was bidding a last farewell to the man whom she could not bring herself to forget or to despise, and an acute feeling of unbridled jealousy shot through him like a poisoned dart – jealousy even of the dead.

3

A mounted scout led the way, to clear the road of any encumbrance that might retard progress. After him came the standard-bearer. Twelve Spanish halberdiers followed, the shafts of their halberts swathed in black velvet, behind them one hundred cavaliers, who were armed with muskets, and a hundred more carrying lances. Then came the litter, which was covered in leather with richly stamped leather curtains, at the sides, the shafts, front and back, supported by heavy Flemish horses, which were sumptuously caparisoned and plumed. The Lord of Stoutenburg rode on one side of the litter and Nicolaes on the other, and behind it came two more companies of musketeers and lancers.

The way lay through the Koppelpoort and then straight across the Veluwe, on the road which runs to the north of Amersfoort, thus avoiding any possible encounter with the Stadtholder's vedettes. Stoutenburg's intention was to await Maurice of Nassau's coming at the *molen*, not to offer him battle in the open.

The road was lonely at this early hour, and a cutting wind blew across from the Zuider Zee, chasing the morning mist before it. Already on the horizon above the undulating tableland, the pale, wintry sun tinged that mist with gold. Stoutenburg's keen hawklike eyes searched the distance before him as he rode.

A little after seven o'clock, Barneveld was reached, and a

brief halt called outside the city whilst the scouts went in, in search of provisions. The inhabitants, scared by the advent of these strangers, submitted to being fleeced of their goods, not daring to resist. Though closely questioned, they had but little information to impart. They had, in truth, heard that Ede was in the hands of the Spaniards and that Amersfoort had shared the like fate. Runners had brought the news, which was authentic, together with many wild rumours that had terrorized the credulous and paved the way for Stoutenburg's arrival. His sable standard, with its grim device, completed the subjugation of the worthy burghers of Barneveld, who, with no garrison to protect them, thought it wisest to obey the behests of His Magnificence with a show of goodwill, rather than see their little city pillaged or their citizens dragged as captives in the train of the conqueror.

Gilda did not leave her litter during the halt. Maria, who had been riding on a pillion behind one of the equerries, whom she roundly trounced and anathematized all the way, came and waited on her mistress. But Stoutenburg and Nicolaes kept with unwonted discretion, or mayhap indifference, out of her way.

The halt, in truth, lasted less than a couple of hours. By nine o'clock the troop was once more on the way, and an hour later on the high upland, out toward the east, the lonely *molen* loomed, portentuous and weird, out of the mist.

4

The spies of the Stadtholder, who had, according to Diogenes' statement, spoken of the *molen* as Stoutenburg's camp, where he had secreted great stores of arms and ammunition, had in truth been either deceived or deceivers.

The *molen* was lonely and uninhabited, as it had always been. No sign of life appeared around it, or sign of the recent breaking of a camp. True, here and there upon the scrub in the open, the scorched rough grass or a heap of ashes, indicated that a fire had been lit there at one time; whilst under the overhanging platform, the trampled earth converted into mud, and certain debris of straw and fodder, accused the recent presence of horses and of men.

But only a few. As to whether the stores of arms and ammunition were indeed concealed inside the mill-house itself, it was impossible to say from the mere aspect of the tumble-down building. Whatever secret the *molen* contained, it had succeeded in guarding inviolate up to this hour.

Standing as it did upon a high point of the arid upland, the *molen* dominated the Veluwe. Toward the west, whence the Stadtholder would come, a gentle, undulating slope led down to Barneveld and Ede, Amersfoort and Utrecht; but in the rear of the building toward the east, the ground fell away more abruptly, down to a narrow gorge below.

It was in this gorge, secluded from the prying eyes of possible vedettes, that Stoutenburg had put up his camp ere he embarked upon his fateful expedition to Amersfoort, and it was here that he disposed the bulk of his troop: horses, men and baggage, under the command of Nicolaes Beresteyn; whilst he himself, with a bodyguard of fifty picked men, took up his quarters in the *molen*.

The plan of action was simple enough. The fifty men would remain concealed in and about the building, until the Stadtholder thinking the place deserted, walked straight into the trap that had been laid for him. Then, at the first musket shot, the men from the camp below were to rush up the sloping ground with a great clatter and much shouting and battle cry.

The Stadtholder's troops wholly unprepared for the attack would be thrown into dire confusion, and in the panic that would inevitably ensue, the rout would be complete. Stoutenburg himself would see to it that the Stadtholder did not escape.

'Welcome home, *myn engel!*' had been his semi-ironical, wholly triumphant greeting to Gilda, when her litter came to a halt and he dismounted in order to conduct her into the *molen.*

She gave him no answer, but allowed her hand to rest in his and walked beside him with a firm step through the narrow door which gave on the interior of the mill-house. She looked about her with inquiring eyes that had not a vestige of terror in them. Almost, it seemed, at one moment as if she smiled.

Did her memory conjure back just then the vision of that other *molen,* the one at Ryswick, where so much had happened three short months ago, and where this arrogant tyrant had played such a sorry role? Perhaps. Certain it is that she turned to him without any defiance, almost with a gentle air of appeal.

'I am very tired,' she said, with a weary little sigh, 'and would be grateful for a little privacy, if your lordship would allow my tire-woman to attend on me.'

'Your wishes are my laws, *myn schat,*' he replied airily. 'I entreat you to look on this somewhat dilapidated building only as a temporary halt, where nothing, alas! can be done for your comfort. I trust you will not suffer from the cold, but absolute privacy you shall have. The loft up those narrow steps is entirely at your disposal, and your woman shall come to you immediately.'

Indeed, he called at once through the door, and a moment or two later Maria appeared, reduced to silence for the nonce by a wholesome fear. Stoutenburg, in the meanwhile, still with that same ironical gallantry, had conducted Gilda to the narrow, ladder-like steps which led up to the loft. He stood at the foot, watching her serene and leisurely progress.

'How wise you are, *mejuffrouw,*' he said, with a sigh of satisfaction. 'And withal how desirable!'

She turned for a second, then, and looked down on him. But her eyes were quite inscrutable. Never had he desired her so much as now. With the gloomy background of those rickety walls behind her, she looked like an exquisite fairy; her dainty head wrapped in a hood, through which her small, oval face appeared, slightly rose-tinted, like a piece of delicate china.

The huge fur coat concealed the lines of her graceful figure, but one perfect hand rested upon the rail, and the other peeped out like a flower between the folds of her cloak. He all but lost his head when he gazed on her, and met those blue eyes that still held a mystery for him. But, with Stoutenburg, ambition and selfishness always waged successful warfare even against passion, and at this hour his entire destiny was hanging in the balance.

The look wherewith he regarded her was that of a conqueror rather than a lover. The title of the English play had come swiftly through his mind: 'The Taming of the Shrew.' In truth, Nicolaes had been right. Women have no use for weaklings. It is their master whom they worship.

Just one word of warning did he give her ere she finally passed out of his sight.

'There will be noise of fighting anon, *myn engel*,' he said carelessly. 'Nothing that need alarm you. An encounter with vedettes probably. A few musket shots. You will not be afraid?'

'No,' she replied simply. 'I will not be afraid.'

'You will be safe here with me until we can continue our journey east or south. It will depend on what progress de Berg has been able to make.'

She gave a slight nod of understanding.

'I shall be ready,' she said.

Encouraged by her gentleness, he went on more warmly:

'And at the hour when we leave here together, *myn schat*, a runner will speed to Amersfoort with orders to Jan to evacuate the city. The burgomaster will be in a position to announce to his fellow-citizens that they have nothing to fear from a chivalrous enemy, who will respect person and property, and who will go out of the gates of Amersfoort as empty-handed as he came.'

Whereupon he made her a low and respectful bow, stood aside to allow the serving woman to follow her mistress. Gilda had acknowledged his last pompous tirade with a faintly murmured, 'I thank you, my lord.' Then she went quickly up the steps and finally passed out of his sight on the floor above.

Just for a little while he remained quite still, listening to her footsteps overhead. His lean, sharp-featured face expressed nothing but contentment now. Success – complete, absolute – was his at last! Less than a fortnight ago, he was nothing but a disappointed vagrant, without home, kindred, or prospects; scorned by the woman he loved; despised by a successful rival; an outcast from the land of his birth.

Today, his rival was dead – an object of contempt, not even of pity, for every honest man; while Gilda, like a ripe and luscious fruit, was ready to fall into his arms. And he had his foot firmly planted on the steps of a throne.

5

And now the midday hour had gone by, and silence, absolute, reigned in and around the *molen*. Stoutenburg had spent some time talking to the captain in command of his guard, had himself seen to it that the men were well concealed in the rear of the *molen*. The horses had been sent down to the camp so as to preclude any possibility of an alarm being given before the apportioned time. Two men were stationed on the platform to keep a look-out upon the distance, where anon the Stadtholder and his troop would appear.

Indeed, everything was ordained and arranged with perfect precision in anticipation of the great coup which was destined to deliver Maurice of Nassau into the hands of his enemy. Everything ! – provided that blind informer who lay dead in the banqueting hall of the stately house at Amersfoort had not lied from first to last.

But even if he had lied, even if the Stadtholder had not planned this expedition, or, having planned it, had abandoned it or given up the thought of leading it in person – even so,

Stoutenburg was prepared to be satisfied. Already his busy brain was full of plans, which he would put into execution if the present one did not yield him the supreme prize. Gilda was his now, whatever happened. Gilda, and her wealth, and the influence of the Burgomaster Beresteyn, henceforth irrevocably tied to the chariot wheel of his son-in-law. A vista of riches, of honours, of power, was stretched out before the longing gaze of this restless and ambitious self-seeker.

For the nonce, he could afford to wait, even though the hours crept by leaden-footed, and the look-out men up on the platform had nothing as yet to report. The soldiers outside, wrapped up in horse-blankets, squatted against the walls of the dilapidated building, trying to get shelter from the cutting north wind. They had their provisions for the day requisitioned at Barneveld; but these they soon consumed for want of something better to do. The cold was bitter, and anon an icy drizzle began to fall.

6

Stoutenburg, inside the mill-house, had started on that restless pacing up and down which was so characteristic of him. He had ordered the best of the provisions to be taken up to the *jongejuffrouw* and her maid. He himself had eaten and had drunk, and now he had nothing to do but wait. And think. Anon he got tired of both, and when he heard the women moving about overhead, he suddenly paused in his fretful wanderings, pondered for a moment or two, and then went resolutely up the stairs.

Gilda was sitting on a pile of sacking; her hands lay idly in her lap. With a curt word of command, Stoutenburg ordered the waiting woman to go below.

Then he approached Gilda, and half-kneeling, half-reclining by her side, he tried to take her hand. But she evaded him, hid her hands underneath her cloak. This apparently vastly amused his lordship, for he laughed good-humouredly, and said, with an ardent look of passionate admiration:

'That is where you are so desirable, *myn engel*. Never twice the same. Awhile ago you seemed as yielding as a dove; now once more I see the young vixen peeping at me through those wonderful blue eyes. Well!' he added with a sigh of contentment, 'I will not complain. Life by your side, *myn geliefde*, will never be dull. The zest of taming a beautiful shrew must ever be a manly sport.'

Then, as she made no sign either of defiance or comprehension, but sat with eyes strained and neck craned forward, almost as if she were listening, he raised himself and sat down upon the sacking close beside her. She puzzled him now, as she always did; and that puzzlement added zest to his wooing.

'I was waxing so dejected down below,' he said, and leaned forward, his lips almost touching the hood that kept her ears concealed. 'Little did I guess that so much delight lay ready to my hand. Time is a hard taskmaster to me just now, and I have not the leisure to make as ardent love to you as I would wish. But I have the time to gratify a fancy, and this I will do. My fancy is to have three kisses from your sweet lips on mine. Three, and no more, and on the lips, *myn schat.*'

In an instant his arms were round her. But equally suddenly she had evaded him. She jumped up and ran, as swift as a hare, to the farther end of the loft, where she remained ensconced behind a transverse beam, her arms round it for support, her face, white and set, only vaguely discernible in the gloom.

The dim afternoon light which came but shyly peeping in through two small windows high up in the walls, failed to reach this angle of the loft where Gilda had found shelter. With this dim background behind her, she appeared like some elusive spectre, an apparition, without form or substance, her face and hands alone visible.

When she escaped him, Stoutenburg had cursed, as was his

wont, then struggled to his feet and tried to carry off the situation with an affected laugh. But somehow the girl's face, there in the semi-darkness, gave him an unpleasant, eerie sensation. He did not follow her, but paused in the centre of the loft, laughter dying upon his lips.

'Am I to remind you again, you little termagant,' he said, with a great show of bluster, 'that Jan is still at Amersfoort, and that I may yet send a runner to him if I have a mind, ordering that by nightfall that accursed city be ablaze?'

He was looking straight at her while he spoke. And she returned his glance, but gave him no reply. Just for the space of a few seconds an extraordinary stillness appeared to have descended upon the *molen*. Up here, in the loft, nothing stirred, nothing was heard above that silence save the patter of the rain upon the roof overhead and against the tiny window panes. For a few seconds, whilst Stoutenburg stood like a beast of prey about to spring, and Gilda, still and silent, like a bird on the alert.

And suddenly, even as he gazed, the man's expression slowly underwent a change. First the arrogance died out of it, the forced irony. Every line became set, then rigid, and more and more ashen in hue, until the whole face appeared like a death-mask, colourless and transparent as wax, the jaw dropping, the lips parted as for a cry that would not come. And the sunken eyes opened wider and wider, and wider still as they gazed, not on Gilda any longer, but into the darkness behind her, whilst the whole aspect of the man was like a living statue of horror and of a nameless fear.

Then suddenly, right through the silence and above the weird patter of the rain, there rang a sound which roused the very echoes that lay dormant among the ancient rafters. So strange a sound was it that when it reached his ear, Stoutenburg lost his balance and swayed on his feet like a drunken man; so strange that Gilda, her nerves giving way for the first time under the terrible strain which she had undergone, buried her face against her arms, whilst a loud sob broke from her throat. Yet the sound in itself was neither terrifying nor a tragic one. It was just the sound of a prolonged and loud peal of laughter.

'By my halidame!' a merry voice swore lustily. 'But meseems that your lordship had no thought of seeing me here!'

Just for a few seconds, superstitious fear held the miscreant gripped by the throat. A few seconds? To him, to Gilda they seemed an eternity. Then a hoarse whisper escaped him.

'Spectre or demon, which are you?'

'Both, you devil!' the mocking voice gave reply. 'And I would send you down to hell and shoot you like a dog where you stand, but for the noise which would bring your men about mine ears.'

'To hell yourself, you infamous *plepshurk!*' Stoutenburg cried, strove to shake off with a mighty effort the superstitious dread that made a weakling of him. He fumbled for his sword, succeeded in drawing it from its scabbard, and cursed himself for being without a pistol in his belt.

'Where you came from, I know not,' he went on in a husky whisper. 'But be you wraith or demon, you –'

He seemed to speak involuntarily, as if sheer terror was forcing the words through his bloodless lips. Suddenly he uttered a hoarse cry:

'*A moi!* Somebody there! *A moi!*'

But the walls of the old *molen* were thick, and his voice, spent and still half-choked with the horror of that spectral apparition, refused him effective service. It failed to carry far enough. The tiny windows were impracticable; the soldiers were outside at the rear of the building, out of earshot; and down below there was only the old waiting woman.

'That *smeerlap!*' he cried, half to himself. 'Either a wraith or blind. In either case –'

And, sword in hand, he rushed upon his mocking enemy. A blind man! Bah! What had he to fear? The rogue had in truth thrust Gilda behind him. He stood there, with one of those short English daggers in his hand, which had of late put the fine Toledo blades to shame. But a blind man, for all that! How he had escaped out of Amersfoort, and by whose connivance, Stoutenburg had not time to think. But the man was blind. Every phase of last evening's interview with him – the vacant eyes, the awkward movements – stood out clearly before his lordship's mental vision, and testified to that one fact; the man was blind and helpless.

Crouching like a feline creature upon his haunches, Stoutenburg was ready for a spring. His every movement became lithe and silent as that of a snake. He had marked out to himself just how and where he would strike. He only waited until those eyes – those awful eyes – ceased to look on him. But their glance never wavered. They followed his every step. They mocked and derided and threatened withal! By Satan and all his hordes! those stricken orbs could see!

At what precise moment that conviction entered Stoutenburg's tortured brain, he could not himself have told you. But suddenly it was there. And in an instant his nerve completely forsook him. An icy sweat broke all over his body. His head swam, his knees gave way under him, the sword dropped out of his nerveless hand. Then, with a quick hoarse cry, he turned to flee. His foot was on the top step of the ladder which led to the room below. A prolonged, mocking laugh behind him seemed to lend him wings. But freedom – aye, and more! – beckoned from below. There was only an old woman there, and his soldiers were outside. Ye gods! He was a fool to fear!

He flew down the few steps, nearly fell headlong in the act, for his nerves were playing him an unpleasant trick, and the afternoon light was growing dim. At first, when he reached the place below, he saw nothing. Nothing save the welcome door, straight before him, which led straight to freedom from this paralysing obsession.

With one bound he had covered half the intervening space,

when suddenly he paused, and an awful curse rose to his lips. There, in the recess of the doorway, two men were squatting on their heels, intent upon a game of hazard.

One of these men was long and lean, the other round as a curled-up hedge-hog. They did no more than glance over their shoulder when His Magnificence the Lord of Stoutenburg came staggering down the steps.

'Five and four,' the lean vagabond was saying. 'How many does that make?'

'Eight, you loon!' the other replied. 'My turn now.' They continued their game, regardless of his lordship, who stood there rooted to the spot, trembling in every limb, his body covered with sweat, feeling like an animal that sees a trap slowly closing in upon him.

The situation was indeed one to send a man out of his senses. Stoutenburg, for one brief instant, felt that he was going mad. He looked from the door to the steps, and back again to the door, marvelling which way lay his one chance of escape. If he shouted, would he be heard? Could his men get to him before those two ruffians fell to and murdered him? Dared he make a dash for the door? Or – It was unthinkable that he – Stoutenburg – should be standing here, at the mercy of three villains, utterly powerless, when outside, not fifty paces away, the other side of those walls, fifty men at arms were there, set to guard his person.

And suddenly fear fell away from him. The trembling of his limbs ceased, his vision became clear, his mind alert. Even around his quaking lips there came the ghost of a smile.

His senses, keyed up by the imminence of his danger, had seized upon a sound which came from outside, faint as yet, but very obviously drawing nearer. In the semi-darkness and with his head buzzing and his nerves tingling, he could not distinguish either the quality of the sound nor yet the exact direction whence it came. But whatever it was – even if it was not all that he hoped – the sound was bound to set his soldiers on the alert;

and if he could only temporize with those ruffians for a minute or two, the very next would see the captain of his guard rushing in to report what was happening: The Stadtholder sighted, the signal given, Nicolaes Beresteyn coming swiftly to the rescue.

Therefore, in the face of his own imminent peril, the Lord of Stoutenburg no longer felt afraid, only tensely vitally expectant. The two caitiffs, on the other hand, appeared to have heard nothing. At any rate, they went on with their game, and the flute-like, high-pitched tones of the fat loon alternated with the deep bass of his companion:

'Three and two make five!'

'No, four, you varlet!'

'Six!'

'Blank, by Beelzebub! My luck is dead out today.'

And the sound drew nearer. There was no mistaking it. Men running. The clatter of arms. horses, too. A pawing, and a champing, and a general hubbub, which those two ruffians could not fail to hear. Nor did any sound come down from the left. Yet Gilda was there with the miserable *plepshurk* who, whatever else happened, would inevitably stand before her now as an informer and a cheat. This, at any rate, was a fact. The man had betrayed his master in order to save his miserable life, and the burgomaster had connived at his escape through an access of doltish weakness. But the fact remained. The Stadtholder was approaching. The next few minutes – seconds, perhaps – would see the final triumphant issue of this terrible adventure.

Stoutenburg, like a feline at bay, waited.

Then, all at once, a musket shot rang through the air, then another, and yet another; and all at once the whole air around was alive with sounds. The clang of arms; the lusty battle cries. Men out there had come to grips. In the drenching rain they were at one another's throats.

The two caitiffs quietly put aside their dice and rose to their feet. They stood with their backs to the door, their eyes fixed upon his lordship.

'Stand aside, you dolts!' Stoutenburg cried aloud; for he thought that he read murder in those two pairs of eyes, and he had need of all his nerves to assure himself that all was well, that, though his captain had not come to him for a reason which no doubt was sound, his soldiers were at grips with the Stadtholder's vanguard, and Nicolaes was already half-way up the slope.

But he, Stoutenburg, was unarmed, and could not push past those two assassins who were guarding the door. He bethought himself of his sword, which lay on the floor of the loft. He turned with a sudden impulse to get hold of it at all costs, and was met at the very foot of the steps by the man who had baffled him at every turn.

Diogenes, sword in hand, did not even pause to look on his impotent enemy. With one spring, he was across the floor and out by the door, which one of the ruffians immediately closed behind him.

It had all happened swifter even than thought. Stoutenburg, trapped, helpless, more bewildered in truth than terrified, still believed in a happy issue to his present desperate position. The thought came to him that he might purchase his safety from those potential murderers.

'Ten thousand guilders,' he called out wildly, 'if you will let me pass!'

But the fat *runnion* merely turned to the lean one, and the look of understanding which passed between them sent an icy shudder down his lordship's spine. He knew that from these two he could expect no mercy. A hoarse cry of horror escaped his lips as he saw that each held a dagger in one hand.

Then began that awful chase when man becomes a hunted beast – that grim game of hide-and-seek, with the last issue never once in doubt. The Lord of Stoutenburg trapped between these narrow walls, ran round and round like a mouse in a cage; now seeking refuge behind a girder, now leaping over an intervening obstacle, now crouching, panting and bathed in sweat, under cover of the gloom. And no one spoke; no one called. Neither the hunted nor the hunters. It seemed as if a conspiracy of silence existed between them; or else that the nearness of death had put a seal on all their lips.

Out there the clang of battle appeared more remote. Nothing seemed to occur in the immediate approach of the *molen*. It all came from afar, resounding across the Veluwe, above the patter of the rain and the soughing of the wind, through the rafters of the old mill. Drumming and thumping, the jangle of armour, the clang of pike and lance, of metal against metal; the loud report of musket shot, the strident grating of chains and wheels. But all far away, not here. Not outside the *molen*, but down there in the gorge, where Nicolaes had been encamped. My heavens, what did it mean?

Already the trapped creature was getting exhausted. Once or twice he had come down on his knees. His eyes were growing dim. His breath came and went with a wheezing sound from his breast. It was not just two murderous brigands who were pursuing him, but Nemesis herself, with sword of retribution drawn, in her hand an hour-glass, the sands of which were running low.

All at once the miscreant found himself at the foot of the steps, and, blindly stumbling, he ran up to the loft – instinctively, without set purpose save that of warding off, if only for a minute, the inevitable end.

7

Gilda was standing at the top of the steps with neck craned forward, her hands held tightly to her breast, her whole attitude one of nameless horror. She had been listening to the multifarious sounds which came from outside, and the natural, womanly fear for the safety of her beloved had been her one dominant emotion.

She had heard nothing else for a times until suddenly she caught one or two stray sounds of that grim and furtive fight for life which was going on down below. She had reached the top of the steps, and tried to peer through the gloom to ascertain whose were the stealthy, swift footfalls so like those of a hunted beast, and whose the heavy, lumbering tread that spoke of stern and unwavering pursuit. At first she could see nothing, and the very silence which lay like a pall upon the grim scene below struck her with a sense of paralysing dread.

Then she caught sight first of one figure, then of another, as they crossed her line of vision. She could distinguish nothing very clearly – just those swiftly moving figures – and for a moment or two felt herself unable to move. Then she heard the laboured breathing of a man, a groan as of a soul tortured with fear, and the next instant the Lord of Stoutenburg appeared, stumbling up the narrow steps.

At sight of her he fell like an inert thing with a husky cry at her feet. His arms encircled her knees; his head fell against her gown. 'Gilda, save me!' he whispered hoarsely. 'For the love of Heaven! They'll murder me! Save me, for pity's sake! Gilda!'

He sobbed and cried like a child, abject in his terror, loathsome in his craven cowardice. Gilda could not stir. He held her with his arms as in a vice. She would have given worlds for the physical strength to wrench her gown out of his clutch, to flee from the hated sight of him who had planned to do her beloved such an irreparable injury. Oh, she hated him! She hated him worse, perhaps, than she had ever done before, now that he clung like a miserable dastard to her for mercy.

'Leave the poltroon to us, *mejuffrouw*,' a gentle, flute-like tone broke in on the miscreant's ravings.

'Now then, take your punishment like a man!' a gruff voice added sternly.

And two familiar faces emerged out of the gloom, immediately below where Gilda was standing, imprisoned by those cringing arms. The man, in truth, had not even the primeval pluck of a savage. He was beaten, and he knew it. What had happened out there on the Veluwe, how completely he had been tricked by the Englishman, he did not know as yet. But he was afraid to die, and shrank neither from humiliation nor contempt in order to save his own worthless life from the wreck of all his ambitions.

At the sound of those two voices, which in truth were like a death-knell in his ears, he jumped to his feet; but he did not loosen his hold on Gilda. Swift as thought he had found refuge behind her, and held her by the arms in front of him like a shield.

Historians have always spoken of the Lord of Stoutenburg as extraordinarily nimble in mind and body. That nimbleness in truth, stood him in good stead now; for whilst Socrates and Pythagoras, clumsy in their movements, lumbering and hampered by their respect for the person of the *jongejuffrouw*, reached the loft, and then for one instant hesitated how best to proceed in their grim task without offending the ears and eyes of the great lady, Stoutenburg had with one bound slipped from behind her down the steps and was across the floor of the *molen* and out of the door before the two worthies had had time to utter the comprehensive curse which, at this unexpected manoeuvre on the part of their quarry, had risen to their lips.

'We had promised Diogenes not to allow the blackguard to escape!' Pythagoras exclaimed ruefully.

And both started in hot pursuit, whilst Gilda, seeking shelter in a dark angle of the loft, fell, sobbing with excitement and only half-conscious, upon a pile of sacking.

16

The Final Issue

Pythagoras and Socrates failed to find the trail of the miscreant,who had vanished under cover of the night. We know that Stoutenburg did succeed, in fact, in reaching de Berg's encampment, half-starved and wearied, but safe. How he did it, no one will ever know. His career of crime had received a mighty check, and the marauding expeditions which he undertook subsequently against his own country were of a futile and desultory nature. History ceases to trouble herself about him after that abortive incursion into Gelderland.

How that incursion was frustrated by the gallant Englishman, known to fame as the first Sir Percy Blakeney, but to his intimates as Diogenes, the erstwhile penniless soldier of fortune, we know chiefly through van Aitzema's *Saken von Staet*. The worthy chronicler enlarges upon the Englishman's adventure – he always calls him 'the Englishman' – from the time when a week and more ago, he took leave of Nicolaes Beresteyn outside Barneveld to that when he reached Amersfoort, just in time to avert a terrible catastrophe.

The author of *Saken von Staet* tells of the ambuscade on the shores of the Ijssel, 'the Englishman's' swim for life through the drifting floes. On reaching the opposite bank, it seems that he was so spent and more than half frozen, that he lay half unconscious on the bank for awhile. Presently, however, alive to the danger of possible further ambuscades, he re-started on his way, found a deserted hut close by, and crawled in there for shelter. As soon as darkness had set in he started back for Zutphen, there to warn Marquet not to proceed. The whole of the Stadtholder's plans had obviously been revealed to de Berg by some traitor – whose identity Diogenes then could not fail but guess – and it would have been sheer madness to attempt to cross the Ijssel now at any of the points originally intended.

To reach Zutphen at this juncture meant for the undaunted adventurer two leagues and more to traverse, and with clothes frozen hard to the skin. But he did reach Zutphen in time, and with the assistance of Marquet, then evolved the plan of an advance into Gelderland by effecting the crossing of the Ijssel as far north as Apeldoorn, and then striking across the Veluwe either to Amersfoort or to Ede, threatening de Berg's advance, and possibly effecting a junction with the Stadtholder's main army.

After this understanding with Marquet, Diogenes then proceeded to Arnheim, where the garrison could now only be warned to hold the city at all costs until assistance could be sent.

In the meantime, de Berg's troops were swarming everywhere. The Englishman could only proceed by night, had to hide by day on the Veluwe as best he could. Hence much delay. More than once he was on the point of capture, but succeeded eventually in reaching Arnheim.

Here he saw Coorne, who was in command of the small garrison, assured him of coming relief, and made him swear not to surrender the city, since the Stadtholder would soon be on his way with strong reinforcements. Thence to Nijmegen on the same errand. A more easy journey this, seeing that Isembourg had not begun his advance from Kleve. After that, De Keysere and Wageningen.

Van Aitzema says that it was between Nijmegen and Wageningen that 'the Englishman,' lurking in a thicket of scrub, overheard some talk of how the Stadtholder was to be waylaid and captured on his return to camp from Amersfoort. This fact the chronicler must have learned at first hand. By this time the forces of de Berg were spreading over Gelderland. 'The Englishman' gathered that the Archduchess's plans were to leave Isembourg's army to deal with Arnheim and Nijmegen for the present, whilst de Berg was to march on Ede, and, if possible, push on as far Amersfoort. But as to how the coup against the Stadtholder was to be effected, he could not ascertain. At the time he did not know that his Highness intended to visit Amersfoort again. But for him, that little city where Gilda dwelt was just now the hub of the universe, and thank Heaven his errand was now accomplished, all his Highness's orders executed, and he was free to go to his young wife as fast as his own endurance and Spanish vedettes would allow.

This meant another tramp across open country, which by this time was overrun with enemy troops. Fugitives from Ede were everywhere to be seen. 'The Spaniards. They are on us!' rang from end to end of the invaded province, and the echo of that dismal cry must by now have been rolling even as far as Utrecht.

It meant also seeking cover against enemy surprise parties, who threw the daring adventurer more than once out of his course, so that we hear of him once as far south as Rhenen, and then as far east as Doorn. It meant hiding amongst the reeds in the half-frozen marshes, swimming the Rhyn at one point, the Eem at another; it meant days without food and nights without rest. It meant all that, and more in pluck and endurance and determination, to which three qualities in 'the Englishman' the worthy chronicler, though ever chary of words, pays ungrudging tribute.

He reached Amersfoort, as we know, just in time to see the Stadtholder leave the city in the company of the traitor, Nicolaes Beresteyn, and, struck by that same treacherous hand, fell, helpless for a moment, at the very threshold of the burgomaster's house.

After which began the martyrdom which had ended in such perfect triumph and happiness.

The daring adventurer, left lonely and stricken upon the moorland, did in truth go through an agony of misery and humiliation such as seldom falls to the lot of any man. Indeed, what he did suffer throughout that terrible day, whilst he believed himself to be irretrievably blinded, was never known to any one save to the two faithful friends who watched lovingly over him. Socrates, after he had accompanied the Stadtholder, returned to sit and watch with Pythagoras beside the man to whom they both clung with such wholehearted devotion.

It was not until late in the night that a faint glimmer of light, coming from the fire which the two caitiffs had managed to kindle as the night was bitterly cold, reached the young soldier's aching limbs, and seemed to him like a tiny beacon of hope in the blackness of his misery. By the time that the grey dawn broke over the moorland, he had realized that the injury which he had thought irremediable, had only been transient, and that every hour now brought an improvement in his power of vision.

Whereupon, three heads were put together to devise a means for using the Englishman's supposed blindness to the best advantage. One wise head and two loyal ones, not one of them even remotely acquainted with fear, what finer combination could be found for the eventful undoing of a pack of traitors?

Ede was in the hands of the Spaniards, Amersfoort on the point of sharing the like fate. These facts were sufficiently confirmed by the stray fugitives who wandered homeless and distracted across the moorland, and were in turn interrogated by the three conspirators.

With the woman he loved inside the invaded city, and with that recreant Stoutenburg in command of the enemy troops there, Diogenes' first thought was to get into Amersfoort himself at all risks and costs. As for the plan for freeing the town and punishing the miscreants, it was simple enough. To collect a small troop of ruffians from amongst the fugitives on the moorlands and place these under the command of Socrates, was the first move. The second was to send Pythagoras with an urgent message to Marquet to hurry eastward with his army from Apeldoorn, to the relief of Amersfoort, taking on his way the lonely *molen* on the Veluwe, where an important detachment of enemy troops might be expected to encamp. The one thing with which Diogenes was, most fortunately, amply provided, was money; money which he had by him when first he started out of Amersfoort on the Stadtholder's errand; money which was needful now to enable Socrates to recruit his small army of ne'er-do-wells and to assist Pythagoras on his embassy to Marquet.

Thereafter Diogenes, feigning blindness and worse, made his way into the presence of the Lord of Stoutenburg, who held Gilda at his mercy and the whole city to ransom for her obedience.

To dangle before the miscreant's eyes the prospect of capturing the Stadtholder's person, and thus make himself master of the Netherlands, was the pivot around which the whole plan revolved. The bait could not fail to attract the ambitious cupidity of the traitor, and verisimilitude was given to the story by Socrates' band of ruffians, whose orders were to spread the news of the Stadtholder's advance both on Ede and Amersfoort, and to silence effectually any emissaries of Stoutenburg's who might be sent out to ascertain the truth of those rumours.

We may take it that Socrates and his little troop saw to it that none of these emissaries did return to Amersfoort, for the Lord of Stoutenburg marched out of the city at dawn, with his sinister banner flying, with his musketeers, pikemen and lancers, and with Gilda Beresteyn a virtual prisoner in his train.

That the daring adventurer risked an ignominious death by this carefully laid plan cannot be denied; but he was one of those men who had gambled with life and death since he was a child, who was accustomed to stake his all upon the spin of a coin; and, anyhow, if he failed, death would have been thrice welcome, as the only escape out of untold misery and sorrow.

Chance favoured him in this, that at the last he was left face to face with the burgomaster, to whom he immediately confided everything, and who enabled him to escape out of the house by the service staircase, and thence into the streets, where no one knew him and where he remained all night, effectually concealed as a unit in the midst of the crowd. He actually went out of Amersfoort in the train of Stoutenburg; and whilst his lordship's troops made a long halt at Barneveld, 'the Englishman' continued his way unmolested across the Veluwe to the lonely *molen*, which was to witness his success and happiness, or the final annihilation of all that made life possible.

2

All this and more, in the matter of detail, hath the meticulous chronicler of the time put conscientiously on record. We must assume that he was able to verify all his facts at source, chiefly through the garrulous offices of 'the Englishman's' two well-known familiars.

What, however, will for ever remain unrecorded save in the book of heroic deeds, is a woman's perfect loyalty.

During those hours and days, full of horror and of dread, Gilda never once wavered in her belief in the man she loved. From the moment when Nicolaes tried to poison her mind against him, and through all the vicissitudes which placed her face to face with what was a mere semblance of her beloved, she had never doubted him, when even the Stadtholder seemed to doubt.

She knew him to be playing a dangerous game – but a game for all that – when first she beheld him, sightless and abject, in the presence of their mutual enemy, and had rested for one brief second against his breast. That his eyes, still dazed by the poisonous fumes, could vaguely discern her face, even though they could not read the expression thereon, she did not know. The fear that he was irremediably blind was the most cruel of all the tortures which she had undergone that night.

When her father came to her in the small hours of the morning to tell her that all was well with the beloved of her heart, but that he would have all the need of all her courage and of all her determination to help him to complete his self-imposed task, she realized for the first time how near to actual death the torturing fear had brought her. But from that time forth, she never lost her presence of mind. With marvellous courage she gripped the whole situation and played her role unswervingly until the end.

Everything depended on whether Marquet reached the *molen* before the Lord of Stoutenburg, or his captains suspected that anything was wrong. True, Pythagoras had brought back the news that he had met the loyal commander at Apeldoorn, and that the latter, despite the fact that he and his troops intended to take there a well-earned rest, had immediately given the order to march. But, even so, the future of the Netherlands and of her Stadtholder, as well as the fate of the gallant Englishman and his beloved wife, lay in the hands of God.

One hour before dusk Marquet's vedettes first came in contact with the outposts of Beresteyn's encampment in the gorge below the *molen*. There was a brief struggle, fierce on both sides, until the main body of Marquet's army, four thousand strong, appeared on the eastern heights above the gorge.

Whilst the Lord of Stoutenburg ran round and round the narrow space wherein he was a hunted prisoner, trying to escape that shameful death which threatened him at the hands of two humble justiciaries, his few hundred men were falling like butchered beasts beneath the pike-thrusts and musket shots of Marquet's trained troops.

Nicolaes Beresteyn was the first to fall.

It was better so. Dishonour so complete could be only wiped out by death.

When, a day or two later, after Marquet had driven the Spaniards out of Amersfoort, the burgomaster heard the news of the death of his only son, he murmured a humble and broken-hearted: 'Thank God!'

17

The Only World

Out there, in the lonely *molen* on the Veluwe, Gilda had remained for a while, half numb with nerve strain, suffering from reaction after the terrible excitement of the past few hours. Presently her old serving-woman came to her, still raging with choler at the outrage committed against her person by those two abominable rascallions.

With great volubility, she explained to her mistress that they had fallen on her unawares when first she had been sent downstairs by his lordship – whom may God punish! – They had bound and gagged her, and then told her quite cheerfully that this was an act of friendship on their part, to save her from a worse fate and from the temptation of talking when she should remain silent.

She had been thrust into a dark angle of the mill-house, from whence she could see absolutely nothing, and where she had lain all this while, entirely helpless, hearing that awful din which had been going on outside, expecting to be murdered in cold blood at any moment, and tortured with fear as to what was happening to her mistress. Only a few moments ago, the two ruffians had reappeared, running helter-skelter down the steps and thence out through the door into the open. Fortunately, one of them, conscience-stricken no doubt, had thought, before fleeing, to release her from her bonds.

288

Maria was stupid, uncomprehending and garrulous; but she was loyal, and had a warm and ample bosom, whereon a tired and aching head could find a little rest.

Gilda, her body still shaken by hysterical sobs, her teeth chattering, her senses reeling with the horror of all that she had gone through, found some measure of comfort in the old woman's ministrations. A mugful of wine, left over from the midday meal, helped her to regain command over her nerves. Holding her young mistress in her arms, Maria, crooning like a mother over her baby, rocked the half-inert young form into some semblance of sleep.

2

And here Diogenes found her a couple of hours later, curled up like a tired child in the arms of the old woman.

He came up on tiptoe, carrying a lanthorn, for now it was quite dark. This he placed on the floor, and then, with infinite caution, he slid into Maria's place and took the beloved form into his own strong arms.

She scarcely moved, just opened her eyes for a second or two, and then nestled closer against his shoulder, with a little sigh, half of weariness, but wholly of content.

She was just dead tired after all she had gone through, and now she slept just like a baby in his arms; while he was as happy as it is possible for any human being to be, for she was safe and well, and nothing could part her from him now. He was satisfied to watch her as she slept, her dear face against his breast, her soft breath coming and going with perfect evenness through her parted lips.

Once he stooped and kissed her, and then she woke, put her arms around his neck, and both forgot for the time being that there was another world save that of Love.

Baroness Orczy

The Elusive Pimpernel

In this, the sequel to *The Scarlet Pimpernel*, French agent and chief spycatcher Chauvelin is as crafty as ever, but Sir Percy Blakeney is more than a match for his arch-enemy. Meanwhile the beautiful Marguerite remains wholly devoted to Sir Percy, her husband. Cue more swashbuckling adventures as Sir Percy attempts to smuggle French aristocrats out of the country to safety.

The Laughing Cavalier

The year is 1623, the place Haarlem in the Netherlands. Diogenes – the first Sir Percy Blakeney, the Scarlet Pimpernel's ancestor – and his friends Pythagoras and Socrates defend justice and the royalist cause. The famous artist Frans Hals also makes an appearance in this historical adventure: Orczy maintains that Hals' celebrated portrait *The Laughing Cavalier* is actually a portrayal of the Scarlet Pimpernel's ancestor.

Baroness Orczy

The League of the Scarlet Pimpernel

More adventures amongst the terrors of revolutionary France. No one has uncovered the identity of the famous Scarlet Pimpernel – no one except his wife Marguerite and his arch-enemy, citizen Chauvelin. Sir Percy Blakeney is still at large, however, evading capture…

Leatherface

The Prince saw a 'figure of a man, clad in dark, shapeless woollen clothes wearing a hood of the same dark stuff over his head and a leather mask over his face'. The year is 1572 and the Prince of Orange is at Mons under night attack from the Spaniards. However Leatherface raises the alarm in the nick of time. The mysterious masked man has vowed to reappear – when His Highness' life is in danger. Who is Leatherface? And when will he next be needed?

BARONESS ORCZY

THE SCARLET PIMPERNEL

A group of titled Englishmen, under the leadership of a mysterious man, valiantly aid condemned aristocrats in their escape from Paris to England during the French Revolution. Their leader is the Scarlet Pimpernel – a man whose audacity and clever disguises foil the villainous agent Chauvelin. Who is he and can he keep one step ahead of the revolutionaries?

THE TRIUMPH OF THE SCARLET PIMPERNEL

It is Paris, 1794, and Robespierre's revolution is inflicting its reign of terror. The elusive Scarlet Pimpernel is still at large – so far. But the sinister agent Chauvelin has taken prisoner his darling Marguerite. Will she act as a decoy and draw the Scarlet Pimpernel to the enemy? And will our dashing hero evade capture and live to enjoy a day 'when tyranny was crushed and men dared to be men again'?

Printed in Great Britain
by Amazon

58186305R00169